BREAKING FAITH

BREAKING FAITH

JO BANNISTER

St. Martin's Minotaur 🐾 New York

www.minotaurbooks.com

ISBN 0-312-34301-9
EAN 978-0-312-34301-9

First published in Great Britain by Allison & Busby Limited

First U.S. Edition: August 2005

10 9 8 7 6 5 4 3 2 1

Chapter One

LAND IS LIKE PEOPLE: it has a skeleton under its cloak of flesh. Also like people, some landscapes carry more flesh than others. As gardeners from Lyme Regis to Eastbourne know to their cost, much of the south coast of England is a poverty case, the chalk bones never far below the skin, ready to break through whenever an injury occurs. All you can do is make the most of what topsoil you have and plant as deep as you can before you hit the layer of impenetrable clunch.

Midway through a dry summer the surface was like dust over iron, but that would be true wherever he went. At least here there was scant chance of being disturbed, however long the job took. The man found a spot beside the trees where centuries of leafmould had worked a little softness into the earth and, avoiding the thick roots that mirrored below the ground the spread of branches above, he began to dig.

At this time of year the day's heat persisted long into the night and soon he was sweating under his clothes. But he didn't break the steady rhythm of his labour. It was important to get the job done: he could rest later. As the Book of Ecclesiastes observed, there's a right time for everything. A time to be born and a time to die; a time to plant and a time to pluck that which is planted. A time for every purpose under heaven.

Which may not have been the perfect analogy, he recognised as he toiled. Some purposes have precious little to do with heaven; and some things are planted with the intention that they remain buried.

A little after two, like a tiny miracle sandwiched between the scorching days, a light rain began to fall, throwing a halo around the moon. The cool was a blessing but the man had no time to admire the optical effects. Before the moon paled he had to be away from here. Before the sun rose he wanted to be in another county.

When he hit hard chalk he considered briefly whether he had depth enough and decided he had. He extended his trench lengthways between the tree-roots. Wrapped in bin-bags, tied with string, he laid his offering in the hole and covered it. Then he spread the leafmould over the top till all there was to see was a gentle hump like another root growing under the surface.

He bent once more, still panting from his exertions, and patted the top of the hump. 'I'm sorry about this,' he murmured softly. 'I know it isn't what you hoped for. It isn't what I wanted either, it's just the best I can do.' Then he turned his back on her and left.

Chapter Two

'Demon Rock,' said Daniel Hood thoughtfully, his yellow head tilted to one side like a puzzled labrador. 'What is that exactly?'

Brodie Farrell looked up from her screen with a grin. Her teeth were so perfect they were almost predatory. Sometimes when she did that grin, and the brown eyes gleamed at him out of the forest of dark curls, Daniel had the uncomfortable sensation of looking down the barrel of a panther.

She regarded him fondly. She knew she intimidated him sometimes and was untroubled. It was a long time since she'd thought Nice Girl was a compliment. She said, 'You're out of touch. I bet you knew all the pop groups when you were teaching.'

He shook his head sadly. 'Not me. I was always out of date. I'm the guy who brought a Beatles LP to the Christmas party only to find everyone else had George Michael tapes. The next year I took tapes and everyone else had CDs.'

Brodie didn't doubt it. Daniel never lied, even about trivia. Also, it was utterly in character. For a man of twenty-seven he had a curiously old-fashioned quality that only made sense when she discovered he'd been raised by his grandfather. His virtues were the postwar ones of honesty, moral courage and personal responsibility that society still valued then. His vices were, by and large, the same things.

'How far back do I have to go?' she asked. 'Punk? Heavy metal? Grunge?'

'Grunge?' he echoed doubtfully, as if she might be making it up.

Brodie sighed. 'OK. Demon Rock is essentially heavy metal music – think loud: thumping bass-line, crashing guitars – with sex and death lyrics and New Gothic staging. Put it this way: Dracula could go to a demon rock concert and no one would notice.'

'Sex *and* death?' Daniel echoed faintly.

'Oh yeah.'

'In that order?'

'Not necessarily.'

Considering, he turned the flier on her desk with a fingertip. 'So this is your new image. Brodie Farrell – research done, *objets trouvées*, mysteries solved, necrophilia by arrangement.'

She laughed out loud. That was what she liked about Daniel: just when you'd got him pigeon-holed – the thick glasses, the why-pay-more? haircut, the outdated manners and gentle self-deprecating humour, even the fact that he could get really excited about the space programme – just when you'd bundled it all up in a box labelled *Nerd* he said or did something to make you think again. It wasn't even that the label was wrong, just that the whole was more than the sum of the parts.

'I'm working for him,' she explained. 'Jared Fry, the lead singer. He wants to buy a property round here. Somewhere secluded, where sacrificing virgins on the lawn won't upset the neighbours.'

'Cheyne Treacey,' Daniel said immediately. 'That's pretty much a mainstream interest in Cheyne Treacey. I believe the parish council has a sub-committee dealing with it.'

'That and hanging baskets,' nodded Brodie. 'And well-dressing.'

Daniel looked at the flier again. 'So what is the well-dressed Satanist wearing this year? Ah – black leather, silver chains and – what would you call that?'

'Body-piercing,' said Brodie, straight-faced. 'And I didn't mean...' She let it go. 'It's all an act, you know. They're not really evil, they're just pretending. They're entertainers. When he leaves the stage and takes off the greasepaint he'll look as normal as...'

She'd meant to say *You and me* but thought better of it. Daniel was small and unremarkable, and the glasses, the mop of fair hair and the boyish enthusiasm had led every class he'd ever taught to call him Joe 90 behind his back. Brodie was tall and dramatically good-looking with strong features, a cloud of dark hair and a taut curved figure. Each of them, alone, drew glances. Together, on their way to a pub lunch or any of the little everyday pleasures they shared, they made an absurd couple.

Brodie didn't care. Daniel was her best friend – not only because she liked him but because she liked herself better for knowing him. He brought out the best in her – reserves of kindness, patience and tolerance that she would never have found alone. He was the cricket on her shoulder: amiable, good company, a friendly voice in her ear, and a conscience for times when it would be easy to ignore her own. He bullied her when she needed bullying, encouraged her when she needed encouragement, held her fast when she needed an anchor. He was the brother she never had but without the baggage that blood relatives bring. There was history between them, of course, and some of it had to do with blood, but the only obligations were those they created for themselves and were the stronger for it.

Daniel hadn't noticed her hesitation. 'Why doesn't he go to an estate agent?'

'Hm?' Brodie looked at the flier and remembered what she'd been saying. 'He did. They couldn't find anything suitable.'

'What made him think you will?'

'*I* made him think that,' she said firmly. 'This is how I make my living, yes? Finding things that other people can't. Buying things that weren't actually for sale. It works for Meissen shepherdesses and it works for houses.'

Daniel thought about this. 'You mean, you're going to knock on people's doors and say, "Someone's going to give me a lot of money if I can get you to move"?'

'Pretty much. Slightly different emphasis, maybe. I tend to stress that my buyer will pay above market value, and if they need help moving I'll do that for them too, but yes, that's pretty much the pitch. It doesn't always work. There are people who won't move at any price, but most people will if the deal is sweet enough. By the time a buyer's desperate enough to come to me, he's ready to sweeten the pot to the point where fillings fall out.'

'I take it they're pretty successful then.' He was reading the flier upside down. 'Ghouls In Satin'.

'Souls For Satan! Jesus, Daniel, even I'd heard of Souls For Satan, and I'm too old for demon rock and Paddy's too young. Some people are famous enough to transcend the boundaries of their own genre.'

'That's probably true,' Daniel agreed slowly. 'Of Albert Einstein, and Albert Schweitzer, and Alexander Fleming, and David Livingstone, and Pierre and Marie Curie. I'm not sure it applies to pop singers.'

'I think they *think* it applies to them. I think their accountants do too.'

'Now you're confusing wealth with importance,' said the man who'd never earned more than a living wage and now earned rather less. 'How many pop singers' names will still be part of the language when they've been dead for fifty years?'

'Precious few,' conceded Brodie. 'But they don't expect to be. Right now Souls For Satan are making obscene amounts of money playing loud music to teenagers across half the world. The bubble may burst tomorrow, or they may be around for another few years before a new New Thing finishes them. Just possibly they'll still be on the A-list in their sixties, like the Stones. But even if they're not they'll have made more money in a few years of doing what they're good at than most of us manage in a career. Maybe that isn't your idea of importance but it's certainly success. Not everyone can split the atom. It's enough to find one thing that, for one brief shining moment, you're better at than anyone else.'

Daniel's mild grey eyes danced with amusement. 'You're a groupie!'

Brodie chuckled. 'I'm ten years and one child too old to be a groupie. I'm all grown up, Daniel: I have property of my own, and a business, and taxes to pay, and if I can find a Home Sweet Home for a demon rocker with an income like the GNP of Belgium I shan't care how fleeting his fame or whether he could be doing something more worthwhile with his time. All I care is he pays my commission before demon rock is the last big thing and what the kids in the music stores are queueing up to hear is singing hamsters.'

Daniel didn't look over his glasses at people because he couldn't see them if he did. He marked his disapproval by peering through the upper edge. 'Now you're just being silly.'

Eric Chandos didn't wear silver chains and body-piercing. He wore an expensive suit, a vicuna overcoat against the January chill and handmade shoes, and he drove a white Mercedes. He parked it on the double yellow line in Shack Lane immediately in front of the burgundy door with its slate shingle inscribed *Looking For Something?* because he could afford to pay parking fines. He went to open the door and seemed surprised to find it locked against him.

Brodie knew Jared Fry's manager was there. She waited until he rang the bell before answering. This was a consulting room, not a shop – people didn't wander in off the street, if they didn't make an appointment they risked her not being free to see them. People approached her with a variety of problems and requests, few of which they would be happy to make public, and she didn't ask her clients to share a waiting-room.

'Mr Chandos,' she said coolly, blocking the doorway with the curve of her body. 'I wasn't expecting you.'

He was a tall man, taller than her, not heavy but powerfully built, his angular face defined by a well-shaped black beard. He had commanding dark eyes with a spark of mischief in them, and when he spoke his voice had a musical timbre that set a quiver in her stomach, like the deep roar of a tiger. He might have been forty.

'I took pot-luck.' His lips, sculpted by the beard, spread in a smile. 'I wondered if you were making any progress.'

Brodie glanced at her watch. 'I have an appointment in twenty minutes,' she said untruthfully. 'But I have a couple of possibilities for you to consider. I'll print them off, you can take them with you.' She stood back and let him in, the door closing behind them.

In fact, if Chandos hadn't called with her this Tuesday morning she'd have called him this afternoon. The urgency of the quest was reflected in the terms of their agreement. Brodie couldn't imagine why a demon rocker with three other homes in the UK and elsewhere was so keen for a fourth in the Dimmock area, but nor did she waste time wondering. The sooner she met Fry's arcane list of requirements, the better she got paid.

And she had hopes of a property that had just come to her notice. It wasn't for sale. It was the subject of a planning application and a neighbour had been telling *The Dimmock Sentinel* why an old coaching inn which had already been redeveloped as eight flats should not suffer the further indignity of having an extra block of four built in the stable-yard. Subdivided among nine owners, none of whom had expressed an interest in selling, the idea of reuniting it under one title would have scared off the bravest estate agent in Dimmock – which was Edwin Turnbull and therefore not saying a great deal. But Brodie relished a challenge, especially a lucrative one.

Before she showed him The Diligence, though, she made Eric Chandos read the particulars for two other properties she had on her spike. They met some of Fry's criteria, fell short on others. As she expected the manager shook his head. 'If I was looking for myself, Mrs Farrell, I'd want to view both of them. But Jared doesn't know the meaning of the word compromise. It makes him a good musician and a bad house-hunter.'

Brodie tried to look disappointed. She hadn't expected him to go for either property. She'd shown them to soften him up for The Diligence and the problems it brought. She said, 'Explain the set-up to me. You've got me looking at big, big houses. Will the whole band be moving here?'

Chandos chuckled. 'Mrs Farrell, I try to avoid having them in the same town, let alone the same house. Johnny Turpin – the keyboard player? – lives about an hour from here and that makes me nervous. The band as a whole gets together for rehearsals, gigs and recording sessions, and it's as much as I can do to stop them breaking one another's fingers in the coffee breaks. If they shared a house I'd have a band for about three days. After that I'd have a solo artist, three bumps in the lawn and policemen at the front door. No, this is for Jared. But he has staff, and he needs places to write, play music and entertain. His home is the head office of a big business.'

'What about you, Mr Chandos? Will you be living there?'

Chandos did the handsome smile again. But he knew the question was designed to peg him in place. 'That's right, Mrs Farrell, I'm a member of Jared's staff too. He has the courtesy to call me his manager but we both know where we stand. I'm a good businessman. But it's musicians who fill concert-halls, not managers.'

'I didn't mean to pry,' Brodie demurred insincerely. 'It's just, I've seen another property that meets most of your requirements pretty well. It's a bit unconventional, but if there are going to be a number of people living there it might be an advantage that it's currently divided into flats.'

One eyebrow rose like a circumflex up his forehead. 'Do you have a picture?'

It was the right question. The extensive work done to convert The Diligence Hotel to flats as recently as eight years ago had been mostly internal. A few new doorways, extended down from existing windows so as to disturb neither the structural nor aesthetic rhythm of the half-timbering, a fresh coat of butter-coloured paint and a new roof of Wealden tiles had in no way diminished the charm of a property so picturesque it was only saved from winsome by the fact that it had been a working building most of its life and it showed. Brodie put the file in front of Chandos and waited for a sharp intake of breath.

The photographs showed a long two-storey building running parallel to the road, an L-shaped wing and what had once been a stable-block creating a courtyard at the rear. The steep pitch of the roof suggested it had originally been thatched, and a gallery ran round the courtyard at upper-storey level. The outer, public facade was broken by a double row of small windows, cross-hatched with leading, looking over the Downs towards the distant Channel. In the centre part of the building a false floor had been fitted – and could be as easily removed – in what had clearly been a double-height hall. Immediately above it, rising through the roofline like the lamp-room of a lighthouse or the lantern of a very small cathedral, was a solar – a structure comprised almost entirely of glass. Anyone up there would feel to own not only half of southern England but half the sky as well.

'It's beautiful,' said Chandos at length. 'How does it measure up?'

Brodie had answered the question comprehensively in the file but didn't mind spelling it out again. 'Surprisingly well. The location is just this side of Cheyne Warren, in the heart of the Three Downs. Do you know the Dimmock area?' He shook his head. 'The Three Downs form the hinterland to this strip of coast. Chain Down, Menner Down and Frick Down are part of the whole range of the South Downs, with all the advantages that brings – an expansive rural setting sandwiched between the coast and the road to London. The villages are small and traditional, but you're only fifteen minutes from the Guildford road which makes it a fifty mile commute to the city. Except at rush-hour you'd do it inside the two hours you specified.'

She was watching him. He was being so careful not to react that she knew she had him hooked. And she wasn't finished yet.

'Cheyne Warren's in a dip of the Downs. But The Diligence is on top of the first rise to the south, which gives it a sea-view at the front as well as farmland all round. Mr Fry was anxious for a view of the sea?'

Chandos nodded, still said nothing.

'There are no immediate neighbours so rocking round the clock won't be an issue. There's a couple of acres of grounds, half of it woodland, which should be enough trees for anyone. And the property is on two storeys with a cellar underneath. What was the cellar for again?'

The manager had the grace to look faintly embarrassed. 'So I can tell the pop press Jared sleeps in a crypt.'

Brodie forbore to comment. 'As you see from the pictures, it's an old property – probably developed from a mediaeval hall house although the earliest reliable record of it is in 1650. But it's structurally sound: it was thoroughly surveyed at the time of the conversion.'

'And now it's flats,' said Chandos, reading the print-out. 'Eight of them. Won't that be a problem?'

'A problem, yes, but not an insuperable one. I'll do the negotiating. Set me an upper limit and I'll deal with each owner individually. I've done this before, Mr Chandos. It takes time, it takes a lot of meetings, a lot of discussion, a certain amount of persuasion and a degree of lateral thinking. But I haven't been beaten yet. If Mr Fry wants The Diligence, I'll get it for him.'

Chandos was still thinking. 'What an odd name for a house.'

Brodie had wondered about it too. 'Apparently it was the name of the stage-coach that crossed the Three Downs. It was The Diligence Inn, then it was The Diligence Hotel, and when they did the conversion they just called it The Diligence. You could change it but it is a piece of history.'

'Quite.' Done thinking, he shut the file and stood up. 'I'll put it to Jared. It's the closest we've come to what he wants. I'll get back to you tomorrow. If he goes for it, can you arrange a viewing?'

For what she was going to make from the purchase of The Diligence Brodie would have arranged for the current residents to swing naked from the jettied upper storey. 'Leave it to me.'

Chapter Three

When word got out that Brodie was negotiating the purchase of a property for the dark lord of demon rock, a number of totally predictable events occurred.

Small gangs of teenagers, biased towards the female by a ratio of two to one, gathered in Shack Lane, and nudged one another until a volunteer knocked on her door to offer their combined savings in return for the address. They trickled away disconsolate when she explained, with a restraint Daniel would have admired, that Jared Fry was paying her even more than £16-30 to protect his privacy.

Then Tom Sessions from *The Dimmock Sentinel* arrived to ask the same question. He didn't offer her money, and didn't sulk when she gave the same answer, but he did point out that it wouldn't be long before someone sold the story to the London papers and when they did he'd be back. She promised for old times' sake that she'd talk to him before she talked to anyone else, and on that note they parted amicably.

Every estate agent in Dimmock snubbed her in the street – except Edwin Turnbull, who regarded her as a man might who's been let down by a favourite niece but can't bring himself to disown her. These days Mr Turnbull wasn't just an estate agent: he was someone whose specialist knowledge and reckless courage in opening his front door at two in the morning helped save a woman from certain death. His picture was in the paper. His wife Doreen bought a dozen copies and sent them to everyone she knew. He owed that to Brodie Farrell, and she'd have to do worse than come between him and a potential client, even a rich one, to forfeit his goodwill.

Eric Chandos came down from London once a week to discuss progress over a meal and a bottle of something pretentious. Jack Deacon, who in recent months had become so nonchalant with the idea of a good-looking woman making room in her life for a bad-tempered policeman that he was starting to take her for granted, re-acted sourly the first time Brodie cancelled their regular night out at his favourite restaurant because it was the only time Chandos could see her. The second time he was, if anything, grumpier.

Negotiations to buy The Diligence proceeded as smoothly as a transaction involving eight residents, a free-holder and a purchaser could be expected to. The development company which owned the freehold and had wanted to build more flats in the stable-yard was happy to sell up. It had not anticipated resistance to its plan and was glad to walk away before its profits went on legal wrangling. Of the eight householders, four signalled their willingness to sell right away while three held out for a better offer. The last, who seemed genuinely reluctant to leave his flat, finally caved in when his fellow residents, keen to get their hands on the money, made a pariah of him. Brodie promised to find him something equally desirable and leave him with cash in his pocket, but sullenly he declined. He intended to invest in a business and live above the shop.

With the deal finalised it was inevitable that the news would break. Brodie persuaded Chandos to give Tom Sessions an interview and he got it into print twelve hours before the London tabloids, which left *The Sentinel* basking in self-admiration for a month.

The day after *The Sentinel* broke the story the chairman of Dimmock Architectural Heritage Society – the indomitable Mrs Fitch-Drury, sixteen stone of well-meaning thuggery surmounted by a silly hat – cornered Brodie on the Promenade and hugged her, oblivious to the sniggers of onlookers or the surprise of Brodie herself.

'Don't get me wrong,' she said, somewhere between a boom and a chortle, 'I'm not what you'd call a Rock Chick myself.' She managed to pronounce the capital letters. 'Given the choice I would not have put an important historic property into the hands of a man who puts obscenities to music for a living. But at least he won't be building more flats, and one owner has to be better for The Diligence than nine.'

'I'm glad you're pleased,' said Brodie, struggling for breath. 'I think you're right. I doubt he's gone to so much trouble to buy that kind of property in order to change it into something else.'

'Over my dead body,' avowed Mrs Fitch-Drury stoutly.

Brodie smiled and moved on. 'Well, round it,' she murmured under her breath. 'Or maybe a fly-over...'

On the first of April ownership of The Diligence passed to Jared Fry. His manager took Brodie out to lunch and settled her account en route to Cheyne Warren to set the builders and decorators to work.

'Have you much work to do before you move in?' Brodie had been too busy dove-tailing the various deals to worry about the décor.

'Not really. I want to get Jared's rooms ready before he sees them but everything else can be done once we're in.'

Brodie wondered if she'd misheard. 'You mean, before Jared sees them again.'

Chandos's smile was no less attractive on longer acquaintance. 'No. He hasn't been there yet.'

Brodie blinked. 'Eric – I know what The Diligence cost him. Are you telling me he hasn't actually seen it?'

'He's seen pictures,' said Chandos calmly. 'And the specs and all the rest of it. But he's been busy, he hasn't had the chance to get down.'

'I hope he's going to like it,' said Brodie fervently.

'Of course he'll like it,' Chandos assured her. 'And if by any chance he doesn't…'

'He'll buy another one somewhere else?'

'No – level it and build a nice block of flats.'

He was of course joking. Brodie was almost sure.

The builders completed Fry's quarters in three weeks. The decorators painted out all sign that they had been there, then stencilled sigils over the paint; then painted over the stencils because Mr Chandos said Mr Fry was a demon rocker, not a fortune-teller.

On the first Friday in May Brodie was closing up when she found the white Mercedes parked outside her door again. She peered through the tinted glass and Eric Chandos nodded back.

'I've cashed the cheque,' she said by way of greeting.

He chuckled. 'It's all right, we haven't found rats in the cellar or a ghost in the attic – and we'd probably have paid more if we had. I've brought an invitation.'

'Oh yes?' Brodie was already weighing up in her mind if she could get away with standing Deacon up again now her job was done.

'We're having a party at The Diligence tomorrow night. Jared wondered if you'd come.'

'Jared did?' Not once in the months she'd worked for him had they met.

'Certainly. He appreciates people who do a good job.'

It's always nice to hear a compliment. Brodie just found it hard to believe a man with Fry's resources ever accepted second best. 'I'm glad he's satisfied. But I rather assumed he always was.'

'Mrs Farrell, there are huge advantages to being rich – it may not make you happy but you can be miserable in real comfort – but there are drawbacks too. One is that a lot of people can't resist trying to cash in. They know you've been massively successful at something but still they take you for a fool. When you find someone who does exactly what she promised, doesn't try to spin the job out or negotiate a whole range of creative add-ons, and doesn't just happen to have a friend who writes for the Sunday papers, you remember. In the short term you ask her to your house-warming. Longer term, you keep her number for next time you or someone like you needs someone like her.'

'I *am* good at what I do,' agreed Brodie with a winning lack of modesty. 'And I do like a good bash. But won't I be the only one there whose party-frock didn't start life as a shroud?'

Chandos laughed out loud. One of the reasons he courted Brodie Farrell's company was, of course, that no man minds being seen with an attractive woman. Another was that she continually surprised him. She didn't state the obvious. She kept him on his toes.

'There are two things to remember about the music industry,' he said. 'First and foremost, it's theatre. Jared Fry on stage and Jared Fry in his own kitchen are two different men. Catch him when he's not spitting obscenities and french-kissing a microphone and there's a lot about the guy to like. Well, some things. The publicity stunts are exactly that – stunts, for publicity. "Demon Rocker Ate My Gerbil" is news. As a headline, "Demon Rocker Feeds Gerbil Before Putting In A Long Day At The Recording Studio" just hasn't the same impact. Off-duty, guys in bands are a lot more like everyone else than they like to admit. On the whole, demon rockers check their shrouds at the stage door.

'And the other thing is, the guys on stage are the tip of the iceberg. For every one vomiting into his drum-kit there are gangs of managers, technicians, roadies, publicity people, sponsors, record producers, DJs, journalists and celeb-collectors everywhere they go. You'll fit in fine. Usually, the one who looks most like a fish out of water is Jared.'

Brodie didn't need much persuading. 'I'd love to come. Can I bring a friend?'

'Of course,' said Chandos. 'I'd like to meet Detective Superintendent Deacon.'

A doubtful eyebrow scaled Brodie's forehead. 'Really?'

'Really. We've only just moved in, Brodie, the police can't possibly want us for anything yet.'

'Um – I'm just flying a kite here,' murmured Brodie, 'but policemen aren't always the most popular guests at functions where the intoxicant of choice may not come in bottles.'

His eyes were measuring her, assessing her. It should have been an unpleasant experience – he was not merely undressing her, he was checking the labels on her underwear – but the lick of his gaze evoked a response that startled her. Almost a thrill. She felt herself purring like a stroked cat. When she realised she was coiling her body round his wing-mirror, shocked, she hauled herself up straight. She had nothing against flirting, but usually it was a conscious choice.

Chandos's brown-velvet voice was low, provocative. 'I thought the police force of today wasn't going to concern itself overmuch with substances kept for personal use.'

'Ah yes,' grimaced Brodie. 'Well, that's the problem. Jack doesn't hold with this *Policing For Today* lark. Part of his soul hankers back to when hanging really was considered too good for criminals so they were drawn and quartered as well. Asking Jack Deacon to turn a blind eye to recreational drug use would be like asking a man-eating tiger to settle for a nut cutlet.'

Amusement made Chandos's eyes sparkle in a quite extraordinary way: at once knowing and surprised, warm and slightly dangerous. Brodie had to check she wasn't crawling in through his window again. 'Bring who you like,' he said. 'We'll be there from about ten. Come early: Jared wants to meet you.'

'Isn't he staying?'

'Yes. But after midnight he transmits better than he receives.'

Brodie stood back from the car. She glanced down at its perfect lines and pristine paintwork. 'I thought black was the colour of choice for demon rockers.'

Chandos gave a delicate little shudder. 'I'm not a demon rocker and I never was. I'm a businessman. I make good deals. Pass me a guitar and I'll only hold it the right way up eight times out of ten. But pass me a road map and I'll put together a tour that'll have a band playing for more hours to more punters in more cities than anyone else in the business. I can't tell Jared Fry anything about entertaining people, except this: you've got to reach them where they are.'

'And the white car?'

He shrugged offhandedly. 'It was what they had.'

'When you walked into the showroom.'

'Well...'

She had him on the run. 'So how long did you wait for it?'

Eric Chandos knew he was beaten. 'All right! Three months. I fancied white. I don't see any point blending into the background. I can afford a car like this, I want to make sure people know. Does that make me a bad person?'

Brodie grinned and walked away. Over her shoulder as she went she called, 'Ask me again when I've known you longer.'

'Will you come with me?'

Daniel shuddered. 'Brodie, I can't. There'll be hundreds of people there. You know I can't do crowds.'

They were in Brodie's kitchen. She left what she was doing and sat facing him across the table. 'You see, I think you could. Now. At least, I think it may be time to find out.'

'Last time I tried I lost it,' he said in a low voice. 'Totally. My old headmaster had to knock me down and sit on me.'

Brodie had heard. 'That's a while ago now. Also, it was where you used to work, a place you weren't free to get up and leave when you needed to. This would be different. We could leave if you started feeling uncomfortable.'

'I feel uncomfortable just thinking about it,' he confessed.

She smiled. 'You're not getting off that easily. Look, I don't need an escort to go to a party. If you don't come, it won't ruin my evening. I just see it as an opportunity. You're a lot better now than you were six months ago. Restaurants, pubs, the supermarket – ordinary crowds in everyday situations don't bother you any more. Maybe it's time to find out what else you can cope with now that you couldn't have done six months ago.'

'A party?'

Brodie nodded. 'It'll be noisy, but there'll be no one there you know and no one'll care if you want to go out in the garden for a bit. No one'll notice if we go home after half an hour.'

Behind the thick glasses Daniel's pale eyes slid out of focus. She knew he was trying it out in his head, wondering how far he could get before panic set in. She thought he was surprised at his lack of anxiety.

'But a party,' he complained after a minute. 'I don't *do* parties. I never did. Even before...'

He didn't finish the sentence; but then, he didn't have to. Daniel Hood's life changed utterly a little over a year ago. Before he'd even heard of Brodie, though not before she'd heard of him. On certain readings of the facts, what happened to him was largely her fault. When she started *Looking For Something?* she would undertake to find anything, including people. It never occurred to her to wonder what might happen to the young man in the grainy photograph if she managed to trace him for her client. Seeing him clinging to life in a hospital bed, a bullet-wound in his chest and his body pock-marked with burns, was what changed her mind about finding people.

These days they hardly spoke of it. They talked endlessly about everything under the sun, but not that. That didn't mean either had forgotten; and, though Daniel had long ago forgiven her, Brodie had not forgiven herself. It wasn't the reason for their friendship but perhaps it explained its importance, to both of them. And why Brodie's motives on this occasion were genuinely unselfish.

'You must have gone to parties when you were at college.' As far as she could remember, Brodie's university years consisted almost entirely of the things.

'Not really. I mean, I used to meet people in bars and bedsits and places, but the object was to talk. Exchange ideas. You can't do that at parties. You can't hear what people are saying. I always ended up in the kitchen, washing glasses and talking mathematics to a girl in sensible shoes. I gave up parties after the first term.'

Brodie sighed. 'That was your chat-up line, was it? Mathematics?'

'I'm a mathematician – what else? Fermat's Last Theorem slays them every time.' He gave a wry, self-deprecating grin.

For a moment Brodie didn't reply, her mind's eye fully occupied with the picture of a solemn student teacher in thick glasses, huddled in a dark corner where the fun wouldn't get him. 'Hot stuff, is it?' she asked then.

'I thought so. There are those who can't see it.'

'Imagine,' said Brodie evenly. 'Well, what do you think about the party?'

'Maybe Jack will want to take you.'

She shook her head. 'If you're not enjoying yourself, you'll go and wash some glasses. If Jack isn't he'll start arresting people.'

Daniel could see how that might make a policeman an even poorer escort than a man who took panic attacks. 'You think I should do this, don't you?'

'I do,' she said honestly. 'I think it'll be all right. But if it isn't, we'll try something easier next time.'

'All right. I'll give it a shot.'

'Good,' said Brodie. 'Now: have you *anything* decent to wear?'

Chapter Four

When rich men build homes they build them in private grounds where commoners can't stare at them. But inns are not residences and The Diligence was built fronting onto what was at that time a main route from the south coast to London. But that was long ago, before motor-cars let alone motorways, and what was once a main arterial had slipped down the rankings in the last century. Now it served only Cheyne Warren, looping back to the Guildford road north of Menner Down, and was quiet enough for people to ride horses and bicycles past The Diligence's mullioned windows.

Brodie had thought that might be a problem. All she knew of pop-stars was gleaned from television, but for people who made their money in the spotlight they seemed inordinately keen on privacy and she couldn't see how a coaching inn fronting a public road could be made private. But Chandos was unconcerned, merely gave instructions for raising the garden wall, topping it with wrought iron and backing it with a bank of mature shrubs. It didn't turn The Diligence into a fortress, but when the iron gates were locked it would take a determined paparazzo to get in.

Tonight the gates and all the doors were flung wide, light and music bursting out in all directions. Following the signs, Brodie parked in the stable-yard behind the house among cars worth more than her flat. She changed her shoes and picked up her bag; but halfway to the door she realised she'd forgotten something. She went back and yanked Daniel bodily out of the car.

'This is a once in a lifetime experience,' she hissed at him. 'You will never get an opportunity like this again.'

His plain round face was unhappy. 'Promise?'

Inside was bedlam. Entering The Diligence they hit a wall of sound – shouts, laughter, music and argument layered and tossed as if by a cement mixer, packing the available space so densely that all meaning was lost. Visually, the same chaos reigned. Far from the funereal atmosphere Brodie had expected, colour was everywhere, weaving and throbbing as two hundred birds of paradise flocked and wheeled, displaying to one another and mobbing the bar. It was im-possible to pick out individuals, and the patterns they wove were no sooner formed than broken up. The effect was a sensory explosion. Anyone prone to seizures would have been worshipping the skirt-ing-board by now.

It should have been an affront to a building as ancient as The Diligence. But actually this was what it was made for: not the mono-chromatic poor who pretty much stayed where they were born but the travelling classes who had money and displayed it every way they could – on their backs and in their entourages and in what they poured down their throats. The Diligence would have seen parties on this scale before. It would take more than a few demon rockers to shock these timbers.

Brodie stole a quick glance at Daniel. She didn't want him to know she was anxious about him. 'How're you doing?'

'Fine,' he said. He sounded surprised.

'There's Eric.' Brodie forged a way through the spectacle and fetched up beside the tall man in the grey silk suit. It wasn't the only suit in the room but it might have been the only one that anyone outside the entertainment industry would have been seen dead in.

The man he was arguing with, on the other hand, would have attracted uneasy looks in *The Rose*, which was the closest thing Dimmock had to a speakeasy. He was ten years younger than Chandos but his skin was sallowed by hard living, his beard a mere neglect of shaving. The fingers with which he gesticulated in the manager's face were stained by nicotine, the angry eyes sunk in dark pits like bruises. By his frame he should have been a sturdy man but his way of life had left his cheeks hollow and the tendons of his throat exposed. Where everyone else had dressed for the occasion – if not in the best of taste, at least with élan – he seemed to have set-tled for the first things he found in the right colour. Against the motley black his pallor glowed like a fever. He looked as if he had an imminent appointment with destiny, and not in a good way.

Brodie didn't like to interrupt them, partly from politeness but mostly because she wanted to eavesdrop, but it was almost over. The younger man threw her a furious glance before yelling his parting shot. 'It hasn't even got a swimming pool!' Then he was gone, a bun-dle of black rags swept away by the multi-coloured tide.

Realising she was there, Chandos turned to her with a restrained smile. 'It's nice when the host takes the trouble to greet all his guests.'

She indicated the departing man with a blood-red fingernail. 'I take it that was…'

'Yes, that was Jared. Spreading charm and good-fellowship wher-ever he goes. Among ourselves, you know, we call him Pollyanna.'

Brodie laughed aloud. 'And I thought all that sexy glowering was part of the act.'

'Oh no. That's real.'

'Well, let me introduce my friend Daniel,' said Brodie. 'He doesn't do a lot of sexy glowering but I'm fond of him anyway.' Seeing the faintly puzzled expression on Chandos's face she turned and found she was alone. She sighed. 'A pound to a penny he's in the kitchen, washing glasses.' She was hoping that was all it was.

Now Chandos laughed. 'Not what you'd call a party animal?'

Brodie considered. 'Perhaps a party hamster.'

Chandos collected a bottle and glasses and found them somewhere to sit out of the carnival. Brodie said, 'He didn't ask for a swimming pool. I'd have found him one if he had.'

'Don't give it a thought,' said Chandos. 'This is Jared all over. You bust a gut for him and he wants to know why you still have two functioning kidneys. *I* didn't know he wanted a swimming pool until today. He doesn't swim. Demon rockers don't – it's something to do with crossing water.'

'That's vampires,' murmured Brodie.

'Anyway, there's a couple of acres outside – if he wants a pool he can have one. It's not that he wants a pool: it's that he wants to complain. It would kill him to say he was pleased with something.'

Brodie eyed the tall man speculatively. 'That must make it difficult working together.'

'It does. Do you know what makes it easier? All the money.' They chuckled together like friends. Brodie thought fleetingly of Daniel, that he might be in trouble, that rather than talking mathematics and washing glasses he might already have been overwhelmed by the fairground atmosphere and be standing out in the dark garden unable even to get himself home. Then she forgot him.

Daniel was fine. And then all at once he wasn't.

When Brodie took off into the raucous crowd in pursuit of her client and the chaos swirled between them, he stood alone in the eye of the maelstrom and waited, breath abated, to see how he would fare. Seconds passed. He had to take another breath. Still he was just a man standing in a crowd, not a panic-flayed brain imprisoned in its own skull hammering to get out, every muscle knotted, every pore streaming, existence concentrated in a silent scream that started in the pit of his belly and swelled to encompass the universe.

He breathed again. Brodie was right. Three months ago he couldn't have done this. He'd healed without knowing, and would never have known if she hadn't pushed him to find out. He breathed again.

Someone put a drink that he didn't recognise into his hand. He risked looking round. They were just people: dressed like parrots and making the same kind of noise but still just people enjoying a night out. There was nothing to be afraid of. He knew where the door was, could be out of here in six seconds if he had to be, but really there was nothing to flee, no reason to panic.

Then the music changed.

At one end of the mediaeval hall was a raised dais where its first owner had conducted his business. The more things change, the more they remain the same: the new owner was using it for the same purpose. Spotlights that a moment earlier had been focused on a DJ with a set-up like Mission Control at Houston suddenly switched to centre stage and picked up a figure which no one – to judge from the sharp intake of two hundred breaths and the chorus of delighted cheers – had noticed until just then. Intrigued, Daniel watched between the shoulders of people taller than him.

In the confluence of the spotlights Jared Fry was something different to the ragged ruffian Brodie had almost met ten minutes earlier. He hadn't changed his clothes but now the black rags shimmered, and mostly it was the light but some of it was the kind of internal energy that fuels stars. His face, paper-white in the bath of brightness, shone like marsh-light. In their cavernous hollows his eyes burned like coals. And when he sang... when he sang...

The voice was as rough as concrete, raw as a wound, and it tore from his throat like a brute birth, marvellous and monstrous. It wasn't so much an energy that drove it, Daniel thought, as a desperate need to get it out there, to be rid of it. The man sang from the depths of his soul in every sense of the words, as if the music festered within him and without venting would spread its poison. Singing was an emetic.

Before Fry sang Daniel had hardly noticed the music except that it was loud. Now it was like a presence in the room, a great dark creature spreading membranous wings over all their heads, making the air throb with its heartbeat. Daniel was astonished. All he knew about music was that there was a lot of it he didn't like. Until now he'd never suspected how much sheer power could be crammed into sound-waves. Enthralled and appalled in equal measure, he stood frozen, mineralised like Lot's wife, while the demon rock bludgeoned his soul; and he never noticed the tight fluttering starting up in his chest.

And what Jared Fry sang was:

I am the timber, the tree that was growing,
the king of the mountain, the pride of the wood.
I am the iron, the ore that was taken
by deep-delving men who knew iron is good.
Men cut me and sawed me, and smelted and poured me,
and now a man's paying in praying and blood.

Millennia pass, and the wood is still growing,
the ore is still glowing in furnace and fire,
and men are still bleeding, and begging and pleading,
and nobody's leading them out of the pyre.
The promise is broken, the words were a token,
the smoke from the burning mounts higher and higher.

We crucify women whenever we take them.
We shake them and break them and leave them in blood.
We plough them and seed them whenever we need them.
They smile through the tears and say it was good;
and don't feel betrayed at having been nailed
to the cross of our wanting, the dream of our rood.

There is no redemption, there is no salvation.
The future is only a come-again past.
The skies are still clouding, the darkness is crowding,
the death-knell is sounding, the dice are all cast.
The strongest are shaken, the truest are broken,
the kraken is waking. The void is vast.

In the dense pack of bodies below the dais people were driven to dance. It wasn't dance music, but in any bacchanalia there's always someone willing to try. Like an electric current, the pulsing beat galvanised bodies and limbs. Immediately in front of Daniel a girl threw her arms to the beamed ceiling and her wits to the wind, and pirouetted into him, spinning him into the surging crowd.

He didn't just lose his balance. He lost all sense of direction so he no longer knew where the door was. He lost the sense of autonomy, that he was here from choice and was free to leave, that no one had an interest in staying him. From a grown man escorting a friend to a noisy but essentially benign social gathering, in an instant he was reduced to a frightened child in a situation he could neither understand nor control nor escape. The old panic rose behind him like the wicked wizard in a pantomime, throwing its cloak over his head, laughing at his helpless burgeoning terror.

Either those around him didn't see he was in trouble or no one cared. They may have thought he was drunk. They may have thought he too was moved to dance by the insistent crash of the music and just wasn't very good at it. He saw sweat-shiny faces leer at him and then move away. He saw the rainbow colours of their garb spiral around him. He tried to ask for help but couldn't find the words.

He looked desperately for Brodie but couldn't see her. Now he couldn't breathe. The harder he tried, the less oxygen he got. He gasped in the sterile air, pulse thundering in his ears until it drowned out even the crowd, even the thumping music. He thought he was going to die. The rational core of him knew the danger was illusionary, that you can't die of panic unless you happen to be half-way across Niagara on a high-wire, but those parts of his brain that were still operating honestly believed he was going to die.

Of all the people crammed into the mediaeval hall, only one was looking Daniel's way. And he had other things on his mind, but by degrees the awareness of another human being in distress brought his focus back from wherever it was Jared Fry went in the throes of his music. He threw the microphone to the DJ and vaulted off the dais, forcing his way through the crowd; and they, thinking it was part of the act, cheered louded and stamped harder and wore the marks of his elbows with pride.

At the heart of Daniel's not-so-private hell a new face loomed out of the mayhem, a voice out of the chaos. 'You OK?'

Daniel shook his head. In fact his whole body shook. He was mortally afraid the man wouldn't understand, would walk away and leave him alone.

But strong hands gripped his shoulders, steering him through the crowd, a harsh voice by his ear clearing a path. The riot of colours parted, the arch of a doorway appeared, and then he was out of the press of people and into an oasis of calm and, when the door closed behind them, quiet. A kitchen. There was a table with bottles on it and already a stack of used glasses beside the sink. Weak with relief, Daniel gave a faint, half-hysterical chuckle. This at least was a situation he was familiar with.

The man holding him hooked out a chair with his toe and dropped Daniel into it. He swilled out a glass and filled it from the tap. 'Drink.' Daniel's teeth rattled on the rim. It took time to unclench them enough to do as he was told. When he did the panic began to subside.

He found an unshaven face peering into his own from a range of inches. 'What happened?'

Daniel panted softly, recovering his breath. His face was wet with sweat and he was damp under his clothes. 'Panic attack. I'm sorry. I thought I could do this.'

'It's happened before?'

'Oh yeah,' sighed Daniel. 'Not so much recently.'

'I thought it was a bad trip.'

'In a way. Thanks for your help. I couldn't have got out of there alone.'

The man shrugged. Dressed in black – worn jeans, torn shirt – he looked as if he'd come to sweep the chimneys and got caught up in the party by accident. 'I thought I was going to end up talking to guys in pointy hats. I don't mind people bringing their own stuff, but if they're going to kill themselves I'd rather they did it somewhere else.'

Daniel was putting it together. 'You're Jared Fry.'

Fry's expression was still. 'You didn't recognise me?'

'I don't think we've been introduced,' said Daniel, with that old-fashioned solemnity that made old ladies want to pat his head and had Jack Deacon reaching for his truncheon. 'I've seen your picture but you were wearing mascara. And, um, chains.'

Fry barked a laugh. He wasn't a big man but his voice was pitched a couple of tones lower than expected. 'Professional attire.'

'Ah. Like a bowler,' said Daniel.

Fry didn't know quite what to make of him; adding his name to the end of a long list. 'What made you lose it?'

'Somebody stumbled into me. But I think mainly it was the music.'

'My music?' He almost seemed pleased.

'I suppose.'

Fry grinned. 'It's nice to know I still have an effect on people.'

'It's powerful stuff,' said Daniel. 'I had no idea.'

'You're not a fan then.'

'No. Sorry. I thought I was too old for pop music.'

'It's not pop, it's rock.'

'Sorry.'

Fry was still trying to make sense of it. 'If you don't know me and you're not a fan, what are you doing here?'

'I came with a friend. Brodie Farrell – she found this house for you.'

A glower crossed his brow. 'Oh yeah. She's with Eric. Do you want me to get her?'

Daniel shook his head. 'I'll be fine here. Let her enjoy the party. I'll wash some glasses.'

'All right.' Fry looked sourly at the kitchen table, groaning under the weight of bottles. There must have been hundreds of them, all the same. 'Have you seen this?'

'It's cola,' said Daniel, not understanding.

'Yes it is,' growled Fry. 'And if I had a house full of twelve-year-olds and a clown called Mr Chuckles to entertain them, it would be exactly what I meant when I said to get in enough coke for everyone.' Shaking his head, the black hair dancing lankly around his face, Fry left Daniel to his washing-up.

Chapter Five

In the timbered hall events had taken an unexpected turn. Thunderous music was still playing but no one was dancing now. Two hundred party-goers, oblivious of the treat awaiting them in the kitchen, were gathered round the open doors and windows along the front of the house.

Brodie and Chandos joined them; and because Chandos was the sort of man for whom crowds part they were soon standing at the front.

A demonstration was taking place in the road outside, illuminated by the spill of light from the house. It wasn't a large demonstration. What was remarkable about it was that none of those demonstrating was under fifty and some of them were wearing lisle stockings.

They were also carrying placards. They were hand-made. Some of the placards said *Demon Rockers go to Hell.* Some of them said *Sinners Come Home.* One of them said *Philbert's Healing Oils: Because Granny Knew Best* – until the demonstrator realised he had his bit of cardboard back to front and turned it round, at which point it said *Get Thou Behind Me, Satan.* A woman in stout brogues was orchestrating a chant of 'Souls Yes, Satan No!' with a tambourine.

When Eric Chandos emerged out of the grinning crowd the chanting first lost its beat then petered out in a confusion of defiance and uncertainty. The demonstrators watched the bearded man as if they saw something genuinely demonic in him.

Chandos said mildly, 'Is there a problem?'

The little gathering didn't have to nominate a spokesman: his garb did that. Chandos thought the white insert in his black collar made him a Catholic priest, but the narrow man with the bald pate and zealot eyes belonged to a much smaller and even less liberal establishment. 'I am the Reverend Gilbert Spender,' he announced with gravitas, 'and these are members of my flock at the New Brethren Chapel in Cheyne Treacey.'

'Pleased to meet you. My name is Eric Chandos and these are my friends. What can we do for you?'

Reverend Spender hadn't expected courtesy. It's easier to hurl insults at someone who's hurling them back, and for a moment the welcome wrong-footed him. But a man didn't get to be a chaplain of the New Brethren, even in Cheyne Treacey where the competition was limited, by lacking words on the big occasion. He drew a deep breath, swelling like a balloon.

'You can begin by ceasing that infernal racket!' He meant the music once more pounding from the sound system. 'Then you can send these harlots home with instructions on how to dress decently in future. And then, if you have any hope of salvation, you can get down on your knees and repent the outrages you commit daily against our poor bleeding saviour!'

'Hm,' said Chandos thoughtfully. He pivotted slowly on his heel and looked at the faces behind him, expectant and not at all offended. 'Well, Mr Spender. Thank you for coming. But I don't think I'll be doing any of those things any time soon.' He turned back to the house.

'You might well flee the Lord's name!' thundered Reverend Spender. 'You *should* be afraid to face Him. Don't think I don't know who you are, what you do. Imps of the Devil you are, all of you. Taking clear young voices that should be raised in praise and twisting them to idolatry! Taking fresh young hearts that should be filled with joy and turning them to evil.

'You don't like that?' He warmed to his theme as Chandos looked back. 'I know evil when I see it and I call it by its name. I know it's not the modern way. I know we're supposed to be tolerant and inclusive. To say that any man's creed is as good as my creed, and if it involves sacrificing goats and dancing naked round a bonfire, who's to say that his way is less precious to the Lord than mine?'

He drew himself up to his full if modest height. 'I told you who, Mr Chandos. I am the Reverend Gilbert Spender of the New Brethren of Cheyne Treacey. I do the Lord's work. I am not among the first of his ministers, but if I thought that naked heathens garotting goats could be anything but an insult to the Lord my God I'd leave my vocation today and go sweep the road instead. That's who I am, and what I do, and why I do it.'

His eyes narrowed dramatically. 'I'm not sure why you follow your path. How much you understand of how the Devil uses you. Are you sworn to him, as I am to God? Or do you think it's just a bit of nonsense that does no one any harm and makes you rich? A bit of a laugh.

'Look around you, Mr Chandos. These are the sons of Adam, the daughters of Eve. They had a birthright – life everlasting. The Lord Jesus Christ died to guarantee it. And you take it from them. You steal their immortal souls, and give them in return music that beats like a fever in their blood to make them forget. And you do it for a *laugh*?'

Watching him sideways, Brodie saw the moment at which Chandos had heard enough. It passed through his eyes like a bird crossing the sun, no sooner glimpsed than gone, and all the evidence of its passing was a slight lifting of the corners of his mouth in a tiny, hungry smile. But before he had been willing to let this foolishness go unpunished and afterwards he was not. 'You don't like our music, Mr Spender?'

'Like it? It is an abomination. A fart from the bowels of hell. No decent man would foul his ears with it. No respectable woman could hear it without blushing.'

Chandos nodded slowly. A backward glance gathered his guests as co-conspirators. 'So which notes it is that offend you? A? G-sharp? Maybe it's E-flat. It's a sneaky little sod, that E-flat, I always had my doubts about it. Is *that* the one the Devil uses and God abhors?'

He waited for an answer, just not quite long enough for Spender to formulate one. Then he shrugged, as if the minister had let him down. 'The dictionary defines music as the result of modulating sound-waves in an organised and harmonious fashion. Now, I can see how we might argue over whether a particular musical form is harmonious or not, but moral? How can a modulated sound-wave either have or lack morality? It's like accusing a chair of being wicked. It isn't wicked, it isn't good, it's just a chair. It's good for sitting on. It's bad if you throw it through somebody's window, but it's still just a chair.

'If you don't like demon rock, don't buy it. Buy *Songs of Praise: the Album* instead. Buy *The Dominican Choir Nuns Sing-along*. Buy Cliff Richard, for all I care: it's a free country and there's enough music out there for every possible taste, even yours. But if that's the price for getting into heaven, I think I'll be happier in hell.'

'You admit it! He admits it!' The chaplain was dancing with a terrible triumph. 'He's going to hell and he's taking all you people with him. But he won't burn, oh no. There's a right cosy welcome waiting for him. The number of innocents he's corrupted, Lucifer himself will shake his hand. Dear God, he advertises what he's up to on every disc he sells! Souls For Satan – that's not the name of his band, it's his job description!'

Chandos rather liked that. The smile broadened within the well-shaped confines of his beard. 'Maybe it's not the music that's a problem so much as the lyrics. Is that what's getting you all of a tizzy – the words of the songs?'

'Songs?' Reverend Spender's voice soared till it cracked. 'In better days than these a man who wrote such filth would have had his hand cut off. He'd have been burnt at the stake.'

'Have you ever read the Song of Solomon?' asked Chandos.

'Of course I have.'

'All that about the garden? About the winds blowing in the garden, making the spices thereof flow out? About the man coming into his garden to eat his pleasant fruits, and his fruits being sweet to her taste.'

'Yes,' said Spender in a low voice.

'You don't *really* think it's about gardening, do you?'

To his credit, Spender didn't hesitate. 'I think it's about love.'

'*I* think it's about sex.'

The little minister turned his nose up. 'Answer not a fool according to his folly, lest thou also be like unto him. Proverbs 26, verse 7.'

'He that hateth dissembleth with his lips, and layeth up deceit within him,' countered Chandos. 'Also Proverbs.'

'Curse God and die,' snapped Spender. 'Job, chapter 2, verse 9.'

'A stone is heavy and the sand weighty. But a fool's wrath is heavier than them both.'

Brodie had no idea if Chandos was quoting accurately or making it up as he went along, but Spender knew. 'You damned popinjay,' he yelled, abandoning the last vestiges of dignity, 'will you bandy words with a minister of God? This has become a house of iniquity in the midst of the righteous. Get from hence, and take your abominations with you. We don't want your kind here. We have families to protect.'

The closer the chaplain came to losing control, the more Chandos was enjoying himself. A throb of power came from him as if from a generator. His eyes sparkled with the joy of conflict.

In truth, making a fool of a pompous little cleric was not something an intelligent man should have been proud of. Brodie felt a quiver of unease that so demeaning someone, even someone who was asking for it, should give him such pleasure. But another more primitive instinct rejoiced at his deftness.

'Well, I don't see us doing that either,' said Chandos cheerfully. 'This is our house and we're going to be here a long time; and what we do here is none of your business. Will it involve Satanic orgies? –

certainly. Is there any danger of your wives and children getting involved? – if they play their cards right. Are we a threat to the church's ideals of pious decency? – I do hope so.'

Spender had his mouth open to retort, but Chandos was on a roll now and wouldn't let him in. 'You think your opinions are worth more than another man's because you're quoting from a book written thousands of years ago. If your doctors treated you according to best practice in Bible times you'd sue them – if you lived long enough. If scientists had learned nothing for two thousand years there'd be no power, no communications, no travel. Education would be what your dad remembered his dad telling him. Most children would die in infancy, most women in childbirth. Most men would die before middle age from minor illnesses and trivial injuries.

'The people who wrote your book lived in squalor and peril, and looked to a power beyond themselves to make a world they couldn't control a little less scary. But times have moved on. What made sense to them really shouldn't still make sense to you.' Chandos's beard jutted like a black finger driving home his point. His voice rang with authority. 'They were a primitive and frightened people who understood nothing of the world they lived in, and their God was a bloody tyrant. And that's the thing you worship? You know the biggest difference between you and Jared Fry, Mr Spender? He rides his demons. You kneel to yours.'

The argument might have gone on, though not to a resolution. Neither man was about to compromise. There was no middle ground. For Chandos, ridiculing the little minister was like pelting an Aunt Sally with a wet sponge: facile but still fun. And, while Spender's beliefs were too deeply ingrained to be shaken, sheer outrage rendered him incapable of response. By now he could hardly put words together without gibbering.

A cheer went up from the crowd at The Diligence. They thought it was entertainment. They sounded like a little corner of the Colosseum at the first sight of blood.

If the demonstrators needed any more convincing that demon rockers were the seed of Satan, that served. They were going home before the Devil himself appeared in a puff of smoke. They set off down the road at something between a stalk and a trot, leaving Spender no option but to follow his routed flock. The party-goers helped him on his way with a round of applause.

Afterwards they drifted back into the house. Someone changed the music, someone else opened some more bottles. A voice called from the kitchen, 'What's all this cola for?' The drama was forgotten, and nothing in Chandos's manner suggested he'd done anything to be ashamed of.

He ushered Brodie back inside, closing the door behind them. A sideways glance at his face told her nothing. She took the glass he offered and they picked up the conversation pretty much where they'd left it, Brodie trying not to let the tumult in her breast show in her face. Half of her was appalled at what he'd done – shredding a pompous but essentially harmless little man in front of those who respected him for no better reason than that he could. But the other half felt quite differently about it, and that startled and alarmed her.

Chapter Six

The events at The Diligence preyed on Brodie's mind all the following week. Every time she saw Daniel she apologised again. He accepted her apology, because it was undoubtedly due, and afterwards considered the matter closed. That Brodie couldn't do the same made him wonder if there was something else she felt guilty about.

Twice he created opportunities for her to talk about it if she wanted. She side-stepped them with a kind of desperate adroitness that was not reassuring. He thought she was avoiding the issue not because she thought it too trivial to discuss but because it loomed too large. When he thought of some of the things they'd managed to talk through, the fact that she couldn't talk about this troubled him.

Then she began avoiding him. When he suggested lunch she claimed to be busy; when he called at her office she said she was rushing out. Finally on the Sunday evening he went to her flat in Chiffney Road, uninvited and timing his arrival just before Paddy's bedtime. He didn't see how she could avoid speaking to him then.

Paddy was delighted to see him, Brodie less so. He saw her looking for an excuse to send him away. Ignoring her, he offered to tell Paddy a bedtime story, and by the time the little girl was asleep – head full of an unusual mythology in which dragons were the good guys and their trusty sidekicks were all mathematicians – Brodie knew they had to talk and had put the kettle on. They took the coffee into the living room. Brodie curled up on one sofa and Daniel, kicking his shoes off, on the other.

'So what's going on?' he asked patiently.

At least she didn't insult him by lying. 'Oh Daniel,' she sighed, 'I don't know whether I'm coming or going.'

'This isn't still about the party?'

'Yes,' she said, 'and no. Not what I did to you. I am sorry about that, but you know that.'

Daniel nodded. 'What do I not know?'

He thought she was changing the subject, but actually she wasn't. 'After John left me, I didn't think I'd ever trust a man again. He was my husband, we'd been married for five years, we had a little girl. I thought I *knew* him – but I didn't know he'd fallen for a librarian. I thought, if even John, who I knew best of anyone in the world, who had *Mr Reliability* tattooed on his forehead, could let me down like that I could never count on anyone ever again.'

'Then you met Jack,' Daniel prompted gently.

Brodie smiled. After everything that had passed between them – perhaps because of everything – he could still touch her heart in ways no one else could. 'I was going to say, Then I met you. Daniel, I don't think you're aware of the effect you've had on my life. I had a pretty jaundiced view of the world. If we hadn't met I'd have been a sour, disappointed old woman by the time I was forty.

'Finding you changed that. Provided options. It's impossible to be around you for any length of time without starting to feel a little optimistic. I was locked in my own bitterness and you freed me. Opened me out; unfolded me. I'm not sure how you did it, I'm not sure it's something you set out to do, but it happened. You showed me how to be happy again.'

'I'm glad,' he said softly. But he knew she hadn't finished.

'It was the trust I had in you – the confidence, the strength I drew from our friendship – that gave me the courage to risk being hurt again. If I hadn't known you first I wouldn't have dared get involved with Jack. And that's given me a lot of pleasure, as you know. Neither of us has used the word but I was coming to think of it as love. I was beginning to think in terms of commitment, of a future.'

The brow wrinkled above Daniel's glasses. His voice was low. 'Brodie – are you trying to tell me Jack's let you down? Been unfaithful?'

'No.' She shook her head, the cloud of dark hair storm-tossed about her shoulders. There was a thin despair in her voice as if a crack was opening in her heart. 'Jack's a good man. He'd never knowingly hurt me.'

'Then... ?' He didn't understand.

'I thought we were happy,' said Brodie softly. 'I thought *I* was happy. I thought we could be happy together maybe for the rest of our lives. Somehow it never occurred to me I might meet someone else.'

Whatever Daniel was expecting, it wasn't that. He only realised his mouth was hanging open when his lips went dry. He moistened them and hunted for something to say. 'Have you told Jack?'

'No!' exclaimed Brodie. 'Daniel, I don't want him to know. I don't think what I'm feeling now is real. I don't think it's going anywhere. I don't want to throw away what I had a month ago for something that might blaze like a firework and spend itself as quickly.'

Daniel was a mathematician: he could put two and two together. 'You're talking about Eric Chandos.'

Brodie nodded, face shielded by her hair. 'Yes.'

'Did anything happen? Anything you owe it to Jack to tell him about?'

She shrugged. 'Sparks flew. I really enjoyed being with him. Of course, you know that.' She looked at him, one lip caught between her teeth, but he said nothing. 'I want to see him again. But I'm not going to. I don't see any future in it. Fireworks are great for half an hour's entertainment, but what you really want on a cold winter's night is a big log fire.'

'Brodie...'

She met his gaze bravely. 'You're wondering if I slept with him. No, I didn't. Not on the night of the party and not since. I've *thought* about him – almost, I've thought of nothing else. I know better. Both my head and my heart know that what I have with Jack is worth more than a fling with Eric Chandos.' The problem was – and she knew it was dishonest to say that much and not finish – her loins weren't subscribing to the majority view.

'All right,' said Daniel, not quite steadily. 'Good. You've made your choice. I don't suppose you can forget this happened, but you can make a conscious decision to put it behind you. For what it's worth, I think you're right not to tell Jack. If nothing happened there's nothing to tell: you'd be hurting him for no good reason.'

Brodie squirmed. 'He may have guesed there's a problem. I let him think it was that time of the month, but even Jack started wondering after three weeks.' Daniel chuckled and Brodie cast him a wry grin. 'Listen: I'll sort this out. I feel better for talking to you about it. I *always* feel better for talking to you. I guess that's why...' She stopped abruptly.

He knew he probably shouldn't ask. 'Why what?'

'Why it never occurs to Jack there could be another man in my life. He thinks there already is.'

By Monday afternoon Norman Wilmslow the builder was already having a difficult week.

His seventeen-year-old son Jason had looked at him with a new respect when he mentioned one suppertime, between passing the salt and declining to fund a round-the-world trip in a gap year between doing nothing and doing nothing with a sun-tan, that he'd won the contract to renovate Jared Fry's house up on the Downs. The only-begotten Wilmslow had volunteered to mix cement and push wheel-barrows for a few days in the hope of meeting the demon rocker, until he realised Fry wouldn't arrive for weeks, at which point honest toil lost its appeal.

Until Wilmslow happened to remark that Fry had now moved in and given instructions for the building of a swimming pool. Nothing more was said, but Jason appeared at breakfast on Monday morning and by eight o'clock was waiting in the pick-up with his guitar on his knee. The builder said nothing. However much Jason wanted to be discovered – snatched away from his home, his family and the occasional urge to get a job, and projected into an alien world of raw music, rapacious women and foreign travel – his father wanted it more.

But immediately the work began he hit problems. Excavating beside the stables as per instructions he found both pipes and cables. He tried digging a few metres out into the garden and hit the septic tank, which was not where it was shown on the deeds. He looked around. Digging too close to the house would risk disturbing the foundations, which on old buildings can be a bit rudimentary. Mostly what kept The Diligence up was habit. Anything which caused the ground to dry and shrink, or to get wetter and swell, could have disastrous consequences.

Most of the day passed in bad-tempered consultations with the client, the surveyor and the building control officer. Wilmslow remained phlegmatic. It wasn't his fault, it wasn't his house, and it was only his problem if he was getting paid for it to be. Finally the decision was taken to relocate the pool further down the garden, far enough from the house that there should be no associated structures lurking under the soil. It would mean piping the water further, but Fry would be able to swim without fear of the gable-end of his house falling on his head. While Jason strummed hopefully in the back of the pick-up, Wilmslow began to dig.

You need a big hole for a swimming pool. Long before there was a deep end Wilmslow had shut down the digger and he, Jason, the surveyor and everyone else on the site were peering into the gritty trench.

'Hm,' said the surveyor. 'Well, you know what that is, don't you?'

Norman Wilmslow nodded glumly. 'That's my crew sitting on their arses for the next three days, that's what that is.'

'Shall I call the police?'

If he'd been here alone the builder would have been tempted to fill in the hole and try again somewhere else. He probably wouldn't have done it, but he would have been tempted. 'Go on then. Tell them we've got a body.'

Given the age and history of The Diligence, Detective Superintendent Jack Deacon thought there was every chance the murderer had escaped justice by three hundred years. It wouldn't be the first time a murder squad had been assembled only to be shooed off the site by archaeologists. It wouldn't be the first time a murder squad had been assembled to investigate the death of a sheep.

But as soon as he moved through the screens he knew it wasn't a sheep. He didn't think it was archaeology either. The remains were skeletonised and there was nothing identifiable as clothing, but to his policeman's eye – which was less scientific than other tools at his disposal but could see the whole picture and make an informed guess in a way that, say, a proton magnetometer could not – the grave just looked too new. Not a week last Wednesday new, but not fifty years old.

'One for me?' he asked the Forensic Medical Examiner.

Dr Roy, a big man in baggy white coveralls, straightened up and nodded. "'Fraid so. She's been here a few years, but probably no longer than you've been in Dimmock.'

'It's a woman?'

'Yes,' said Dr Roy, 'and no.'

Aditya Roy was the bane of Deacon's life. Not because he wasn't a good FME: he was. He was meticulous, intelligent, articulate and helpful. Deacon knew FMEs so fresh from medical school they knew less about cadavers than the policemen they were advising, and others so set in their ways they hadn't opened a textbook in years. He knew of some who were clever and didn't want anyone to know, and others who were deeply ignorant and underlined the fact every time they opened their mouths.

Dr Roy wasn't any of these things. But he was incurably jolly, and though Deacon wasn't the most sensitive soul on the planet even he cringed sometimes when the big Asian speculated on the tragic last moments of some poor soul's existence as if commentating on a village cricket match. He laughed often, gesticulated, made inappropriate witticisms – mainly because there are so few appropriate ones – and would one day hold up a skull and shout, 'Howzat?'

And today he wanted Deacon to search Missing Persons for

hermaphrodites? 'What do you *mean*?' asked the detective with heavy patience.

Roy smiled sunnily, untroubled by Deacon's glower. 'I mean, she may have been a young woman or she may have been a teenage girl. It's not a fully mature skeleton.'

'How did she die?'

'Not sure yet. There are no obvious injuries. I'll know better when I've cleaned her up.'

'But we're probably talking about murder?'

Roy shrugged white plastic shoulders. 'Couldn't say, Superintendent. People do commit suicide. Of course, they don't often bury themselves in an unmarked grave afterwards.'

Deacon reminded himself that over the next two days this man would give him most of the information he needed to work out who the girl was, how she came to be buried here and who was responsible. As long as he kept that firmly in mind he could resist the urge to hit Roy with a plank.

In the trench opened by Wilmslow's digger, Sergeant Mills – the Scenes of Crime Officer – was already on his hands and knees, scooping samples into little bottles and evidence bags and labelling them. Neither man needed Deacon's help. All they asked was to be left to get on with their jobs. 'Let me know as soon as you've got anything,' said Deacon.

Detective Sergeant Voss had gathered everyone at The Diligence in the big kitchen: the builders, Fry, his housekeeper and PA, a couple of gardeners and someone called Mike who was wiring up a sound studio. He'd spoken to each of them but expected the superintendent would want to question them in more detail. So he was surprised when Deacon stuck his head through the kitchen door and said, 'Wrap it up, Charlie Voss, we're heading back to town.'

'Er – fine,' said Voss, shutting his notebook. 'OK, everyone, thanks for your help. We know where to find you if we've any more questions.'

Once in the car he said to Deacon, 'You don't think any of them's involved, then?'

Deacon shook his head. 'She's been there too long. Fry's been here a month and the builders not much longer. We should be talking to people who were at The Diligence in the late nineties.'

'I'll get a list together.'

'Don't trouble yourself, Charlie Voss, I know someone who

already has one.' As he turned for Dimmock Deacon added, with what can only be described as a smirk, 'And I mean that in the Biblical sense.'

When Deacon told her that evening what had been found at The Diligence, Brodie's immediate reaction was to be glad she'd cashed the cheque as soon as she got it. She didn't see how this could be considered her fault. But if Jared Fry already blamed her for not guessing that, along with the items on his long list of requirements, he'd meant to include a swimming pool, perhaps he'd feel that the removal of sitting tenants before completion was also her responsibility.

'Who was she?' she asked. 'Have you any idea?'

Deacon shrugged. 'When Roy can tell me a bit more about her I'll look for a match from Missing Persons. Until then the goal's too wide. All I know for sure is that she's been there longer than the present owner – so if you're worried I'm about to arrest your client, relax. There is something you can do for me, though. I need details on all the people who lived at The Diligence until you made them offers they couldn't refuse.'

Brodie thought for a moment, but there was no reason she shouldn't help. The information was a matter of public record, she was only saving him – or more likely Charlie Voss – the trouble of collecting it. Moreover, a girl was dead. There were times when she had to remind Deacon she didn't work for him, but this wasn't one of them. 'You stay with Paddy while I nip back to the office.'

Deacon wasn't a man who was comfortable with children, even sleeping ones. 'I'll come too. Marta'll sit with Paddy.'

Marta Szarabeijka in the upstairs flat would always sit with Paddy, even if she had better things to do. And it was an opportunity to do a little fence-mending.

From her desk Brodie called up the Diligence file and printed off the list of former owners while Deacon sat on her sofa, filling it.

He glanced at the list but the names meant nothing to him. He folded it into his pocket. But he didn't get up and head for the door. He was waiting for her to ask what was on his mind.

Brodie knew what was on his mind and didn't really want to broach it. They hadn't talked much recently. He wanted to know why and she didn't want to tell him. She hoped her restlessness would pass and leave them where they were before, comfortable with a relationship which – surprising as it was to on-lookers – had met both their needs for nine months now. She knew Deacon: when he mood passed he wouldn't enquire too deeply into the reasons for it. She left the desk and squeezed onto the sofa beside him, and wished he'd stop thinking and jump her bones.

He hadn't got to be a detective superintendent without developing an instinct for secrets. He had the scent of one now. But he knew better than to corner her. 'Typical, isn't it? I've seen nothing of you for three months because of all the time you've spent at The Diligence. And I'm going to see nothing of you now because of all the time *I'll* be spending there.'

He saw a flicker of disappointment cross Brodie's face; which would have pleased him but for the knowledge that – this being Brodie – it should have been more than a flicker of annoyance. She was tiptoeing round him. That had never been part of their relationship before and he wanted to know why. 'What?'

'I was hoping we might go out some evening. It seems ages.'

'It *is* ages,' he agreed, a shade gruffly. 'But not because I've been too busy.'

'I know.' Her smile had a wistful quality. 'It was a big deal for me – not just for the commission but for the contacts it might bring. I had to pull out all the stops.'

Deacon knew about pulling out stops. More than once he'd left Brodie alone in a restaurant and run out the door so quickly he'd left her with the bill. He had no right to criticise.

That didn't stop him. He shrugged dismissively. 'A nice fat cheque and some good contacts is what pulls your chain. Well, a body in the ground pulls mine.'

'Of course.' Brodie let her gaze drop to her lap, leaving Deacon feeling he'd somehow won a battle and lost a war.

He backtracked awkwardly. 'Mind, it's different when the killer fled the scene anything up to ten years ago. Er – when you saw Marta, did she ask you to hurry back?'

'No.'

'She didn't say she was heading out anywhere?'

'No.'

'Ah.' He nodded and just went on sitting there.

A slow smile spread across Brodie's features. 'Why?'

'Stay with me tonight.'

Chapter Seven

By Tuesday afternoon Dr Roy had firmer information on the girl at The Diligence.

'She was aged between eighteen and twenty-five and 163 centimetres in height – about five foot five; lightly built, with short fair hair – natural, not dyed – and good teeth. Good for her,' he added with an avuncular smile Deacon could hear all the way across town, 'not for you, because you're not going to identify her from dental records.'

'DNA?'

'That won't tell you who she was, only if you're right when you find a candidate.'

'How did she die?'

'I'm not sure. The soft tissue is gone so the only injuries I'm going to see are those serious enough to affect the skeleton. Knife-cuts on the bones, fractures, that sort of thing. All I've found so far is some minor damage in the right temple area. I doubt it killed her but it might suggest she was involved in a struggle. It might only suggest that she walked into a door.'

'You don't bury people in secret because they walked into a door!' Deacon said forcibly.

'Not usually,' agreed Roy, cheerfully unabashed. 'Superintendent, I don't know how she died but I can tell you some ways she didn't. She wasn't the victim of a frenzied attack with either a blunt or sharp instrument. She wasn't pushed off a building or run down by a car. She wasn't strangled, she wasn't burned, she wasn't in an explosion...'

Deacon scowled at his phone. 'Are you saying she may not have been murdered?'

The FME clucked at him. 'You know that isn't my province. She could certainly have been murdered. She could have been asphyxiated – by gas, smothering or drowning. Someone could have stabbed her really carefully so that she bled to death. The blow to the head may have been to stun her so the killer could take his time. I don't know. I don't think I'm going to know. I don't think this body's going to tell me much more.'

His tone brightened. 'Except maybe where she came from. I'm running a test that'll give us some idea where she grew up.'

Deacon appreciated the help he got from the forensic laboratory but not understanding how it all worked made him uneasy. You shout at a man until he tells you the truth, you know where you stand. But all this business of atoms and elements and *Therefore you're looking for a left-handed Irish Guard with a fondness for cheroots, Superintendent* – it was all black magic to him. 'You'll be able to say where she grew up before you know who she was?'

'Probably,' said Roy. 'The proportions of certain elements in the environment vary from place to place. These differences are recorded in our teeth. We can take a thin section from a tooth and be fairly sure that this person came from the south coast and that one came from the Welsh borders. Of course, it's harder when people feed their kids baked beans and fish-fingers rather than local produce. But it's pretty difficult to avoid the local water. I'll get you an idea of where she came from – at least if she was local or not.'

'When?'

'Leave it with me,' said Roy; as if Deacon had a choice.

'The other thing I need pretty soon is when she died.'

It was the question policemen always ask and FMEs hate answering. Science is about trends, not moments: to a detective the moment is everything. Roy did his best. 'The grave fauna are proving helpful' – Deacon was horribly afraid he meant maggots – 'but you'll have to be patient while I work out what they're telling us. If you want my best guess, she's been there between five and ten years. If you want science you'll have to wait a little longer.'

Deacon knew things about this girl now that he hadn't half an hour ago. Enough to call up the long sad lists of missing persons and rule out most of the people on them. A young woman in her late teens or early twenties, of average height, with short fair hair and good teeth. Though this was his job and he didn't get emotionally involved, he was aware that there was a middle-aged couple out there somewhere who, before this week was out, would have the news they'd been waiting for, and dreading, for years. 'OK, Dr Roy, thanks for your help. Get back to me if there's anything new.'

'Rest assured,' said Aditya Roy jovially, setting Deacon's teeth on edge.

Brodie lived in fear that one day Mrs Campbell-Wheeler would discover the junk-shop at the top of Fisher Hill; or else that Miss Timoney who ran the junk-shop would learn of Mrs Campbell-Wheeler. Because at that point Brodie would lose what's known in the trade as a nice little earner.

She'd got away with it thus far because the women moved in different circles. Mrs Campbell-Wheeler didn't go to junk shops. Mrs Campbell-Wheeler didn't even go to antique shops. She occasionally went to antique galleries, but that was all right because there wasn't an antique gallery on the south coast that would let Edith Timoney through the door.

She looked like a tramp. She looked, in fact, like a mad tramp, in her twin-set of ill-matched woollies, the cardigan always buttoned up wrong, and her ancient kilt that ended two inches of grubby ankle above where her men's socks began. On her feet were either galoshes or trainers, depending on the season. Her long grey hair was usually tied up with a scarf though at different times Brodie had seen a row of beads, a length of upholstery fringe and a piece of orange baler-twine pressed into service. She claimed to have Romany blood. It may have been true, though if she had the aquiline features of the true Gypsy they were hidden under the doughy complexion of a pie-eating champion from Wigan.

So the two women were not exactly social equals. It was hard to imagine Edith Timoney having a social equal. What she did have was a good eye for glass. Brodie never knew where she found it or how much she paid, only that it would be less than Brodie gave her for it and an even smaller proportion of what Mrs Campbell-Wheeler would give Brodie. If the leading light of Dimmock Ladies' Lunch Club but knew it, most of her admired collection of Victorian cranberry glass had passed through the hands of dumpy, grubby Miss Timoney.

Most of the local dealers would phone Brodie if they had something to interest her. Miss Timoney didn't have a phone. She didn't have electricity either, and there was scant evidence that she had a water-supply. When she wanted to see Brodie she sent a message with Wee Maurice who did her Heavy Lifting and was accompanied everywhere by a cat on a length of string. People assumed the string was to prevent the cat wandering off. Brodie suspected it was to stop Wee Maurice wandering off.

It was a half mile climb up a steep hill: Brodie took the car and told herself she'd need it to carry her purchases. Miss Timoney didn't disappoint her. They dickered over the price but Brodie took the lot. She'd feed it to Mrs Campbell-Wheeler a piece at a time over the next few months, giving the impression that she was constantly scouring the market on her client's behalf and earning every penny of her commission.

When she turned back into Shack Lane, her first thought was that someone had left her a parcel. Her second was that it was a bin-bag dumped in her doorway. Only after she'd parked the car did she recognise it as a human being. She had her phone out to call the police and have it moved before she realised this bit of human detritus was someone she knew.

Or at least, someone who'd recently given her a cheque for a great deal of money. Though their business was done, it seemed ungrateful to betray a demon rocker in a highly illegal state to his natural enemies. Brodie stepped over the mumbling body, unlocked her front door, put a hand on his collar and yanked.

She'd seen drunks before. She'd seen people out of their heads on assorted drugs. The sight of Jared Fry passed out on her office floor annoyed rather than alarmed her. She phoned his manager.

When Chandos didn't answer his mobile she phoned The Diligence. PC Vickers picked up. 'That you, Reg? It's Brodie Farrell. I'm looking for Eric Chandos.'

'I haven't seen him today,' said Vickers. 'Hang on a minute while I check.' She heard voices in the background, then the constable was back. 'He's up in London. The housekeeper isn't expecting him back till late.'

'Thanks, Reg. It'll keep.'

Actually, though, it wouldn't. She had to get rid of Fry before Deacon arrived. He'd asked her to stay over again and she'd refused; she'd asked him to tea with her and Paddy and, if grudgingly, he'd accepted. If Fry was still here in half an hour so that Deacon tripped over him he'd wake up in a cell. Since that would be the end of any repeat business she might get from him, Brodie looked for options.

She put on the kettle in the tiny kitchen behind her office and brewed coffee so strong the smell was enough to make Jared Fry open his eyes. But the pupils remained distant and unreactive, and after a moment the heavy lids fell again. He mumbled indistinctly into his chest.

Brodie hauled him into a sitting position against the wall, his head colliding with the plaster. She knotted her fingers in his lank black hair, tipped his face back and dribbled some of the fearsome liquid between his lips. When he coughed most of it down his front she repeated the process.

Finally she saw the beginnings of reason in his eyes. She sat back on her heels. 'Jared, do you know where you are?' He nodded. There was no way of knowing if it was true. 'So what are you *doing* here?'

'Leave. Leave him alone. He's mine.'

Even with her brows knitting Fair Isle Brodie couldn't make sense of that. 'Leave who alone?'

'Eric,' mumbled Fry. 'He's mine. I need him. Leave him alone.'

'*I* haven't got him,' she snorted indignantly. 'What are you talking about?'

'I know what you're up to.' Enough of the caffeine was reaching his brain that he was starting to make sentences, if not sense. 'You think you can flash your... flash your...' Just in time he opted for discretion as the better part of valour. 'Flutter your eyelashes at him and he'll fling himself at your feet. You don't know *anything*. I've known him for years. I've made more money for him than you'll see in your lifetime. He's never going to dump me for the likes of you.'

Brodie's eyebrows arched sharply. For a moment she felt herself getting competitive with a demon rocker for the soul of a man she didn't even want. Probably didn't want. She took a deep breath. 'So why are you here?'

The ravaged face twisted in a scowl. Fry was just alert enough to see he'd strayed into a trap, too woolly to get out of it. 'I'm telling you,' he slurred fiercely. 'Telling you. Leave him alone. He's no use to me if the only thing he can think about is you.'

Brodie blinked at him in astonishment. '*Me*? Eric Chandos is thinking about *me*?'

'Brodie this, Brodie that. Brodie says. Like a kid with his first girl-friend.' His tone was bitter. 'I need him. I need his mind on his job. Get out of his head.'

Brodie wasn't often lost for words. But this was... unexpected. It took a moment to regain her balance. 'You've misunderstood. Nothing is going on between Eric and me. I haven't seen him since the party.'

'What party?' Then Fry remembered. 'At the house. Yeah. You found me that house.'

'That's right,' said Brodie, hoping he was now circling the airstrip ready to touch down.

'You're good at finding houses.'

'Thank you, Jared,' she said.

But it wasn't a compliment. 'Find yourself a new one. In another town. I'll make it worth your while.'

Even knowing the state he was in, Brodie couldn't believe what she was hearing. 'Jared – are you telling me Dimmock isn't big enough for the two of us?'

But to Fry it was no laughing matter. 'Get out of my life. Out of Eric's life. I'll pay you. Or you can wait for the fire insurance to come through.'

Brodie had been threatened before. Most threats can safely be dismissed as wishful thinking; one in twenty is serious and warrants immediate police intervention. She wasn't sure about Fry's. Possibly he knew and no doubt he could afford that kind of help, and right now he seemed disturbed enough to want to hurt her. But he was a junkie: he was threatening her from a position half-prone on her office carpet because he hadn't the strength or co-ordination to get up. Whatever threats he slurred at her now would be forgotten by the time he was sober enough to do something about them.

As a kind of acid test she asked herself if she felt in danger from him, and the answer was no.

Still, she had to do something about him. She reached for the phone. 'You remember my friend Daniel. He had a funny turn at the party and you helped him.'

Fry sniffed, curling his lip in way that reminded her of Deacon. 'He didn't like my music.'

'That's because he has post-traumatic stress disorder, not conductive deafness,' explained Brodie as she dialled. 'Daniel? It's me. Listen, I need a favour...'

It was a few minutes' walk from Daniel's house on the beach to Brodie's office. For fifteen months that had been a constant source of pleasure to him. It made it easy to drop in on one another unannounced, and share a fisherman's lunch (like a ploughman's but with added sand) sitting on his iron steps, and talk about the myriad things that amused or troubled or interested one or other of them in the course of a normal week.

Just occasionally, though, there was a downside, and this was it. Like many people who enjoy more than their fair share of personal magnetism, Brodie could impose shamelessly on those who were attracted to her. Neither Deacon nor Daniel had ever found a way of saying no to her that (a) didn't sound churlish and (b) stopped her in her tracks. Mostly she proceeded as if they'd said yes so the end result was the same.

It was the exam season and Daniel was busy tutoring, devoting hours each day to preparing and giving lessons. He had pupils with him when the phone rang, a couple of fourteen-year-old girls who'd come to him struggling with long division and were now at home with logarithms and Pythagoras. He tried to explain that he couldn't just evict them but Brodie wasn't listening.

Finally the girls took pity on him. One of them leaned over – a little closer than was strictly necessary – and whispered in his ear, 'Give us an extra half hour next week.' They packed their books away, and their feet rang on the iron steps and their laughter on the salt air.

Daniel sighed. 'I'll be there in five minutes.'

Brodie had the nerve to sound faintly aggrieved. 'I *knew* you were only pretending to be busy!'

'I've been pouring coffee into him but he isn't sobering up much.'

Daniel stood with his hands in his pockets and his chin on his chest, gazing at the dishevelled heap on Brodie's sofa. 'I don't think he's drunk.'

Brodie nodded. 'Me neither, I just couldn't think what else to do. What do you suppose he's taken?'

'What am I, a sniffer dog?' Daniel took Fry's arm by the wrist and slid the cuff of his black shirt above his elbow. Fry watched disdainfully and did not resist. Daniel winced. 'Whatever it is, he's injecting.'

'I don't know what to do with him,' said Brodie. She was the least helpless person Daniel knew so when she played for sympathy he felt a little as Androcles must have when the lion held up its paw. 'I can't take him to The Diligence, the place is full of coppers, and I can't get hold of Eric. And Jack'll be here in ten minutes. I'd dump him on Marta but she's got Paddy. I can't just chuck him out, not in this state. I wondered…'

Daniel knew exactly what she'd wondered. 'Bring the car round. I'll keep him out of harm's way till Scotty beams him down.'

Deacon hadn't quite given up on Plan A, which to his mind was a great deal better than the Plan B Brodie had countered with. It was why he wasn't driving to her house but begging a lift instead. He'd told her the Area Car would pick him up sometime between Paddy's bedtime and his. Of course, if the Area Car was busy elsewhere she'd ask Marta to step downstairs again and run him home. And once there… Deacon wasn't a man to count his chickens, but he'd had a shower and changed his shirt and his underwear in the locker-room before leaving Battle Alley.

It was twenty past six now, so he had ten minutes to get to Shack Lane. He was spending them trying to forestall the myriad emergencies that might lead to urgent phone-calls, mumbled apologies and a night spent kicking himself. It was, he was well aware, optimistic trying to run a social life and a murder inquiry at the same time. The only thing that made it possible was that, whoever she was, the girl at The Diligence had been dead for years.

It's the first forty-eight hours that matter. That's when the body will speak almost as clearly as it did in life, when the scene will yield real clues, when neighbours will remember seeing an argument under the street-lamp, when a panic-stricken killer will stumble home with blood on his clothes and never realise he's leaned against the gatepost, the door and the hall wallpaper.

For forty-eight hours you throw as much manpower at the problem as you can muster, talk to everyone you can find, whistle up every specialist you can think of and subject every piece of evidence to every scientific method you know, because if you want to crack this every hour counts. With the clock ticking you don't stop for meals and you don't stop to sleep: you snatch both in bite-sized chunks at your desk, in your car or occasionally in the autopsy room, and the first one to call his wife is a sissy.

This long after, the need to find out what happened at The Diligence was no less but the urgency was. Whoever killed the girl wouldn't still have her blood under his fingernails. He could be on the other side of the world by now; and if he wasn't it probably meant he wasn't going anywhere. It would take time to get to the bottom of this, but after so much of it time wasn't really the issue.

Except for that bit of it between six-thirty and about eleven tonight, when any untoward breakthroughs – welcome as they would be at any other time – could quickly render the clean underwear superfluous.

So he spent a last few minutes checking that all the bases were covered. Detective Sergeant Voss was in Deacon's office, which was the best insurance against interruption he could arrange; partly because Voss was capable of dealing intelligently with most things that might arise, and partly because he knew how long Deacon could hold a grudge.

As Deacon was finally heading for the door the phone rang. Voss beat him to it by a split second, waving him on his way. Deacon didn't go, hung around anxious and scowling like a bogie-man when someone's vacuuming under the bed.

It was Dr Roy. 'I've done the autopsy on your girl.'

Another reason Voss was good at covering for Deacon's absences was that he could think very quickly if the need arose. 'Hello, Aunty,' he said. 'Listen, I keep telling you, you shouldn't call me at work.'

Deacon gave a gruff little chuckle, mimed 'You've got my number' and headed downstairs.

'Sorry, Dr Roy,' said Voss. 'Mr Deacon was just on his way out. Should I call him back?'

'No, no,' said Aditya Roy amiably. 'Just a bit more detail to flesh out the bones. Sorry,' he added, the avuncular smile audible in his voice, 'pathologist's joke.

'So. She was in good physical health and always had been – no signs of old injuries, or any around the time of death except that bump to her temple. I'm not convinced it killed her, although it's hard to be sure with head injuries. People head-butt cars and walk away; others die because a book fell off a high shelf.'

'You think someone hit her?'

'It could have been a blow,' agreed Roy. 'Or a fall, or she might have walked into something. It could have been an accident, only why then was she buried in secret?'

'What about the time of death? Can you narrow it down any?'

'A little. I'd say she was alive in 1995 and dead three years later. And she went into the ground in summer.'

'How do you know that?'

'The little beasties,' said Roy cheerfully. 'Different beasties at different times of year. The ones that started work on this girl are active in summer: June to August, depending on the weather.'

Voss was taking notes. 'Anything to help identify her?'

'Sorry, Sergeant. Not a stitch of clothing on her and nothing in the grave. Unless she was a nudist, she was stripped before she was buried.'

On the face of it Roy's information wasn't much help. She was still an unknown girl who died in one of three months in one of three years in a manner that was uncertain. All the same, the time-window was progress. Now CID could establish who was at The Diligence in that period and start asking questions. A detective with no one to question is one of the saddest spectacles in nature.

On the desk was a list of the eight residents with whom Brodie negotiated the purchase of The Diligence flats. She'd made a note of how long each had lived there, probably because it affected how much money she'd offered them. Voss had a lot of respect for Brodie Farrell, not least because he knew an operator when he saw one.

As he read down the print-out he saw something else, and for a couple of minutes wasn't sure if it was a help or a hindrance. Actually it was neither, but it was useful to know. None of the residents at The Diligence had been there as long as ten years. Ten years ago it was still The Diligence Hotel.

Some of the names on Brodie's list had lived there for eight years, some for seven. More recent arrivals than that Voss felt justified in dismissing from the inquiry.

He wasn't going to do anything about it tonight. But first thing tomorrow he would contact the developers who converted The Diligence to flats and ask them for dates and details. When the hotel closed, when they moved on site, how long the work took, and when the first purchaser moved in. It occurred to Voss that, if you had a body to dispose of, a building-site was a good place to do it.

What he could do this evening was start a systematic search through the various data-bases for fair 163-centimetre-tall girls in their late teens or early twenties who were reported missing in the summer between 1995 and 1998.

It sounded simple. But Voss had done this too often to expect a quick result. One complicating factor is how many people are reported missing every year. And the other is that, as most murders are domestic, not all disappearances are reported.

Chapter Eight

For most people, waking from a drugged sleep in a place they didn't know to a face they barely recognised would be the worst kind of nightmare. For Jared Fry it was routine.

As his system metabolised the heroin his body came back to him. He was cold and his mouth tasted like an old sock. He had a vague recollection of climbing some stairs, or being dragged up them, but couldn't work out where he was.

He knew he wasn't at The Diligence: neither in the cellar which Chandos had invited the music press to photograph, nor in his actual bedroom, nor even in the solar on top of the house where he commonly slept – still in most of his clothes as often as not, an old quilt pulled around him, the heavy metal thumping from the music centre numbing his mind, keeping him from thought till exhaustion intervened. He knew that someone came into the airy moonlit room about then, turned the music off, took his boots off, lifted his legs onto the sofa and tucked the quilt around him, but he didn't know who it was. Chandos perhaps, or Miriam the housekeeper. He'd never asked.

Nor was it an hotel room, this place where he was now. The best of them had a certain smell; the worst of them were bigger than this, and came equipped with mini-bars and trouser-presses not wall-sized posters of the night sky. When he opened his eyes and saw stars, his first thought was he'd passed out in a ditch. That wouldn't have been a first either.

But he was definitely indoors: sprawled on a bed with a lamp nearby banishing the shadows to the corners of a grey and white room. Though cold he was out of the rain and seemed to be safe, so Fry lay still and waited to see who wanted his babies this time.

Though he'd seen some pretty plain groupies before, the girl with the yellow hair, thick glasses and round, frankly simple face came as a bit of a shock. Only when Daniel told him to sit up and drink some orange-juice did he realise his mistake.

Fry hadn't realised how thirsty he was until he started. He drained the glass and it was refilled. He peered again at the face, its edges blurred by the opiate still in his bloodstream, and his brow corrugated with the effort to remember. 'I know you.'

'Yes. I'm the one who freaked out at your party.'

'You got a name?'

'Daniel Hood.'

'Where are we?'

'My house.'

Fry looked round again. There were two windows, two doors. 'All of it?'

Daniel laughed. 'A significant proportion.' He pointed. 'The bathroom's through there, the living room's through there. Get cleaned up and I'll make some supper.'

'Screw supper. Get me a drink.'

Daniel wasn't sufficiently interested in celebrity to be awed by it. If he'd had Patrick Moore hung-over on his bed he just might have felt a *frisson*, but a popstar was just a man who made noise for a living. Jared Fry had been kind to him when he needed it and he was returning the favour, but that didn't include fawning on him. He knew Fry was feeling fragile and sympathised, but only to the extent of providing what he needed, not what he wanted.

'Finish the orange-juice. Or there's water in the tap. Or, if you ask nicely, I'll make a pot of tea. Anything else can wait till you get home.'

People didn't often speak to Fry that way. He was unsure how to respond. 'So drive me home,' he growled.

'What's the magic word?'

Fry regarded him in disbelief. Of course, he didn't know Daniel was a teacher. His eyes, deeper and darker than always, smouldered and crackled. Daniel headed for the door.

'*Please* drive me home?' said Fry. It was like pulling teeth.

'I don't have a car,' said Daniel pleasantly. 'I can call you a taxi.'

Fry was sober enough to know he wasn't sober enough to make that a good idea. 'I'll call Eric, he can come for me.' He patted his clothes but there was no sign of his phone.

'Use mine,' said Daniel.

Fry didn't know the number. Defeated, he slumped back on the bed. 'I'll stay here, then.'

'You're welcome,' murmured Daniel.

He made tea and toast and carried it into the living room. He didn't wait for Fry, but within a couple of minutes the demon rocker appeared looking both fresher and steadier, and took one of the mugs, drinking fiercely.

'It must have come as a bit of a shock,' said Daniel, making conversation.

'What must?'

'Moving into your new house only to have the builders unearth a body.'

'It's bloody inconvenient, I'll tell you that much,' grunted Fry. 'God knows when I'll get my pool now.'

Daniel said nothing; and when he kept saying nothing, Fry finally realised it was the silence of disapproval. 'What?'

'I know she's nothing to do with you, that she's been there a lot longer than you have. But she was a human being, and someone ended her life and shovelled dirt over her, and he probably did that because she was bloody inconvenient to him too. It's not much of an epitaph. It's not much of a reason to die.'

Fry thought. 'People die for stupid reasons all the time. You can't bleed for them all.'

'You're a poet. You're *supposed* to bleed for them.'

Fry stared as if he'd been accused of something unnatural: giving to charity perhaps, or helping lost dogs. 'A poet?'

Daniel hadn't expected an argument. He gave the word some more consideration, then nodded. 'You weave a structure of words that conveys more than the words themselves. What's that if not poetry?'

'I write songs,' said Fry.

'A song is a poem to music. Why do you think it's different?'

There was a longer pause as Fry ordered his thoughts. Daniel suspected he wasn't used to engaging in discussion, not just about poetry but about anything. Giving orders but not talking. 'Because there was a time when I wrote poetry or something like it,' he finally said, his voice low. 'And now I don't. So yes, I know the difference.'

'What changed?' Fry didn't understand, shrugged. 'You were a poet, now you say you're not. What changed? Do meaningless songs sell better? Your fans get all they need from the album cover, songs that say something would just confuse them? So you beef up the obscenities and dumb down the content, and that way you can write a song in a day and still have the afternoon free. Is that how it works?'

Fry was familiar with sycophancy, with envy and with fear. He wasn't accustomed to having to justify himself. He wasn't sure why he felt the need to now. He had nothing to gain. In the unlikely event that he made a fan of Daniel Hood the effects on his career would be microscopic. Hood wasn't a music journalist, a record producer or a

DJ; he wasn't a booking agent, a festival organiser, even a fan club secretary. If he went out and bought every disc Souls For Satan had ever cut, the benefit to Fry's fame and fortune would be negligible. He didn't matter. So what if Hood thought what he did was trivial? Fry could buy Hood and everything he owned, and everything he'd ever done, with the small change from his pockets.

In spite of which, he found he did care that Hood considered him a fraud. It was because, while it might be true now, it wasn't always true and Fry remembered what it was like to have real talent. Part of him would have given back the money to be writing now the songs he wrote when he was twenty. So he tried to explain.

'*Now* that's pretty much exactly how it works. All the creativity is done. I have a name; the band has a name. People buy a Souls For Satan album, they know what's going to be on it. That's what they want. They're not looking for a challenge: you want to please them, you keep recyling the same stuff. The same themes, emotions, ways of expressing those emotions; the same obscenities. The perfect new release is as close to the last release as you can get without using the same title. And yes, it takes about a morning to write. Allowing for a coffee-break.'

A distance opened in his eyes that was quite different to the vacancy of drug dependence. 'I used to write good songs. Hell, I used to write *great* songs: songs that sent a shiver up your spine, that brought the sweat to your brow. Before I had a name. When I was writing for me, and people like me – people who listened to the words. Nobody cares about the words now. They care about the volume, the make-up, the stage set and the video. Get those right and you could sing the phone-book for all anyone cares.'

'Are you sure? Don't get me wrong,' Daniel said quickly, 'I know nothing about rock music. But if the words matter to you, what makes you think they don't matter to your fans?'

Fry gave a bitter little laugh. 'Experience, that's what. You think I haven't tried? You think the first record deal I signed, I threw away my pen and stopped trying to say things? That I was happy to write to a formula from then on? I wasn't; I'm still not. But any time I try to say something important the industry says, "Gee, thanks, Jared, that's… interesting, it's really cool you're still writing this stuff, but basically we've got a million fans lined up who don't want to have to think too hard. So what do you say, Jared? You gonna give us another take on vampire lovers?" So I do. I've been doing it so long I've forgotten how to do anything better. So maybe I was a poet once but I don't think I am any more.'

'The way you talk,' Daniel said softly, 'you could still write anything you wanted.'

'I'm not interested in writing songs that no one buys,' Fry said shortly. 'It was never a *hobby*, even when I couldn't make a living at it.'

'No. It was a need.'

Fry glowered at him. He didn't understand how someone he didn't know could know him. 'What do you know about it?'

Daniel gave a little smile. 'I have no skill with words. None. Little kids get the better of me in a fair argument. One of my friends is a Polish woman who learned English off a Rumanian with a speech impediment, and even she expresses herself better than I do. Because she isn't afraid of words. She fires them off like a scatter-gun, and if they don't do what she wants she fires off some more. I try too hard. I think so long about what I want to say that by the time I've got the right word the conversation has moved on. I can't tell you how many times I've come up with the *mot juste* only to find everyone else has gone bowling.' He blew out a sad little sigh that lifted his front hair.

'Numbers are different. Numbers I can do. There are no nuances, no room for debate. They always and only mean one thing: you can't twist them to mean something else. The smartest mathematician on the planet can't win an argument with a snappy *nombre juste*. They're the perfect means of communication for the anal retentive. An equation is either right or wrong: a quick thinker can't cheat by slapping down a number no one else knows.'

The scowl had vanished from Fry's face, leaving him attentive, trying to follow almost as hard as Daniel was trying to explain.

'How you feel about words, I feel about numbers. They light up my universe. The kids I teach see maths as a hurdle to be overcome, not a beauty to be owned. For most people it's like Latin: an anachronism. If you pay attention you might get a grade that'll let you study what you're actually interested in – anything from veterinary science to astro-physics. But when it comes to practical applications, a pocket calculator is your best bet every time.'

He did the gentle, self-deprecating smile that melted the backs of Brodie's knees. 'But not in my head. In my head it's a ticket to the cosmos. It takes me to the stars. The telescope in the corner there, it shows me pretty pictures – but I know what the pictures mean because of mathematics. I know how the world began, and how it will end, because of mathematics.

'I'm a pretty dim guy,' he admitted wryly. 'There's a lot going on around me that I don't understand. I'm running so hard to stay in the same place I haven't time to notice that actually I'm on the wrong escalator. It worries me, that all this stuff is going on and doesn't make any sense to me. But numbers I understand. Numbers keep me safe.'

Jared Fry said:

The guy upstairs is playing too loud
the music of the spheres.
My plea to him to turn it down
has fallen on deaf ears.
He's riding on a beam of light
out where the planets play
and never thinks his taste of joy
is ruining my day.

Daniel gave a delighted chuckle. 'Who wrote that?'

'That poet we were talking about. A long time ago.'

'It's not very demon rocky.'

Fry shrugged. 'I was more original then.'

'Did you record it?'

'Even then, putting the General Theory of Relativity to music was considered a minority interest.'

'I'd have bought it.'

'Hey, I'd have been rich by now,' said Fry, with an irony that only seemed to emphasise the weariness of his soul.

Inexplicably, Daniel found himself feeling sorry for the man. He was rich and successful; he'd scaled the peak of his profession; and for all the pleasure it gave him he'd have been better working in a carpet show-room and keeping his songs for a few friends in bedsits.

That may have been largely his own fault. Maybe it was part of the drugs package, that compared with that chemical high even the achievement of a lifetime ambition seemed banal. Maybe long days on the road and long nights on the stage had burned him out. Maybe even talent is finite: the faster the river flows, the sooner the lake empties. Daniel didn't know enough about drugs or rock music, or talent, to be sure.

But he knew about disappointment, and Jared Fry was a disappointed man. Still in his twenties, he believed his best days were already behind him. 'Why do you do it?' asked Daniel.

'What?'

Daniel lifted one shoulder in a delicate little shrug. 'Sing; write music; take drugs. Put so much effort into the things you like least about your life that you've nothing left for what matters to you. What's your motivation? If it's the money, why isn't it making you happier?'

'*Happy*?' Fry spat the word out. 'Jesus, Daniel, where *do* you get your ideas? If there's one thing demon rock is *not* about it's happiness.'

Daniel's tone was dismissive. 'Demon rock is what you do, not who you are. It's a performance: even I know that. And if the performance doesn't make you happy, and the money doesn't, I'm even less sure why you do it.'

From the look on Fry's face, he'd never been asked before. That he was looking for an answer was due in part to Daniel's trademark brand of gentle, obstinate persistence, and in part to a vein of honesty in his own character. He hadn't wondered till now, but now he wanted to know.

'Because the songs want to be heard. They're not just scribbles on paper: once they're written, once they're right, they have an existence of their own. They make demands. They want to be acknowledged. If gods become real by being prayed to, songs become real by being heard. The more people who hear them, the more real they are.'

He struggled to explain to someone who thought numbers the apex of creativity. 'When you first write a song you think you'd be satisfied if you could get somebody – anybody – to listen. But when you do it isn't enough. Even a busker at a bus-stop expects a few coins. If the songs are good, people should pay for them. It's a way of showing respect.

'So you keep working at it. And because the songs are good, and you've worked hard, and you've been lucky, eventually the offers start coming. A gig in the back of a pub. Warming up for somebody more famous. Finally you get a recording contract.'

Fry leaned back on the sofa, hands behind his head, legs stretched out on the rug, eyes closed. His cheeks and the hollows of his throat were sunken, sucked in by the vacuity of his existence.

'But there's a price to pay. As other people get involved there are more demands to be met, more needs to be satisfied. It's not just the songs now, it's the accountants. And the bigger the market for your work, the bigger the risk: if you crash you crash big-time. So everyone's telling you to be careful. Stick to what worked last time. You've all these people making a living out of you – it's not just you now, if you go down other people are going to get hurt, and they're never going to forgive you.'

His voice grew bitter and oddly helpless as he spoke. 'And the more you listen to them, the less you heed the songs. And songs are jealous gods. If you don't flatter and feed them, and do their bidding, they go away. They seek out new talent, teach new songwriters their craft. Make them hungry for success, because that's what gets the songs heard.

'Songs are parasites. They infect their host, suck his blood till he's weak, then move on. All they leave behind is a husk, a burnt-out singer who's spent ten years getting where he is and can't remember why.'

Daniel didn't know what to say. If Fry thought he'd lost his skill with words he was mistaken.

'I think you're tired,' Daniel said at last. 'You need a break. Not just a few weeks between tours but a couple of years doing something else. Recharging your batteries. It's not enough to be able to write if you've nothing to write about. If your whole life is about singing, what do you write the songs about? You need to get grounded again.'

'And live on what?'

Daniel blinked. 'Jared, you can't possibly have money problems! You've just spent two million pounds on a new house!'

'Two and a half,' growled Fry. 'And it still doesn't have a swimming pool.'

'There are salt-walter baths in Dimmock, you can buy a season ticket for twenty quid! Focus on what's important. This is your *life* we're talking about, and it looks to me you're flogging yourself for the benefit of people who don't know or don't care what matters to you. Let them wait. If you're as good as they say they'll still be there in two years' time: if you're not you'd be finished by then anyway. Take the risk. Maybe you'll never again make the kind of money you're making now, but you don't need to. You've done that. Use the time it bought to do what makes you happy. Write your songs. *Your* songs – the ones that matter to you. If you're not doing that, I doubt the rest of it is worth doing.'

'That's easy for you to say,' gritted Fry.

'Well yes,' admitted Daniel, 'perhaps it is. I haven't a talent to my name. I had one once. I was a good teacher. It was never going to make me rich but it felt good. And then... well. I can't do it any more.'

'What happened?'

Daniel side-stepped the question by answering one that hadn't been asked. It wasn't lying. He was just tired of telling the story, of the shock and sympathy in the eyes of people who would never again see him as a whole person. 'You've seen what happens. I panic in crowds. You do that in front of thirty twelve-year-olds, somebody takes you aside and says that, for you, the summer holidays are starting early.'

'Will you get back to it sometime?'

Daniel flicked him a fragile smile. 'I don't know.'

'You miss it?'

Again the one-shouldered shrug. There was something wistful about it, although in purely practical terms it was the legacy of a broken collarbone. 'It was my song.'

Brodie took an almost malicious pleasure in watching Deacon with her daughter. Paddy enjoyed the company of adults, even the grumpy detective, but Deacon – with no children of his own – was never sure how to treat her. As a pet? As a rather short person of limited vocabulary? As a different species entirely? At various times he'd tried being jolly – a seriously scary prospect – and he'd tried ignoring her, which went down as well with the daughter as it did with her mother. Now he was like a man walking to work across an area marked on the map as 'former minefield': not confident, but a little happier every time he got away with it.

While Brodie was putting Paddy to bed, Deacon shifted onto the sofa. When she returned – story read, bedclothes tucked in, child and dragon companion dutifully kissed – she sat down beside him, leaning into the warmth of his bulk.

The awkwardness that had crept into their dealings with one another had begun to ease in the last few days. She was glad but she was left wondering if it was entirely due to the time she'd spent with Eric Chandos or if she and Deacon had reached a natural cooling-point in their relationship. In a way it was a wonder it had lasted till now. It would be hard to imagine a man less like the husband she'd chosen and been happy with for five years than Jack Deacon. He was a lot older than her; also he was rough in his manner, stubborn, bad-tempered, often crude and occasionally cruel. He was not a nice man by any conventional yardstick. He wasn't a rough diamond: he was a rock.

In spite of which he was a good man. It was the only thing he and John Farrell had in common; and that was surprising too. Brodie hadn't known she was drawn to probity. It wasn't the sexiest attribute in men or women. When you meet someone who sets your blood racing, you might be attracted to their looks, their physique, the power they wield or the wealth they've accumulated, but you don't normally go weak at the knees over their integrity. It's an attribute you only discover – or sometimes miss – in people you've known for a while.

And the reason is that it's irrelevant to a passing fancy, however intense. Where it comes into its own, and in doing so overshadows all the more obvious kinds of appeal, is when you contemplate marriage.

The recognition that at least part of her was thinking along those lines hit Brodie like a sock full of wet snow. The inference was that, without consulting her conscious, choice-making self, her instincts were sizing up Deacon as husband material. Now she understood her sense of confusion. When her brain got wind of what her heart was up to it locked the doors and windows, took the phone off the hook, packed a bag and had someone bring its car round.

But she didn't want the emergency exit: only panic was suggesting she did. She wasn't afraid of commitment, just didn't want to be rushed into it. She could imagine herself settling for Jack Deacon. She wasn't sure she was ready to settle yet.

Spending last night with him – and it wasn't just the sex, it was the talking and not talking and simply being together – had helped. The unease she'd been feeling in his presence, that she was sure he must be aware of, began to dissipate. They ate at Deacon's favourite restaurant, where Deacon gave the wine waiter a lesson in distinguishing the genuinely good from the merely pretentious and the wine waiter gave Deacon tips on solving murders. Her arm linked through his, they strolled back to Deacon's house as the restaurant closed, and were still chuckling together after the last of the clothes were off.

Today she felt more relaxed in his company than she had for weeks. She leaned into his solidity and after a moment his arm went around her. His voice was a bear's growl in the pit of his stomach. 'Better now?'

'Mm.'

After a while he felt emboldened to raise Plan A again. Brodie hugged his arm but he didn't get the answer he wanted. 'I can't ask Marta again.' She felt his disappointment and smiled. 'But Paddy's going to her father's this weekend.'

Deacon's ears pricked at that. 'Saturday? Sunday?'

'Friday night to Monday morning.'

Deacon's expression was pontifical. 'I think it's important to let a child spend quality time with her father.'

'So do I,' said Brodie. 'So will John when I tell him.'

About eleven Deacon called to ask where the Area Car was, and was unsurprised to learn it would be passing Chiffney Road shortly. Brodie kissed him goodnight and headed for bed.

She was taking her make-up off when her phone rang. She glanced at the clock, and wouldn't have answered except that she recognised the number. 'Eric? I was trying to get hold of you earlier.'

'I know. I've been up in London all day.' He didn't sound apologetic so much as alarmed. 'I was going to call you tomorrow. Then I got home and found Jared's missing, and I'm hoping like hell you know something about it.'

'It's all right,' she reassured him, 'he's fine. He's with Daniel. If he hasn't come home yet it's because he's staying there. Do you want to phone Daniel to check?'

Chandos took the number. But he plainly didn't understand. '*Why's* he with Hood, again?'

'Because he couldn't stay with me and I couldn't reach you,' said Brodie. 'He turned up at my office as I was closing up. He was out of his skull, he'd no idea what he was doing. I'd have driven him home, but The Diligence is full of policemen – I was afraid that if he rolled up there singing Puff the Magic Dragon they'd throw him in a cell for his own protection. So I called Daniel. I tried to let you know.'

'You didn't try very hard!'

She bristled. 'I phoned you: you didn't answer and you didn't get back to me. So I made other arrangements. Keeping your milch-cow from straying is your job, not mine. I've done what you paid me for, I have no further responsibilities to Jared Fry. I could have left him stoned in the street, in which case he'd certainly have ended up in the Battle Alley bed-and-breakfast. I got him safe and out of sight – and if that isn't good enough, maybe you should invest some of his money in a babysitter. One who won't leave him wandering the streets in a daze waiting for someone to take pity on him!'

From the quality of his silence she suspected people didn't often shout at Eric Chandos. After a moment he said, chastened, 'Yes, OK. I'm sorry I woke you. I'll call Hood.'

'You do that,' she snapped; and added, for no better reason than devilment, 'But just for the record, we weren't sleeping.'

For an hour after he'd rung off she lay awake in the dark, wondering why she'd said that. Why had she felt, let alone succumbed to, the urge to make Eric Chandos jealous?

First thing on Wednesday morning Deacon and Charlie Voss divided Brodie's list in half.

Cynthia Bush owned The Diligence Hotel for twenty-two years until it closed at the end of the 1996 season. It was then purchased by the Ferndale Partnership who put their plans in the hands of local

builder Norman Wilmslow. The first flats were finished the following summer and bought by Mr and Mrs Edward Rollins, Mr Corin
Hurley and Miss Agnes Venables. The rest were completed by the
end of the year. It made sense to begin by interviewing those who
were at The Diligence at the earliest time the girl could have gone
into the ground – summer 1995 – and work forward chronologically.

'I'll take Mrs Bush,' said Deacon. 'And...' He was going to say the
builder but thought better of it. 'And the Rollinses. You take
Wilmslow and Hurley. He'll be the hardest to find – he was only at
The Diligence for three years, God knows where he is now.'

'What about Miss Venables?'

'God knows where she is too,' said Deacon, 'but actually so do I.
She died three years ago. She was a local councillor, it was a big
funeral. She must have been in her late sixties when she went to The
Diligence. I think we can probably discount her as a murderer of
young women.'

'Stranger things have happened,' said Voss. He considered.
'Though probably not many.'

'In all likelihood,' said Deacon, 'none of the residents was
involved. She probably moved in before they did, when the hotel was
lying empty and the grounds were overgrown. Her killer could have
chosen worse: she went undiscovered for years, it was a fluke she
was found when she was. But we've got to start somewhere.
Someone may have seen something – disturbed earth in the garden,
the tracks of a vehicle, a suspicious visitor. If we ask the right questions we might jog memories.'

'It would be easier if we knew who she was.'

'Only if she was murdered because of who she was: somebody's
wife, somebody's girlfriend. If she was a random victim – a girl he
met in a pub, a hitchhiker he picked up on the road – identifying her
won't help us find him. Except that it'll narrow the time-frame.'

Voss nodded. 'I'll make a start then.' He glanced at his notebook.
'You're sure you don't want Wilmslow? After Mrs Bush he was the
next person to spend much time at The Diligence.'

Deacon shook his head like a Newfoundland emerging from a
river. 'The more time I spend with those people' – he didn't mean the
builders – 'the more likely it is I'll deck one of them. No, I'll leave
hob-nobbing with the celebrities to you. I've always thought you
were a bit of a hippy, Charlie Voss. You should blend right in.'

Detective Sergeant Voss was a hippy in the same way that Eddie the Eagle was a ski-jumper: only someone with no experience of the real thing could have been confused. But he'd been called a great deal worse in his time. 'Yo man,' he said obligingly, and went down to his car.

Mrs Bush closed The Diligence Hotel only when she saw no way to keep it open. Ten years ago the walkers and cyclists who for most of her incumbency had thought a country hotel on the South Downs a desirable holiday base began heading for more exotic climes.

'I tried to sell as a going concern,' she told Deacon as they sat in the conservatory of her retirement bungalow beside the River Barley. 'I didn't want to make my staff redundant. But the sums worked out the same for everyone else. What we were doing made more sense in the 1960s than the 1990s. Finally I had no choice. We saw out the summer of 1996, then shut the door. Most of the staff found work pretty quickly, which was a relief. I knew I'd be able to sell the building – it was a good piece of real estate.'

She was a widow in her early seventies with a floss of soft white hair and a sugar-almond complexion. She was softly spoken, too, but there was something about the way she said 'real estate' that told Deacon she was a businesswoman to the bone.

'The period we're most interested in,' he said, 'is from 1995 onwards. Can you remember back ten years?'

'Certainly,' said Mrs Bush, happy to confound his expectations. 'I've also kept my books. I can tell you everyone who stayed there until we closed. Would that be helpful?'

A slow smile softened Deacon's craggy features. 'Indeed it would, Mrs Bush.'

Which gave him another list of names, but no reason to set the dogs on any of them. Mrs Bush recalled nothing untoward happening around that time.

'Could someone have got into the garden without being seen?'

Mrs Bush nodded. 'If he came through the wood. The only boundary between our bit of it and the rest was a split-rail fence. There's a wall there now, the new residents wanted their privacy, but I liked people wandering in from the wood. I used to sell them afternoon tea.'

So a man burdened with a girl's body could have parked his car down the road and walked through the wood looking for a place to bury her. 'But why your garden? The fence would have warned him he was entering private property. Why not bury her in the wood?'

'You're not a countryman, are you, Superintendent?' observed Mrs Bush. 'I can think of two good reasons. The roots make it hard to dig under trees. Your girl was buried on the edge of the wood – which happened to be in my garden but was a good hundred yards from the hotel on the far side of the stable-block. Even if we'd still been there we wouldn't have noticed anyone down there late at night. But we would have seen the damage to the lawn the next day. I think she was buried after the hotel closed.'

'And the other reason?' Deacon wasn't being polite, he wanted to know what she thought. The woman knew the area better than anyone: she might easily set him on the right track.

'Dogs,' said Mrs Bush briskly. 'People walk their dogs in the wood. A body in a shallow grave wouldn't stay buried for long.'

Deacon nodded. Mrs Bush had given him a much clearer picture of what was going on at The Diligence around that time than he'd had before. And she didn't believe the girl could have been buried while the hotel was open, which meant summer 1997 at the earliest. That took two years out of the time-window. 'You've been very helpful. Call me if you think of anything else, however trivial.'

'I will,' she promised. 'But I don't think I've forgotten anything.'

'I bet you haven't, Mrs Bush,' said Deacon.

Voss phoned The Diligence to see if the builder was still there, but with the pool on hold he'd taken his digger elsewhere. PC Batty had his mobile number: Wilmslow answered from the top of the Firestone Cliffs, overlooking Dimmock from the east.

He was waiting beside his digger, looking worried, when Voss drove up. 'Should I have gone back to The Diligence this morning? I did ask – they said there was no point. So I came here. They want security gates putting up.' He looked doubtfully at a stack of wrought-iron.

The builder was, thought Voss, the perfect example of the self-employed tradesman. The overalls that came in contact with the big Case digger were oily and disreputable, but underneath he wore – in deference to his status as proprietor – a crisp white shirt which his wife washed and ironed daily. Voss had a lot of time for people like Norman Wilmslow. If he was in the gutter it was only because he was repaving the thoroughfare. His eyes were on the stars because he'd taken someone's roof off to install a skylight.

Voss was quick to reassure him. 'No, that's fine. You can't hang around all day waiting for someone to think of a question to ask you.

I've got one now, though. I understand you did the work when The Diligence was sub-divided.'

'I did. And that,' added Wilmslow pointedly, 'is all I did.'

'Can you give me some facts and figures? How long you were there, how many people were working on the site, when you went home at night and how you locked up – that sort of thing.'

Wilmslow Construction had done a lot of work for the Ferndale Partnership and they'd told him they'd need him at The Diligence before they'd actually bought the place. He moved onto the site with a crew of five in February 1997 with four months to convert the first three flats.

'We nearly did it, too,' he added with a touch of pride, as if nearly doing what he'd contracted to was a rare mark of distinction.

'How nearly?' asked Voss.

'The first flat was ready for occupation at the end of May, the third by mid-August.'

Voss wrote it down. 'Were they occupied right away?'

'Pretty much. The first couple moved in while we were still snagging. Eddie Rollins and his missus – he's in hardware. They'd been living in digs, reckoned it was worth putting up with us still on site in order to get in. She was a right bobby dazzler, that Mrs Rollins,' he remembered with a slow smile. 'She used to bring out tea and biscuits, and her in a dressing-gown that wouldn't have kept a babby decent.'

Voss grinned. 'One of the perks of the job.'

'No,' said Wilmslow carefully, 'the only perk of the job. Unless you've got a use for second-hand sanitary ware.'

'So the Rollinses moved in at the start of June. Until then your crew were the only people at The Diligence?'

'Pretty much. Except for the Ferndale people, of course – and the architect, the building inspector, the suppliers, the estate agents and people looking at the flats. I wasn't responsible for everyone who came on the site between February and June.'

'But you probably saw more of them than anyone else. Did you see anything odd? Suspicious?'

'What, like some bugger down the back garden with a roll of carpet over his shoulder and a shovel in his hand?' Irony thickened Wilmslow's local accent. 'Sorry, Mr Voss, but if I'd seen that I'd have mentioned it before now.'

Voss nodded apologetically. 'I've got to start somewhere and you're probably my best witness.' He thought for a moment. 'So what happened at night?'

'We knocked off about six mostly. You can work later in summer but long days mean people getting tired and that's when accidents happen. At the start of the job we worked from eight till four, and maybe a few of us would stay on to catch up with some inside work.'

'Until the Rollinses moved in the site was vacant overnight?'

'We used to lock up, of course,' said Wilmslow. 'But you can't turn it into Fort Knox. To start with we still had people wandering in from the woods looking for a cream tea. That stopped when we put the wall up, but we still had stuff go missing. It's the same everywhere. You lock away the small valuable stuff, and the big stuff is too hard to filch, but you always lose lengths of timber, enough bricks for a barbecue and any tools that didn't get put away at the end of the day. We had mesh up till the Rollinses moved in but it won't keep out a determined thief.'

But it wasn't a thief they were concerned with: it was a man with a body over his shoulder, who wouldn't have been interested either in climbing a two metre wall or breaking down Mr Wilmslow's mesh fence. If the girl arrived that summer she came in via an open front gate, almost certainly in a car. 'Do you remember seeing any vehicles on site that you didn't recognise? Or tyre-tracks down the garden that shouldn't have been there? Any freshly turned earth?'

Norman Wilmslow was a patient man, and the death of a young woman was important enough for him to try to answer honestly however foolish the question. 'I don't remember seeing any vehicles I couldn't account for. But tyre-tracks – Mr Voss, have you never been on a building site? The whole damn thing's a mass of tyre-tracks, there's no way you'd notice extra ones. Same goes for holes. I never noticed someone had been digging down the garden, but there were so many trenches and ditches and heaps of earth round the place I couldn't swear to it.'

Voss accepted that. 'Thanks for your time, Mr Wilmslow. I'll get back to you if I need to.'

'Do you know who she was yet?'

'We will,' Voss said with more confidence than he felt. 'We'll find out who she was and what happened to her.'

Chapter Ten

The sign over the shop read *Edward Rollins Hardware*. In the window were trays of tools, pyramids of paint, brushes in every imaginable size and shape, and a garden parasol from the days of the Raj. And it was all new. The name, the window, the stock. Rollins had taken the money from the sale of his Diligence flat and put it into this shop.

No, thought Deacon, looking at it, he probably called it a store. Not unreasonably: it bore as much resemblance to a corner hardware shop where you could buy a pound of mixed nails and a mousetrap as McDonalds did to a chip-van. A year ago Eddie Rollins ran the hardware department in the Dimmock outlet of a national home supplies chain: today he had his own store. For a man passionate about hardware it was the realisation of a dream.

Somehow, he didn't look like a man living his dream. When Deacon introduced himself he reacted with a startled glance. After a quick word with the girl on the till he ushered the policeman into a back office. 'We can talk in here. It's quieter.'

Out front the store was all bright and shiny and eager to please: in here half the office equipment remained to be unpacked and the manager's chair was a garden seat with the price-tag still on it. There was nowhere else to sit. Rollins offered Deacon the garden seat, himself leaned against the wall looking wary.

'Business doing well?' asked Deacon, hoping to put the man at his ease.

On the television, Deacon had noticed, it was immediately clear who the murderer/rapist/forger/diamond thief was because policemen made him nervous. In reality, being questioned by the police makes perfectly innocent people nervous. Those who remain calm are those who've had the most practice.

Perhaps Rollins relaxed a little. He was a man in his late thirties, of average height and spare build, with a thin face and receding hairline. He'd gone for a corporate image of white drill apron (businesslike, knowledgeable) over denims (casual, approachable) but it worked rather better on the young woman at the till than it did on him. He looked like a trendy butcher.

'Pretty well,' he said. 'We've only been open a month, we're still at sixes and sevens, but we're getting plenty of people in. Sales are better than I expected this soon.'

'It was a good decision then,' said Deacon. 'To put the money from your flat at The Diligence into this place.'

Rollins nodded. His face was closed, uncommunicative. 'It's something I've wanted to do. Selling the flat made it possible.'

'You made a good deal there,' said Deacon. 'Better than the people who settled sooner. Comes of being a businessman, I suppose – knowing how long you can hold out without killing the deal.'

Rollins shrugged. 'I wasn't keen to move. It was only when my so-called friends and neighbours put the pressure on that I gave it any real thought. They wanted the cash, which meant my moving out too. So I considered my options. Staying put with seven households hating my guts was the least attractive, so I made the best deal I could.'

'Where do you live now?'

Rollins gestured upwards. 'It was a house before it was a shop. There's another two floors up there.'

'Plenty of room for a family,' said Deacon. 'Do you have children?'

'Actually,' Rollins said stiffly, 'I'm on my own.'

Deacon glanced at his notes. 'I'm sorry, I understood you were married.'

'We're separated. We have been for years.'

'But you were together when you bought into The Diligence.'

'Just about.'

Deacon raised an eyebrow that indicated Rollins should elaborate.

There was a quiet savagery in the man's eyes. 'Six weeks after we moved in she moved out. She left me for an Italian truck-driver. I promised her a new suite for the living room. She picked something in Italian leather. It came in a lorry all the way from Turin. She left the same way. I got home from work to find a new suite, an empty wardrobe and an apologetic note. His name, apparently, was Luigi.'

Not trusting himself to find an appropriate expression, Deacon concentrated on his notebook. 'I expect you heard what's happened at The Diligence. We're trying to establish when the body was buried and if anyone saw anything suspicious. You and Mrs Rollins were the first to move in, you saw the other residents arrive. Do you remember a teenage girl or maybe a woman in her early twenties visiting any of them?'

Rollins considered. 'Your best bet would be Corin Hurley. He moved in at the beginning of July. He was a student, his parents bought him the flat to finance his course. He rented rooms to two other guys and between them they went through a lot of girlfriends.' He looked up quickly. 'I'm not suggesting they murdered any of them. They were decent enough lads. Noisy, a bit heavy on the late-night revels, but decent. But they were much the youngest in the house, then and since. If your girl knew someone there, it seems likely it was one of them.'

Deacon nodded. 'Of course, we're not sure yet that she knew any-one at the house. Someone may just have thought an overgrown gar-den behind a building-site was a good place to leave her.'

'You think she was buried during the redevelopment?'

'Possibly. Or maybe the following summer.'

Rollins frowned. 'I don't think that's possible. There were over twenty people living there from the autumn of 1997 onwards. Someone would have seen something.'

Deacon made a note. 'What about the builders? They were on site for some time after you moved in. Did they give you any problems?'

Rollins shook his head. 'There was a fair bit of noise and mess, of course, vans parked all over the place and lorries delivering materi-als, but I expected that. We wanted to get in, that was the price we had to pay. And before you ask, I wouldn't have thought Norman Wilmslow was the sort to go burying people on his building sites.'

Deacon flicked him half a smile and didn't comment. 'There's nothing else you can tell me that might help?' Rollins shook his head. Deacon handed out another of his cards. 'If anything comes to mind, give me a call.' He turned to leave.

With his hand on the door he turned back. 'One thing more: I'll need Mrs Rollins's phone-number. I don't expect she saw anything strange either but I'll need to ask her.'

Mention of his wife made Eddie Rollins's expression shut like a box. He spoke through his teeth. 'I don't have a number for her. I haven't communicated with her since she left.'

Now Deacon's eyebrow angled upwards, surprised. 'You never filed for divorce?'

'I don't know where she is.'

'There are procedures...' But it was clear from Rollins's face that he didn't want the information. 'If you ever want to remarry you can chase it up then. So the suite came from Turin. Maker's name?'

Rollins didn't know. 'It'll be under the sofa. But...?'

'With the maker's name and the date I can find the carrier. They'll give me Luigi's other name, and maybe Luigi can tell me where your wife is. What's her first name?'

'Michelle.' He said it as if it was a terminal disease.

It was becoming something of a habit, Brodie thought, getting back to the office to find someone waiting on her doorstep. At least this one was fully conscious. Eric Chandos looked up quickly at the sound of her step. 'Can we talk? I owe you an apology.'

'Yes, you do,' she said calmly. She'd seen the white car – he still didn't believe that parking restrictions applied to him – as soon as she turned the corner so she was ready for him. She wasn't going to be startled into a schoolgirl blush and end up apologising to him instead.

She reached past him to unlock the door. Only then did she look him full in the face. 'That was it? Very well, I accept your apology. Good afternoon.'

She must still have had him on the back foot or he'd have followed her, relying on his strong arm and stronger charm to get him inside. Instead he hovered uncertainly on the step. 'Brodie...'

Relenting, she held the door open. 'Come on in then. But make it quick: I've got things to do before I can call it a night.'

Dropping her bag on the desk she went through to the tiny kitchen and put the kettle on. For a moment she hesitated, then put two cups on the tray. Now she'd let him in she couldn't really do anything else.

Chandos stood in the middle of the office, and if he wasn't exactly shifting his weight from foot to foot he looked distinctly ill at ease. Brodie gestured at the sofa, herself sat behind her desk. 'Did you round up your golden goose?'

He nodded. 'Last night you called him a milch-cow,' he said, subdued.

She remembered. 'So I did. Is he all right?'

'He's fine. As much as he ever is. He takes heroin; and other stuff. I imagine you guessed.'

'I realised he was on something. For how long?'

'Nine years, on and off. Mostly on.'

'Why?' Brodie brought the coffee.

Chandos sighed. 'Because the whole industry's riddled with dope and Jared has an addictive personality. Some people can take it when they want it and stop before it becomes a problem. Jared isn't one of them. The only question is how much he's taking: just enough to prevent withdrawal or sufficient to paralyse an ox. Yesterday was an ox day.'

'Why?' asked Brodie again.

'Too much going on at The Diligence, and too much of it out of his control. Policemen coming and going make most people nervous – but Jared doesn't just get nervous, he shoots up. Maybe if I'd been there I could have kept him either calm or out of sight, but the first anyone knew he was sprawled at the foot of the stairs, grinning a silly grin and waving a loaded syringe, pretending to inject everyone who went past.

'Miriam – our housekeeper, you've met her? – did what you did and tried to call me but she couldn't get through either. So she and Tommy the driver decided the next best thing was to get him off the place before the joke got out of hand and he found himself behind bars, coming down fast with nothing to break his fall.'

Chandos drank the coffee fiercely. 'They put him in the back of the car. Tommy was going to drive round for a couple of hours to give Jared the chance to sleep it off. It seemed to be working: Tommy thought he was out for the count. So coming through Dimmock he stopped in the Promenade car-park for a smoke and a leak. When he returned to the car Jared had gone. Tommy drove around town for an hour looking for him, without luck. Eventually he went home.'

'He couldn't spot him,' said Brodie, 'because we had him off the street by then. I found him passed out on my doorstep a bit after six. Jack was on his way round: the best I could do was put Jared somewhere he could surface in his own good time. I thought he'd call you when he did.'

'You'd think so, wouldn't you?' Chandos put his cup down with a weary sigh. 'He doesn't know my number. He dropped his phone in the car, and he didn't know either my number or his own home-number.'

'If he was high…'

'No, not because he was high. Because he's Jared. Because he's the great Jared Fry, the famous Jared Fry, Jared Fry the demon rocker, and he always thinks sorting his mess out is someone else's job. I suppose it is: I suppose it's mine. But I can't be in two places at once, and you shouldn't have to watch a grown man as if he was a child.'

Brodie hadn't wanted to forgive his rudeness but found herself doing so anyway. He'd been frantic when he got home after midnight and found Fry had been missing for six hours. Knowing the condition he was in when he vanished, and the trouble he could get into like that. In the same circumstances she might not have opened conversations with 'Hello, how are you, how was your day?' either.

She pursed her lips, wondering how much to say. 'I'm not sure why he came here. I think he was warning me off.'

Chandos looked surprised. 'Off what?'

'Actually, off you.'

His eyes dropped quickly and he had the grace to blush. 'When he's like that he doesn't know what he's saying.'

'He's afraid you might leave him.'

'I work for him,' Chandos said shortly. 'I manage his career. We're not married.'

'He's dependent on you. I think he feels too dependent on you.'

'He's nothing to worry about. I'm not going anywhere.'

'Eric?' She waited till he looked at her. 'He had the idea that you and I were...some kind of an item. Did you give him that idea?'

Finally he admitted it. 'We were talking about you the previous night. *I* was talking about you. At length, I suspect. I must have given him a false impression. I'm sorry. I'd had a drink, it was just wishful thinking – I never imagined it would get back to you.' He peered at her through the parted curtain of his hair. 'You could try taking it as a compliment.'

Brodie gave a scornful laugh. 'You're right: it's pathetic when a grown man behaves like a little boy.'

He chuckled too, uncomfortably. 'I am sorry. For that – for everything. I don't usually behave like this.'

'No. You don't usually apologise. Where's Jared now?'

'I took him home first thing this morning. He needed a fix by then but he's OK. Your friend looked after him pretty well.'

'Daniel's good at looking after people. Which is why I impose on him the way I do. Have you tried to get Jared sorted out?'

'A couple of times. No, more than that, but a couple of times we got him clean and kept him that way for six months. But it's a life's work, beating an addiction, and his heart isn't in it. He thinks what it gives him is worth what it costs.'

Brodie frowned. 'What can it possibly give him that's worth that?'

'His music. He's at his most creative when he's high. When he's clean the spark is missing. What he writes is...pedestrian: you and I could write it. You want people in half the civilised world to listen to what you have to say, you need that spark. It's Jared's tragedy that he's never been able to reproduce sober what he can do when he's on drugs.'

'A lot of addicts feel that way. It isn't usually true.'

'For him it is. I don't know where he goes on a fix, but he comes back with words and music running out of him. At least...' He stopped.

Brodie finished the sentence for him. 'At least, he used to.'

Chandos nodded wryly. 'What he writes now is good enough for someone who's already got a name. It isn't good enough to make one.'

Whatever the morality of the situation, it was hard not to sympathise. 'Do you think he knows?'

'He knew before I did.'

Brodie got up to make more coffee. Chandos thought it was his cue to leave and clambered out of the sofa. They met in the narrow space beside her desk.

It wasn't a big office. Even though she spent limited time here, it wasn't big enough for the job she needed it to do. She was trying to acquire the building behind in order to extend. In the meantime she told clients that her other office was a Richard Rogers – which amused her, even when she had to explain the joke.

But the narrowness of the space had never seemed so acute as it did now, and never less of a problem. She felt the man's proximity as an elemental force, hot and electric. She was intensely aware of how he filled the room, invading her personal space. Of the scent of his body. Of the power emanating from him, making the air swell and throb.

Whatever chemical reactions were burgeoning in the little office, Chandos was as much aware of them as Brodie was. She saw it in his eyes, a mixture of surprise and urgency. His shoulders widened and curved, enclosing her body with his. His face tipped to meet hers: when a lock of his hair touched her cheek her whole body jolted.

She opened her mouth to say something sensible, something humorous and situation-defusing. She got as far as, 'Er...' Everything after that he swallowed.

Chapter Eleven

Detective Sergeant Voss was studying his computer screen when Deacon got back to Battle Alley. There was nothing unusual about this. Deacon had noticed that the younger policemen tended to think crime could be solved online. Not a bad detective in many ways, Charlie Voss was still the wrong side of thirty and so liable to be led astray by a sexy piece of electronics flashing her bits at him.

'Turn off the Playstation,' Deacon growled as he passed Voss's open door, 'and come and tell me what you got out of Wilmslow.'

'Nothing,' said Voss, neither moving nor looking round. 'But I think I've got something here.'

Deacon back-tracked. 'Where?'

'It's the Missing Persons index on the PNC. It turned up a few possibilities but this is the front-runner.'

Leaning over his shoulder, Deacon studied the file with him, all the while wishing it was a printed page. Sensing his superintendent's discomfort, tactfully Voss read off the relevant information. 'She's in the right age group – nineteen – and she disappeared in the summer of 1997 – last seen June 14th. She's the right height and build, she has short fair hair and she lived in Brighton.'

Deacon was looking at the photograph. It wasn't big enough to identify her from, even if she'd still been alive. Dr Roy would need something better to work with. But some sense of her was there, and there had been times in the past when Deacon had looked at a fuzzy family snap and known what he was still days and detailed forensic tests from being told officially.

What he'd seen on Roy's table was a skeleton with scraps of skin adhering and a cap of short fair hair about the skull. He studied the photograph for a trace of kinship. But this time the magic failed him. It was a passport-type photo of a teenage girl who looked like a million others, whose experiences were probably pretty much like theirs until the day that she didn't go home. It might have been the girl they'd found, it might not.

'Sasha Wade,' he read aloud. 'What's Sasha short for?'

'I don't think it is,' said Voss. 'I think it's Russian.'

'You think she's a Russian?'

Detective Superintendent Deacon was clearly an astute man, but not all the time. Voss said patiently, 'It's one of those names that was trendy thirty years ago. The sort of name hippies gave their children.'

Deacon was looking blank. 'You think her parents are Russian hippies?'

Voss straightened from the screen and regarded at him levelly. 'You're winding me up, sir, aren't you?'

Deacon chuckled. 'Just a little bit. Well, I'd better go and talk to them. Print me the address, will you? I'll take Jill Meadows. In case I find Mrs Wade on her own.'

'After eight years she may be quite relieved.'

'To know that her daughter's been murdered? I don't think so, sergeant!'

Voss was unapologetic. 'Yes. To know. Not to be worrying any more. Not to be wondering if she's safe, or in trouble, or wanting to call home but too embarrassed. Not to be constantly listening for the phone. When we get a positive ID she won't be afraid of the phone any more.'

Deacon considered. 'When I was at Hendon, basic training was about getting a shine on your boots and *Always finish what you start so don't start anything you don't want to finish.* Amateur psychology must have come in later.'

Voss hadn't come from the Met so was never at Hendon. 'Don't know, sir,' he said stoically. 'I got mine from Chinese fortune cookies, mostly.'

It was a nice day for a drive but Deacon took no pleasure in it. Whatever Voss thought, the reality was he was about to tell two people there was a good chance their daughter had been lying in a muddy hole on the Downs for the last eight years. Then he was going to ask them to help identify her.

Thank God, there was nothing they could tell him from looking at the remains. Nor were there any personal effects – no clothes, no jewellery, no watch. If there'd been anything they might have recognised he would have asked them to look, but he was glad there was not. It was always a deeply upsetting moment.

Deacon himself had seen much worse than a gently decomposing skeleton. He'd witnessed the results of unspeakable cruelty – people in terrible suffering, dying people for whom nothing could be done, and those so newly dead their agony was etched both on their ravaged faces and on the backs of his eyes. Pain was the real horror. Death was an end. He investigated murder with all the energy, ingenuity and resources at his command not because someone was dead but because someone else was a killer.

Beside him, Detective Constable Jill Meadows was anticipating the coming interview with quiet dread. It was a routine part of the job, much commoner than being shot at or taking part in high-speed chases, but still hard to deal with. Crises come from nowhere and you react with a blend of instinct and training, and usually there's only time to be afraid afterwards. Breaking bad news is difficult because you know you're going to have to do it.

'What if they ask if we could be wrong?'

Deacon shrugged. 'Tell them the truth. It could be someone else, but the odds are it's Sasha.'

Meadows nodded sadly. 'Eight years? She'd have been my age.'

A few miles passed. Deacon enjoyed driving normally, found it therapeutic. His mind split itself neatly in half when he drove, one half managing the road, the car and whatever arose while the other quietly kicked a football around. Sometimes the football was work, sometimes his private life. Usually it was work.

Today he wasn't sure what it was. Something someone had said. Someone had said something, and he couldn't think who or what or when, but the little Deacon in the back of his mind who had time to kick a football around thought it was significant. Thought he ought to give it some consideration. Was jumping up and down trying to attract his attention. Deacon could see him, but he couldn't think what he was on about.

And then he could.

The first Meadows knew was the car slowing down. When she looked at him enquiringly his face was closed for stock-taking, please call again later, and his eyes were turned inward. 'Sir?'

He found somewhere to stop. Actually, he just stopped and let the traffic behind shift for itself. 'She'd have been twenty-seven?'

Meadows nodded. 'If she was nineteen eight years ago.'

'But she could have been twenty-five eight years ago,' mused Deacon. 'That's what Roy said – she was eighteen to twenty-five. By now she could have been thirty-three.'

'Sir?'

Deacon went on thinking. 'We still need to see the Wades. But if they ask about the odds, tell them their daughter is one of two young women it could be.'

'Who's the other?'

He was already on the phone to Voss. 'Charlie, have you spoken to Corin Hurley yet?'

'Not yet. I was going to do that next. Why?'

'Ask him about Michelle Rollins.'

Corin Hurley bought his flat at The Diligence, his parents guaranteeing the loan, when he was eighteen and starting a photography course at Dimmock Polytechnic. He owned it for the three years of his studies, letting the second bedroom to two fellow-students in order to pay the mortgage. After graduation he sold it and put down a deposit on a London flat.

All this Voss learned in the course of a phone conversation with the elder Mr Hurley who still lived in Bognor Regis.

Mrs Hurley answered the phone. Voss had learned not to begin conversations with, 'Good morning, I am a police officer,' because it took ten minutes to calm the other party down enough to answer questions. Instead he said, 'There's nothing whatever to worry about, Mrs Hurley, but I'm a police officer and I need a quick word with your son Corin. Can you give me his current address and phone-number?'

Mrs Hurley did not yield to hysterics but she did put her husband on the line. She stayed at his elbow, listening. Voss could hear her prompting him.

'Has something happened to Corin?'

'No,' said Voss, 'nothing. Something's come up' – he could have worded that better – 'at The Diligence where he used to live and I want to ask him about his neighbours.'

'Tell him he hasn't lived there for five years,' urged the whisper in the background. 'He hasn't lived there for five years,' said Hurley dutifully.

'I know that, sir. If you could give me his address?'

'Tell him he's married,' came the whisper. 'Got a good job. And two little girls.'

'He's married now,' said Hurley. 'He's...'

'... Got a good job and two little girls,' said Voss patiently. 'Yes, I know, sir. I still need to talk to him.'

If Corin Hurley had still lived in London Voss might have paid him a visit. Phoning would take ten minutes, travelling up to town half a day. On the other hand, there are risks with interviewing people over the phone. You can't see their eyes. Plus, there's always the chance that as soon as they put the phone down they're going to head for the nearest airport. He wasn't expecting Hurley to confess to murder, but if he did Voss would be in a difficult position. You can't arrest someone over the phone, and while he could tell Hurley to stay put while he despatched the local CID it was asking a lot.

The matter became academic when Hurley turned out to be in Aberdeen, working for the public relations department of an oil company. So the phone would have to do. After all, Voss had no reason to suspect him. It was only information he was after.

The marvels of modern technology allowed him to speak to Hurley as the North Sea hammered the boat carrying the photographer back from an oil-rig.

'I thought you used helicopters,' said Voss.

'From a helicopter the sea always looks flat and the rigs look like toys. For a decent photograph you need to get up close and personal.' Also, the manic cheerfulness in his voice suggested that Corin Hurley liked being tossed about in boats.

'There's been an incident at The Diligence,' Voss said. 'A body's been discovered. It seems likely she was buried around the time you moved into your flat.'

'She? A girl?'

'Late teens, early twenties. Does that mean something to you?'

'No. There was an elderly lady living there – Miss Venables – and a couple, the Rollinses. Other people arrived later, but I don't think I ever saw a girl.'

Voss cleared his throat. 'Mr Hurley, you and two other male students were living there. You're telling me you never took a girl home?'

'Of course not. But we never mislaid one. We counted them all in and we counted them all out again.'

'Was Sasha Wade one of them?'

Hurley had to think. Voss listened to the waves boom along the steel hull. 'Not one of mine. I don't remember either of the other guys going out with a Sasha. To be sure you'd need to ask them. But like I told you...'

'... You counted them all out again. Still, I'll speak to your flatmates. Do you know where they are now?'

'Can I call you back from home? I've got them both in the address book. Or call my wife and ask her. Jonathan Scott and Mark Parsons. Mark's doing glamour photography in Amsterdam. Jonathan, oddly enough, went into the church.'

'Did you ever see anything strange or suspicious at The

Diligence? Perhaps something that didn't seem significant at the time but does now you know we've found a body.'

Hurley didn't remember anything. '*We* were pretty strange but I don't think anyone thought we were suspicious. I was a late-flowering hippy, Jonathan was seeing cosmic meaning in everything, and Mark had a down on clothes. He could get some girl to pose naked anywhere, any time. As part of the course we had to photograph a multi-storey carpark. Mark shot it from a roof three miles away with a telephoto lens, between the legs of a girl called Mindy. It was the most erotic image from the whole damn course.'

'I don't suppose Mindy suddenly disappeared?'

'No, sergeant. She's Mindy Parsons now, she runs his studio in Amsterdam's red-light district.'

Even without being able to see his eyes, Voss was content that Corin Hurley knew nothing about a murder. Which didn't mean he couldn't still be helpful. 'Did you see much of the Rollinses?'

'Not a lot. Eddie was older than us – just enough to disapprove of our beards and clothes and late-night parties. We tried to keep the noise bearable but he still complained regularly. I've every sympathy for him *now*. *Then* I thought he was my dad in disguise.'

'What about Michelle?'

'Never really got the chance to know her,' said Hurley. 'We moved in in July, about a month after they did. We introduced ourselves, asked them to our house-warming, borrowed the odd cup of sugar, then she ran off with an Italian truck-driver.'

'They weren't happy together?'

'I'm not sure Eddie does Happy. I thought they were OK. We didn't hear them argue and he seemed to be fond of her. He bought her a nice new suite. Of course, that could have worked out better.'

'What was she like?'

'Bubbly. She was fun, I liked her.'

'Tall – short?'

'Not tall. She had short blonde hair, huge mascara eyes, and a silly giggle. She was a hairdresser. She was a bit younger than Eddie – early twenties, maybe. Oh, she was the original dumb blonde, and I guess she was what my mother would call common, but from the little I saw of her she was a nice girl – kind, you know? I don't know what she saw in Eddie. Security, probably – he was always going to be in work. But I don't think married life was all she'd expected. Hence the Italian.'

'Did you see him?'

'Alas, no. Eddie told us a few days later. To avoid speculation, he said. So we wouldn't think...' Hurley's voice died as the implications caught up with him.

'Think what?'

There was a shell-shocked note in the voice on the phone. 'It's just what he said. That Michelle had left him and wouldn't be coming back. That she'd gone off with an Italian truck-driver called Luigi. That he didn't want us thinking something had happened to her.'

'It's a reasonable thing to say,' said Voss mildly.

'That's what we thought. At the time. When we didn't know there was a girl buried in the garden!'

As soon as he'd finished with Hurley, Voss called Deacon back. 'Have you seen the Wades yet?'

'Not yet.' Deacon's voice dropped a note. 'Are you telling me I shouldn't bother?'

'No. But if they want some hope to cling to, Michelle Rollins is as good a match for the girl in the ground as Sasha.'

Which was a policeman's lot all over, thought Deacon grimly. Too many suspects or none at all; a victim with no name or one with a choice of two. 'I'll take DNA samples from the Wades, that should tell us if it's Sasha. If it isn't we'll need to check that Luigi the truck-driver isn't a figment of Eddie Rollins's imagination. Get onto the Italians again. The last they heard we were looking for a potential witness: they need to know Michelle Rollins could be the victim.'

It was now after six and Deacon hoped to find both of the Wades at home, if only to save one the agony of telling the other after he'd left. He wasn't by nature a thoughtful man but every so often he surprised people.

It was a comfortable semi in a post-war housing development and everything about it celebrated the basic decency of the owner-occupying lower middle class, the salmon paste in the Great British sandwich. The outside was painted every five years, and every weekend the lawn was mown and the mid-range hatchback on the drive was washed and waxed. It was living at its most respectable, and people who wash their net curtains twice a year and polish their doorstep shouldn't have to learn that their daughter has been dug up by a builder.

When a policeman calls, most people do an urgent head-count. Is everyone here, has someone had an accident? Deacon thought that Alice Wade knew why he was there before he introduced himself. 'We're from Dimmock CID. We'd like to talk to you and your husband.'

She was older than Deacon had expected, with long greying hair tied back in a loose plait and bones like a bird. Her voice was soft. 'You've found her, haven't you?'

'We don't know yet, Mrs Wade,' said Jill Meadows gently. 'It'll be a couple of days before we're sure.'

'Where was she?'

By then her husband had shown them through to the sitting room. Deacon took the proferred seat and summarised events at The Diligence. 'We don't yet know who it is we've found, and we don't know how she died. We're here because there's nothing in what we know of Sasha that says it *couldn't* be her. We'll know for sure if mouth-swabs from you two match her DNA.'

The Wades exchanged a quick, significant glance. 'That could be a problem,' said Philip Wade.

'Why?'

'Sasha was adopted,' said Alice. 'As a baby. She was ours almost all her life but she won't have our DNA.'

'Ah.' Deacon sat back, momentarily nonplussed. It was salutory how quickly even a detective like him, a man who swore by old-fashioned, sweat on the brow, blisters on the feet police work, could be seduced by a scientific advance. Deacon learnt his job when genetic profiling was laughed off as science fiction by policemen who thought solving crimes would always depend on asking suspects questions and preferably thumping them till they answered. Of course, a hundred years earlier the same doubts had attended the new science of finger-printing.

In just ten years, though, the primacy of DNA as arbiter of identity had seeped so deeply into the collective consciousness that, for a moment, he couldn't think what to do next. He gave himself a mental shake and thought back to when he was Voss's age. 'What about old injuries? Did she ever break a bone?'

Mrs Wade shook her head.

'Who was her dentist? Dental X-rays are pretty foolproof.'

The woman went to a bureau drawer, came back with an address book. 'Try him by all means, but I don't think Sasha ever had an X-ray taken. She had a couple of minor fillings. She was only nineteen, superintendent.'

DNA, bones, teeth… Thumping someone was almost all that was left. 'A good photograph might help. Taken not too long before she disappeared.'

'That would still be useful?' murmured Mrs Wade. 'After eight years in the ground?'

Tragedy takes people different ways. Some are overwhelmed by it. Others get through by attending to the minutiae almost like part of the professional team. Neither was right or wrong, more or less appropriate. Deacon had seen enough of violent death to know that anything which helped those left behind was valid.

'The lab will measure the distances between fixed points on the face and compare them with those on the body. It's pretty reliable. The proportions vary between one individual and another.'

Sasha Wade's mother nodded. 'I have a picture. Only, I would like it back.'

'Of course,' said Jill Meadows, standing up. 'Shall I come with you?' She wanted to see Sasha's room. In all probability it would be as it was the last night the girl slept there.

Left alone, Deacon turned to Philip. 'There's a note on the file to the effect that Sasha was missing once before. Went off with a boyfriend, came back later. Is that what you thought had happened this time?'

Wade shook his head. 'Not after the first couple of days.'

'Why not?'

'She called us the other time. She didn't want us to worry. She said she had her own path to follow but she didn't want us worrying.'

'And you thought she'd have done the same again, if she'd been safe.'

'Yes. We waited for two days, then we went to the police.'

'What did she take with her?'

'Her guitar, a change of clothes and her purse. The clothes were the only reason we waited two days. We thought they might mean she intended to be out overnight.'

'Wouldn't she have said something to you?'

'Not if she was doing something we'd have disapproved of.'

'Was she prone to doing that?'

'She was a bit of a free spirit, superintendent,' said the girl's father. 'People who didn't know she was adopted wondered how Alice and I managed to produce someone like her. We don't know who her birth parents were, but one of them must have been musical and I've always suspected the other was an elf.' He gave a wan smile. 'There was something other-worldly about her. When she ran you weren't quite sure her feet touched the ground.'

That wasn't something Deacon could comment on. But he felt a twinge of sympathy for the older man. Adoption had never been an easy option. He'd gone to a lot of trouble to have this child, and after nineteen years he'd lost her, and he didn't know why. 'How much money did she have?'

'She drew sixty pounds on her credit card.'

Deacon back-tracked. 'How old was she the first time she went off?'

'Sixteen. Not a child any more, not yet a woman.'

'And the boyfriend?'

'Twenty-four. He was a professional footballer. She thought they were going to be rich and famous. She desperately wanted to be famous. But they split up after a couple of months and Sasha came home.'

Deacon took down the name in no expectation that it would help. Three years had passed, an aeon to a teenager. Sasha Wade hadn't gone running after her footballer. But she might have found another ticket to fame and fortune, someone who treated her less kindly when he got bored with her. 'Did she take her clothes that time?'

'All of them,' said Wade. He knew the significance of that. He'd had eight years to think about it.

Meadows came downstairs with a square parcel under her arm. 'Thank you very much, Mrs Wade. I'll take great care of these and get them back to you as soon as I can.'

On the way out to the car Deacon said, 'Photographs?'

'And a book of her songs. She wanted to be a singer. I thought her songs might give us an insight into who she was.'

Deacon sniffed disparagingly. 'All teenagers think they're going to be the next Elton Jones, don't they? But they still end up working in building societies.'

Meadows was trying to think who Elton Jones was. Then she realised he was testing her, waiting for her to correct him. 'These are good. Well, I think so. Maybe even good enough.'

'So she took her guitar,' said Deacon, 'and sixty pounds off her credit card and a change of clothes in a carrier bag. Even eight years ago sixty pounds wouldn't have taken her far. She wasn't heading for

Las Vegas to seek her fortune. She planned to be away one night. When she left home she thought she was coming back.'

Chapter Twelve

Spring was beginning to stretch the evenings: astronomy was increasingly a task for insomniacs. At ten o'clock Daniel set up his equipment on the iron gallery that ran around his upper storey and started looking for the other Russian comet.

People who hadn't known him long marvelled that he'd managed to find – and even more remarkable, to afford – a house so perfectly matched to his needs, almost as if it had been built for him. In fact, to a large degree it was. After standing on this foreshore for two hundred uneventful years, a lot had happened to the netting-shed in just the last three. When Daniel first rented it, soon after moving to Dimmock, it had been not much more than a beach-hut on steroids: a tall black timber-clad structure with one large room above, reached by an outside staircase, and a boat-house below. When Dimmock still had a fishing industry, this was one of perhaps twenty such strung along the beach just above the historic high water mark. Three of them survived into the twenty-first century.

Quickly appreciating that he wasn't going to do much better for the funds he had available, Daniel put in an offer and bought the thing outright. After twelve months he had a small but comfortable home with unparalleled views of the English Channel and the sky above it.

A year after that he had a smouldering ruin, and if he'd been in it when the mob arrived he'd have been spared the trouble of rebuilding. But he wasn't so he did; and while he was at it he found enough money to augment the insurance and give himself two things he'd wanted – more living space on the ground floor, and an outside gallery running round the entire house at first floor level giving him a viewing platform from which he could observe any part of the night sky.

Tonight he set up the telescope at the north end of the house. Observing conditions weren't as good as on the seaward side because the lights of Dimmock got in the way, but north was where the other Russian comet was growing.

The original Russian comet, so called because only those familiar with the Cyrillic alphabet could pronounce its name, had come and gone; this one, equally unsayable, had been spotted the previous month. It was expected to become a naked eye object over the next few weeks, but there's no fun in that for the genuine astronomer. He wants to be in at the birth, when it's nothing but a fuzzy pinprick that doesn't correlate to any known body. Daniel hadn't the gear for serious comet-hunting and would never put his name on one. There was still enormous satisfaction in seeing it early. If not at the birth, perhaps at the christening.

But it wasn't a good night for comets. At first glance the stars appeared to be shining brightly, but through the telescope it became clear there was enough cloud in the atmosphere to mask anything as amorphous as an embryo comet. He turned his attention to the southern sky where it sheeted down all the way to the Channel and the great recumbent lion that dominated it. He was focusing on the binary system of Algeiba in Leo's mane when he became aware that he was no longer alone. This far from the Promenade there wasn't enough light to see by, and he hadn't heard footsteps on the shingle. But he knew there was someone out there in the darkness watching him.

He straightened slowly and moved away from the telescope. 'I know you're there,' he said quietly.

Something moved in the dark, the stones of the shore chiming their familiar warning. 'It's only me.'

She didn't need to say any more. Daniel reached inside the open door to turn the lights on and Brodie was standing at the foot of the iron staircase. Since the rebuild his front door was at ground level like everyone else's, but the iron stair had been too much a feature of the netting-shed to remove it. Visitors went to the new door; friends usually came straight up and tapped on the one opening onto his living room.

'Brodie? What are you doing down there? Come on up.' He'd been on the gallery for half an hour and could not have missed hearing her arrive. 'How long have you been there?'

She didn't look at her watch. 'Oh, about an hour.' She sounded exhausted.

'You've been watching me for an hour?' He didn't understand. 'Is everything all right? Has something happened? Is Paddy all right?'

'Paddy's fine,' she said quickly. 'Marta's with her. But yes, something has happened; and no, everything is not all right.'

He kept a couple of deckchairs on the gallery: Brodie slumped into one as if she hadn't the strength to make it inside. Daniel lowered himself carefully into the other. 'Tell me what's happened.'

In the chiaroscuro world of black night and white light her face was haggard. She waved a weary hand. 'Could we have the light off again?'

He did as she asked without question. Then he said, 'What did you come here to tell me?'

She couldn't get started. He wanted to take her hand but was afraid. He said softly, 'I don't need to say this but I'm going to. Whatever has happened, we'll deal with it. Whatever you've done, we'll sort it out. Are you in trouble?'

That made her laugh, a despairing little chuckle that Daniel could make no sense of. He wished he could see her face. 'Brodie?'

She was contrite. 'Sorry. It's just, that's what Victorian mistresses used to ask their maids. No, I'm not in trouble – at least, I'm not going to be dismissed without a reference. I've seen Eric again.'

If he was disappointed Daniel kept it out of his voice. 'You went to The Diligence?'

'He came to my office. He was... brusque when he called last night. He was worried about Jared, didn't know what was going on. When he realised everything was under control and it was thanks to you and me Jared wasn't up in court this morning he wanted to apologise.'

'But you were still angry with him.'

'Not so much. I made him coffee. He apologised, I accepted.'

That wasn't what she needed him to know, that she'd stood in the dark for an hour cranking up the courage to tell him. He wasn't sure how much to press her. If she needed to talk it was for her to set the agenda. If he made it too difficult she might change her mind and go home still unburdened. He tried a change of tack. 'Jared Fry isn't what I expected.'

She gave a little sigh. 'What did you expect?'

'I don't know. Something more glamorous, I suppose. More of a celebrity.'

He heard her wan smile. 'Disappointed, Daniel?'

'Reassured. Even that much money and success don't stop a man worrying about his future. He's afraid he can't write songs any more.'

'He's a heroin addict,' said Brodie, as if that told the whole of a man's tale.

'Yes, I know. He says that's how he writes best. Of course it isn't, but he thinks it is. And the longer he's addicted the more his brain deteriorates, the harder it is to get something worthwhile out of it, the more he feels the need for a fix. He's going to kill himself.

'And it's a pity, because deep inside where the garbage can't get him he's a decent man. He thinks without it he'd never write another word. I think it's all there waiting for him, but he's too scared to take the risk. The fear of losing it forever is what stops him, not the misery of detox.'

'He has kicked it, a couple of times,' said Brodie. 'If the results had been what he wanted he wouldn't have gone back.'

Daniel stared at her outline, just visible in the darkness. 'That's a harsh judgement.'

Her shoulders framed a shrug. 'I haven't much patience with people who spend good money destroying themselves. I don't know if it's an illness or a weakness of character. I do know most people face the same trials and tribulations and don't yield to dependency. If you think Jared Fry would make a noble cause, Daniel, I have to tell you I don't think you can save a drug addict. Every so often one manages to save himself, but mostly their life is over the first time they inject or sniff or smoke something because they need it rather than because they want it.'

Daniel wasn't sure what he was hearing. He knew Brodie was a tough, resilient woman, partly because she'd had to be and partly because the capacity had always been there. He knew she held some fairly robust views. He didn't believe she was a natural fascist. 'I don't think you'd be saying this if someone you cared about was hooked on drugs.'

'Probably not. That doesn't mean I'm wrong. No one's at their most objective when their emotions are involved.'

'No,' he agreed softly. 'Brodie, what's this about? What happened after you gave Eric his coffee?'

It was now or never: she got it out in one breath. 'We fucked each other's brains out.'

Deacon needed to hear from the Forensic Medical Examiner before he made his next move. If measurements of the girl's skull matched the photograph of Sasha Wade they had an ID and, except for the urge to find answers to questions which bothered him the way midges bother campers, there was no need to concern himself further with the whereabouts of Michelle Rollins.

If, on the other hand, Dr Roy's measurements meant the body

couldn't be Sasha's, the need to establish Michelle's whereabouts became urgent. It didn't mean she was the girl in the ground, but it meant she could be.

He toyed with the idea of paying Rollins another visit while he was waiting but decided he couldn't justify it. If Michelle was by now the mother of six bonny bambinos he would be wasting his time interrogating Eddie. And if there were no babies because there was no Luigi because Michelle never actually left The Diligence, all jumping the gun would achieve was to warn Rollins that he was under suspicion.

He'd sat tight for eight years: it might not be enough to panic him into packing a bag and leaving the store unopened tomorrow morning but it wasn't worth the risk. As things stood Rollins was going nowhere: either he had nothing to hide, or he'd weighed up the odds when the body was found and decided to sit it out. Being interviewed as a possible witness would have reassured him. Going back late at night to ask him about Michelle, when Deacon hadn't the evidence to arrest him no matter how unsatisfactory his answers, could only be a mistake. So he sat in his office, the upper floor empty about him, and drank too much coffee waiting for Roy to ring.

The phone went just after eleven. 'Well?' barked Deacon.

'Yes, thank you, Superintendent,' said the FME smoothly, 'how kind of you to ask.'

Deacon gripped his phone as if attempting to strangle it. 'Is it the Wade girl?'

There was a judicious pause. 'It could be.'

Deacon had his next move ready whether the answer was affirmative or negative. He hadn't expected uncertainty. 'You still don't know? What's the problem?'

'Her age,' said Roy. 'I understand the photograph was taken two years before she disappeared. She was still growing. You'd expect minor changes in the bone structure in those two years, and minor differences is what I'm seeing. I think it's the same girl, but if you want me to stand up in court I'd have to say it might not be. I couldn't make a positive identification.'

'Bugger,' said Deacon feelingly. He thought for a minute. 'Is it worth waiting? Will any of your tests clarify matters one way or the other?'

'The DNA's as clear as crystal,' said Roy with mild reproof.

'For all the help that is! Are you telling me you can't ID someone who was adopted?'

'Eight years is a long time. If she'd just died we could take hairs from Sasha's brush and see what other traces she'd left around the house. After eight years...' His tone was regretful.

'What about that tooth thing, that says if she came from another part of the country?'

'Yes, I've got that back,' said Roy. 'It says she didn't. Do you know if the Wade girl... ?'

'Lived in Brighton from infancy. Along, of course, with thousands of other people.' An idea struck Deacon. 'If I can get DNA relating to the other possible victim, presumably you could run the rest again?'

'Of course,' said the FME. 'Get me a living close relative and I can tell you something.'

'I'll find out where Michelle Rollins's parents are, and if she has any brothers or sisters. But not tonight. Tomorrow, as someone said, is another day.'

'Scarlett O'Hara,' said Aditya Roy helpfully.

'I knew that,' growled Deacon.

With no wind behind it the tide was creeping in like a burglar, just the faint chink of a dislodged pebble and the hiss of foam to warn of its approach. It would stop, even on a spring tide with a gale behind it, thirty metres from the netting-sheds; still, its approach always made Brodie uneasy. She had it at the back of her mind that one day it would do something different – keep coming until the occupants of the little house were marooned on the gallery. She was aware of it now, stealing up on them trying not to be heard. And for this she desperately wanted to be alone with Daniel.

It was a long time – and that wasn't just how it felt to Brodie, longing for him to break the silence and afraid what he might say – before he spoke. He sat beside her like a statue, and only the flicker of starlight on his eye when he blinked was evidence of the life within him.

She wanted to scream, to shake him, to shout 'Say something!' into his moonwhite face, but dared not. Given time, she knew, reason would prevail. Daniel Hood was a rational man. He would say nothing until the shock had subsided and he was able to see the situation clearly. Then what he had to say would be sensible and humane and immensely helpful. If she forced him to speak before he was ready, her soul shrank from the judgement he might pass.

She heard him draw breath. He still didn't look at her. His voice was low. 'You're not saying he raped you?'

'No,' she said immediately. 'I wish I could. I wish I could tell you he misunderstood a bit of harmless flirting and didn't hear when I told him to stop. I can't. I wanted him. I wanted him as much as he wanted me. If he'd tried to leave I'd have stopped him.'

'Have you told Jack?'

'No. I came straight here. Well – after I got my breath back and worked out which way was up. Eric wanted me to go back to The Diligence with him. I said I was going home, but I didn't do that either. I phoned Marta to say I'd be late, and after that I just sat in the office on my own for two hours. Not doing anything, not even thinking, just sitting. Then I came here.'

'An hour ago.'

'Or rather more. I wanted to come up. I couldn't face you.'

Daniel sighed. 'Brodie, you don't owe me an explanation. You're a grown woman, if this is what you want you can have it. But it wasn't the last time we talked. Is it now?'

He had an uncanny knack almost of reading her mind. Brodie shook her head, her hair tossing wildly. 'No! It isn't. So why the hell do I behave like a nymphomaniac whenever that man comes near me? I don't love him. I don't want to spend my life with him and have his babies. I hardly know him. I don't understand!'

There was genuine distress in her voice that Daniel could not have ignored if she'd come to him with a much more shocking tale than this one. She needed comfort, and when she was calmer she might need some advice. Of course, he knew the reason she felt able to ask his advice on her sex-life was that she saw him as a disinterested party, outside the boundaries of the electric triangle, and it was hard to take that as a compliment. But she was his friend, and if this was the help she needed from him he was glad she'd come. 'Pheromones,' he said.

She blinked. 'What?'

'Pheromones. Chemicals given off by one individual that affect the behaviour of others. They're part of what makes us attractive to one another – or not,' he added wryly. 'I imagine Eric Chandos produces pheromones that match the receptors in your brain.'

Brodie stared at him open-mouthed. 'You're telling me love is a matter of chemicals?'

'No, I'm telling you sex is. For casual sex, or for someone to fertilise an egg for you, pheromones are probably a good guide to choosing a partner. If the biology is favourable you're more likely to have a strong baby. I dare say most animals don't think any further than that.'

He looked at her sidelong. 'Some people don't either, but most do. Most people want a partner who makes them laugh. Someone who respects them, someone who's kind. They aren't really survival attributes and I don't expect you can give off a chemical that says, "Hey girls, drop everything, here comes the best mower of lawns, mender of domestic appliances and picker-up of dry cleaning you'll ever meet." But if you're looking for someone to spend your life with, those things matter.

'Which is why it's a good idea to get to know someone before starting with the biology. Sexual magnetism is just your hormones telling you the bits are going to fit. By the time you're ready to think in terms of love your brain's ticked off a check-list and is confident you're compatible in a lot more ways, and a lot more important ways, than just chemically.'

Brodie managed a shaky little laugh. 'Daniel – is there anything I could throw at you that you couldn't put me straight on?'

He did the rueful one-shouldered shrug. 'Nothing you can get out of books, anyway.'

She didn't ask herself if he was right: it made too much sense. It explained why her body kept doing things that she – Brodie Farrell, mother, businesswoman and person in her own right – didn't approve of. Iron filings don't ask themselves if they love the magnet: they feel the pull and react. It was like that. She was addicted to a chemical as much as Jared Fry was.

'So what do I tell Jack?'

She thought he'd tell her, Everything. Daniel's addiction was the truth: he had to have it even when he knew it was bad for him. He surprised Brodie by thinking long before answering. 'How do you want this to end?'

'The same way I did last time you asked. I've no interest in Eric Chandos. I don't know if I love Jack but I like being with him. I want to be with him after this is history.'

'Is that what he wants?'

'I think so.'

'I think so too. What do you think will happen if you tell him?'

Brodie didn't have to think. 'It would finish us. He wouldn't forgive me for being unfaithful. He might want to, he might try to, but he wouldn't succeed.'

Daniel chewed his lip. 'Is there any chance you're pregnant?'

That at least she knew the answer to. 'No.'

'Then I think, if you tell him, the one who'll suffer most from all this is the one who had no responsibility for it. I think if you told him you'd be doing it not for Jack's benefit but for yours, to clear the air.'

She was astonished. 'You think I should lie to him?'

'No,' said Daniel with conviction. 'I think if he asks you have to tell him the truth and take the consequences: what happens next is his call. But splitting up will hurt him more than it'll hurt you. I think what you have to do – and do to the best of your ability, put your heart and soul into doing – is make sure he never has a reason to ask.'

She sat quietly, taking it in. It wasn't an easy way he was offering her. She'd have her conscience to deal with as well as her addiction, and she couldn't let Deacon see she was troubled by either. It couldn't be a factor when they argued: she could never, *ever* say, 'I don't need this crap, there are other fish in the sea,' for fear he'd answer, 'What fish?' However long the road they travelled together there would be potholes every mile, and the job of avoiding them would be hers.

It would be easier to tell him what had happened, apologise, and shovel up the debris after the explosion subsided. But Daniel was right: she wasn't the one who stood to lose the most. She could walk out of this relationship and into another whenever she chose. Deacon couldn't. He'd been alone for eleven years before she knew him. She knew how much making a go of this meant to him. Not enough to humiliate himself, but perhaps enough to wonder if he should.

'All right,' she said quietly. 'Yes. Thanks. Daniel, I don't know where I'd go if I couldn't come to you.'

'Any time,' he said with a sort of thin breeziness that, if she hadn't been so wrapped up in her own concerns, she'd have recognised as grief. 'Any time you need to tell someone how you've shafted one guy by sleeping with another, I hope you'll think of me.'

Brodie laughed. She thought it was a joke. She kissed him lightly on the cheek, then she was on her way down the iron stairs. 'I'm going home now. I'll see you tomorrow. Thanks again, Daniel.'

He heard her footsteps up the shingle beach, soon afterwards he heard her car. He went on sitting in the darkness for a long time, oblivious now of the stars or the cold. Finally he realised he was shivering, and climbed out of the deckchair and went inside.

He went straight to bed. But he didn't sleep. Alone in the dark, with the galaxies westering unconcerned beyond his ken, with the duvet pulled about his chilled body, with his glasses on the bedside table and his eyes wide with images he had not sought but could not escape, he lay silent until the tears came. Then he wept as if his heart was breaking.

Chapter Thirteen

Like a manic depressive Deacon swung between opposite poles.

For twenty minutes at a time he was convinced that the girl at The Diligence was Sasha Wade. Still in search of fame and fortune she hitched her wagon to the wrong star and paid with her life. She left home with her guitar, her credit card and a change of clothes, and went to meet someone who'd offered her the world. It didn't work out that way. It turned out what he was actually offering Sasha didn't want. She tried to leave and he hit her. Maybe that was all it was: one blow. There were no signs of a sustained attack. It was too late to know if there had been a sexual assault.

Whatever happened, she died and left her killer with a body to dispose of. If he wasn't a local man he had another reason to know about The Diligence. A man with a body in his car doesn't go for a drive looking for somewhere he can dig. He goes to a place he knows, and he knew about the empty hotel in its wooded grounds. Possibly he knew about the builders whose activities would soon erase all trace of his.

Security on the site had never been absolute. By June 1997, with the first flats ready for occupation, there was nothing to stop the killer driving round the back of the building and down to the bottom of the garden where he pulled a pick and spade from his car and dug a hole as close to the trees as the roots would allow. If he drove over it a few times after he filled it in, anyone who noticed at all would blame the builders. Anyone who saw his car there late at night would think the same thing. It was a brave move, but in fact he'd have attracted more attention in a more secluded spot.

His gamble paid off. No one disturbed him as he buried his victim, no one even noticed, and for eight years nothing came to trouble her or threaten him. Finally it was only bad luck that led to her discovery. Even if he was a local man he might have moved on in eight years; if he was just passing through there might be nothing linking him to the area. If the girl was Sasha Wade, Deacon thought her killer had probably got away with murder.

But after twenty minutes or so the pendulum swung back and he was drawn to the possibility that the body was that of Michelle Rollins. Bubbly, uninhibited Michelle. In that case he knew who the killer was: her husband Eddie, dour and hardworking, who found while the ink was still wet on his mortgage that he was busting a gut to make a home for a trollop. Perhaps he caught her *in flagrante*, perhaps in an angry moment she threw her infidelity in his face. He reacted with a fury that startled them both and Michelle ended up dead on the carpet.

It was the only reason for Eddie to lie about her disappearance. Luigi the truck-driver indeed! Rollins should be behind bars for that alone. Michelle was the right age, build and colouring. She moved into The Diligence with her husband in May 1997 and a few weeks later, one way or another, she moved out again.

The builders were still on site, only one of the other flats was occupied and that by three students. Rollins would have had the place to himself most evenings. He put his wife's body in one of Wilmslow's wheel-barrows, trundled her down the garden and buried her on the edge of the wood. He'd seen the plans, he knew no one else would be digging down there.

But why did he stay? He could have sold up soon afterwards, citing his wife's desertion, and put miles or countries between them. But then, as long as he stayed he had some control over the situation. If his neighbours had wanted a swimming pool there, or any construction that meant excavating, he would have vetoed the proposal and suggested an alternative site. Miles wouldn't save him if Michelle came back. Keeping her underground was the key to his safety.

And Rollins was the one who held out longest. Who wanted to stay when all his neighbours wanted to sell. Who only succumbed when his obstinacy began making him conspicuous.

Deacon was going to have to contact Michelle's parents for a DNA sample. He didn't know her maiden name, and didn't want to ask Rollins for fear of alerting him. But the marriage would have been registered and these wonderful new computers should be able to get him the information. Jill Meadows was computer literate. She was also his newest DC and still glad of an opportunity to please Sir.

Of course, finding Michelle Rollins's parents wouldn't help if the body was that of Sasha Wade...

He was about to page Meadows – he did this by the simple expedient of filling his lungs and bellowing 'Meadows!' – when Charlie Voss wandered in from his office next door with an odd expression and a large book. 'I've found something funny.'

'Oh good. I could do with a laugh.'

Voss didn't respond to his sarcasm. Often these days he didn't even notice it. 'It's Mrs Bush's register, from when The Diligence was an hotel.'

'I'm sure a lot of murders get planned on holidays,' said Deacon bleakly. 'I dare say a few get committed. Ten days of rain and she says "We should have gone to Miami" once too often. But you wouldn't bury her in the hotel grounds.'

Voss opened the ledger on Deacon's desk. 'The hotel closed at the end of September. All that last month there were only a handful of bookings – except for six days when all eight rooms were booked to one account.'

Deacon tried to read the script without his glasses. 'A conference? A small one?'

'A band.'

Deacon stopped peering at the book and stared at Voss instead. 'You're kidding me!'

'No. Souls For Satan stayed at The Diligence Hotel for six days in September 1996.'

It was hard to know what it meant. They sat and stared at each other, neither offering an opinion. It might be no more than one of those off-the-wall coincidences that do occur, even in murder inquiries, that seem at first to be of deep significance but turn out to be nothing more than fate taking the piss.

'After all,' ventured Voss at length, 'both the girls we know about were alive then, and for at least nine months afterwards.'

'But why hasn't somebody said something?' demanded Deacon. 'We weren't interested in Fry because he's only just bought the place. Wouldn't it be natural for him to say, "Of course, I was here once before"?'

'Maybe he thought it was irrelevant,' suggested Voss. 'If he knew we were interested in what happened after the hotel closed.'

'*I'm* the investigating officer,' snarled Deacon, '*I'll* judge what's relevant. And if he knew we wouldn't be interested, why hide the fact?'

'He may not be hiding it. He may genuinely not have thought to mention it. Do you want to ask him about it?'

Deacon hesitated. 'I'll have a word with Brodie first, see if she knows. If she does it's not a secret, Fry just didn't mention it. If she doesn't know – if she spent three months negotiating the purchase of a property for the man and he never told her he stayed there once – you'd have to wonder why.'

'But if he's hiding something, what is it? He didn't kill anyone when he stayed there. And if he came back the next summer with a body to bury, why buy the place eight years later? He should have severed any connection he had with The Diligence. He certainly wouldn't have had someone digging holes in the garden if he knew what they were likely to find.'

Voss was right: it made no sense. Bizarre coincidence was a likelier explanation than a killer behaving *that* stupidly.

Voss went to leave, taking the ledger with him. In the doorway he slowed to a halt. 'She took her guitar.'

'What?'

'Sasha Wade. When she disappeared, she had her guitar with her.'

'Yes. And a change of underwear and sixty pounds.'

'She's a singer, and she set off carrying her guitar – and the next time anybody sees her she's buried in the grounds of what used to be an hotel and was once visited, and is now owned, by a rock star. There's a pattern there.'

Deacon thought about it. 'If the body's Sasha. Do you think it is?'

Voss had momentarily forgotten there was some doubt. 'If she's still alive, why haven't her parents heard from her in eight years?'

'She could be dead without being dead at The Diligence. She could just have gone her own way. People do.'

'You think it's Michelle.'

'The situation's simpler if it's Michelle,' said Deacon judiciously. 'Any word from the Italians?'

'I'll go chase them up.'

He could have phoned Brodie. It was a one line question demanding a one word answer: if the telephone had never been invented he could have done it by semaphore. But Deacon welcomed an excuse to get out of the office for half an hour. He walked the short distance from Battle Alley to Shack Lane.

Brodie knew his knock and answered promptly. 'You're not busy then?' he asked.

'Paperwork,' she said. 'I'd rather see you.'

When he first started dating Brodie Farrell he was on tenterhooks waiting for the second shoe to drop. He couldn't believe that a woman like her was interested in a man like him, and he steeled himself for the disappointment when he found out what she was up to instead.

As time went on it became clear that she enjoyed his company in the same way that he enjoyed hers. He didn't know why. Given her choices, *he* wouldn't have spent much time with him. These days he didn't look into the mystery too deeply. He was just glad to be able to knock on a door and have an attractive woman drag him inside.

'I can't stay long,' he said. 'I'm still trying to put a name to this body. And Voss has found something odd. When you first showed The Diligence to Fry and Chandos, did they tell you they'd been there before?'

'No.' She sounded surprised and her brow gathered in a frown. 'Though to be fair, I never did show it to Jared. He bought it, believe it or not, sight unseen.'

'Did he indeed?' There was a significant note in Deacon's voice. 'He left it to his manager to find a place and he only saw it after the deal was done?'

'Yes. Crazy or what? But that's what they wanted to do so that's what we did.'

'Was Fry pleased with it?'

'Eric said he was. I can't say it was obvious. Jack, what's this all about?'

He had no reason not to tell her so he told her. 'It might mean nothing. But it struck us as odd, and I wondered if they'd said anything to you.'

'Nothing. Of course, it is nearly nine years ago. I imagine a band stays in a lot of hotels in nine years.'

'Yes. But I can't see why they wouldn't mention it. In the course of conversation. Over one of those dinners you had with Chandos,' he added unnecessarily. 'All he had to say was, "You know this house you've found for us? We stayed there, years ago when it was an hotel." End of mystery. Why wouldn't he say that?'

'Ask him.' Her voice was a fraction strained: Deacon wondered if she and Chandos had had words.

'I will. Or maybe I'll get Charlie to do it. He gets on with these long-haired types better than I do.' He sniffed disparagingly. 'I suppose I'd better go do some work.'

'Right now?'

He didn't understand. 'Right now?'

'I mean, is anybody going to die or suffer unreasonable hardship if you don't go right now? Is anybody going to get away with murder, mayhem or sedition?'

He considered. 'Probably not. Why do you ask?'

'Because there's something I need you to do for me.'

'Sure,' he said. 'What?'

'I need you to make love to me. Right here, right now.'

His expression hardly flickered. '*Right* now?'

'This very minute.'

He looked round the little office critically. 'Your sofa can't be more than five feet long.'

'No,' said Brodie, expressionless. 'But the wall is eight feet high.'

While Deacon was otherwise engaged and Voss was on his way to The Diligence, an hour's intelligent work at the computer led DC Meadows to Thomas and Ellen Vincent, parents of Michelle Rollins, sometime of Bexhill and now resident in Chapel St Mary. And likely to remain so: it was one of the largest cemeteries in the area.

'They were in a car crash last year,' said Meadows when her superintendent returned. 'Both killed instantly.'

'Never mind,' said Deacon, crossing as he often did the boundary between single-minded and crass, 'we can get an exhumation order and get DNA that way.' Something in the constable's silence drew his gaze. 'Unless of course ..'

Meadows nodded. 'They were cremated.'

'Any other children?'

She shook her head. 'Mr Vincent had a brother. He was a radio officer on a Panamanian supertanker.'

'Was?' echoed Deacon suspiciously.

'Yes, sir: she broke up in a typhoon in the Pacific in 1991. To prove the body is Michelle's you'd need to test a close blood relative, and she doesn't have any left.'

'Of all the rotten luck,' growled Deacon.

'I know,' said Meadows. 'How unfortunate can one family be?'

He stared at her. 'I didn't mean theirs. I meant ours.'

Eric Chandos met DS Voss at the front door and steered him down the garden like a rodeo clown distracting a bull. He'd left Fry upstairs but that was no guarantee he'd stay there, and Chandos didn't want him talking to policemen.

Sergeant Mills was back at the trench, still taking measurements and samples. Voss couldn't think what more a hole in the ground could tell anyone, but that wasn't the point. All excavation is destruction. Open a grave and you get one chance to hear everything it has to say. A detective can go back weeks later to re-interview a witness and get as much as, or more than, he did the first time. But a hole in the ground fills with water, fills with mud, fills with nature, and will never again be as it was when first opened. Anything it has to say you have to hear at the start. A week later is too late.

The Scenes of Crime Officer nodded amiably to Voss as he and Chandos came down the lawn. 'You got my second-best wellies, Charlie?'

Voss considered. 'Should I have?'

'Reg Vickers said he'd send them up with whoever was coming next. These have sprung a leak.' He lifted an enormous foot out of the trench to demonstrate.

'He didn't know I was coming,' said Voss. 'I've got mine in the car. What size are you?'

'Thirteen,' said Mills proudly.

Voss could have got both his feet into a size thirteen Wellington boot. 'Sorry.' He and Chandos walked on. 'I wanted to ask how you first heard about The Diligence.'

Chandos shook his head. 'I didn't. Mrs Farrell saw something about it in the local paper. There was a planning application to build some more flats and the locals were protesting. She thought the developers might be glad to wash their hands of it. She asked if we were interested, and the rest is history.'

History was certainly what interested Voss. 'Was that the first you'd heard of the place?'

'Yes. Why?'

'Souls For Satan stayed at The Diligence Hotel eight years ago.'

Chandos could not have looked more surprised if Voss had slapped him. His eyes went to the trench where Sergeant Mills was once more labouring leakily. 'Eight years?'

'Yes,' said Voss. And then, in the interests of honesty: 'Actually, a little more. In September 1996.'

'Really?' Chandos was thinking. 'But you think she died the following summer.'

Voss nodded. 'It may have no bearing on the case, it just seemed strange. That you stayed here for a week and nobody thought to mention it.'

Chandos understood. 'I dare say that does seem odd. It's because of how we work. I book the hotels but I don't travel with the band. I'm up ahead at the next venue, getting ready for the next gig.

'By September '96 the band was making a name for itself but it wasn't mega-big. We didn't need special security or police escorts. I

probably picked the hotel because it was midway between two venues. If I look back at the records I could tell you which. Before they
set off I'd brief the roadies on where they had to be when, where
they were playing and where they were staying, and that would be
the last I'd hear of the place. I was never here until Mrs Farrell
brought me. Maybe I should have remembered the name, it's
unusual enough, but I didn't. It was just an hotel booking – one of
maybe a hundred I made that year and every year since.'

'But Fry stayed here for a week,' said Voss reasonably. 'He should
remember it.'

Chandos chuckled. 'When we do a European tour there are whole
countries Jared doesn't remember. He remembers gigs. He remembers audiences. The stage is pretty much his whole life. An hotel
room is just somewhere to sleep. He'd get in a bit before dawn and
sleep most of the day. He may never have seen it in daylight until we
moved in.'

Voss nodded slowly. It seemed plausible in the circumstances. 'I
expect that's it. I'll have a word with Mr Fry, see if I can jog his memory.'

'Sure,' shrugged Chandos. 'Though I don't see how it'll help.'

Voss gave a wry grin. 'Making sense of things is pretty much my
whole life. I find something weird, I have to find out how it fits.
Sometimes it doesn't, but I need to know that. It's kind of an occu-
pational illness: we live in fear of missing something. We'd rather
waste days ruling something out than dismiss it too soon. I'll have a
word with Mr Fry before I go back to town. It's the first thing Mr
Deacon's going to ask me.'

'I'll go find him,' said Chandos. 'I'll get Miriam to bring you some
tea in the sitting room.'

Charlie Voss had been a policeman for nearly ten years, he knew
when he was being got rid of. He didn't want Chandos coaching Fry
on what to say. If he wanted to; if there was any need to. Voss was
aware of another reason Chandos might want to see Fry before the
detective did. He needed a tactful way to say he wouldn't search Fry
for banned substances even if he found him playing air guitar and
singing *The Good Ship Lollipop* in a slurred falsetto.

'That's all right,' he said, 'I'll come with you. Who knows, he
might be sober enough to answer a few questions.'

The manager cast him a slightly uncertain grin and led the way
back to the house.

Chapter Fourteen

Sometimes fate takes a hand.

Night long, unsleeping, Daniel had thought of nothing but Brodie's revelations. He felt – not just emotionally but somehow physically too – as if he'd been kicked senseless. His mind raced and froze by turns. His body ached.

He couldn't explain it, even to himself. Brodie was his friend, she owed him certain kinds of loyalty but not that. He had no claims on her sexuality. Seeing her on Jack Deacon's arm hadn't pained him like this. He had no idea why he felt betrayed, but that was it. Through the endless dark it sawed at his heart. What made it worse was that she had no idea, and never would know, how her actions had affected him.

Before dawn he washed and dressed, and made breakfast, and watched while it went cold. He sat motionless, unaware of the Channel breeze picking up or the turn of the tide, recycling the same facts and feelings until they slumped to acid sludge in his brain.

Finally he realised he had to get out of the house. He gave himself a couple of tasks to do – going to the bank was one, shopping for food another. Neither was urgent: he was trying to take his mind off things.

The money he drew at the bank he spent at the supermarket on things that he didn't need and, later, wouldn't know why he'd wanted. He arrived on the pavement with his arms full and a fifteen minute walk through busy streets ahead of him. So when the area car from Battle Alley pulled up and PC Vickers offered him a lift, he took it.

Police cars aren't meant to be used as taxis. But every cloud has a silver lining and events of the last fifteen months had left him on friendly terms with the local police. For that, right now, he was grateful. He put his shopping on the back seat and climbed into the front.

'Are you in a hurry?' asked Vickers. 'Only I've a call to make on the way.'

'Suits me,' said Daniel. Anything was better than sitting alone at home, pondering developments and the unexpected feelings they had stirred in him. 'Where are we going?'

'I've got something to take to The Diligence.'

If the next traffic lights had been red Daniel might have bailed out, leaving a month's food behind. They were green. Vickers kept driving, unaware of his passenger's dilemma.

And when his heart steadied and his brain was making sense again Daniel realised he was over-reacting. He would wait in the car. Even if he saw Chandos, the only awkwardness would be in Daniel's head. There was no reason for Chandos to suppose he knew what had happened. It was none of his business. He could stay out of the shambles Brodie was making of her life without avoiding large chunks of the Three Downs.

Vickers parked behind The Diligence and ferreted under Daniel's shopping for a pair of white rubber boots. 'I'll just take these down to Billy Mills. Shan't be five minutes.'

Left alone Daniel opened the door and swivelled sideways, tapping his feet on the cobbles. He needed the air.

A voice close at hand made him start. 'What are you doing here?'

By daylight Jared Fry looked even worse than he did at night. His face was drawn, pallid but for dark smudges like bruising under his eyes, his frame skeletal under his clothes. But his gaze was placid, his mood amiable. Daniel guessed why.

'I got a lift home with a policeman,' he said. 'We're taking the scenic route.'

Fry didn't question that. Curiosity is not a feature of drug addiction. 'They're everywhere,' he shrugged. 'I'm avoiding them.'

'That's probably a good idea.'

'And Eric. I'm avoiding Eric as well.'

Daniel sighed. 'Me too.'

Fry gave him a conspiratorial grin. 'Come with me.'

Daniel gestured weakly at the car. 'I'm waiting for Constable Vickers…'

'Got something to show you.'

He wasn't off his head – after so long it took a lot to do that: too much, not much less than it would take to kill him – but he was clearly intoxicated. It was like talking to a child, thought Daniel: the short attention-span, the simplistic thought-patterns. Fry took drugs to expand his consciousness but what they actually did was shrink his world. It was the man's tragedy. That, and having talent but perhaps not quite enough.

In the end Daniel did as he was bid. He could see what Fry wanted to show him and be back before Vickers was ready to leave.

The demon rocker – but there wasn't much demonic about him

now, a forlorn figure with his baggy clothes and thin jauntiness – led the way through the high hall of The Diligence and up the stairs. And up, and up: through the first floor with its range of bedrooms and on through the roof, terminating in a single room perched on top of the house, more window than wall, a glass cage with views across the Three Downs to the distant sea.

It wasn't a bedroom, although plainly someone slept here some-times – on the beanbag sofa, amorphous enough to make the tight turns of the stairs, were jumbled cushions and a quilt. Instead of cur-tains, lengths of shimmering voile like saris whispered in the breeze. There was a television on the floor in one corner, a mismatched music system in another. A guitar leaned drunkenly against a low table.

'This is my room.' Fry slumped onto the beanbag, leaving Daniel nowhere to sit.

'It's your house.'

''Course it is,' agreed Fry. 'But this is *my* room. No one else comes here.' On the table were a tray, a plate, an empty vial and a used syringe.

Daniel nodded. 'I see.' His lips were tight but the heart within him gave a little twist. It wasn't a bedroom so much as a retreat. The beanbag sofa, the old quilt, the pretty fabrics, the spare TV and stereo: in all his multi-million pound house, this attic room with its bedsit scraps was where Jared Fry felt safe.

'They won't find us here,' he said as if it mattered.

The guitar was like the rest of the junk-shop furnishings: cheap and unremarkable. Not a demon rocker's instrument, wired to the moon for decibels to make an otologist weep, but a scratched and battered acoustic guitar with the ends of strings protruding from the keys like untrimmed whiskers. Daniel nodded at it. 'Play something.'

Fry's mind might be fogged by what was in his bloodstream but the short strong fingers knew their job. From a slow start they moved with mounting tempo up and down the frets and across the strings, trailing increasingly complex threads of sound, chords piled on chords, notes throbbing and soaring like a wailing child.

Daniel knew nothing about music. Marta Szarabeijka had tried to teach him some basic piano but he never progressed beyond *Chopsticks*. She said he had a tin ear but that wasn't true. He could appreciate music. He knew that this impromptu concert on a cheap guitar was something rock fans the world over would have killed for.

He knew that Jared Fry was a genuine musician. When the lights went down, the make-up came off and the band went home, you could argue he was no longer a rockstar, but he was still a musician. Daniel was impressed, and sorry it didn't make Fry happier.

With no sign of Vickers returning, he lowered himself cross-legged on the wooden floor, rested his chin on his arms across his knees and listened.

'That's what you were playing at the party,' he said when Fry finished. 'When I...' Embarrassed, he fell silent.

Fry nodded. '*Crucifiction*. It's a kind of signature-piece. It's what most people want to hear.'

'Is it new?'

'I wish. No, it's from way back. When I was eighteen I wrote songs to die for but nobody listened. Now I dash them off so quickly I don't even remember writing half of them, and people throw money at me. Where's the sense in that?'

'Where do you get your ideas?'

Fry gave a lazy, druggy smile. 'There's this warehouse in Walthamstow – you send them a fiver and they send you four ideas, one of them a guaranteed show-stopper...'

'All right, stupid question,' acknowledged Daniel with a grin. 'Look, I'm a mathematician, I've never had an original thought in my life. I can't imagine how you create something entirely new. And not just once but time and again. Is your brain wired differently to mine? Am I not using mine properly? Were you born able to write songs – is it something you learned – if so, *how*?'

Jared Fry had heard the question a thousand times. Only very occasionally did he think the answer might be understood. 'It's like evolution. Your brain is a primaeval soup with proto-ideas swimming round in it. They collide all the time and nothing happens, but every so often the right two meet and start to reproduce. If you were a biologist you'd understand.'

'It happens in physics too,' said Daniel. 'That's a chain reaction. It's what makes nuclear bombs explode.'

Fry snorted. 'Sex and death, hey? Where else would demon rock get its ideas?'

'Play some more.'

Chandos was ready to admit defeat. He turned to DS Voss with a wry smile. 'I think he's given me the slip again.'

'Is his car gone?'

Chandos speed-dialled Tommy the driver who was polishing chrome in the garage. 'Nothing's missing. He must be about somewhere.'

They were back in the stable-yard. Suddenly the sound of the guitar hit them like a missile arriving. Tight-lipped, Chandos glared up at the glass turret. 'Jared, get the hell down here now!'

The man was worth millions. He was the beating heart of a business that employed a lot of people, including the one in the yard. But when Chandos raised his voice, Fry stopped mid-riff like a child caught raiding the fridge. Daniel looked at him in surprise and saw two expressions flit across his face. The first was guilt, the second fear.

Fry put down the guitar and unfolded from the beanbag, glancing awkwardly at his guest. 'We'd better go down.'

'Why?'

'Eric…' The hand that had been thumping out music to wake the dead and make the dying cheer waved a sheepish gesture towards the stair. 'He's looking for me.'

'I think he's found you. I imagine, if you don't go down, he'll come up.'

Fry gave a rueful grin. Then he headed for the stairs. Sadly, Daniel followed.

Chandos met them with his arms tightly crossed. 'I was calling you. Didn't you hear me?'

'No.' Fry didn't look at him. 'I was…'

'I know what you were doing,' interrupted Chandos. 'Dear God, there's a brand new state-of-the-art studio in the house, and you play on a matchwood guitar on a roof!'

'Daniel wanted to hear…'

'If Daniel wants to hear you he can buy a CD like everyone else! Detective Sergeant Voss wants a word with you. Try to give him what he needs and save him the trouble of coming back.'

There aren't many places where you'll see one grown man berate another publicly. A police station is one, and Voss was less taken aback than Daniel was. He'd seen Jack Deacon lay into errant DCs as viciously and with not much more excuse.

It wasn't quite the same, though. Mistakes by detective constables can have repercussions out of all proportion to their scale, and sometimes the fear of a superior's anger is more effective at focusing the mind than the evanescent risk of letting an offender escape. Also, while Deacon might blow off steam at those who answered to him, Voss had never heard him swear at Superintendent Fuller.

There were lines not to be crossed. While everything was going smoothly, Battle Alley was like any workplace where the staff were friends as well as colleagues and rank was a secondary consideration. But when the shit hit the fan, suddenly the formalities applied because they protected all concerned. Lower ranks were protected by those above them taking control; those in authority were protected by knowing their orders would be carried out without question. So while Deacon might humiliate a deserving constable in front of his colleagues, if he wanted to argue with Fuller they did it behind closed doors.

The exchange he'd just witnessed told Voss two things: that Chandos was a bully, and that Fry was his man, not the other way round. Neither had, so far as he knew, any relevance to his inquiries; all the same he wouldn't forget.

He said, 'Something odd came up and I wondered if you could explain it. It seems you stayed here when The Diligence was still an hotel.'

Fry's face was blank. 'Did I?'

'According to the hotel register. Eight rooms booked for six days to Souls For Satan in September 1996. Mr Chandos says he wasn't there so that would be you, the band and the roadies, would it?'

'Probably.'

'You don't remember?'

'One week in an hotel eight years ago? Jesus, I've forgotten way more important things than that!'

'You didn't remember it when you moved in?'

'No.' But something was stirring in his eyes: not memory but alarm. 'Eight years ago? Are you saying I had something to do with that girl? You're crazy! I never met her.'

'If you don't remember being here,' asked Voss reasonably, 'how can you be sure?'

'I'd remember if I'd killed someone!' yelled Fry. 'A hotel's a hotel, it's just somewhere to sleep, I don't remember any of them. But if something happened here – if someone got hurt – *that* I'd remember.'

It could have been the truth. Police work is full of coincidences: a man could go mad trying to incorporate them all into an Integrated Theory of What Happened. Sometimes the dog did nothing in the night because it never woke up. 'All right,' said Voss, shutting his notebook. 'Well, I expect I'll be back at some point but that'll do for now.'

'We are trying to help, sergeant,' Chandos pointed out. 'If it doesn't always seem like it, that's because we don't know anything.' He walked Voss to his car. 'Perhaps you'd give Mr Hood a lift back to town.'

'Sure. Daniel?'

Daniel hadn't moved. He appeared to have no intention of moving.

Most of the time Daniel Hood seemed so deeply unremarkable he was easy to overlook. People said things in front of him that they shouldn't because they forgot he was there. In normal circumstances he didn't make much impact on the world.

But Voss had known him long enough to realise there was another side to him: a kind of moral obstinacy that made him stand his ground against all odds when he thought he was right. It didn't make the quiet, gentle, unassuming Daniel a deceit, but it did temper one's view of him. Voss knew him better than Chandos and had some idea what was coming.

'I'll hang on here for a while,' said Daniel. 'If that's OK, Jared?'

Chandos turned slowly, looking not at Daniel but at Fry. 'You and I have work to do.'

'Then I'll wait till you're free.'

'We may be some time,' said Chandos coldly.

'I can wait some time.' Now there was no missing that tiny, polite steeliness in Daniel's tone.

A small crowd was gathering. Reg Vickers was helping to carry Sergeant Mills's samples to the car. SOCO's civilian staff assistant, a girl actually called Trisha but universally addressed as Morticia, was there too. Miriam the housekeeper, constitutionally unable to see a new face without trying to feed it, was taking orders for lunch and the gardener was crossing the yard with a strimmer over his shoulder and his eyes averted, trying not to notice the mess these people had made of his lawn.

If there's one thing a bully can't resist, it's an audience. 'Hell's teeth.' Framed by the beard, Chandos's smile was a thing of cruelty. 'You're a God-botherer. You want to save his soul.'

Daniel shook his yellow head. 'No.'

'Oh yes. I'd know that *Jesus Saves* expression anywhere. I bet you've got a Bible by your bed. I bet you say your prayers every night – properly, down on your knees. I bet you ask God to make you a better person.'

'You're mistaken,' said Daniel quietly.

'No,' said Chandos confidently, 'I know your type. Youngest child, yes? Parents a bit long in the tooth by the time you came along? Their idea of a night out was polishing the altar-rails. Proudest day of their life when you joined the choir. I'm guessing now but tell me if I'm right: your first solo was *Jesus wants me for a sunbeam*.'

Daniel smiled. 'Guess again.'

'Don't be embarrassed – the world's full of people like you. Small and afraid. You believe in God in the hope that'll make God believe in you.

'And you think you're going to convert Jared Fry. That would be the ultimate, wouldn't it – bringing the quintessential demon rocker to God! Your name would be spoken with awe wherever prayer-books are dropped. There'd be Daniel Hood Halls in the back-streets of small northern towns and a Daniel Hood Scholarship to one of the less popular seminaries. You'd finally have done something to justify the space you take up on the planet.'

His expression hardened. Daniel glimpsed a bitter dis-appointment, as if Chandos had tried to salvage Fry once and failed. 'Only it isn't going to happen. Jared doesn't have a soul. He sold it years ago and shot the proceeds up his arm. There's a vacuum there now. Take away the devil's music, the foul mouth and the glitter make-up and you aren't left with Jared Fry – you're left with noth-ing. You couldn't make a worthwhile person of him if he wanted you to. A demon rocker isn't just what he is. It's all he is.'

That Chandos was irritated with Daniel, Voss could understand. Almost everyone who met him wanted to slap him sooner or later. There was a kind of intellectual superiority about him that got under people's skins. Many of them would have applauded Eric Chandos's attack on him.

What was astonishing was how the vitriol had spilled over. Fry was his employer and his meal-ticket, and Chandos had ripped him apart in front of people he hardly knew to show that he could. To show that Fry would take anything Chandos doled out, because behind the wealth and fame he was too weak to survive alone. It reminded Voss of the lion act in a circus, where a man with a whip reduces the king of beasts to a shambling spectacle: up on the stool, roar for the people, jump through the hoop, back in the cage.

Daniel was white with fury. He didn't shout when he was angry, he didn't throw either objects or punches. Behind the thick glasses his eyes went diamond-hard, and regardless of the risk he went for the throat. He didn't say things he didn't mean. He sometimes said things which would have been better left unsaid precisely because they were true. When he was angry the truth stopped being his shield and became his morning-star.

Deliberately he turned his back on Chandos. His voice was quiet but utterly serious. 'You don't have to take this,' he told Fry. 'You have options.'

That thought seemed to trouble Fry more than the abuse. Voss saw expressions form and dissolve in his face, as if he didn't know how to feel or didn't dare let the feelings show. His lips started to frame words that then eluded him. His gaze strayed round the yard, unable to look either Daniel or Chandos in the eye. He looked trapped. Like an animal caged so long it has become afraid of the outside.

Finally, a dull flush on his hollow cheek, he marshalled a few mumbled words, his eyes dipped to the cobbles. 'It's all right. He doesn't mean it.'

'Yes, he does,' said Daniel flatly. 'Jared, you're entitled to better than this. The least he owes you is respect. If you're not getting it – well, you're not married to him, and if you were you could get divorced! Don't let him grind you down because you haven't the guts to walk away. Call your solicitor. Whatever contractual obligations you have, meet them – but get rid of him. He's eating you alive.'

Voss saw Chandos knot his fists by his sides and suspected that, but for his own presence, Daniel would be eating dirt by now. But if the thought had occurred to Daniel it did not stay him. He plunged on, reckless with righteous indignation.

'You want to know why you can't write any more? Because he's sucking the life out of you. He's a parasite: he's got his teeth into you and he wants you to think you can't do without him. But you don't need him to get you work – you're a star, promoters will queue up to stage you. In the short term all you need is a secretary to handle the paperwork and an accountant to handle the money. Hell's bells, I'll do it myself until you get organised. *You're* the success, Jared – you and the band. This man wants you to think otherwise because you're worth a fortune to him. And a good manager's worth his cut. So try to find one.'

Chandos's face was like thunder and his voice, when he found it, venomous. 'He's right, Jared, you do have options. Maybe you should think about them. You can ask me to throw Hood out, then stop behaving like a spoilt child and get back to doing what you're good at. Or you can ask me to leave. You won't have to ask twice. I'll have another job by the end of the month, but you'll never play in public again.' It was more than a threat: it was a prediction.

'Hood has no idea what it takes to get a rock show on stage, but you have. You know you can't do it, and you sure as hell know he couldn't. He's an unemployed teacher, for God's sake! And he's telling you to throw away your career. Be clear about that. If you want to find out if he's right, it's your call. But I won't hang around waiting to rescue you. It's time to make your choice.'

He sucked in a deep breath, fighting down the anger. 'Look, I know I'm hard on you. *You* know it's because I want the best for you. I want to see you achieve everything you're capable of, not slip into obscurity for lack of proper guidance. Maybe I go too far sometimes, but you wouldn't last ten minutes without me.'

Daniel knew he'd lost – saw it in Fry's face – before Chandos had finished speaking. It wasn't that he'd thought and decided that, after all, Eric Chandos was the best he could do. He was afraid to think about it. He was bound to the stronger man and lacked the courage to break free. Ashamed and embarrassed and quite unable to help himself, Fry said to the cobbles, 'Eric knows what he's doing. We'll be all right.'

There was nothing more to say. He'd offered to help and been rebuffed. Daniel shook his head regretfully. 'Every battered wife who's ever been through A&E said the same thing.'

Chandos laughed out loud. It was impossible to hear it without thinking of a cock crowing on a dunghill. 'I only said you had no soul. He thinks you've got no balls!'

Daniel was halfway to Voss's car. He paused and turned round, and said quietly, 'If you hurt him I will be back.'

It was so absurd a threat that the only thing keeping all who heard it from laughter was the certainty that he meant it. The thing you have to remember about David and Goliath is that David won.

If Chandos had held his tongue another ten seconds those few brave words would have been all that remained of his enemy and the field would have been his. But he wouldn't give even that much quarter. Pitching his voice to be heard he said, 'Don't think I don't know why you came here. Jared thinks you're concerned for his welfare, but you and I both know that your only interest in him is as a weapon against me.'

Daniel said nothing. He turned away and waited for Voss to get in the car, and wished he'd hurry.

His face puzzled, Fry asked the fatal question. 'Why would Daniel want to hurt you?'

Chandos had known someone would ask. He was prepared to volunteer the information, but he knew people well enough to know someone would make it easy for him. 'Because I've had what he hasn't been able to get in a year of trying,' he sneered. 'He thought that made her unobtainable: the virtuous woman whose price is above rubies. Now he knows different. She wanted it. She just didn't want it from him.'

Chapter Fifteen

Daniel phoned Brodie from the car. 'Are you in the office?'

The urgency in his voice startled her. 'Yes. Why?'

'I need you to do something for me. And I need you not to ask questions. I'll be there in ten minutes. Until then, don't open the door or answer the phone.'

'If I don't answer the door,' she said reasonably, 'how will I know you've got here?'

'Brodie, please! I can't explain now but it really matters. Humour me.' He sounded close to tears.

'All right,' said Brodie. 'We'd better agree on a special knock.' But he'd already rung off.

Voss drove and said nothing. Once he stole a sidelong glance at his passenger, and Daniel had his glasses off and the heels of both hands pressed into his eyes. Apart from using the phone, he hadn't spoken since leaving The Diligence. But he looked as if Chandos had taken him behind the stable-block and kicked seven bells out of him.

When the car stopped in Shack Lane Daniel reached over the seat back to collect his shopping. His hands were unsteady and cans kept rolling out of the plastic bags. Voss said quietly, 'Leave them. Give me your key, I'll drop them off.'

Daniel only had one key. He stared at it in confusion until Voss took it from him. 'I'll leave it under the wind-vane on the gallery, all right?' Daniel nodded.

Brodie had heard the car and opened the door as Daniel went to knock. Whatever she'd promised him, she wasn't about to check out her callers through a chink in the curtain. He pressed her inside and shut the door behind him, then he went to her desk and took the phone off the hook, all without a word.

A quiver of unease caught her under the heart. 'Daniel, whatever's the matter?'

So he told her.

Midway through the telling Brodie's long-fingered hand, the nails bloody talons, stole to her face, covering her mouth. Above, her eyes were stretched with horror. Her breast rose and fell as she took the air deep into her lungs, fighting panic.

When Daniel was done the silence in the little room grew until it packed every corner, muffling the sound of the street and the steady tick of the clock, probing every cavity with tendrils that swelled to fit, like fog or rot. The silence enveloped them.

Finally Brodie broke it with ragged words that caught in her throat. 'Daniel – how *could* you?' Her eyes, that had not left his face, nailed him to the wall.

'I didn't,' he mumbled unhappily. 'At least, I didn't mean to. I didn't mean to go there. I wasn't looking for Chandos and I wasn't looking for a fight. But Jared was getting hurt – either I had to say something or watch it happen. I expected him to hit out at me. I didn't expect him to bring you into it.'

'No,' she said slowly, 'I don't suppose you did. Who would? Why would he do that to me? In front of people I know – people Jack works with.'

'That's why I didn't want you answering the phone,' said Daniel. 'I didn't want you talking to Jack before I'd had the chance to explain. I didn't want you to find yourself denying it out of sheer surprise.'

'Well, this is it, isn't it?' She braced herself. 'Decision time. If I know anything about police stations, it'll be canteen gossip by now and Jack will have heard within the hour. I have to talk to him first.'

Daniel agreed. 'However bad it gets, it'll be worse if he hears it from anyone else.'

'What do I tell him?'

'What you told me. That you don't know why it happened. You didn't want Eric Chandos before, you don't want him now, but for a moment something in your body chemistry took over.'

'Will he believe it?'

'It's the truth, isn't it?' She nodded disconsolately. 'The question isn't whether or not he'll believe you, it's what he'll do about it.'

Her head came up quickly. 'Jack would never hit me!'

'I don't think he would. I do think he might go up to The Diligence and take a swing at Chandos, and if he does that he's probably looking for a new career.'

'Oh God,' moaned Brodie. 'I never wanted to hurt him, Daniel. If I've robbed him of what matters most to him in all the world – more than me, more than what we have together – I'll never forgive myself.' She reached for the phone. 'I have to talk to him, right now, face to face. Here, where if he blows up there'll be no one to see, where I can keep him from storming out and heading for Cheyne Warren.'

When there was nothing else to admire, Daniel could still admire her courage. 'Do you want me to stay?'

She thought for a moment then shook her head. 'It'll be difficult enough with just the two of us. Having a witness won't make it any easier for Jack, and he's the one who matters. In the end we'll do what he wants. The most I'm hoping for is to buy some time for him to calm down and make a rational decision.'

'I'll be at home: call me if you need me. If Jack needs someone to shout at…'

'Thanks, Daniel, but I think you've done enough already.'

Brodie didn't mean it as a slap in the face but that was how it felt. He nodded quickly and let himself out onto the street before she saw his eyes fill.

It was amazing, he thought as he walked, how two people who were important to one another could manage to keep hurting each other. He didn't think he was to blame for Brodie's present distress but he knew he was the cause of it. He knew she didn't mean to punish him by what she'd said, but it had slid under his ribs like a dagger.

What she hadn't said had, if anything, cut deeper. She hadn't even asked if Chandos had stumbled on the truth.

Back in Shack Lane, oblivious of how the ripples of her actions had spread to hurt someone else she cared for, Brodie was dialling Deacon's mobile number. She got voice-mail and her heart stopped. He didn't turn his phone off when he was driving or at night, only when he was dealing with a transgressor.

Deacon was not, as Brodie feared, on his way to The Diligence with his heart full of mayhem. He was in the flat above Eddie Rollins's hardware store, looming over the man like a storm and trying to put the fear of God into him while still complying with the PACE regulations. To the letter: the spirit of them troubled him not at all.

Rollins had been unwise enough to ask where he'd got with his inquiries.

Deacon's voice was barred with import. 'To the point, Mr Rollins, where I now know you're lying to me. Where we go from here is one of two ways. You tell me the truth, the whole truth and all that crap, and maybe it's not as bad as it looks, and even if it is we can start dealing with it. Or you keep pissing me around, in which case I charge you with murder and set about proving it.'

'Murder!' yelped Eddie Rollins, screwing his apron in his hands.

Deacon considered. 'Yes, I think so. Drunk in charge of a bicycle wouldn't really cover it. Not when I've dug a body out of your garden!'

'But – *murder*? I haven't murdered anyone!' Regaining a little control of his expression allowed him to knit his brows in a frown. 'Who do you *think* I've murdered?'

Deacon breathed heavily. 'Your wife. Michelle. Remember her? Blonde girl, a cheery word for everyone, a negligee for every occasion. One day she's here, the next she's gone, a week after that you tell the students next door she's left you. How was that again?'

'I told you,' hissed Rollins with a kind of fierce terror. 'She took off with a lorry driver.'

'Mr Rollins,' said Deacon disappointedly, 'you're selling yourself short. It was a much better story the first time round. It was the lorry driver who brought your new suite, he was an Italian, and his name…'

'… Was Luigi,' finished Rollins insistently. 'That's all I know. Except I also know it wasn't her in the garden.'

'Can you prove it?'

A hunted look. 'No! How?'

'Didn't she leave you a note?'

'I destroyed it.'

'Why?'

'Because…' He had to think about that. 'I was angry.'

'Naturally enough,' allowed Deacon.

'Damn right! I'd worked every hour God sends to buy a nice home for her. I'd even forked out for the Italian suite she wanted. And the day it came…'

'Oh yes,' said Deacon, 'a man would be angry about that. Angry enough to burn her note.'

'Yes.'

'Angry enough to burn her clothes?'

Eddie Rollins couldn't see the trap being laid for him. 'No, but I threw them out. Everything she didn't take with her.'

The directness of Deacon's gaze was like a finger in his eye. 'Angry enough to kill her?'

Rollins's cheek was white. 'No! I told you, she left me…'

Deacon shrugged. 'It didn't take much to kill her. One blow. Maybe not even a blow so much as a slap. You slapped her, she stumbled, she hit her head on the corner of the hearth… It was only when you told her to stop being such a drama queen and get up that you realised she wasn't going to, ever.'

'No...' whispered Eddie Rollins.

'Look,' said Deacon, suddenly – and disconcertingly – kind, 'can I give you a bit of advice? Obviously we're going to move this down to the police station, and you're going to want your solicitor there and everything you say is going on the record. I'll caution you in a minute, and after that we're into the formalities. So let me say this first. The sooner you come clean about this, the easier it's going to be for people to see your side of the story.

'You did your level best for the woman right up to the moment you lost your temper and hit her. You didn't beat her: you hit her once. She shouldn't have fallen, let alone died. Even angry, you did- n't mean to harm her. She was playing around, you struck out in a moment's fury, the next thing you knew she was dead. That isn't murder. It's manslaughter, and it's not the worst case of that. People will understand. Set the record straight and give us the chance to make it easy for you. You may do a couple of years. You might not, if you tell the truth now.'

'But it isn't the truth!' wailed the hardware tycoon. 'I didn't kill her. I didn't hit her. She left me. And...' He swallowed, hard. 'And I can prove it.'

Deacon blinked. 'Really?'

Rollins's eyes dipped. 'You're right, I lied. About a couple of things, but not that. To the best of my knowledge Michelle is alive and well and living with Luigi. I've had postcards from her. I don't know why I kept them but I did. I also kept the note.'

Deacon was staring at him in rank disbelief. 'You have the *Dear John*? And you didn't produce it even when you were suspected of murder?'

Rollins shook his head wearily. 'I didn't seriously think I was. I *know* that isn't Michelle you found, I thought you'd know it too in a day or two.'

'You could have eliminated yourself from the inquiry. You could have saved me and my officers time and effort as well, and we'll get back to that later. Oh no, Mr Rollins,' said Deacon, 'I'm not buying this. A man who can prove his innocence leaps at the chance. What possible reason could you have for pretending to have burnt Michelle's note when you were in a position to produce it?'

'You'll see,' said Rollins in a low voice. 'It's in the dresser with the postcards. Read it for yourself, then you'll see.'

The postcards were Italian tourist scenes – the Trevi fountain, the Ponte Vecchio, Vesuvius – written in a schoolgirl hand in scratchy biro. It appeared to be the same hand each time. The signature was *Michelle* and the postmarks were seven, six and four years old.

The same hand and signature appeared on the note. It was undated, written hurriedly on the back of an invoice. When Deacon turned it over it was the invoice for the Italian suite.

He read it, then read it again. Then he looked at Rollins, who looked away. Deacon read the note a third time.

'*Now* do you see?' muttered Rollins.

'Not entirely.'

'She was *married* to him!'

'Yes.'

'Before she married me. They never divorced.'

'That makes her a bigamist. Why would it make you risk being charged with murder?'

'We bought the flat as husband and wife. Every penny I had went into it, and I put both our names on it because I loved her. The mortgage was in our joint names.'

Deacon still didn't get it. 'You didn't tell the bank?'

'I told them she'd left. I *didn't* tell them we were never married.'

'Why not?'

'Because I'd have lost everything! The flat *and* the money I'd put into it. I couldn't face that. I told them she'd left me but neither of us was seeking a divorce at present.' He looked up with a tiny flicker of wan humour. 'At least that was true.'

Deacon was trying very hard not to shake him. 'You thought the bank would foreclose?'

'That's what I was told.'

'Who by?'

'A man I know. He knows about financial matters.'

'He's a banker?'

'He's a house remover. I see him down the pub sometimes.'

After a long moment in which he held his tongue, Deacon said, 'You've been lying to your mortgage company for eight years, and you've risked being arrested for murder, because of something a white van man said to you in a pub?'

'He knows about financial matters,' said Rollins again, defensively. Then, belatedly: 'Do you think he was wrong?'

'I think,' shouted Deacon, 'that if he knew much about financial matters he wouldn't be driving a van! Yes, I think he was wrong. I think the bank will have a form that you fill in to say your circumstances have changed from when you first applied for your mortgage, and after that all they'll be interested in is whether you can meet the repayments each month.'

Clearly, Rollins hadn't dared hope as much. 'Really?'

'Look,' snarled Deacon, 'I don't own a white van so I'm not qualified to give financial advice. Talk to your solicitor. Go see your bank manager. Tell him you believed you were married when you took out the mortgage – you had the ceremony and the certificate to show for it – only it turned out Mrs Rollins had married abroad and never divorced. None of it's your fault. You hadn't done anything wrong until you started lying about it.'

Slowly it was dawning on Eddie Rollins that the nightmare was over. He'd resisted selling the flat at The Diligence because it meant reopening the issue of his mortgage. He'd believed that if the bank found out the loan was granted on the basis of a lie they would demand immediate repayment. He'd thought Michelle's fib was going to bankrupt him. A tear trembled on the lip of his eye. 'No...'

Finally, when the fear had passed and so had the euphoria that followed it, Deacon was able to pursue his investigation with the man, not now as a suspect but a witness. Rollins was pathetically eager to help. He made coffee for his visitor, and put lashings of cream and too much sugar in it. And Deacon, bemused by the turn events had taken, drank it without complaint.

Rollins cast his mind back to the early months at The Diligence. 'The students next door threw a party most weekends so there was no shortage of girls around. I imagine some of them stayed over but I don't think any of them moved in, even temporarily. I used to grumble about the noise but there was never anything nasty.'

'Do you remember a girl with a guitar? Slight, fair, about the same height as your...' Deacon stopped himself just in time. 'As Michelle.'

Rollins thought hard. 'No.'

'Then did you see anything odd, at any time? That girl probably arrived at The Diligence either just before you did or soon afterwards. She didn't walk down the garden – somebody carried her or drove her. And he brought tools and spent quite a while digging a hole under the trees. Did you see any of that?'

Again the dutiful pause while Rollins thought. He shook his head and started to apologise. Then he stopped mid-sentence, his expression changing.

'What?' asked Deacon.

'I don't know. Nothing, probably. But one night there was a van, and I never did know who it belonged to.'

'Tell me.'

It was a Monday night in the middle of June. Rollins had begun stock-taking at the store where he worked. Michelle hadn't liked his being out late when she was alone at The Diligence – Miss Venables and the students had yet to arrive – but he had no choice. He got in a little after one o'clock to find the house in darkness. Supposing Michelle was asleep and not wanting to wake her he parked beside the stable-block. As he crossed the yard he noticed a van parked at the bottom of the garden.

'In the morning it was gone. I assumed it belonged to the builders. I asked Mr Wilmslow what it was doing there but he said it was nothing to do with him, he didn't have a black van. We decided it must have been a courting couple who hadn't realised the place was occupied again. I haven't given it a thought from that day to this.'

'What kind of a van?'

'It might have been a Ford Transit. I'm not sure – the only light down there was moonlight.'

'And you think it was black.'

'Dark, anyway.'

'And it was where we found the body?'

'More or less. I didn't look that closely. I thought it was one of the builder's vehicles, I just wanted to check that he wasn't doing anything down there that wasn't on the plans.'

Deacon nodded slowly. 'OK. Well, if you think of anything else, give me a call. If I think of anything else I'll pay you a visit. And for pity's sake, Mr Rollins, get yourself a financial advisor who doesn't shift second-hand furniture on the side!'

As he walked to his car he checked his phone. Brodie's number came up, a couple of times. He thought as soon as he'd got a minute he'd call her.

Chapter Sixteen

By close of play Deacon had confirmation that Michelle Rollins (sic) was alive and well, living in Naples with Luigi and four children, and astonished that anyone might think she'd been murdered.

Which left Sasha Wade.

It didn't mean the body had to be Sasha. There were no clothes, no personal effects, no help from DNA or dental work, no old injuries. If the girl at The Diligence had wanted to stay anonymous she could hardly have done a better job.

Finally Deacon remembered Brodie. It was almost six o'clock: he thought he'd give her a nice surprise and drop by instead of phoning.

As soon as he saw her face he knew they were in trouble. In spite of that she had to spell it out before he understood what kind of trouble it was, and say most of it again before he believed her. The first time he thought it was a bad joke: that if he waited and didn't panic she'd suddenly grin her boyish grin and admit as much. So he stood frozen, refusing to react, waiting for the punch-line; and she, her heart riven, had to go through it all again, a sentence at a time, giving it time to sink in. What she'd done. With whom. Why. At least that part of the story was soon told. She could offer no reason.

Finally Deacon believed what he was hearing. Anger, and even more than that shock, locked him rigid. For much of their relationship he had been afraid of losing her, but not like this – to an affair so casual it hardly merited the name. An animal coupling between strangers, a mere scratching of mutual itches, in an office where the paperwork overflowed the desk and the sofa was barely five feet long.

But the wall was eight feet high.

She saw him recoil as the thought hit him. 'When was this?' His voice was like gravel.

'Yesterday afternoon.'

The magnitude of her treachery rocked him. 'You were with me the night before!'

'Yes,' she said simply.

'And again this morning...' He looked around the little office incredulously. 'Right here. You *asked* me...'

'Yes, I did,' Brodie said. 'I needed you.'

'What, for comparison?'

She'd told Daniel he wouldn't hit her: now she almost wished he would. She thought anything would be better than the dumb pain in his face, and the knowledge that he loved her and she'd done that to him, for no reason. On a whim. A chance presented and she'd taken it without regard for the hurt it would cause. They weren't married, but after a year together it was disingenuous to consider herself single. Jack Deacon was her partner, she owed him fidelity. She could end their relationship with a word, but until then she wasn't free to respond when another man's hormones serenaded hers.

When her husband told Brodie there was someone he loved more than he loved her it was as if the earth had opened. As if nothing could be trusted any more. She'd screamed and cried; she'd berated him from the depths of her terrified soul; she'd begged him to stay. She'd reduced him to tears too – because John Farrell was a good man and only love would have made him let her down. He'd gone beyond scrupulously fair to guiltily generous in the divorce settlement, and when he was free to do so he'd married his plump little librarian. If there was scant consolation for Brodie in that, at least it proved his reason for hurting her wasn't trivial.

She hadn't fallen in love. She hadn't agonised for weeks over how to square the circle, to be fair to all concerned. She'd felt a surge of lust for an attractive man, and instead of burying herself in her VAT returns till it passed she'd grabbed him and impaled herself on him as if nothing in the world mattered more than satisfying her desire. She'd behaved like a bitch in heat. She was ashamed of herself in a way she had never been before. As if she'd been caught shop-lifting, she was mortified by her own dishonesty.

'There is no comparison,' she said, as calmly as she could with her voice breaking. 'Jack, I know it can't seem so right now but I care deeply for you. And I feel nothing for Eric Chandos, and I didn't even before he used my name as a weapon. Maybe that makes it worse: I don't know. I don't know why it happened. I know whose fault it was, but I don't understand why I did it. I was never unfaithful to you before. You've no reason to believe me but it's true.'

If she was hoping he'd contradict, say roughly that of course he believed her, she was doomed to disappointment. He said nothing. His face was graven with deep gullies of anger and pain, and his eyes were hot.

Brodie struggled on. However difficult it was, she had to get this said. 'I didn't want to hurt you. I wasn't thinking one second ahead. It was as if I was caught up in something outside my control. I didn't just forget about you: I forgot about me too – who I am, what I want, where I want to be. It was like being run down by a truck.

'And no.' She saw the thought burrowing like a worm in his raw flesh and squashed it. 'It wasn't that I had no choice. He didn't force me, and he didn't make me think he was going to. I think he was as startled by what happened as I was. But your quarrel isn't with him, Jack, it's with me. Eric Chandos didn't owe you better.'

They'd been standing here maybe fifteen minutes by now and Deacon had hardly spoken. He was going to have to, and both of them were afraid of what he would say when he did. Even in normal circumstances he wasn't a man who weighed his words carefully. He caused a lot of offence by saying what he thought. Here and now, saying what he felt would throw up a barrier between him and Brodie that might block all future communication.

Angry as he was, hurt as he was, Deacon knew that there was more at stake here than his outraged dignity. That he hadn't lost Brodie yet, but that didn't mean he wasn't going to.

It broke her heart to see him doing what he never did: treading cautiously, considering the consequences, trying to ignore his pain because once he acknowledged it his only choice was between vengeance and acceptance, and each would diminish him and put an end to them. There was nothing she could do to help. She had already betrayed his trust and injured his pride: telling him what to do now would strike at his very manhood. He might eventually forgive the rest, but not that.

After a long time he managed a tiny, deeply uncharacteristic little smile. 'I have no idea where we go from here.'

'You could tell me how you feel,' murmured Brodie.

Deacon considered. 'No, I don't think I'd better. I think if we go down that road I'll end up wrecking your office.'

'If it makes you feel any better…'

'It wouldn't, though, would it?' He wasn't shouting. His restraint was worse, in the same way that a rumbling volcano may be more disturbing than one in eruption. 'It's not your filing cabinet that dumped on me.'

'I am so very sorry,' said Brodie softly. 'I don't expect that helps much right now but I still want you to know.'

'Yes,' he said, 'I imagine you are. And no, it doesn't help much. I thought… I thought we were strong. I don't know about permanent, but I thought we were going somewhere. It felt like something real. To me: that's how *I* felt. And you felt it could be put aside for half an hour, for a man you didn't even care about. What does that make me, Brodie? Someone who matters less than a man you don't care about?'

Brodie shook her head. Her voice was shaking too, now. 'You do matter to me, Jack. If you didn't we wouldn't be having this conversation. I wouldn't be feeling this way. If I can I want to put this right. If it's going to take time I'll wait. Anything it's going to take I'll do. But if what you want is not to see me again, I'll understand and I'll do that too.'

'Feeling what way?'

'Like trash,' she said honestly.

Deacon nodded. 'You should.'

The silence grew about them again. Brodie didn't want to be the one to break it. She watched the ghosts of expressions flit through Deacon's face as his emotions churned. She knew he wanted to rage at her and didn't dare. She knew he could see no further ahead than getting outside without breaking something.

Until this moment she'd had no sympathy for battered women. She'd thought anyone who submitted to violence as the price of a relationship was unworthy of compassion. Now she saw how it might work. How the black eye, the split lip, the bruised ribs might seem a price worth paying to clear the air. She found herself thinking, 'If that would do it – if after that we could get back to where we were – if he'd settle for that…' And her blood ran cold at what she was reduced to.

Finally Deacon pushed the hair off his brow with a thick hand. 'I can't think about this any more. I'll call you tomorrow.'

'Promise?'

That was a mistake. She saw the anger he'd managed to suppress, the huge justifiable rage he hadn't dared give rein to, kindle in his eye. His voice was harsh. 'You don't have the right to ask for promises.'

'No,' she agreed, subdued. 'But I'm going to ask for another one.'

'Well?'

She thought he knew what it was. 'Don't go anywhere near Eric Chandos.'

He almost managed to laugh at her effrontery. 'I thought you didn't care about him! Now you're worried I might ruin his pretty face?'

'You're entitled to be angry,' she shot back, spurred by his tone, 'but not stupid. I don't give a damn what happens to him. I care what happens to you. Pick a fight with him and he'll get a bloody nose but you'll blow your career. He's not worth it. *I'm* not worth it.'

He almost said that she was. He almost said that even when she let him down, even when she hurt him, she was the best thing in his life. He came palpably close to saying, 'We'll get through this, because what happened yesterday matters but not as much as everything that went before.' He almost got it right.

Words and tears would have saved them. But Deacon had no fluency with either. On the brink of redemption he balked. Afraid of demeaning himself, of delivering himself into another person's hands – because if he took this from her there was nothing he couldn't take, couldn't be expected to tolerate – he stepped back both literally and figuratively and reached for the door behind him. 'I'll call you.'

'Jack…' Her voice was a plea.

'I won't go looking for him. But he's involved, if only marginally, in a murder inquiry and I won't avoid him if it means not doing my job.'

Perhaps it was as much as Brodie could have expected. If she'd felt any confidence in either man's desire to avoid a confrontation she might have let Deacon go with a grain of hope in her heart that tomorrow they'd do a better job of talking about it. But she hadn't. Her heart was telling her that tomorrow was indeed another day, and it had the potential to be worse than today.

Deacon returned to Battle Alley with a fox gnawing at his vitals.

'What's your gut feeling?' asked Voss. 'We know it isn't Michelle Rollins. Is it Sasha Wade?'

Deacon's instinct said that it was. In his experience names didn't come from nowhere: once someone's name comes up in connection with an inquiry – as a suspect, a witness or a victim – the odds are they'll turn out to be involved. With Michelle out of the frame he put the probability at around eighty percent. The chances that he was wasting his time concentrating on Sasha were only one in five.

He could have said that. He didn't have to bite his sergeant's head off for asking an entirely reasonable question. But sarcasm was his default position. 'Gut feeling? I'm a detective superintendent, sergeant, not a god-damned clairvoyant. I'm waiting for some evidence of her identity. With all the experts on the payroll it shouldn't come down to guesswork!'

People who knew him less well than Voss thought Deacon was always difficult, bad-mouthed and hard to please. Voss knew he was all those things, but not all the time. He also knew why his fuse was burning so short at the moment.

'Maybe we have to proceed on an assumption for now. If we can find someone with a reason for killing Sasha Wade, he can tell us whether he buried her at The Diligence.'

'Of course he can,' agreed Deacon nastily. 'He got away with it for eight years, he must have thought he was in the clear, the way we're carrying on he probably still thinks that – but if we put it to him straight I'm sure he'll take pity on us and confess. Maybe we don't even have to find him. We could put an ad in the personal column of *The Dimmock Sentinel* and see if he replies.'

'Murders got solved before there was forensic science,' said Voss evenly. 'We work with what we have. You told me that.'

'You talk like you remember when detective work was what solved crimes,' mocked Deacon. 'No one under thirty has a notion what "we work with what we have" *means*!'

Even Voss, who was famously even-tempered, was starting to pique at his superintendent's rancour. He knew he didn't deserve it; he knew Deacon didn't think he did; he knew sniping at him was displacement activity for taking a meat-cleaver to Eric Chandos. He could take a bit of abuse in a good cause, but he needed Deacon thinking more like a detective and less like a cuckold. He allowed the least edge to sharpen his tone. 'Then perhaps this would be a really good chance to show us, sir.'

People didn't often talk back to Deacon: even this mild rebuke was enough to make him blink. He took a deep breath, ready to give Voss both barrels. Then he remembered that the detective sergeant was not only not his enemy, he was actually his friend. He sighed. 'I'm sorry, Charlie. I'm in a foul mood. It's not your fault. Problems at home.'

'I know.'

It wasn't a conscious decision in the sense that Voss weighed up the pros and cons before speaking. But nor did it slip from him in an unguarded moment – stunned at receiving an apology, perhaps. Either he had to pretend ignorance or admit to knowledge, and he respected Deacon too much to lie to him even if it would have been easier.

Deacon stared at him, heavy brows gathering. 'Yes, you do, don't you? How?'

'I was there when Chandos blew his mouth off. Just for the record, it wasn't Daniel's fault. He didn't bring it up, and he didn't give Chandos a reason to bring it up.'

Deacon knew what had happened at The Diligence. He knew he had officers buzzing round the place like wasps. Until that moment he hadn't put the two facts together. Now he did, and the sum of the parts crashed through his expression like an avalanche. 'God damn! And you weren't there alone, were you?'

Silently, Voss shook his head.

'Who else?'

But Voss wouldn't say. 'A couple of people.'

The ripples had stopped spreading. Deacon's expression hardened. Now as he looked at Voss his eyes were dark with resentment. 'Why didn't you tell me?'

'It was none of my business.'

'Didn't you think I'd want to know?'

'I thought there were better places to hear it.'

'You were waiting till the canteen gossip reached me? Thanks, Charlie, that's just how I want to hear I've been made a fool of! Christ, what it is to have friends!' He shook his head in disgust.

Voss hung onto his temper. 'Did you hear it in the canteen?'

'No, I heard it from Brodie.'

'Who was the right person to tell you. It wouldn't have made it easier for either of you if I'd told you before she could. I heard something that shouldn't have been said in front of me, and I didn't consider it any part of my job to pass it on. I thought I owed it to you *and* Mrs Farrell to say nothing. As far as canteen gossip goes, I don't think there's been any.'

He'd managed to knock the wind out of Deacon's sails. 'You told them to sit on it?'

'No,' said Voss, 'I didn't have to. Everyone reached the same conclusion – that gossip would only make things worse. As far as friends go, I think you have more of them in this nick than you care to admit.'

Deacon's experience of detective sergeants was that they were, on the whole, a necessary evil. The more responsibilities an officer had, the less feasible it was for him to see each of them through personally and the more necessary it was to delegate. The advantage of sergeants was that you could delegate the donkey-work without them coming over all pre-menstrual when you wanted the interesting bits for yourself. The disadvantage was that they were either on the way up, in which case they saw senior officers as competition, or had already fulfilled their ambitions and were marking time till they could draw their pension. Prior to Voss, Deacon had gone through detective sergeants the way beat coppers used to go through boot-soles.

Voss was something else: a DS who was certainly on his way up but in less of a hurry than some of his contemporaries, an intelligent man taking every opportunity to learn. In a profession more notable for the broadness than the sophistication of its approach, Voss was an unusually subtle detective and it took Deacon twelve months to realise there was more going on behind his amiable expression than the red hair and freckles suggested.

These days, if he was honest with himself, he recognised that Voss brought almost as much to their partnership as he did himself. This in no way blurred the distinctions between them, but it did remind Deacon of his good fortune in finally acquiring a DS he could work with.

It in no way prepared him to be lectured by a man young enough to be his son. He felt his jaw drop and a flush rise in his cheeks. What Voss had said was hardly insubordination; nonetheless Deacon felt himself diminished by it. He knotted his hands on the desk and his voice was thick. 'Get out.'

'Sir.' Voss left the room quietly, closing Deacon's door behind him.

Deacon sat alone in his office until his fury abated. At that point a more gracious man would have begun to feel embarrassed and looked for a way to apologise. Deacon looked for someone else to vent his anger on.

He'd told Brodie he wouldn't go out of his way to confront Chandos, and he had no reason to interview the man at this point. But there's more than one way to skin a cat. If Deacon's weak spot was Brodie, Chandos's was Jared Fry. Deacon picked up the phone.

Left alone, Brodie locked the office and went home. She collected Paddy from Marta and made tea while she listened to the child chatter about her day; with one ear because the other was listening for the phone. She hoped Deacon would call.

The phone remained silent but a little after eight, with Paddy tucked up in bed, the doorbell rang. Brodie whispered, 'Thank God,' hurried out into the hall and threw open the massive front door.

It wasn't Deacon. It was Chandos.

He wasn't expecting much of a welcome. For a moment, before her expectations adjusted, Brodie's face glowed with hope. A man as proud as Eric Chandos could not fail to notice how that changed when she recognised him. It said something that he went on standing there, his head bowed.

In the moment that she saw him, sandwiched between disappointment and bitter recrimination, she felt a twinge of shame. She had to remind herself it was he who betrayed her, not the other way round. In front of Deacon she had every reason to be ashamed. In front of Chandos she was entitled to be angry, and her gaze turned to knives as she drew herself up tall.

His voice was low. 'We need to talk.'

With her little girl in the back bedroom Brodie didn't want to start shouting. 'Do you know, Eric, I think you've said enough already.'

'You heard then…'

She stared at him in disbelief. 'Since you boasted of getting into my knickers in front of friends of mine, I'd have been surprised if I hadn't.'

'I didn't mean to…' He stopped as if she'd interrupted him. But she hadn't. She was quite interested to hear what it was he hadn't meant to do.

'Do please explain. What exactly was it you were trying to say that, due to a slip of the tongue, came out as "Brodie Farrell is a tart"?'

'Please.' His voice was supplicant. 'Can't we talk inside?'

'Oh Eric, that's so touching. You're concerned for my reputation.' But she stood back from the door and let him into the hall. No further. Not into her home and her child's.

'I let him goad me into…'

'*Daniel*?' Her voice soared. 'Daniel doesn't goad. Daniel's never goaded anyone in his entire life. And everyone else who was there,' she added, and although it wasn't exactly true she didn't expect him to deny it, 'reckons Daniel was leaving when you hurled my name at his back.'

He didn't attempt to say otherwise. And she needed no corroboration to know Daniel had told her the truth.

'I was angry by then. We argued. He was telling Jared he'd be bet-

ter off without me. I just… lost it. I didn't mean to involve you. I
didn't know what I was about to say until I'd said it. If there'd been
any way of taking it back…'

Brodie didn't believe him. She thought he'd found himself armed
with a weapon against which his enemy had no defence and used it
with purpose and relish. She thought it was as off-the-cuff as an
Oscar Wilde riposte and that he'd do it again, and as often again, as
would serve him. She thought her behaviour in succumbing to his
charm had been breathtakingly, culpably stupid.

She said briskly, 'Well, there isn't. I gave you something precious
to hold and you smashed it. It was my fault – I shouldn't have
handed it to anyone else and I sure as hell shouldn't have trusted you
with it. I'll deal with the consequences: just don't expect me to care
that you feel bad about it. You *should* feel bad.'

Chandos said, 'I suppose Deacon heard… ?'

'Of course Deacon heard,' retorted Brodie. 'I told him. Daniel
told me and I told Jack. And he hasn't spoken to me since, and I
don't blame him. Look, Eric – why exactly are you here? To apologise? Fine, you've done it. If you want me to forgive you, you're
wasting your time. And I don't think we've anything else to talk
about.'

But he made no move to go. He darted furtive glances at her but
dropped his gaze before she could meet it. There was something on
his mind but Brodie was damned if she knew what.

Finally Chandos said what he'd come to say. 'What happened…
I'm not sure where it came from but it wasn't just sex. It meant
something, at least to me.'

'I know exactly what it meant to you! A trophy. And the thing
about trophies is, they're for public display. For putting on the man-
tle-piece.'

He was shaking his head stubbornly. 'I know that's how it must
look. I don't blame you for being angry. But I wasn't using you.
Something happened between us that neither of us had the power to
control.

'I'm not used to feeling out of control, Brodie. I don't like it and
I don't know how to handle it. What I said to Hood was partly
because I was feeling overwhelmed. The point is, whatever it was we
both felt it. We both responded to it. I'm not sorry it happened.
Maybe you want to make up with Deacon but I don't want you to. I
don't want him to forgive you.'

Now their eyes met, and Brodie felt the pit dropping out of her stomach as if she'd boarded an express elevator. His gaze devoured her. She had no way of knowing if it was the truth or just what he wanted her to believe, but the words were enough to make the blood thump in her temples and her juices run. Being this close to him was like venturing too near a precipice: one more step and she was going to fall...

'Forget Deacon,' he urged, 'forget Hood. You don't need them. I don't think you need anybody, but I need you. What we felt: we didn't imagine that. We shouldn't run away from it because it scares us. We have to follow it through.'

Waves thundered and creamed at the foot of the precipice. Gravity sang its siren song. If she fell, the rocks at the bottom would smash her. But for a few seconds first she'd be flying.

'Tell Deacon you're sorry. You can tell him I'm sorry if you like, but tell him you're with me now.'

Somehow, in the middle of a murder inquiry, DS Voss found himself with nothing to do except stay out of Deacon's way. For half an hour the next morning he sat in his office with his fingers laced behind his head, going through what they knew.

He was aware as he did it that Deacon was probably doing the same thing next door and they should be doing it together because – like painting a wall – two people thinking at different angles get better coverage. For the moment, though, Deacon's mind was elsewhere. Voss hoped the anger between them would pass in time, but nothing he knew of Deacon suggested he would be quick to drop the grudge.

They knew that Sasha Wade was last seen on Saturday morning, June 14th 1997. That she left home with her guitar, a few clothes and a little money. They knew that the girl who went into the ground at The Diligence, probably around that time, was a physical match for Sasha.

They knew that two nights later Eddie Rollins got home around one to see a dark van – that he was never able to identify, that was gone the next morning – at the bottom of the garden. They knew the dead girl had suffered a head injury, and though it was unclear if it killed her there were no other signs of trauma. They knew that she was raised on the swathe of chalkland that ran along much of the south coast.

They knew that Sasha wrote songs and craved fame. She ran away once before in pursuit of celebrity. They knew that Jared Fry and Souls For Satan stayed at The Diligence eleven months before she disappeared, and that Fry bought the house eight and a half years later without mentioning this.

Now matters became speculative. Voss didn't mind speculating but it was a tricky thing to do alone. With no one to point out the flaws in your case it was easy to become attached to a theory and find yourself defending it in the face of the evidence. He looked towards the door. But it was too soon for Deacon's fury to have abated. He'd try again tomorrow.

There was the band. He wanted to talk to the other members of Souls For Satan who stayed at The Diligence. He was waiting for a call from the original drummer, who'd left the band six years ago and now had his own label in San Diego. Bass guitarist Zack Quaid was still with Souls, except that he was currently on a month's retreat in Tibet and his PA wasn't sure when she could get a message to him. Only keyboard player Johnny Turpin was currently close enough to meet. He lived in Hove, but Voss had been told he never got up before midday. Not for policemen; not for fires.

Deacon wouldn't have taken that for an answer. Voss headed out to his car.

Anyone who thought Jared Fry looked like the wreck of a human being should have seen Johnny Turpin hauled from his bed at half-past nine on a Friday morning. His face looked like a cake left so long in the sun that the icing had run off the edges. His eyes were like piss-holes in snow. The t-shirt and joggers that served him as pyjamas were less flattering than the leathers he wore in perform-ance and it was already clear he was in for a battle with middle-age spread. Only his hands appeared well-cared-for. He was thirty-one years old.

A mug of strong coffee later Turpin was beginning to make sense. Or Voss was beginning to understand him: he spoke with a Birmingham accent thicker than the coffee. He came over as a down-to-earth individual with no reservations about talking to the law. Of course, his vice was a legal one.

'Beer,' he said, rubbing his stomach gingerly. 'Bit of a booze-up last night.'

'Showbiz bash?' asked Voss brightly.

'Me brother's darts team.'

He remembered that tour of the south of England. He even remembered the hotel where they stayed. 'A bit of a dump. All bits of wood holding it up.'

'Half-timbering,' nodded Voss, deadpan.

'The old biddy who ran it seemed to think we should be in bed by midnight. We tried to tell her, we were still on stage at midnight.'

'You were there for six nights. Eight rooms. Who would that have been?'

Turpin needed his fingers to work it out. 'Four band members, sound engineer, electrician and two roadies. Yeah, eight of us.'

'Wasn't Eric Chandos with you?'

Turpin shook his head. His hair fell in rat-tails to his shoulders. 'Nah. He'd be a couple of hundred miles away, setting things up for the following week.'

Everyone agreed on that point. 'What about groupies? Any of

them stay with you at The Diligence?'

Turpin considered. 'There was my wife Sharon.'

Voss grinned. 'I think we can safely discount Mrs Turpin. You married young then?'

'Twenty-one. She travelled with us for a couple of years, till she started with the kids.'

'How many have you got?'

'Five,' said Johnny Turpin proudly.

'I imagine the other guys had girlfriends.'

''Course they did. And sure, they brought them back to the digs. All the time.'

'Can you remember who was at The Diligence with you?'

Turpin shook his head again. 'I can't remember any of their names. I'm not sure I ever *knew* their names.'

'Would you recognise a photo?' He produced a copy of the one Mrs Wade had supplied.

The keyboard player took another long swig of coffee, studying the picture. He didn't return it until he was sure. 'I don't think I ever saw her.'

Voss moved on. 'I know the band is the same except for the drummer, but what about the road crew? Who was travelling with you about then? Any idea where I'd find them?'

'Well, you'll find one of them in Jared's garage. Tommy Bell.'

'Fry's driver?'

'Driver, roadie – it's the same job, he just thinks it sounds smarter. When we're touring he drives the wagon, when we're not he drives Jared around.'

'Wagon?'

Turpin waxed enthusiastic. 'Yeah, it's great. It's like a damn great bus. It's got bedrooms and a sitting room and a kitchen: it's not like travelling at all. You can sleep all day and wake up at the next gig. We used to shift everything in a couple of vans. This is better.'

'So Mr Fry has a driver. Can't he drive himself?'

Turpin regarded him frankly. 'There's this law about not doing it while you're under the influence of drink or drugs.'

Voss nodded. 'So there is. OK. So, do roadies get groupies too?'

Johnny Turpin laughed until he spilled the last of his coffee. It blistered the varnish on the floor. 'You haven't met Tommy, have you? Decent guy, what he doesn't know about distributors and things you don't need to know, and you come to want an all-night dry-cleaners – and believe me, there are times you desperately want an all-night dry-cleaners – you couldn't be in better hands. But the answer to a groupie's prayer? Let's put it this way. When we were first on the road we couldn't afford hotels so we slept in the back of the van. I used to sleep in one of Tommy's sweatshirts.'

Voss wasn't sure what Turpin was telling him. 'Instead of pyjamas?'

'Instead of a sleeping-bag.'

Voss didn't know how much use this information was going to be, but then you never did. You just kept piling it up until something slid into place. 'Tell me about Jared Fry. What kind of a man is he?'

'He's a bloody good songwriter.'

'Yes. And a friend?'

Turpin had to think about that. 'He's never done me a bad turn. The success I've had, I got it on his coat-tails. But a friend? I'm not sure. We work well together.'

'Who would he call friends?'

Turpin grimaced. 'I don't think he has any. But then. I don't think he ever wanted them. What some people get from friendships, Jared gets from Eric.'

'Have they always lived together?'

There was a bleary twinkle in Turpin's eye. 'You mean, are they extra special friends? No. But Eric knows which side his bread's buttered on. Any of the rest of us walk – like Kevin Michaels, the original drummer – we'd be replaced in a week. But if Jared stopped singing, or stopped writing, we'd all be queueing down the Job Centre and so would Eric. No one in the world has more regard for his own best interests than Eric Chandos. When the time comes that the only way to get Jared on stage is to carry him, he'll do that too.'

Heading back to Dimmock Voss thought of another call he should make. Not in a professional capacity but because DS Voss was a decent human being who didn't like to see people hurting.

'Hi, Daniel. I was passing, I just wondered how you were.'

For the second night running Daniel had barely slept. It showed in the dark smudges under his eyes, the hollowness of his cheeks, the way every movement seemed an effort. But he ushered Voss inside as if he was glad to see him. 'I'm OK, Charlie, thank you. Maybe a bit shell-shocked.'

'I bet,' said Voss feelingly. 'How's Brodie?'

Daniel gave an unhappy shrug. 'I haven't seen her today. She hasn't called. I don't think she's talking to me.'

'What happened wasn't your fault. You couldn't have guessed Chandos would do something like that.'

Daniel shrugged. 'Jared's worth a lot of money to him. I should have realised I was pushing him into a corner. I knew about him and Brodie: I should have guessed it would come out if he got angry enough.'

'My dad's an undertaker,' said Voss, apparently changing the subject. 'It's a traditional trade and he's a very conventional man. He's fifty-six but really he's the last Victorian. When I left home he sat me down in the front room and gave me three pieces of advice. I still think they're pretty good. He said, Always pay your bills on time. Never drink so much you don't know what you're doing. And be aware that you can hurt a woman without laying a finger on her.

'What happened between them put a duty on Chandos to take care of Mrs Farrell. To put her needs above his own. And not to throw her name into the middle of an argument as if it was a grenade. He behaved like a cad. Nothing anyone did or said, or could have done or said, alters the fact.'

Daniel was grateful for that. He'd rerun the encounter endlessly in his mind, as if finding another way to play it would let him rewrite the ending, but he never found the point at which he should have seen and could have avoided what was coming. Still he carried the burden of Brodie's unhappiness, if only because it mattered more to him than to the man who caused it. He sighed. 'Jared's right: we crucify women whenever we love them.'

At the same moment they heard the tattoo of footsteps on the iron stairs. Daniel was on his way to the door before Brodie had the chance to knock.

Voss was about to excuse himself but she waved him back as if it was her flat. 'Stay where you are, Charlie, I want your opinion on this too.'

'What's happened?' asked Daniel softly.

'I'm not sure. It might be just my nasty suspicious mind at work again.' She paused long enough for someone to demur; when no one did she rolled her eyes and continued. 'Eric came to my house last night. No,' she added, knowing what both men would be wondering, 'nothing happened – we just talked. Mostly, he talked. He says he's in love with me.'

Neither man knew how to respond. Neither was quite sure she

wanted a response.

After a moment Brodie gave a gruff chuckle. 'I was hoping to surprise you – I wasn't expecting you to be dumbstruck! Does it seem entirely beyond the bounds of possibility, then?'

Charlie Voss was shaking his ginger head and saying, 'No, no,' very quickly. But Daniel, who knew her better, knew she was teasing them.

'Did you believe him?'

'Well – no,' she admitted. 'A bit of me wanted to, but actually I haven't fallen for a line that thin since I was about sixteen. People don't *say* when they love you, they show it.'

Daniel bit his lip. 'Then what… ?'

'That's what I asked myself. I went to bed wondering, and I still didn't know when I got up this morning. So I thought I'd come round here and ask you. What does Eric Chandos stand to gain by pretending to be in love with me?'

One answer was so obvious Voss was reluctant to voice it. 'He may have thought he stood to gain you.'

She gave him a smile like patting his head. 'Nice try, Charlie Voss. Sucking up to the boss's girlfriend is never a bad move. Unless it turns out she's his ex-girlfriend,' she added in wry parentheses. 'But no. He's an intelligent man: he must know I'm not going to forget what he did even if he lays on the sex appeal with a trowel. So if it isn't me he wants, what is it?'

'Perhaps he wanted to apologise,' said Daniel.

Brodie laughed aloud. 'He did that too, but I don't think he risked a thick ear to give me an apology. I hope not, because it wasn't a very good one.'

'So not love and not guilt. What's left?'

Brodie regarded him sternly. 'Don't come the cynic with me, Daniel Hood, you're no better at it than Eric is at apologies. Get your brain in gear and tell me what he was up to.'

Daniel accepted the rebuke graciously. Behind the thick glasses his pale eyes slid out of focus, went distant with thought. 'You think he has an ulterior motive.'

'I'm sure of it. What he's done, what he's said, makes no sense otherwise.' She made herself look at him. 'I never thought it was love. I thought it was desire. But if you want something so much you have to have it regardless of the cost, you take better care of it. You don't throw it away. Not that quickly, anyway.'

'You think he's using you?'

'I think he's trying to. But I don't know what for.'

Daniel had the glimmerings of an idea. He struggled to put it together. He was hindered in this by his own hopes, because if he was right the episode at The Diligence was nothing to do with him: if he'd never gone there it might have happened differently but it would still have happened. But if it wasn't desire motivating Eric Chandos, it was something altogether nastier. 'What if he's using you to get at Jack?'

'What?' said Voss, startled. 'How? *Why?*'

Brodie said nothing. But her attention was absolute, her gaze like claws in his face.

Daniel didn't want to spell it out. However carefully he chose the words they would hurt and humiliate her. He bit his lip until he tasted blood.

Brodie may have behaved like one but she wasn't a fool. She knew that two and two never make five. There was a missing factor in all of this, and she thought Daniel had found it, and his very reluctance to explain suggested what it might be. Her voice was hard, metallic. 'Spit it out, Daniel. What do you think Eric's up to?'

'I don't know. It just occurred to me that maybe what he really wants is to take Jack's mind off his job.'

Voss's eyes widened with shock. 'But that would mean...' He fell silent then, but not in time.

'*Yes*,' Brodie said crisply, following the trail of barbed wire. 'That everything between us was a lie. The only reason he was interested in me was that I was involved with Dimmock's senior detective. Jack Deacon's soft spot, the best place to attack him.'

Wanting to spare her pain Daniel tried to back-pedal. 'We don't know that. This is pure speculation...'

'Yes,' she agreed wearily, weighed down by understanding, 'but it makes more sense than the alternative. I know he was lying when he said he loved me: I think he was lying before that. I was bowled off my feet, stupid with what I felt for him, but Eric never was. I think he knew what he was doing all along. He was making it impossible for Jack to treat him like any other suspect.'

'Suspect?' echoed Voss, startled. 'What are we supposed to suspect him of? There's no connection between him and the girl in the garden. Is there something else he's hiding?'

'I don't know what he's hiding,' said Brodie, 'but I'll wager cash money he's hiding something. Something that would damage him if it came out. Something that, if it started to come out, would be investigated by Dimmock CID.'

'A crime,' said Voss.

'It has to be.' Now she was thinking faster even than Daniel. 'Jack has, you'll agree, a certain reputation. Eric wasn't sure he could take him if they went head to head. But he could put Jack off his game. He needed a distraction, something to stop Jack thinking like a policeman.'

'If it really was a ploy, if Chandos made a play for you specifically to upset Jack,' Daniel said quietly, 'Jack had to know about it.'

Her jaw clenched hard, Brodie nodded. 'He had to make Jack aware of what he'd been up to – what we'd been up to – without actually telling him. You gave him the opportunity, but if you hadn't he'd have made his own. He needed Jack to know I'd been unfaithful. He wanted Jack thinking about that. Seeing him as a rival, not a suspect.'

Voss knew things about police procedure that neither of the others did. 'If Division get to hear about this they'll take Mr Deacon off the case – the murder and anything else Chandos might be involved in. They'll say there's a conflict of interests. If I had something to hide, I'd rather face almost anyone than Jack Deacon.'

Brodie was not blind to what that meant: that her behaviour had left a man she cared about barely able to function professionally. That she'd crippled him. But there'd be time to agonise over it later: now she was seeking a way to make amends.

Voss was a detective: he needed to relate the theory to the facts. 'But what are we actually suggesting here? That even though we've been unable to connect them, Eric Chandos did in fact murder Sasha Wade?'

Brodie shook her head. 'How could he have done? I don't think it's anything to do with your case, Charlie. I think he was just unlucky: turning up a body in his back garden meant everybody's actions were going to be under the microscope, and something he thought he'd got away with was in danger of coming to light.'

'What?'

She shrugged. 'Who knows? Except that it mattered to him to keep it quiet. Mattered enough to go to a lot of trouble and a fair bit of risk to distract attention from it.' Her lips were tight.

Daniel was reviewing what they knew. 'Drugs, maybe? We know

Jared's an addict. Maybe Chandos is his supplier.'

But Voss wasn't convinced. 'Jared Fry is worth a lot of money to Eric Chandos. When he finally dissolves his brain with that stuff he'll be worth nothing. Chandos made it pretty clear yesterday that he'll do just about anything to protect that investment. I can't see him actively encouraging Fry to do drugs.'

'So maybe it's fraud,' suggested Daniel. 'He's taking more out of the pot than he's entitled to. Jared would never have noticed, but now other people are involved, and some of them are policemen, he's afraid it'll come to light.'

'Tell you what,' said Brodie, growing tired of the discussion, 'why don't you ask him? Haul him in and ask him.'

'We will have to interview him,' agreed Voss, 'but I'm damned if I know how. If I tell the governor about this he'll do it himself. But if Daniel's right, that's what Chandos wants – a stand-up fight on tape in the interview room. Once their hostility and the reason for it are public knowledge – ie, the topic of meetings at Division – no one, not even his staunchest supporters, will go on backing Mr Deacon's judgement on the subject of Eric Chandos. They'll think he can't possibly maintain a professional detachment, that whatever suspicions he has about Chandos come from...'

He glanced quickly at Brodie. When she refused to look away, he did. 'On the other hand, if I question Chandos without checking with the governor first – well, if he didn't hate me before he would then.'

'You mustn't stick your neck out any further.' Brodie was aware how difficult Voss's position was becoming. 'I'll talk to Eric. Jack'll be angry with me too but he can't sack me.'

Voss's eyes saucered. Daniel shut his altogether.

Brodie was determined. Humiliation made her reckless 'If you can't question him and Jack mustn't, I will. Eric thinks he can use me as a stalking-horse, does he? We'll see about that. I allowed this situation to develop, it's for me to resolve it. If I don't Jack will, and we all know what that means. I won't let that happen.'

'You can't confront an unpredictable man with his back to the wall either!' exclaimed Voss.

'I'm not going to make a citizen's arrest,' said Brodie scornfully. 'But I can do what neither you nor Jack can: talk to him off the record, without him even knowing he's being questioned. If I can get some idea what he's covering up you'll know what to do about it. If it's murder you'll go after him whatever the consequences. If it's drugs, could Drugs Squad take over and keep him and Jack apart? But if he's been fiddling his VAT you can safely back off till everyone calms down.'

Daniel took a deep breath. If he'd learned nothing else in the last year, he knew not to tell Brodie Farrell what she could and couldn't do. But he wanted her to think about this. 'Whatever he's covering up, clearly it matters to him. He could be facing prison. Or maybe he stands to lose everything he's worked for. If he realises you're onto him he'll be scared and angry. He may become violent.'

Her lip curled. 'I can handle Eric Chandos. Daniel, he's used me in the most cynical way imaginable. And he's going to pay for that.'

'How did you part?' asked Voss. 'Did you send him home with a flea in his ear? Or…' He couldn't find a safe way to finish the sentence.

'Or,' she agreed. 'I suddenly realised there was another agenda. I didn't call him on it: I wanted to think about it first. I accepted his apology, said I'd consider his proposition and saw him out.'

'Whether he's trying to keep Mr Deacon on the back foot,' said Voss carefully, 'or he really does want to take you away from all this, he should be happy to see you again. As long as you don't call him a liar you shouldn't be in any danger.'

Daniel remained uneasy. 'If you start quizzing him he'll get suspicious. We can't guess what he'll do because we don't know how much trouble he'll be in if it all comes out.'

But Brodie wouldn't be deterred. 'I won't quiz him, I'll just… steer the conversation. I'll say that before I can make a decision on the future I need to know more about him, and listen out for things he should be saying and isn't. Charlie, you're the detective. If you were also a stunningly attractive woman whose mere presence was enough to make men indiscreet, what would you ask?'

Voss considered. 'He was pretty upset when Daniel came between him and Fry. What if it's not him that's in trouble but Fry? What if all this is to protect Fry, because Chandos stands to lose a packet if he can't keep Fry out of prison?'

'For the drugs?'

'Maybe. I mean, yes, he breaks the law every day and he could go down for it. But it's not exactly a secret, is it? I'd have thought anyone who was interested in prosecuting Jared Fry for possession of Class A drugs would have done it long ago.'

Daniel shook his head stubbornly. 'Jared hasn't the time or emotional capacity for another hobby. He performs, he tries to write songs and he takes drugs. That's about all he has the energy for. I don't think he's hiding any terrible secrets.'

'But you never think the worst of people,' said Brodie. 'He helped you and you're grateful. But I could believe there's something in his past that needs covering up. He's a haunted man. The question is, what's he haunted by?'

'Maybe that's what you should ask Chandos.' Voss heard himself and his eyes shot wide. 'No! I didn't say that. This whole thing is a terrible idea and I want nothing to do with it. In fact, I'm not even here.' He got up to go. 'And I never was.'

Though Daniel was no happier with Brodie's plan, he knew from the glint in her eye that her mind was made up. 'Don't let him…'

'What?'

His voice was low. 'You said yourself, there's something about this man that makes you behave like an idiot. Don't let him convince you that we've misjudged him, he's just a fool for love too. Don't end up in bed with him because this time he wanted to take *your* mind off the job.'

She almost struck him. Just in time she recognised it as fair comment. She nodded tersely. 'I'll be careful.'

'When are you going up there?' Voss really wanted to be somewhere else, was kept here only by a kind of horrid fascination.

Her smile was as bright and brittle as crystal. She felt she'd been stupid and she felt she'd been used, and now she felt like fighting back. 'There's no time like the present.'

She was on the way to The Diligence, Chandos was on his way to her office. They met on the Guildford road, in a flurry of brake-lights and u-turns.

'Brodie!' Even knowing what she did, the smile was as handsome, as winning, as ever. His hands fastened on her shoulders and he stared into her face as if seeking answers there. 'You were looking for me?'

It was not only the truth, it was what he wanted to hear. 'Yes, I was. Eric, you – well, to be honest you rather floored me last night. We need to talk – properly, not in the hall, not in my office between appointments, just us with the time to say what we want from one another. I have time now.'

There was no way he could turn her down and maintain the illusion of desire. His eyes were warm and his hands tightened on her arms in a way that, if she hadn't come here knowing his duplicity, would have turned her knees to jelly. 'What do you want to do? We could drive. Or go somewhere...'

She didn't want to be driving round the open countryside with him, just in case he recognised her for a spy. 'I could use a coffee. There's a tea-shop I know...'

He was half puzzled, half charmed. 'You want to discuss our future in a tea-shop?'

Brodie shrugged ruefully. 'It's all old ladies with hearing-aids, nobody will overhear us.'

He shook his head and laughed. 'Coffee it is.'

In the event, though, they didn't get that far. Passing Poole Lane the car behind her suddenly began flashing its lights, and when she pulled over Chandos's face was dark with anger. 'I'm sorry, Brodie, but we're going to have to do this later. Jared's in trouble.'

'Again?'

'I just had Miriam on the phone. The police are at The Diligence. They've arrested him for murder.'

'You understand,' Deacon intoned woodenly, 'you are not under arrest. You are free to leave at any time. You are merely helping me with my inquiries. Of course, if you should refuse to help in a murder inquiry I'd have to wonder why, and it's not impossible that I could find something to arrest you for. Doing something – possessing something – who knows? But right now you're here of your own free will, meeting your obligations as a good citizen. Yes?'

Jared Fry stared back at him defiantly. But his hands were unsteady, and clasping them together on the table-top only drew attention to the fact. 'Get on with it, Deacon.' His voice was rough.

'*Mr* Deacon,' Deacon corrected him gravely. 'Or Detective Superintendent Deacon. Do let's try to stay civil, shall we, Mr Fry?'

There's nothing cosy about a police interview room. There isn't meant to be. This one was four walls, a table and four hard chairs, a tape-recorder. It was like a stage set with a minimum of props so as not to distract from the performance.

If there was one thing Jared Fry knew about it was dominating a stage. But this mean space with its linoleum floor and small high window managed to shrink him, not only in status but somehow even physically. He sat hunched at the table like a recalcitrant schoolboy, stubborn and resentful, a gaunt shadow of the man who could fill stadia. Deacon almost felt sorry for him. It wasn't as if he was here because of something he'd done. He was here because of something someone else had done, and even that wasn't a crime.

'Last time you were asked you said you'd never met Sasha Wade,' said Deacon. 'I want you to give that a bit more thought. Look at the photograph I'm showing you and tell me if this girl was a friend, or an acquaintance, or part of your circle about eight years ago.'

'I told you,' said Fry, neither looking up nor at the photograph, 'I never saw her before.'

'She was a musician,' said Deacon. 'She sang and played the guitar. Did you know that?'

'I don't know anything about her.'

Deacon ignored him. 'She also wrote songs. This was at about the time your career was taking off.' He managed to say it with a borderline sneer that the tape might not pick up. 'It's not unlikely that you'd know other people who were doing the same things you were.'

'There were a lot of them,' said Fry shortly. 'Some of them I knew. The ones who got somewhere. Got gigs, got recording contracts. It isn't easy, you know. For every one who makes it big – hell, for every one who makes it *small* – there are hundreds of wannabes.'

'Wanna… ?' echoed Deacon with a puzzled frown. He knew exactly what it meant: he wanted to show Fry that he was only important in his own world, and his world wasn't as important as he thought.

'Wannabes,' gritted Fry. 'I wannabe a rockstar.'

'Well, it's what you wanted,' said Deacon reasonably. 'You made it.' If he'd added, 'So it can't be that hard,' he could not have made his opinion clearer.

The speed with which Jared Fry lunged across the table startled him into jerking back. Fry didn't touch him. But he thrust his gaunt face into Deacon's and spoke very distinctly. 'I make a lot of money. I make more money than you. I make more money than anyone you know. It's because I'm very, very good at what I do.'

With difficulty Deacon resisted the urge to shove him back in his seat and after a moment Fry subsided. 'Of course you are, Mr Fry,' Deacon said blandly. 'And what you do is so vital to human civilisation that if you stopped tomorrow the pillars of society would crumble as captains of state and industry proved unable to feed or dress themselves.

'I grant you,' he went on, 'it's funny about the money. Looking at the money you'd think that scoring a goal in a football match was more important than solving a murder. More important than preventing one. Maybe if you asked a capacity crowd at Wembley they'd say it was. But if you asked them one by one if it was more important than preventing *their* murder, or that of their wife or child, you'd get a different answer.'

His head came up sharply and he pinned the demon rocker in his place with the spear of his gaze. 'So don't let's confuse income with importance, Mr Fry. Don't let's confuse the value of what you do with real value. And let's bear in mind that if you end up dead in a ditch tonight it'll be me trying to find out why. And I'll put as much time and effort into it as I am into finding out who killed the girl in your garden. Every bit as much, and not an ounce more.'

Fry rocked his chair back and slouched, staring at the ceiling this time. 'So what do you want to know?' He was trying to look as if being here was cool. But it's hard to feel cool when your body's telling you that pretty soon it's going to need, as a matter of urgency, something you have no way of providing.

'Everything you know,' said Deacon. 'Everything that might help me identify that girl, work out what she's doing in your garden and find her killer.'

'That's all? That's easy.' A bleak smile twisted Fry's lip. 'Nothing. Can I go now?'

Deacon breathed heavily. 'Mr Fry, when you agreed to help me with my inquiries, I hoped you'd be trying harder. Now, there are different ways of doing this. This is the nice way, where I assume we're on the same side. If that doesn't work, we can try the other way where I assume you have something to hide. If you haven't, I'd recommend sticking with the nice way.'

All the arrogance in Fry's gaze – and there was plenty: he'd practised in mirrors – was not enough to disguise the fear that was there too. 'I want Eric in here.'

Deacon sighed. 'Mr Fry, you're too old to need a responsible adult present. You can have a solicitor if you want one.'

'I want one.'

'Which would be an excellent idea if you were expecting to be charged with some offence,' Deacon continued seamlessly. 'Now, I'm not there yet. I thought I was talking to a witness. But if you're telling me that's where we're going to end up, maybe it would save time if you called your solicitor and I prepared some charges. Is that where we're heading?'

He was, as well he knew, straining the boundaries of the Police and Criminal Evidence Act. It wasn't the first time, wouldn't be the last. Usually he got away with it because most people who find themselves in police stations don't know their rights. Those who do are usually guilty of something; those who are guilty of nothing are usually so relieved to get out they won't go back to make a complaint.

Seeing Fry waver he played his trump card. 'Doing it all formally takes longer, of course, but I don't suppose there's anywhere you have to be in the next several hours. Anything you have to do?'

And of course there was, and Deacon knew it when he sent for Fry. The singer wasn't afraid of missing his favourite television programme. He wasn't afraid of Deacon's questions – at least, nothing he'd been asked so far bothered him half as much as the prospect of being here all day. Probably he needed to shoot up every twelve hours or so. The fear of not being able to when the time came would accelerate the withdrawal process.

A good man in many ways, Deacon had a regrettable thread of cruelty running through him. He wasn't vicious but he could be distinctly unkind when he thought people deserved it. And he wasn't always the best judge of who deserved what.

He wasn't leaning on Fry because he believed he had important information. He was doing it because it was in his power to hurt Fry, and through him the real object of his enmity. Fry was vulnerable in a way that Chandos was not. But Chandos would know the trouble Fry was in, stuck in a police station for hours at a time. He'd know who was doing it and why. That was what Deacon wanted. Revenge is a primitive emotion. But as with wine, jokes and vices, the old ones are the best.

Fry turned away with a sneer. But he reached for the photograph of Sasha Wade and looked at it properly for the first time. 'I still can't help you.'

'She doesn't look familiar?'

The demon rocker shrugged. 'She looks like all of them look. I can't guarantee that this one didn't come to a gig or a club or a party, and I may have bought her a drink or danced with her. I may have sat beside her half the night. But I wasn't aware of her. I never knew her name, I never dated her, I never slept with her, and I sure as hell never murdered her.' He looked Deacon in the eye. 'And if I had, and if it seemed like a good idea to bury her in the grounds of an hotel where I once stayed, I wouldn't then have bought the bloody place and paid someone to dig her up!'

Deacon nodded slowly. It was a valid point. 'You wanted a swimming pool.'

'Yes.'

'Why wasn't it on your list of requirements when you sent Mrs Farrell house-hunting? It was a long list: why leave off something as big as a swimming pool if you were determined to have one?'

Fry looked away. 'Eric knew what I needed. I expected him to find something suitable.'

Deacon regarded him impassively. 'So you didn't bother to look at The Diligence before you bought it, and when it turned out not to have a pool you decided to have one installed. Who chose the site?'

Fry shook his head negligently. 'I don't remember.'

'You wanted it so much you were prepared for extra expense and upheaval, and so urgently you started work almost as soon as you moved in, but you don't remember who chose the location? It seems likely it would be you.'

'Maybe it was.'

'Who else could it have been?'

'Eric? The builder?'

'Builders don't tell their clients where to put their swimming pools. And Mr Chandos didn't want a pool enough to ask Mrs

Farrell for one. I think it must have been you, Mr Fry.'

'All right, so it was me.' He couldn't see how it mattered.

'You wanted the pool beside the stable-block. But Mr Wilmslow found he couldn't dig there and started looking at other sites around the garden.'

A sixth sense warned Fry there was a trap here somewhere, but he couldn't see it. 'I didn't tell him where to dig.'

'No,' said Deacon seriously, 'I bet you didn't. If you had you've have said, "Dig anywhere you like but not at the bottom of the garden." Isn't that the truth, Mr Fry? That you were appalled when you saw where he'd dug his test-pit? That you knew what he was going to find before he did?'

Fry didn't flinch. He gave Deacon a tight little smile and shook his head. 'You have nothing on me. If you had you wouldn't be playing *Pin the Tail on the Donkey* like this. Yes, I could have killed that girl, and if I had maybe some of the things I've done in the last eight years would have been significant. But I didn't, and you're trying to make a pattern out of random decisions. Buying this house. Digging in the garden. Whoever had bought the house would have dug in the garden: would you be accusing him of murder? The only reason…'

He caught the thought in time to keep from voicing it but not quite quickly enough to prevent Deacon hearing it. The detective felt his skin prickle. 'Is what, Mr Fry?'

Even with the panic-demons of withdrawal beginning to shout in his head, Fry had too much sense to answer.

Deacon would have answered for him except that common sense finally caught up with him too. If he had – if he'd rapped out, as he almost did, 'The only reason you're here is that your manager seduced my girlfriend: is that what you mean?' – he'd have put two things on tape that would come back to haunt him: Brodie's infidelity and the fact that it was affecting how he did his job.

Shocked at how close he'd come to disaster, for long moments he said nothing more, sitting at the table fighting the fury that had almost betrayed him. He saw Fry's ashen face, the dew of sweat breaking on it and the unsteady rise and fall of his chest, and the shabbiness of his own behaviour tasted bitter in his mouth. He had no case against this man. Fry was only here because Deacon abhorred his choice of friends.

If he'd genuinely suspected him of murder Deacon would have been justified in continuing this until he got at the truth, and if that meant getting Fry medical attention that's what he'd have done. But he had no such excuse. There was no reason to suspect Fry. What seemed like an odd coincidence was probably nothing more than that. Which made his behaviour unconscionable. It wasn't reasonable to subject Fry to the pain of uncontrolled withdrawal, it wasn't clever, it wasn't even helpful. It was mean-spirited and Deacon was ashamed of himself.

He drew a deep breath and let it out as a sigh. 'Do you know, Mr Fry, I think we've achieved as much as we can for one day. I'll have a car take you home.'

There was time for him to see the flicker of hope in Fry's gaze as he looked up, to see the desperate tension of his spare body begin to soften in anticipation.

Then a knuckle beat a quick tattoo on the door and Detective Sergeant Voss was in the room, keen-eyed, looking between Deacon and Fry, looking at the tape. 'You've finished?'

'Yes,' said Deacon, surprised. Generally speaking a senior officer's interview is safe from interruption by excitable young detectives, especially those who, had they any sense, would still be steering clear of said senior officers. 'Mr Fry's helped us all he can for the moment. Will you organise a car for him?'

'No,' said Charlie Voss.

Deacon blinked. This was a triumph of mind over matter: he could hardly have been more astonished if Voss had produced a ghetto-blaster and commenced to strip to the strains of... well, Deacon didn't know what it was called but he'd seen *The Hull Mounty* and he'd recognise it if he heard it. And it wouldn't surprise him as much as DS Voss coming in here uninvited and refusing to do what he was told. One of Deacon's bushy eyebrows climbed. 'No?'

Voss knew he needed to explain. But first he needed to make sure Fry didn't leave while he was doing it. 'Did he tell you he knew Sasha Wade?'

'He told me he *didn't* know Sasha Wade.'

'It's a lie,' said Voss. 'He knew her. I can prove it. He's been singing her songs.'

Chapter Nineteen

Voss returned to Battle Alley deeply uneasy about what Brodie was doing yet aware he had no power to stop her. If he'd thought she was putting herself in danger he'd have gone to Deacon. But that was a high-risk strategy: he could end up with both of them after his blood.

Still, when he heard Chandos arrive at the police station in a flurry of raised voices and banged doors his immediate reaction was relief that he wouldn't be at The Diligence when Brodie got there. But his misgivings remained. He was no longer even sure it was Brodie he was worrying about. Something was rasping away at the edge of his consciousness, persistent as the Count of Monte Cristo armed with a nail-file, and he couldn't work out what it was.

Trying to ignore the itch in the back of his brain, to focus on questions which had answers even if he didn't know what they were yet, he found himself leafing through Sasha Wade's songbook. Afterwards he was never quite sure why. Sheer chance, his fingers that might have passed the time drumming on the scarred desk-top turning the pages of the exercise-book instead? Or something smarter, the bit of his brain that had spotted the anomaly despairing of getting him to listen and communicating directly with his fingers instead?

Either way, the moment Voss saw the handwritten pages he knew what it was that had been troubling him. He'd read the book before, of course, thoroughly enough to recognise that the missing girl was a serious and talented songwriter. If Daniel had quoted accurately, and hadn't attributed them to Jared Fry, he'd have recognised the lines right away.

Voss pored over the scratchy handwriting for another minute, wondering what it meant. Another coincidence – an innocent misunderstanding – something significant? After that he picked up the phone.

'What's the problem?' asked Daniel.

'Something you said. Something Fry said, about men crucifying women. Was it from a song, do you know?'

'Yes. *Crucifiction.* He calls it his signature-tune.'

'And it was definitely that way round – "We crucify women". Not "Men crucify us".'

'Yes.' Daniel frowned. 'It would be a rum song for Jared to sing if it was the other way round.'

'Yes,' agreed Voss. 'But not for Sasha Wade to write.'

The words were there in front of him, unedited, the way they sprang from her mind. *Men crucify us whenever they love us* – a song written by a woman, for a woman to sing. In the cheap exercise-book that Sasha Wade left at home when she disappeared. She might have written it any time up to June 14th 1997. She could not have written it since. 'I need to know when Fry first sang it.'

But Daniel couldn't help. 'Ask him. Or Chandos.'

'I don't want to ask either of them until I know the answer.'

'Ask Jason Wilmslow.'

For a moment Voss couldn't think who he meant. 'The builder's son? *Why?*'

'He lives and breathes this stuff. He may have every rock album ever sold. I talked to him a couple of times when his dad was working on my house, and rock music was his only topic of conversation. I imagine the reason he was labouring at The Diligence was in the hope of meeting Jared.'

'Where do I find him – where does he work?'

Daniel sighed. 'He's seventeen years old with a GCSE in art and a stereo system that interferes with broadcasts to shipping. Midday Friday? – he's probably just getting up.'

Norman Wilmslow had been a builder for thirty years. He was reliable, cost-effective and unimaginative, a combination which made him enduringly popular in Dimmock. Ten years ago he built himself a sturdy, unimaginative mock-Tudor house on River Drive ten minutes from the centre of town.

Jason was indeed at home. In his extensive collection was the first Souls For Satan album to feature *Crucifiction*. Voss checked the copyright imprint. The song was accredited to Jared Fry in 1999, two years after Sasha Wade disappeared.

'That's when it was published – the earliest anyone but a close friend should have heard it,' said Voss rapidly. They were in the corridor outside the interview room and Deacon was listening to every word he said. 'But Sasha had the song in her notebook, that she left at home when she went missing. Even if she was in the habit of copying down songs she liked and passing them off as her own, it was two years too soon.'

Deacon was trying to catch up. 'You're saying Fry stole it from her? That he read the notebook she left with her parents? And they never mentioned it?'

Voss was shaking his head. 'I don't think that's what happened. I think they knew one another before Sasha disappeared. Either they corroborated on the song – and came up with slightly different versions, hers for a woman and his for a man – or she wrote it and sang it for him. She wanted to break into the business, remember. The day she went missing, with an overnight bag and her guitar – what if she was going to meet Fry? What if she sang *Crucifiction* for him?'

'And he liked it so much he killed her?' Much as he wanted to charge somebody – anybody – from The Diligence, Deacon was unconvinced. Even accepting that, in the music business, a good song is the worth a lot of money, it didn't ring true. 'Sasha finished her audition with a last triumphant chord and Fry hit her over the head with his second-best Yamaha? Even if he was desperate for the song, why wouldn't he just buy it?'

'I don't know,' admitted Voss. 'I don't know that he did kill her. I do know that they knew one another – the song proves it. So why is Fry still denying they ever met?'

Deacon went on staring at him from under gathered brows for another half minute. Then he nodded. 'Let's ask him. Er – good work, Charlie Voss.'

In the few minutes since Voss's interruption things had changed. Fry had thought he was about to be released; now he knew he wasn't. He must have thought that, whatever their suspicions, the police had no evidence against him. Now he knew they had. He'd thought he was just a short drive and a minute's privacy from being able to feed his craving. In the space of a few words, that hope died.

Deacon had interviewed a lot of drug-addicts in his time. In some ways it was difficult, in some ways very easy. Uniquely among suspects, you could put the fear of God into them by promising to do nothing to them but talk. And talk, and talk, while the fingers on the clock crept round and the counter on the tape machine clicked up and the chemicals in their blood and brain ebbed and thinned and told them they were going to die in agony. Then, usually, they'd say anything you wanted. It didn't have to be the truth, just what they thought you wanted to hear.

If all you were interested in was the clear-up rate you could get a lot done in that window of opportunity between desperation kicking in and physical collapse. But if you wanted the truth, a withdrawing addict was the worst kind of suspect: one who no longer knew what it was. Deacon wanted to know what Jared Fry remembered, not what he'd dreamt or hallucinated or wanted to be true or was afraid might be true or knew wasn't true but might get him bailed.

Deacon went back to the table and sat down again. His eyes took in Fry's pallor, the slick of sweat on his skin, the hunched attitude as the abdominal cramps kicked in, and decided enough was enough. They weren't playing at this any more. Fry wasn't just an overpaid lout with a bad habit: he was a man facing a murder charge. He needed protecting, and so did the process.

Deacon said, 'I think you need to see a doctor, Mr Fry. I'm going to suspend this interview until the surgeon's had a look at you. I'd recommend you to be frank with him. On the basis of information we now have, you could be with us for some time.'

Fry swallowed. His eyes were at once apprehensive and fierce. 'I don't need a doctor. I don't need to score. I'd like to, but I don't need to. What I need is to get this sorted out. You may think you have evidence against me, but you can't have because I didn't do what you think it proves.'

Deacon frowned. It was a good impression of an innocent man. 'Are you sure? It's no use to me if, by the time we've got your statement typed out, you're not capable of signing it.'

Fry barked a gruff laugh. He knew what he was doing. He knew he'd feel worse before he felt better. But instinct warned against letting himself be typecast. If it went on record that he couldn't get through an interview without chemical support his credibility would be gone. No one trusts the testimony of an addict. Even if it cost him, he had to challenge that perception of him.

'Superintendent,' he gritted, 'let's cut the crap here. I take heroin. I've taken it for a long time. I like what it does for me and I'm not interested in quitting, except for today. Because what it's going to do today is convince you that under its influence I could do anything – however stupid, however vicious – and have no memory of it. So today I do without. It won't be much fun for either of us so I suggest we get on with it. If I want a doctor I'll tell you; if I want a solicitor I'll tell you. If I pass out on the floor you'll have to do whatever the Police Manual says, but until then I don't want to see anyone or do anything that'll spin this out. Whatever the song may say' – he flicked a taut smile – 'time is not on my side.'

Deacon would have suffered dismemberment rather than admit it but he felt a twinge of admiration for this scarecrow of a man, sunken-eyed, sallow-skinned, his health broken by the self-indulgence of his lifestyle. Jared Fry was everything that Jack Deacon despised; and yet... He had no idea if Fry could do what he said. Perhaps he didn't understand how hard it would get. But most addicts have tried to quit, some of them repeatedly, so probably Fry had some idea of what he was letting himself in for. Try as he might, Deacon couldn't avoid feeling a certain respect for him.

'All right,' he nodded. 'But you can change your mind any time. And even if you don't, I'll call the surgeon any time I become concerned about your ability to continue.'

'You worry about the questions,' grated Fry. 'I'll worry about not dribbling while I answer them.'

Brodie had her foot on the bottom tread of the police station steps when someone linked an arm through hers and swung her in a surprised parabola back onto the street. 'Keep walking.'

'Daniel? What... ?'

'I mean it. Keep walking.'

He didn't let her go until they'd turned the corner, out of sight of the CCTV cameras above the station door. When he did she turned to face him. 'Well?'

'You can't go in there. Charlie's found a connection between Jared and the missing girl. Jack's questioning him and Chandos is shouting the odds at the front desk. If you go in there now it'll be like spraying petrol on a bush-fire.'

'And... ?' Brodie was looking for the down-side.

'Did you see Chandos?'

'Yes. We barely got to talk, though, before he heard the news, jumped in his car and headed down here. I followed. Daniel, I'm not going to sit out the fireworks display in an air-raid shelter. I want to know what's going on.'

'That song of Jared's – *Crucifiction*? Sasha Wade wrote it.'

Amazement knocked the breath out of her. 'You're *kidding!* So he did know her. Do you know, I really didn't think he was lying about that.'

'Or me. I suppose there's no other way of reading it?'

Brodie couldn't see one. 'So that's what Eric was covering up. That Fry was telling the truth about things we thought were lies and lying about things we thought were the truth.'

Daniel didn't follow. She explained, her voice on the cusp between sorrow and anger. 'We thought he was pretending to be mad, bad and dangerous. We also thought he was a great songwriter.'

✳ ✳ ✳

'So I'll ask you again, Mr Fry,' Deacon said wearily. 'Did you know Sasha Wade?'

'No.'

'Then can you explain to me how you've spent the last six years singing her song?'

That made him bridle as even the suspicion of murder did not. 'That's my song. I wrote it – every word, every note.'

Deacon shook his head. 'Not according to this.' He had Sasha's exercise-book open in front of him. He turned it with the points of two fingers so Fry could see. 'Read it. Tell me if that isn't, in every essential, the same song.'

Half way through Fry's gaze skipped aside disparagingly. 'She copied it. She heard a song she liked and rewrote it so she could sing it. That's my song, Superintendent. Ask anyone.'

'The problem is – *your* problem is – Sasha left this book in her bedroom at her parents' house when she went missing, two years before you first sang it in public.'

'That isn't possible,' Jared Fry said flatly.

'It isn't arguable,' said Deacon. 'Unless you're saying her mother copied the song down, in a skilful imitation of Sasha's handwriting, more than two years after her daughter disappeared. Is that the basis of your defence, Mr Fry?'

'Don't be bloody silly.'

'Then how did it get there? If you wrote your song first.'

'You're the detective, you work it out!'

Deacon smiled. 'I think I have. I think Sasha Wade came to you with some songs she thought you'd be interested in. And you were. You realised there was some good material in there and offered to buy it. Unfortunately, she knew what she'd got as well. She didn't want a few quid in her pocket: she wanted to be famous. She wanted her name on the songs. She wanted to be up there singing them with you.

'But you didn't want a partner. A nineteen-year-old girl was no part of the hellfire image you were creating. It was a great song, but only if it was your song. And Sasha wasn't interested in being your ghost-writer.'

He sighed. 'You know, Mr Fry, it should be pretty easy to see you as a murderer. You're a rockstar, a Satanist and a heroin addict – I shouldn't be asking myself if you murdered this girl, I should be wondering how many others there were. But the fact is, I don't think you're an evil man. I've known evil men and I don't think you're one. I don't think you killed Sasha Wade because she stood between you and a good song.'

This was Jack Deacon's trade and he knew it well. He knew Jared Fry wanted nothing in the world so much as to ask what he thought instead, but didn't dare to. Deacon was in no rush to give him what he wanted, left Fry hanging. Even when he was ready to proceed he began with a question.

'So what did happen? Was it just a stupid accident? Maybe she got angry when you couldn't agree terms, went to storm out and tripped on the stairs. She banged her head, didn't she? That's all the pathologist could find. But by the time you realised she wasn't getting up and went to see why, she was dead.'

He watched Fry's face for confirmation. However she died, if he killed her that was the best gloss he could hope to put on it – he should have jumped at it. But he said nothing.

A little doubt beginning to nag inside him, Deacon pressed on. 'And because of who you are you thought you wouldn't be believed. You panicked and dumped the body, hoping like hell there was nothing to connect her to you. Perhaps she'd already told you that coming to see you was a spur-of-the-moment decision and she hadn't told anyone what she was doing. She didn't want people to be disappointed if she never even got to see you.

'Is that what happened, Mr Fry? If it is – if it was anything like that – you should tell me. That isn't murder. We can go a long way towards sorting it out.'

Finally Fry looked up at him. For a moment Deacon thought he was going to grasp the lifeline. He'd made it as tempting as he could. There would be time enough, once Fry had confessed to being there when Sasha Wade died, to map the extent of his culpability.

But what Fry said was, 'Do you know when she died? I mean, can you pin it down precisely?'

Deacon nodded. 'Pretty much. Mid June 1997. She went missing on the 14th and we think she was buried on the night of the 16th. Why, have you got an alibi?' He smiled.

By now Fry's breathing was growing ragged. 'I've no idea where I was then – hell, I've no idea where I was last week – but it'll be a matter of record. Ask Eric. If we were on tour you're going to find it hard to make a case against me.'

Deacon resented his manner, but actually it was a good point. Fry didn't work in the local carpet factory. If hundreds of people had seen him strutting his stuff at the Fortwilliam Empire the night Eddie Rollins was late home from stock-taking, someone else buried the girl.

'All right,' he said after a moment. 'Let's find out.'

Chapter Twenty

He was in Ireland.

Chandos didn't have the books with him: he phoned The Diligence and his PA brought them down. Voss took him into the other interview room – keeping him away from both Fry and Deacon – and went through them with him.

The records were clear enough: entries in a ledger written in the same hand, though with different pens, to those before and after. There were no signs of alteration. Fry, the band and the crew were in Ireland for seven days before Eddie Rollins's stock-taking and four days after it. They played four nights in Dublin, two in Cork, one in Limerick, one in Londonderry and two in Belfast. The night the black van was seen at The Diligence, Souls For Satan were rattling the back teeth of several thousand fans in Limerick.

Anticipating the next question Chandos opened a file of press cuttings. *The Irish Times* was typically restrained but *The Irish Press* had a comprehensive review of the gig including an interview with the lead singer.

Chandos looked up with his handsome, confident smile. If he'd done it next door Deacon would have decked him. 'I could probably track down video if you still have doubts.'

'I don't think that'll be necessary.' Voss managed a wry smile of his own. 'It's a pretty good alibi as it stands.'

Chandos shrugged. 'We were lucky. It happened to be a time when I could prove where he was, what he was doing. There are plenty of weeks where the only people to have seen him will be me and other members of his staff.' He looked Voss full in the eye. 'So, sergeant, can I take it Jared Fry is no longer a suspect? Can I tell the press that?'

Voss was surprised. 'I didn't know the press thought he ever was.'

'I'm not sure they do,' said Chandos calmly. 'But they're never far away. As soon as the body turned up there'd be whole teams of them doing what you've been doing – trying to make a connection between Jared and the dead girl. Some of them may think that Jared helping with your inquiries is all the proof they need. Before they print that I'd like to put them right.'

'I'd have thought being a murder suspect was money in the bank to a demon rocker.'

Chandos grinned. 'It's certainly less damaging than to a lay preacher. I don't mind the publicity, I just want to manage it. After all, that's my job.'

Voss nodded. 'I'll need to speak to Superintendent Deacon but it's going to be difficult to show Mr Fry could have buried her.' Which wasn't quite the same as saying he couldn't have killed her, and it occurred to Voss that if he had it might have been smart to make himself visible in another country while a friend disposed of the body. 'Were you in Limerick too?'

'Earlier. By the time the band reached Limerick I was probably in Belfast, making sure things would be ready when they arrived.'

'Can you prove that, sir?'

Chandos shook his head. 'I doubt it. We keep receipts for six years, for tax purposes – the invoices from that tour are long gone. I don't even remember where I stayed. Somewhere near the venue, I expect, but I can't bring it to mind.'

'It would be helpful if you could,' said Voss.

Chandos nailed him with a glance. 'Why, am I a suspect now? Sergeant Voss, I'm trying to help. I'm sorry I can't tell you where I stayed one night eight years ago, but I do know it was a long way from Dimmock.' He thought. 'Besides, how *would* it help? You don't really think Jared killed this girl before he left for Ireland and left her lying around for eight days till I got the chance to bury her?'

Voss changed the subject rather than answering. 'Why did you move to this area? Where were you living before?'

'In London. It was very central, very handy, just a bit too accessible. The south coast is nearly as convenient and a little more private. And also...' He stopped.

'Sir?'

Chandos sighed. 'I'm not going to surprise you, am I, by saying Jared uses heroin. I thought it would be easier to control his habit if we lived out in the sticks than if he was never more than a taxi-ride from the dealers.'

'You're trying to get him off drugs?'

'Good grief, no. After this long? I doubt he could function at all. No, Jared's never going to come clean. He likes it too much. All I try to do is keep him off the downward spiral: taking more and more as his system responds less and less. I doubt if I can save Jared Fry's body any more than I can save his soul, sergeant. I'm just trying to keep him going as long as I can.'

Voss thought it was time to use the powder he'd been saving. 'Mr

Chandos, have you any idea how the same song could appear both in Sasha Wade's notebook that she last wrote in eight years ago and on Jared Fry's albums as having been written by him in 1999?'

He'd thought it was unanswerable; that, if it didn't prove Fry murdered Sasha, at least it proved he knew her. But Chandos's expression wasn't worried enough. 'Really?'

'Yes. *Crucifiction.* The same song, except for a handful of words.'

'Jared wrote that song. I remember him writing it.'

'So how did it get in Sasha Wade's notebook?'

Chandos considered. 'There's one way I can think of. You have to understand, writing a song isn't like making a chair – you have a log and a lathe after breakfast and something to eat your dinner off that night. A song can be a long time growing. Jared was working on *Crucifiction* for a couple of years before he recorded it. He came to me with different drafts half a dozen times. He even sang a few of them – for friends, at private parties – to see how they went down. If this girl was at one of those parties, or knew someone who was, she could have heard a version of the song. She may not have intended plagiarism – she just liked it, wrote it down and played with it in a notebook she never expected anyone else to read.'

Voss had to concede it was a plausible explanation. It could have happened that way. The mere possibility undermined the notebook as evidence linking Sasha and Fry. Disappointed, he moved on to his last question. 'How do you move the band around on tours?'

'We have a big transporter thing, custom-built on a bus chassis. Think Air Force One on wheels. And a truck for the equipment.'

'That wouldn't come cheap.'

'It didn't.' Chandos frowned. 'You want to see the receipts?'

Voss shook his head. 'I'm wondering what you used before the band hit the big-time.'

Chandos understood. 'Say, eight years ago? Vans. The first ones were small and old, and they got bigger and younger as Souls got better known and made better money. Eight years ago? Transits, I think. Two of them.'

Voss would check with the Department of Motor Vehicle Licensing but only because being thorough was a habit. 'What colour?'

'Black.' He shrugged. 'For demon rockers? What else?'

'With the band's name on them?'

'No. You'd get mobbed every time you stopped at traffic lights.'

'Did you take them both to Ireland?'

'Yes. It took both to carry the band and their equipment.'

Voss reflected, but there weren't any questions he hadn't asked and there weren't any Chandos had seemed reluctant to answer. 'OK. I'll have a word with Mr Deacon but I think that's probably it for now.' He left the room still unsure whether these people were involved in the death of the girl in their garden but with no clear idea how to nail them if they were.

When his sergeant asked to see him in the corridor, Deacon was almost glad of the interruption. His interview with Fry was going nowhere. He'd have liked to think it was because Fry had secrets to guard, but actually he believed the demon rocker didn't remember where he was eight years ago.

It made the interview a frustrating and increasingly pointless exercise. Fry wasn't suddenly going to remember anything helpful or let out something damaging, which meant that sooner or later Deacon would have to send him home. It was no pleasure watching Fry come apart in front of him, but it went against the habit of a lifetime to cut a suspect loose in exchange for nothing at all. He went outside hoping Voss could give him either grounds to charge Fry or a reason to let him go.

'If Rollins has the date right, Fry couldn't have killed Sasha Wade. She was safe at home when he left for Ireland, had probably been underground for four days when he got back,' said Voss. 'Even if it isn't Sasha, he'd have had to kill her before June 9th and leave her for someone else to bury a week later.'

'Chandos?' asked Deacon.

'He says he was in Belfast on the 16th. And that the two vans used by the band – which were in fact black – were both with Fry.'

'Can he prove that?'

'No, but we probably can. I'll check with the ferry company.'

Deacon was disappointed. 'I'm going to have to let them go, aren't I? Well, I'd have had to do something about Fry soon anyway – another half hour and we'd have to mop him up and send him home in a bucket.' He stood a moment longer, craggy features twisted in thought. 'What do you reckon, Charlie Voss? Are they involved or not? Am I trying too hard to believe that they are?'

Voss didn't know. He had less reason than Deacon to hate Chandos but no more reason to trust him. Yet he hadn't caught the man out in so much as an evasion; which seemed to make a nonsense of Daniel's theory.

Or did it? Wasn't that the point – that he, not Deacon, had conducted the interview? Because of what had gone before Chandos had been questioned not by a detective superintendent at the peak of his investigative powers but by his sergeant. 'I don't know, sir. I can't say I've much confidence in what they're saying, but I can't fault it either.'

'What did he say about the song?'

Voss repeated Chandos's explanation. 'It sounded feasible. How about Fry?'

'I thought he was going to cry when I suggested he might not have written it. He said it was the best song he ever wrote.'

'Chandos said he was working on it for a couple of years.'

Deacon shrugged. 'Fry didn't tell me that. But then, I doubt if he can remember back that far. I think you're right, Charlie. I don't know if they did it, but I don't think we can prove they did it. We need to catch them out in a lie. Get them to contradict one another. It shouldn't be *that* difficult – there may be worse co-conspirators than a heroin addict but off-hand I can't think of any. Fry can't remember what actually happened, let alone what he's been told to say happened.'

'You want to keep them talking?'

Deacon shook his head. 'Not today. If I don't turn Fry loose now I'll have to get him looked at, and that'll tie my hands. No, send them home. Thank them for their co-operation and send them home.'

'Chandos wants to tell the press we're not treating Fry as a murder suspect.'

For a moment Deacon's eye kindled. 'Does he indeed? Well, he can tell the press anything he likes. If they ask me I'll tell them we have certain lines of inquiry but we aren't currently treating *anyone* as a murder suspect.'

Voss nodded and turned away.

With his hand on his own door Deacon hesitated. 'Charlie?'

'Sir?'

'About earlier. I was ready to shout at someone. You got in the way.'

It was the nearest thing to an apology Voss was going to get. 'OK.'

'OK.'

Daniel thought they should leave. He assumed the police investigation had reached a point where whatever he or Brodie thought, whatever suspicions they held, would be irrelevant. If charges were imminent, the last thing Jack Deacon needed in the middle of cautioning the demon rocker was to hear Brodie's voice raised in querulous enquiry at the front desk.

Brodie thought she'd been left out of the loop. That she'd arrived too late to help settle the case and so missed her opportunity to make amends. It wasn't much to set against her stupidity but she'd thought it was better than nothing. Now it seemed events had overtaken her. If Deacon was formally interviewing Fry he was probably past needing the benefit of her insights into Eric Chandos's behaviour.

On the other hand, she thought, brightening, that needn't prevent her from giving Deacon moral support. Or to phrase it slightly differently, from swanning past Sergeant McKinney on the desk, using her most dazzling smile as a swipe-card, and planting herself in the main corridor of the police station from where she could follow developments. 'Come on,' she said, hooking a finger in Daniel's cuff, 'let's be in at the death.'

'No!' he exclaimed, horrified. 'It's none of our business, Brodie. Jack doesn't need us there and he doesn't want us there. For heaven's sake, come away.'

Which is how, five minutes later, Chandos and Fry heading down the police station steps met Brodie and Daniel heading up them.

She was surprised. She hadn't thought either of them would be leaving any time soon. She'd thought Fry wouldn't be leaving at all. She opened her mouth to ask Chandos what had happened. Then she saw Fry's face, and his sweat-dark shirt, and knew this was neither the time nor the place for conversation. 'We'll talk later.' Chandos registered her presence just enough to nod.

Daniel was looking at Fry and a rage was building within him. He knew Deacon too well to think, as a passer-by might have thought, that helping with police inquiries had meant having the crap kicked out of him in a sound-proof room, but that was how he looked. Only force of habit was keeping Fry on his feet and he seemed scarcely aware of his surroundings. Daniel stared into his white face and found no recognition there. The man was a husk, withered by pain, verging on mental and physical collapse.

The sensible thing would have been to keep quiet and keep moving. Not every tragedy can be averted. Sometimes good men have no choice but to do nothing. Daniel had tried to save Jared Fry – from his history, his manager and himself – and failed: there was no reason to suppose another attempt would succeed. More than that, he recognised that further intervention would only make things worse. Still he couldn't bring himself to take the extra couple of steps that would mean turning his back on the ruined man.

He said quietly, 'If you killed that girl, Jared, tell Superintendent Deacon now. Nothing the law can do to you will compare with what you're doing to yourself.'

Fry's deadfall eyes came round to him slowly, his jangled brain struggling to make sense of the words. Finally he realised that the face before him, etched as it was with sombre concern, was familiar. 'Daniel…'

For Chandos it was the last straw. There was a split second, and Brodie saw it pulse through his expression like a trace on a seismograph, in which he might equally have let fly with his tongue or his fists. She thought her own presence was the only restraining factor.

'Jesus!' he swore, 'here we go again with the Sister of Mercy routine. What is it with you, Hood, that you can't see someone having a bad day without wanting to extend your hand and poke them in the eye?'

Daniel didn't even smile. 'A bad day? That's what you call it? He's dying on his feet, Chandos. Look at him. He made you a wealthy man, and all you care now is that he's good for one more gig, one more album. You could save his life. You could get him into a clinic and make him stay there till he was well. No one in the world has that kind of power over him, except you.

'But that's not what you want, is it? The only thing that's worth more to you than Jared Fry's next album is Jared Fry's last album.'

Chandos flushed darkly. But he'd demolished tougher opponents than a sometime maths teacher with a tendency to panic attacks. And he knew Daniel's weakness, and wasn't above exploiting it even with her standing beside them.

'We both know what this is about, Hood, and it isn't Jared. Last time you rattled my cage I said something I shouldn't have, but that didn't make it any less true. You resent me because you envy me. Dress it up any way you like, but the reason you're interested in men's souls is that you have no luck with women's bodies. Here.' He dug in his pocket, threw down a crumple of notes. 'Buy yourself a short-sighted hooker and all this wanting to make the world a better place will stop.'

Daniel laughed, his mild grey eyes fired with battle. 'No, don't be tactful, Mr Chandos – say what you think.

'You keep getting me wrong, don't you? I don't envy you because you're richer than me, more successful than me, better looking than me and a more accomplished philanderer than me. I don't envy you at all. I despise you. I find you despicable.' He paused just long enough to let the words sink in.

'You like to think you're dangerous, and in a way you are. You corrupt weak people with the glamour of badness. Call it demon rock and stick nails up your nose, and alienated youngsters will be shocked and thrilled and want to be just like you. But you aren't real. You're a paper demon.'

'You know a man's running out of arguments when he plays the religion card,' drawled Chandos. 'Though I have to admit there's something diverting about hearing you preach. It's like Johnson's dog walking on its hind legs: it's not that you're any good at it, it's just amusing to see you try.'

Daniel showed his teeth in a surprisingly wolfish grin. 'You've accused me of religion before. Really, you couldn't be wider of the mark. That's why I can see you for what you are. Christians think Satanism is the antithesis of faith, but actually it's just a different expression of it. It's believers who turn to devil worship. Atheists know that whether you're talking about the inside of a box or the outside of a box, it's the same box.'

'And I keep telling you,' Chandos said lazily, 'all we do is music. He makes it, I sell it. It's good music, and lots of people buy it, but that's all it is. Just music.'

Daniel shook his head knowingly. 'But that isn't all you're selling, is it? People who buy a Souls For Satan album are buying into a whole philosophy of *Do what you want and the devil take the hindmost.* Of course, most of them never try to put the philosophy into practice, but they think you do. They see you as a standard-bearer for rebellion.

'But it's just an act. You're no more a Satanist than I am. That's the slogan on the packet, but when you get the wrapper off there's nothing inside. It's painting-by-numbers Satanism. The great necromancers of the past must be revolving in their unmarked graves at how easy it is to pass as an Antichrist these days.'

Chandos shrugged. In similar circumstances Brodie had felt the confidence radiate from him: now there was a defensiveness. 'Of course we're not real Satanists, any more than ballerinas are real swans. We're entertainers.'

'You're liars,' said Daniel contemptuously. 'You say, *Look at us: we're outlaws, we don't obey the rules; buy the over-priced T-shirt and you can be an Antichrist too*. But it's just words. You haven't the commitment to be genuinely evil so you settle for mere nastiness instead. It has a certain shock value for the emotionally immature, and you can't be done for it.'

'What are you accusing me of?' Chandos was starting to speak through his teeth. 'Being wicked or not being wicked enough? And why should I *care* what you think? You're a confused little man: an atheist with a Church of England soul. You want to believe in goodness without believing in God. Make up your mind, sonny, you can't have it both ways.'

Brodie had never seen Daniel so focused. He seemed unaware of anything except Chandos and his own argument. 'Goodness has very little to do with God,' he shot back. 'Societies thrive on the innate decency of most of their members, not the fear of a beard in the sky. Ethics don't stem from a belief in God. Ethics make God redundant.

'You aren't a threat to society, Mr Chandos. Society is strong and pragmatic, and most of it knows better than to take a bully at his own valuation. The only danger you pose is to people with some growing up to do who think you are what you purport to be: a real alternative, occult souls serving a different theology. But you're nothing of the kind. You're a fraud. A sham.'

Chandos flushed and tried to respond but Daniel was nowhere near finished. 'That cleric from Cheyne Treacey is more dangerous than you. Because he believes something quite terrifying: that people are less important than their God. That our place is in the mud while His is in the sky. It's a disastrous philosophy that not only makes a virtue of mud but deprives human beings of the rights and obligations of free will. If there's a God up there, no one has to think; no one has to take responsibility for his own actions, to hammer out for himself the meanings of good and evil. If there's a God, we are nothing more than children and the last word in any attempt to explore the essence of our existence will always be, *Because I say so.'*

Brodie had to remind herself to breathe. Of all the possible out-comes of this confrontation, this was the least likely – that Daniel Hood would challenge Eric Chandos at word-play and win. Of course, he had the advantage of believing what he was saying. But the eloquence that was suddenly at his command knocked her sideways. It was as if everything he felt, everything he knew in his bones, had backed up behind a dam and the sluices were condensing it into per-fect jets of words.

He still wasn't shouting. But every syllable he spoke rang clear with conviction. 'Human beings are the bravest, strongest, most ingenious, indefatigable creatures the world has produced in four billion years. We can achieve anything we can imagine. Without God, man is alone in the darkness. But he can make fire.

'Of course,' he added scornfully, 'a real Satanist is another kind of religious fanatic and so deeply dangerous. But you're just playing the part, aren't you? Well, at the end of a play the actors come in front of the curtain and take a bow. They don't pretend to *be* the remark-able people they portray. So take a bow, Mr Chandos – it's time to leave the stage.'

Dimmock is not a city like London, humming with industry and enterprise and the sheer electricity of many lives being lived in close proximity all the time, and Battle Alley hadn't much in common with New Scotland Yard. There were quiet times. There were periods during the day when no one was entering or leaving the police sta-tion, or walking in the street or past the end of the street. There were times when there was no traffic noise, and even the dulcet tones of Detective Superintendent Deacon berating a junior officer were not wafting from an upper window. There were moments, sometimes whole minutes, of calm.

Even so, Brodie had never heard the street fall so silent. Now Daniel was done, his extraordinary tirade spent, no sound of any kind escaped any of the four of them. Not a word, not a gasp, not the scraping of a foot on the stone steps. She looked at Daniel's face and saw a blissful, almost arrogant satisfaction; at Chandos's and saw monstrous rage; at Fry's and saw fear.

Of all of them it was Fry who tried to break the terrible silence, avert the coming storm. He reached out a bony hand to touch Chandos's sleeve. 'Eric...'

Chandos pushed him aside. There was no need: his grip was too frail to detain a grown man, Chandos could have freed himself with one of his elegant shrugs. Instead he swept Fry aside with enough force to send him sprawling down the stone steps, fetching up in a heap against the balustrade. And then, as if the sudden movement had released a tiger that wouldn't be penned, that was going to feed before it went back in its cage, he packed all the strength of his upper body into a piston that exploded, firing off a fist.

Daniel never saw it coming. He tried to catch Fry as he stumbled past, failed, and when he turned back he met the hay-maker coming the other way. By accident or design – possibly the former, Daniel was shorter than most people Chandos might have had occasion to strike – the blow connected not with his jaw but with the cheek-bone immediately below his eye. Blood spurted as the broken-spider frame of his glasses ground into his flesh. His vision exploded in a firestorm of red and black, and for a moment the universe got its strong and weak forces confused so that gravity worked sideways while up and down squabbled over who was driving. When they sorted it out he hit the ground.

Brodie was on her knees beside him, filling her lungs to summon help, when she saw Jared Fry's face. He knew what she was going to do, and what it would mean. More interviews, more statements. More time before he could deal with the dragon in his veins. His eyes were smoky with despair.

'Jared.' She caught his hollow gaze. 'Go. This is nothing to do with you. Get out of here.'

He looked at her, and at Chandos. He looked at Daniel, vacant and bleeding. His voice, that had filled hearts and lifted roofs, was something between a moan and a whisper. 'I can't.'

Brodie stared at him in disbelief. She opened her mouth to swear at him. But what was the point? He knew what he was. No abuse she could pile on him would add significantly to the burden of his self-contempt. He knew he was pathetic. He knew he'd had, and squandered, a talent that those who paid to see him would have sacrificed limbs for. He knew the only redemption left to him was the tradi-tional one of dying young, and even that was slipping daily beyond his reach.

He saw himself through her eyes – a ruined idol with feet of clay reaching all the way up to his armpits, stripped of everything that makes a man, even the ability to answer his own most pressing needs – and wished he could have died first. His gaze dropped and he knelt on the steps, his head bowed, his life past amending.

She'd given him one chance more than he deserved: it wasn't Brodie's fault he was incapable of taking it. Again she filled her lungs to call for assistance.

Even without his glasses Daniel had seen enough to understand what had passed between them. The difference between him and Brodie was, Daniel was no good at letting others pay for their own mistakes. She was broadly content to let people make their beds and lie in them; he was constantly trying to tuck them in. He was, she freely admitted, nicer than her. At regular intervals he paid the price of that.

'Let it go,' he said softly.

Still crouching she turned and stared at him, blood and dirt on his face. 'What?'

'I'm all right. We don't need to involve the police.'

'Involve them? He just knocked you down their front steps! They've undoubtedly got it on CCTV.'

'What if they have? I don't need their protection. From him? You don't take something like that to court – you wipe it off your shoe and get on with your day.'

'Daniel, you're bleeding! He broke your glasses and cut your face. He could have had your eye out.'

'But he didn't. All that happened is he ran out of arguments and used his fists as an exit strategy. If he was a child he'd have stamped; if he was a teenager he'd have slammed a door. You want him charged with being sad in a public place? Forget it. I made my point. That was him acknowledging it.'

'But he *hit* you! Assault occasioning actual bodily harm. Malicious damage to a pair of spectacles. He shouldn't get away with it!'

Daniel was up, wiping the dirt off his face with the back of his hand. 'He isn't getting away with anything. You know what he is, I know what he is, Jared knows what he is and even he knows what he is. Would it make any difference if we told a magistrate what he is? If I make a complaint we'll have to go inside and make statements about it, and Jared doesn't need that and neither do I. I don't need to waste another hour of my life on this man. Another hour that isn't coming back – that I could be washing my pots and vacuuming my rug and putting Germalene on my haemorrhoids. He isn't worth it. Let him go.'

So they let him go. Wordless, mortified, he walked away as

quickly as a man can without people saying he's running. Jared Fry glanced back at them once with an mixture of gratitude and desolation, then they were gone.

Brodie drew a deep, steadying breath and looked at Daniel. 'I didn't know you had haemorrhoids.'

Daniel started laughing; and having started, was helpless to stop. 'I haven't. It just seemed to be where the rhetoric was going.'

For no reason she could understand Brodie found herself smiling too. 'Daniel – that was a lie!'

'More a literary device,' he demurred.

'So said the man tap-dancing at the top of the slippery slope.'

'I know,' sighed Daniel. 'I'm a real hell-raiser, me.'

Before Sergeant McKinney had decided what to do about the fracas on his doorstep it was over. Two of those involved were away down the street, the other two were leaning on the stone ballustrade, weak with laughter and searching their pockets for tissues.

He frowned at the TV screen a moment longer, then he picked up the phone and called Deacon. 'You probably want to have a look at this.'

Deacon didn't understand what he was seeing on the CCTV recording either. But he thought he needed to. Three of those involved had good reasons to keep him in the dark; the fourth might talk if provided with the right incentives. Subtlety was not something the detective was famous for but he could do it if he had to. And he'd thump anyone who said different.

So when he left work around nine o'clock, instead of walking round the corner to his house Deacon cut across to the Promenade, crunched down the shingle and clanged up the iron steps of the net- ting shed.

As he lifted his hand to knock Daniel's voice, slightly muffled, called to him. 'Come on in, Jack, it's not locked.'

Deacon let himself into the living-room. 'How did you know it was me?'

Daniel may have been too polite to laugh or just too sore. 'It was you or Nelly the Elephant, and the other circus is out of town.'

He was holding a packet of frozen peas to his face. When he low- ered it Deacon understood why he sounded muffled. 'I won't ask what happened to you because I saw the Director's Cut. Anything broken?'

'Just my second-best glasses.' Daniel's cheek-bone jutted like a cow's hip, stained with bruising. Without the familiar frames his face looked undressed, vulnerable. But his pale grey eyes were still per- ceptive though Deacon knew they saw so poorly his own face was a blur. Daniel looked at his visitor largely from habit. 'If you saw what was happening, why didn't you intervene?'

Deacon sniffed. 'Just because I'm not allowed to deck you does- n't mean I can't enjoy it when someone else does. Plus, it was over by the time I got there. What was it about?'

Again the astute, clouded glance over the frozen peas. 'Have you asked Brodie?'

'Do you think she'd tell me if I did?'

Daniel considered. 'She might. It wasn't about you, if that's what you're wondering.'

'Was it about the murder?'

'No. Oh, it's no secret. I told Eric Chandos what I thought of him. I called him a sham and he punched me in the eye. A predictable enough reaction, when you think about it.'

Deacon thought about it, stopped when he found himself smirking. 'Was it worth it?'

Daniel's blind smile was seraphic. 'Oh yes.'

'*Why* was it worth it?'

'He had it coming. He's a powerful man, and powerful men don't hear the truth about themselves often enough. He's damaged decent people's lives. I wanted him to hear the truth for once, and I wanted Jared to hear it too.'

Deacon regarded him speculatively. 'You wanted him to hit you. You provoked him until he did.'

Daniel shrugged. 'I suppose.'

'And you wanted Fry to see it.'

'Yes.'

'And Brodie.'

Instantly Daniel sensed danger. He wished he had his glasses on. He looked at the blob that spoke with Deacon's voice and wished he could see its expression. 'Er…'

'Because' – this was the reason he was a detective – 'you were afraid she still felt something for him. You wanted her to see him for what he is.'

'I didn't say that.' Daniel's voice was low, his gaze wary.

'You're not denying it either,' Deacon observed quietly. 'You knew what had happened: that something outside her control had taken hold of her. You were afraid Chandos could turn the charm on and have her back. You knew what he was but you were afraid she couldn't see it. That even if you reminded her how he'd used her already she might forget if he looked at her a certain way. But she'd never forget seeing him beat you bloody. That's what you wanted.'

'Put that way it doesn't sound very noble, does it?' admitted Daniel. 'I was worried. She couldn't seem to cut free of him. Even today, knowing all she did, she was still looking for a reason to see him. She said there were things she could ask him that no one else could. But if they'd been alone together for any length of time, I don't know what would have happened.'

'You think she'd have gone with him.'

Daniel shook his head. 'I don't know. I know that isn't what she wants.' He stopped, tried to order his thoughts. 'She was happy before she met him. He took that from her, and not even because he was in love and couldn't help himself. Jack, I think everything that's happened was part of a plan. I think Chandos made a play for Brodie as soon as he realised you two were a couple.'

He'd lost Deacon completely. The big man spread his hands in bewilderment. Daniel realised he would have to explain. 'I think he went after Brodie to distract you from doing your job. Because there's something he doesn't want you finding out.'

Deacon's jaw was hard. 'About the girl in his garden?'

'I can't see how. I wondered if it was something to do with Jared's addiction, or maybe the band's finances. Whatever it is, I think he was scared that once you started asking questions you were going to uncover something he was desperate to keep secret.'

'So he made a play for Brodie?' Deacon's tone was doubtful as he tried the thought for size.

'You're a very effective investigator. He was afraid of you. He had to stop you thinking like a policeman.'

Now he understood. How Chandos had used him and Brodie both. If Daniel was right. Things like this, Daniel had a habit of being right. Deacon's breathing was thick in his throat. 'You discussed this with Brodie? What did she think?'

'She thought she'd been very stupid. She was embarrassed and she was angry.'

'And then she went to see him again.' Deacon's lips were compressed in a hard line.

'She wanted to make amends. She thought she could find out what it was all about. She wanted to be able to give you something useful.'

'Which was also a pretty stupid thing to do,' growled Deacon. 'If he'd realised what she was doing she could have got hurt.' His gaze sharpened. 'But that isn't what worried you, is it? You were afraid he'd win her back. After everything he's done?'

'I know,' murmured Daniel, 'it doesn't make any sense. But somehow this man can reach her in ways she has no defence against. That's why...' He gave a slow, gentle smile. 'I couldn't let him hurt her any more, and I could only think of one way to stop him. I didn't think she'd guess what I was doing. I didn't factor you into the equation.'

Deacon had lowered himself into Daniel's armchair. Resting his elbows on the arms, gazing over his laced fingers, he regarded Daniel in silence for perhaps a minute. To Daniel, half blinded, it felt a long time. He couldn't guess what Deacon would say or do next. He'd angered this strong, touchy man more times than he could remember, usually without meaning to and often without understanding quite how he had. Now he thought he'd done it again. But Deacon just sat in silence with his hands folded and an expression Daniel couldn't fathom even when he put on his other glasses.

Finally Deacon said, 'You wanted Brodie to see Chandos thump you because you thought it would help her and me get back together. Is that right?' There was no clue in his tone as to what answer he wanted.

'More or less.'

Deacon went on eyeing him pensively. 'Daniel, I'm going to let you into a secret. At least, I think it'll come as a surprise. Brodie won't have told you because she doesn't know.

'Eric Chandos threw a spanner in the works of our relationship, and for a while it rained brass cogs and sump-oil and was all very dramatic. But Chandos wasn't the first to come between us. And when he goes, as go he will, we'll still have to work out what to do about the real threat to our future. The real third party. The one who was there before and will still be there when Eric Chandos is just a bad memory.'

Daniel's eyes saucered and his jaw dropped. Even his bruises paled. He could barely string the words together. 'You're telling me – *you* – have someone… ?'

Deacon's head tipped to one side. 'Would that trouble you?'

'If you told me you were cheating on Brodie?' His light voice soared till it cracked. 'You *know* how I'd feel about that. I'd want to kill you.'

One sceptic eyebrow rose as Deacon's gaze took in the frozen peas. 'Lucky for me then,' he said drily, 'I got you on a bad day.'

Deacon's blow had hit him much harder than Chandos's, but even with his mind reeling Daniel knew there was something not right about this. The irony in Deacon's tone. Jack Deacon was a man who could make jokes about many inappropriate things, but Daniel couldn't see him joking about this. 'Hang on,' he muttered, struggling for breath. 'That's not what you're telling me, is it? Then –

what... ?'

'I know,' Deacon said distinctly. Over the laced fingers his eyes nailed Daniel to the sofa. 'What Brodie doesn't. What I think you're only beginning to suspect. I know.'

'Know *what*?'

'That you love her, Daniel. That the real, abiding threat to me and Brodie, the one I can't do anything about, the one that will one day force us apart, is you.'

Voss should have been on his way home too. But his desk was littered with notes and faxes and e-mails, and he didn't like closing the door on it all. It would still be there in the morning, and God knows what else as well.

Because he was a conscientious detective he had sought confirmation of everything Eric Chandos told him. And he'd got it. What records survived supported his account of Souls For Satan's Irish tour. Dates, places, what ferries they used, what vehicles they took, what hotels they booked, for how many people. So far as Voss could tell, Fry had an alibi for the critical week that an innocent man would have killed for.

Which didn't necessarily make him innocent. For a conscientious detective, a water-tight alibi eight years old was enough to raise suspicion where none existed before. It might prove innocence; it might suggest that someone knew that one day he was going to need it. If Souls For Satan had been travelling shoe salesmen, Voss would have been surprised at how well their journey had been documented.

But they weren't reps, they were a rock band, and by 1997 they were just big enough for their activities to be remembered. There was nothing dubious about Fry being able to establish his whereabouts so precisely.

Voss fanned out the papers with his hand, hoping this would make them look fewer. It didn't work. Cover his desk? – he could redecorate his wall with the things. He looked at his watch, with a guilty twinge because he knew his fiancée would also be looking at hers just about now. She'd wait half an hour, then she'd phone him. Just once. She didn't nag. She knew what he did was important. Her restraint only made Voss feel guiltier.

He thought that for once he wouldn't trade on her patience but would get home before she phoned. In twenty minutes he could marshal this blizzard of papers into some sort of order so that first thing tomorrow he could dispose of it and be ready for something more promising. He picked up two sheets at random and, finding both related to the vans, laid one on top of the other in an embryonic pile.

Then he picked them up again and looked closer. His brows knit in a puzzled frown. 'Now,' he asked himself, 'what does that mean?'

'Of course I love her!' Daniel heard his voice soar and tried to bring it under control. 'Dear God, is that your revelation? There are hermits in Anatolia who know I love her. There are amoebas in the seas of Ganymede who've heard a rumour. You're telling me this came as a surprise to you? You've seen the stupid things I've done for her, you must have known why. I think the world of her. Bizarrely enough, she cares for me too. I know you never understood that but I thought you were OK with it. You can't think it's a threat to you.'

Deacon was nodding slowly. 'You're talking about friendship.'

'Of course. That's what it was from the start. You can say that's all it was, but to me that isn't the Wooden Spoon. The friendship of Brodie Farrell is worth having on any terms that it's offered.'

'But still, friendship. Platonic friendship.'

'Yes. Jack, you and Brodie have been together for nine months. You can't really think she's been cheating on you with me all that time.'

The big man shook his head. 'No, I don't think that. Like I said, I don't think Brodie knows what the situation is. As far as she's concerned, you two are just really good friends.'

'That's what I'm trying to tell you!'

Deacon looked up with coals in his eyes and his voice was deep with import. 'Daniel, it's a lie. I know – you don't tell lies. So maybe it really is a secret and I'm the only one who's cracked it. But I'm telling you, if it was a crime I could get a conviction. I know what I'm seeing. What you feel for Brodie: it may have been platonic once but it isn't now. You feel about her the way I feel about her.'

'You're wrong,' Daniel said faintly.

'Look me in the eye and say that.'

But he couldn't. Ignorance was one thing. He'd seen this coming for a little while, had managed to avoid facing it, so it wasn't exactly a lie the first time he told Deacon that friendship was all it was. But it would be a lie if he said it again. He thought sometimes it would be a good thing to learn how to lie, just a little bit, but he wasn't going to start by lying to Jack Deacon about Brodie Farrell.

'You admit it,' Deacon said softly.

Daniel flicked him hunted eyes. 'I thought you said it wasn't a crime.'

Deacon blew out a gusty sigh. 'What are we going to do?'

'We're not going to do anything,' said Daniel with certainty. 'I hope you and Brodie will get back together. I know that's what she wants, I think it's what you want too. Nothing has happened to stop that being the best outcome.'

'Of course it has!' snarled Deacon. 'You expect me to keep this from Brodie? Don't you think she has a right to know?'

'Know what?' cried Daniel, a catch in his voice. 'That I wish I was the sort of man she could fall in love with so I could sweep her off her feet, but I'm not so I won't? You think that's something she needs to know? Jack, what we have – that friendship you don't understand – used to work for both of us. It still works for her, and even if some schoolboy part of me would like more it's a pretty good deal for me too. I don't want to lose it.'

Deacon found himself in the absurd position of trying to encourage his rival. 'You don't know you would lose it. Until she knows how you feel you're not going to know.'

'And by then it would be too late. You say something like that out loud, you can't go back. You can't pretend it was a joke if somebody looks horrified, or laughs. Nobody stands to gain anything by having this out, but nobody else stands to lose as much as I do. I won't risk losing her.'

'You'd rather sacrifice something that would make both of you happy?'

'She's happy now. At least, she was and will be again. And I'm – content. Please, Jack, don't make an issue of this. You made a lucky guess and I was too slow to deny it. Forget it. What matters is what's best for Brodie. I can't give her what she needs. She likes having me around, she enjoys my company, but for some things she's always going to want you or someone like you. I may regret that but I can't change it. And you shouldn't be trying to! If you want Brodie to be happy, put things right between you.'

Deacon's heavy brow was troubled. 'She has the right to know. To make an informed choice.'

'Listen to me.' Daniel was calm now, clear and determined. 'If you say a word of this to Brodie, I will leave here and never see her again. She'll be hurt and confused, and I don't want to do that, but I will do it rather than ask her to choose between two kinds of caring. If you care about her you won't put her in that position.'

Deacon shook his head, bemused and defeated. 'I don't understand you, Daniel. I never did. The more I know you, the less I understand. Are you sure this is what you want?'

'Quite sure.' He even managed a smile. He put the packet of frozen peas to his face again, hiding behind it, and they shifted with a tiny, icy clink like the sound of something dying.

Chapter Twenty-Three

When Deacon went into his office the next morning, for a moment he thought he'd opened the wrong door. Papers like an early snow-fall drifted an inch thick on his desk, making it look like Voss's. Deacon shuddered. Detective superintendents still have paperwork to do, goodness knows, but usually someone has tamed it before it reaches them. Usually their sergeant.

Deacon bellowed, 'Voss!' like a bull moose at the peak of the rutting season.

Voss was at the coffee machine. Though it was now officially the weekend he'd been here since before seven. He hadn't shaved yet, and his stubble was a startling shade of red. He hurried back, holding the polystyrene mug like a peace offering. 'Don't touch anything,' he said; adding a belated, 'Sir,' when he saw the expression on Deacon's face. 'I know where everything is.'

'*I* know where everything is too, Charlie Voss. It's on my desk. It should be on yours.'

It had taken Voss half an hour to lay out the paper-trail in a form that Deacon, a man with all the natural sense of order of a garden hose – which can be carefully coiled and tied and hung on a hook in the shed, and still be full of kinks and missing its connector next time it's needed – could be expected to understand in the small window of opportunity between trying and losing his temper.

'Bear with me.' Voss tapped the first sheet, top left, with a fore-finger. 'This is the two black Transit vans owned by Souls For Satan at the beginning of June 1997. This one they bought new nine months previously, the other they'd had for four years and was then seven years old. Hence the difference in the plates.' He glanced at Deacon, but thus far the superintendent was keeping pace.

'OK. This' – another tap – 'is the same vans booked on the Dublin ferry. And this' – another piece of paper – 'is them making the crossing.'

'Hang on.' Deacon peered closer. Then he put his glasses on and looked again. 'Is that a mistake?'

Voss breathed a sigh of relief. If he'd had to point out the discrepancy it would have taken him another month to get back in Deacon's good books. 'No. Back in May they ordered another black Transit to replace the older of their two vans. It was delivered early in June and they took it to Ireland.'

'What happened to the old one?'

'It was sold via a dealer to a market trader. He registered his ownership on June 18th.'

Deacon was beginning to suspect where this was going. 'When did the band send in the notification that they'd parted with it?'

'June 18th.'

The superintendent thought about it. 'It's not a high priority, is it? You don't rush to catch the post. You fill in the new owner's name and address, then it sits on the sideboard for a week, then you use it as a bookmark for a bit, and sometime after that you stick it in a pillar-box. A week isn't a significant period of time.'

'Any other week wouldn't be,' agreed Voss. 'But that week? OK, so maybe some time went by between the band parting with the van and both parties registering the change of ownership. As you say, it happens all the time. But maybe it didn't happen this time. Maybe the new owner sent off the registration-form as soon as he got it. In which case…'

'In which case,' said Deacon, taking the baton and getting up to speed, 'Souls For Satan actually owned three vans on the Monday that Eddie Rollins did his stock-taking, and only two of them were in Ireland. We need to talk to that market-trader, find out when he actually took delivery.'

Voss nodded. 'He works at Camden Lock: the Met are sending someone round to see him.'

'When?'

The sergeant glanced at his watch. He did it a lot these days, Deacon had noticed – possibly due to a new interest in the passage of time, more likely because it was a present from his fiancée. 'About now, sir.'

But it was another hour before the Met phoned Voss with the information he'd asked for, and by then he'd thought of more questions. He used the number provided by his London colleagues to call the trader direct, looking for greater detail.

It turned out the black van had gone to the great scrapyard in the sky two years earlier. Thirteen years isn't a bad life for a Transit van, particularly one that's been used by a rock band *and* a market trader. 'So you had it for six years,' said Voss. 'What did you use it for?'

'Carrying stuff. To the market. Stuff for sale.' There's a kind of natural wariness between policemen and market traders that's built in at a genetic level.

'What kind of stuff?'

'Antiques of the future,' said Arnold Warboys firmly. 'Eastern European, mostly. Hand-carved stuff – bowls and chairs and the odd bed. They think nothing of it, they'd rather have shiny new plastic. Ship it over here, give it a spray of polish, and the next thing you know it's the latest thing in St John's Wood. It's entirely legal, squire,' he added loftily, 'all above board.'

'I'm sure it is,' said Voss. 'Going back to the van. Did you ever find anything odd in it? Left over from the previous owners.'

'It came from a rock band,' said Warboys, 'the only odd thing about it was it was clean. I had a good look to see if there were any interesting little packets under the seats...' He remembered then who he was talking to, covered his confusion with a cough. 'Not that... I mean, I'm not... Anyway, there wasn't. Nothing. It must have been valeted. You buy a seven-year-old van, you don't often get it valeted first.'

Only if someone has something to hide, thought Voss. Aloud he said, 'Can you remember when you bought it? Exactly when – the day, or at least what part of the week?'

He could have asked a hundred people and eight years on they'd have had no idea. But Arnold Warboys measured his life in market-days. 'It was a Wednesday. I picked it up on my way to a little antiques sale in Pinner. I don't think it's going now but it used to be Wednesday mornings. You'd see stuff sold there on the Wednesday, then on the Saturday it'd turn up, polished and three times the price, in Kensington High Street. Jimmy Patel called me on the Tuesday afternoon to say it was in and I went to see it on my way to Pinner. It was just what I needed: I bought it, phoned my insurance and took it with me.'

When Voss related the conversation to him Deacon tried to do the maths in his head, got it wrong and had to scribble on the back on an envelope. 'So Jared Fry and his band left for Ireland on Monday June 9th, when Sasha Wade was still at home with her parents. He took the new van, and the newer of the other two, and he played most nights between the 10th and the 19th. It might just have been possible for him to come back for a few hours, but so difficult you can't imagine him doing it.

'Sasha left home on Saturday June 14th, and she took a change of clothes so she maybe wasn't expecting to be back before the start of the week.

'Eddie Rollins started stock-taking on Monday June 16th. He worked late and got home around one in the morning – the Tuesday morning – and that's when he saw the dark van parked down the garden. Fry was still in Ireland. Unless we're wrong about almost everything we think we know, Fry didn't kill her.'

Voss hesitated. But it had to be said. 'What about Chandos?'

Deacon took a deep breath and let it out again. 'He says he was in Ireland too, but no one was paying to see him and no one was interviewing him for the papers. He travels ahead of the band. He says he was in Belfast on the 16th. Do we believe him?'

'I'd want some sort of corroboration,' said Voss. 'A hotel receipt, a petrol docket – something.'

'But it's eight years ago and he says they're all gone. They probably are – mine are.' Deacon continued thinking. 'Belfast was the last stop on the tour?'

'Yes. The Wednesday and Thursday nights, 18th and 19th.'

'Right,' nodded Deacon. 'But if Chandos was there to spot problems in time to sort them out, how late would he leave it? If he was in Belfast after, say, midday on Monday 16th he didn't kill Sasha Wade either. But if he was there any earlier there might have been time for him to get back to England, meet Sasha, kill her and bury her at The Diligence on Monday night. Using the old van, which he then cleaned up and delivered to the dealer the following afternoon.'

His eyes flared suddenly wide. 'So we know *somebody* was in London by Tuesday 17th. Fry and the band were still in Ireland. The only one who could have got back to London in time to deliver that van to Patel on the Tuesday was Chandos. And if he was there Tuesday afternoon, maybe he was there by midnight on Monday.' Deacon had the bit in his teeth now. 'How long would it take him to get from Belfast to London?'

'By car? A couple of hours from Belfast to Stranraer, then a full day's driving.'

'Find out when he left Belfast.'

'He can't remember where he stayed,' said Voss apologetically.

'That's convenient,' growled Deacon. 'Then find out when he was at the concert-hall.'

'It's eight years ago…'

'Find out!'

Voss called the King's Hall in Belfast. He was lucky in that there were still people working there who remembered seeing Chandos, but after eight years no one could say precisely when the manager had arrived, how long he had spent scrutinising the arrangements, or when he had left.

Deacon slumped behind his desk, regarding his sergeant from under bushy eyebrows. 'It's not just me, is it, Charlie? It's not just me wanting him to be involved. Reading too much into some random events.'

Voss didn't think so. 'There are too many coincidences. One or two you could accept, but we keep meeting another one. Now there's the black van that was unaccounted for but still the property of the band the night one was seen at The Diligence.

'And there's the song.' He kept coming back to the song the way Deacon kept revisiting his grudge. 'Chandos says Sasha must have been at a party where Fry sang it or else knew someone who was. But it's another point of contact.'

'But why would he buy a house where he'd buried a body?'

'And if by some crazy mischance he found he had,' agreed Voss, 'why would he immediately start digging up the garden? You wouldn't. You'd put a really heavy statue on the spot to discourage anyone from digging there ever again.'

Deacon was trying to remember what they'd been told about the work. 'The pool was supposed to go at the top of the garden, beside the stable-block. The bottom of the garden was Plan B. I wonder who gave Wilmslow the go-ahead to dig there.'

'I'll ask him.'

'You do that little thing, Charlie Voss,' said Deacon. 'Because if Fry told Wilmslow to dig there, probably he didn't know there was any reason not to. But if Chandos did, that's him in the clear. Either way, you and me are taking a run up to The Diligence for another conversation with the pair of them.

'And for heaven's sake,' he added with asperity, 'get a shave first. What's wrong with your generation that you can't get up in the mornings?'

When Daniel heard Brodie's quick step on his stairs his heart plummeted. He knew immediately that Deacon had broken his word and told her. Or not that, because he hadn't given his word, but decided Brodie had to know. Seeing her face he was sure. She looked ill at ease, wound up for an encounter she knew would be difficult but had to be faced anyway. They regarded one another across the little sitting room and neither of them seemed able to start. Daniel couldn't believe it had come to this.

Her long fingers pushed the cloud of dark hair away from her face and Brodie gave him a wry half-smile. 'I'm sorry.'

Daniel's fugitive gaze slipped away, seeking refuge in the cornice and the prints on the walls and the view of the English Channel that was his back garden – anything to avoid meeting hers. He stammered his way towards a response. 'There's nothing to be sorry about. You haven't done anything… Neither have I. There's no need…'

'That's kind,' she said, 'but not entirely true. How you're feeling right now, that's my fault. And Jack's feeling pretty rough, and that's my fault too. I didn't want to hurt either of you, but the fact is you got hurt and I'm the reason.'

'Brodie,' he managed, 'I never meant to put you in this position. I shouldn't have said anything. I wish I'd kept my mouth shut. I wish Jack had. You and me: nothing's changed between us. You know what I want – I want you to be happy. It's all I ever wanted. I'm sorry if I've made it harder.'

There was a great deal about Brodie Farrell to please the eye and linger in the mind. She was tall and lithe, both shapely and strong, with classic features framed by a mass of tight dark curls. She carried herself with an elegance born of confidence, and had a way of wearing clothes that made them look more expensive than they actually were.

None of which made the impression on Daniel Hood that her eyes did. He loved her eyes. The intelligence there, the strength, even the acerbic sharpness. The woman had drawn a winning hand from the genetic pack, but none of it would have mattered to Daniel if she'd had someone else's eyes.

And the moment was coming when he had to meet them. He summoned all his courage and looked up.

Her eyes were puzzled. 'What do you mean, you wish Jack had kept his mouth shut?'

The possibility that he'd made a mistake swept over Daniel like a toxic fog, choking him. He struggled desperately to remember what he'd said, to think what he should say now. 'I… What? What are you talking about?'

She raised her hand and laid a butterfly touch on his bruised cheek. 'This. What's Eric Chandos to you or you to him, that you end up carrying the print of his fist on your face? The only reason you'd know one another in the street is me. The only reason you'd reduce him to a quivering jelly, goading him until he hit back the only way he could, is me. I got you hurt again, Daniel, and I'm sorry.'

His skin registered her touch as spots of cool fire. He put his own hand to his cheek as if to preserve the sensation. He said carefully, 'It was absolutely, positively, worth it.'

Brodie chuckled and her arm went about him in a quick hug. 'So where does Jack come into it?'

This close to the precipice he dared not stumble. 'I said something to Jack that I hoped he wouldn't repeat. I was tired and a bit upset, and I said something stupid. Then when you came here…'

'You thought he'd been telling tales out of school,' finished Brodie with an indulgent smile. 'It's all right, Daniel. You were entitled to be angry – I don't mind you bad-mouthing me to Jack. As for him grassing you up – *how* long have you known Jack Deacon? I don't suppose he was even listening. I'm damn sure he's forgotten everything you said by now.'

Daniel smiled uncertainly and shrugged. 'Maybe.' But he really didn't think so.

Norman Wilmslow remembered the discussions that followed his abortive attempt to excavate beside the stable-block. They involved a number of men who were all eager to avoid the blame, and the longer the debate went on and the hotter it became, the surer Wilmslow was that any time now it would be all his fault.

'So who suggested putting the pool at the bottom of the garden?'
'I did,' said the builder.

Which wasn't the answer Voss wanted. 'Why?'

'Because there were no other structures down there to interfere with it. Why do you think builders like greenfield sites? It's easier and cheaper than building where there are pipes and cables under the ground.'

'Still, I don't suppose you told the clients that was where their pool was going and they could like it or lump it. I presume you got somebody to OK it first.'

'Of course I did. Though there wasn't much to think about. Between building considerations and planning considerations and what-all else, it was put it there or put it on the long finger.'

'So who told you to go ahead?'
'The big man,' said Wilmslow.

Chapter Twenty-Four

The phone rang. Brodie waved Daniel to take it. She had the feeling they weren't entirely done yet, and she slipped off her shoes and curled up cat-like on the sofa to ponder why. Something he'd said, some look he'd had... He'd thought there was another reason for her coming here.

It took Daniel a minute to work out who was calling him. Someone with a comprehensive vocabulary of expletives, certainly, and a sense of grievance fuelling them, but there weren't enough other words – nouns, verbs – for the litany to make sense. All he could be sure of was that he'd managed to annoy someone, and for once he didn't think it was Deacon. He said, 'If you'll calm down for a minute and tell me what the problem is...'

As soon as he'd said it he knew: both the caller's identity and the nature of his problem. He couldn't calm down. The chemicals ravaging his brain left him unable to discriminate between a setback and a disaster, so he could be reduced to incoherent rage by trivial inconveniences then sit and watch a cigarette burn a hole in his thigh because sometimes even pain was a phenomenon that applied only to other people.

'Jared? Is that you? Jared – stop yelling for a minute and tell me what's happened.'

The rage was genuine, thick as curd in his voice, but behind it Daniel heard fear. Perhaps fear lies behind most fury. He still wasn't finishing many sentences, but some gist of a narrative began to emerge. 'You fly bastard! You offer me... And then you rip the rug...! I *know* what you think of him. I know what you think of me. So? It's too late to... it's too... It's just too late. This is it, this is my life. I need him. I can't *manage* alone.'

Daniel said again, 'What's happened?'

'You know what's happened! You sent them. You told them... And they're going to lock him up, and I... I'm...' His voice choked to silence.

'The police have arrested Chandos? What for?'

'Because you told them to, you bastard!'

Daniel sighed. 'Jared, I have trouble making twelve-year-olds do what I tell them, let alone policemen. Whatever they're doing, it's nothing to do with me.'

'I'm supposed to believe that? Eric knocks you down and next morning the police come for him? He was right about you. A man would have got up and hit him back. Telling the police is what little girls do.'

'Jared, you can believe me or not, as you like, but I didn't tell the police anything. They may have seen – it did happen on their doorstep – but after you went home, I went home. If they've arrested Chandos it isn't because of anything I did.'

'Then tell them to let him go!'

Daniel rolled his eyes to the ceiling. He wasn't getting through. He looked questioningly over the phone at Brodie, and she made an impatient gesture then nodded.

'All right,' said Daniel, 'I'm on my way. I don't know what good it'll do, but if you want me there I'll come.'

Jared Fry grunted and put the phone down.

'Such a charming man,' murmured Daniel. He looked at Brodie in some embarrassment. 'I'm sorry to ask but would you take me up there? You needn't wait, I'll get a lift back with someone.'

'We'll see,' said Brodie; which was Brodie-esque for *The shit has hit the fan and someone who let me down has been arrested, possibly for murder, and you expect me to keep a discreet distance? Have we actually met?*

Daniel knew he'd lost that one when she drove round the back of The Diligence and parked in the courtyard. 'So you'll wait for me here?' he suggested hopefully.

'Of course I will,' she said, getting out of the car and leading the way to the kitchen door. He followed like a disconsolate spaniel who hasn't put up a pheasant all day.

Miriam let them in, clearly relieved to see them. As the door opened a barrage of noise hit them. Daniel – who'd been subjected to something similar fifteen minutes earlier – knew what it was: Fry bouncing off the walls. He tracked the rumpus to the hall.

Chandos's PA, a tall girl with straight brown hair and the expression of a dyspeptic camel, was trying to restore some kind of order and failing. Other members of the staff were there too, making token attempts to net Fry as he hurtled past. A sharp uppercut would have stopped him in his tracks, but none of those equipped to deliver one was prepared to and Daniel didn't do fisticuffs. Daniel talked.

He tapped the whirlwind on the shoulder as it passed and said, in an even voice as if nothing much was happening, 'Let's go somewhere quiet and talk.' He headed for the glass turret where he hoped, stripped of his audience, Fry might calm down.

After a moment, rather sheepishly, Jared Fry packed away his tantrum and followed.

To Brodie, anything short of a locked door was an open invitation. She went too.

At the foot of the stairs she came face to face with Deacon, who'd despaired of making any progress with his inquiry when he couldn't hear the lies he was being told and had come through the sitting-room door like the little man in the Bavarian weather-house, red-faced and yelling, 'What the hell is all this noise?'

When he saw Brodie he blinked. He couldn't think what her presence here meant – at least, he hoped he couldn't. She smiled at him, he squinted at her. She leaned forward and kissed him quickly on the cheek, then she was gone.

Brodie had been in every room in The Diligence when she was negotiating the purchase. The solar was part of the central upstairs flat where Miss Carolgee the lecturer in economics had kept her train set. (She'd tried to explain it away as a treat for visiting nephews. Brodie hadn't believed her, and the two women had spent a happy hour on their hands and knees on the floor, whistling *The Flying Scotsman* through Astroturf tunnels.)

The layout was gone now, in its place a beanbag sofa and a low table with a tray on it. When she saw what was on the tray she pursed her lips but said nothing. She sat on the sofa and let the men shift for themselves.

Daniel had his hands in his trouser pockets. Brodie had noticed him do this in heated situations, and finally she'd worked out why. It was an declaration that, however events developed, he at least would not be provoked to violence. Like many things he did, it was a two-sided coin. It should have made him vulnerable. In fact it made him appear in control, of himself and the situation. One day – perhaps today – someone would be sufficiently exasperated with this bit of mindplay to respond with a good thump, but mostly it had the effect of defusing anger and making people take a step back.

'All right, Jared,' he said, 'so what's this all about? Why are you so angry? The police have been here on and off all week. They've talked to you and they've talked to Chandos. You know why: they're trying to make sense of what they found in the garden. They ask questions, you answer them, they go away. Why do you think it's different this time?'

In the same way that Daniel used weakness as a weapon, Fry used anger as a defence. With every step up through his old house it had been seeping away, leaving him unprotected. He sounded like a child. 'They won't let me see him.'

'Why is that a problem?'

'Because... because...'

Because it raised the spectre that if this ended badly Jared Fry could be left alone, and he no longer knew how to deal with that. He depended on Chandos in the same way that he was dependent on heroin.

Brodie hadn't a massive supply of patience and the reserve with his name on it was rapidly running out. But it's hard to remain unfeeling when someone's in that much distress. His predicament might have been of his own making but then, so was hers. A little kindness goes further at such a time than any other. She moved to one end of the sofa and patted the seat beside her. 'Sit down and we'll see if we can help.'

But it wasn't her help he wanted. There was something about Daniel that made it easy to accept his friendship. It might have been the way they met, or what people who didn't know him very well saw as his undemanding nature. But Brodie was different. Fry blamed a lot of his present difficulties on Brodie Farrell. A rational man would have recognised that she was only doing what he paid her for when she brought him to this house of ill omen, but Fry was not a rational man. Common sense is the first casualty of addiction, as instinct is the last. Instinctively he felt that his problems began with her. She'd brought him to this house, she'd bewitched the man he relied on to keep the chaos at bay, finally she'd brought the enmity of a powerful adversary down on them both. He blamed Brodie for Deacon's presence here and for whatever disasters would follow. He looked coldly at her hand patting the sofa and turned his back.

'Don't be childish,' said Daniel, sitting cross-legged on the rug. 'I understand that you're upset. But taking it out on us will get you nowhere. If you want to talk we'll talk; if you don't we'll go home. My life may not compare with yours for glamour and excitement, but even I have better things to do on a Saturday than sit on the floor of someone's loft while they hurl abuse at me.'

Fry was regarding him with the same puzzled expression that Brodie had seen on others confronted by the enigma that was Daniel Hood. People found it hard to stay angry with him – he was too little and too obviously decent – but they never knew quite what to do with him instead. Mostly they ended up liking him. Right now Jared Fry didn't know his left ear from Thursday week, was still breathless from trying to beat up a house, and could as easily have tried to silence the demons in his head by hurting himself or someone trying to help. Brodie would not have felt safe alone with him in this state.

But even through the mayhem he seemed able to recognise that if Daniel wasn't a friend he was probably the closest thing he had to one; if he wasn't a counsellor he talked some sense; and if he threw him out he'd be back where he'd been half an hour ago, bouncing round his big house, angry and afraid. He took a long breath, and if it wasn't exactly steady it was steadier than what had gone before. 'You want to help? I could use some help. Start by telling me why the police have arrested Eric.'

'I don't think they have,' said Daniel.

Fry's mood was on a knife-edge. He actually bared his teeth. 'They're downstairs with him now...'

'Exactly. They had you down at the police station for a couple of hours yesterday but they didn't arrest you. If they'd arrested him I don't think they'd still be here.'

'Then what – ?'

'It's an interview. It isn't very pleasant, is it? Not the way Superintendent Deacon does it.' There was an amused glint in his eye as he glanced at Brodie but she didn't argue. She knew Jack Deacon had given Daniel hard times. She also knew that Daniel had given Deacon some. These days she let them sort out their own differences: if they couldn't, if they ended up hating each other's guts, it was unfortunate but needn't affect her relationship with either of them.

'And you didn't send them here?'

Even Daniel ran out of patience eventually. 'Jared, what exactly do you think I am? An Assistant Chief Constable in a really good disguise? I'm not tall enough to be a policeman! Can we try to stay on nodding terms with reality here? If you think Jack Deacon does what I tell him, that stuff' – he glanced at the tray – 'has eaten up more of your brain than I thought.'

'Then why won't he leave us alone?' It was a child's wail in a man's voice.

'Because he found a body in your back garden!'

It was the wrong thing to say. It reminded Fry of his grievance.

He swung on Brodie as if she'd carefully Tippexed the information out of the property details. 'This is your fault. If you'd found what I asked for, and Eric hadn't been horny enough to take anything you offered, we'd never have come here. Your boyfriend would be turning somebody else's life upside down!'

Some criticism, some insults, Brodie could take with equanimity. Not many, to be sure, but some. But criticising her professionalism was almost like disparaging her child. She swelled with indignation. 'I found you *exactly* what you asked for. To the cellar; to the trees in the garden. Such a long and foolish list I have never seen in my life, but somehow I managed to find you a property with everything on it. If you still didn't like it you shouldn't have bought it. Only you were too idle to actually look at it before you signed on the dotted line!'

'What are you *talking* about,' yelled Fry, close enough in her face for her to smell the sourness on his breath, 'cellars and trees? I wanted a swimming pool. The *only* thing I particularly wanted was a swimming pool. Eric wanted space for a studio, and he may have cared about things like security and privacy, but trees? Do we *look* like tree-huggers?'

Brodie didn't believe this conversation. She shook her head fiercely. 'Listen, Mr Fry, I don't know how the two of you came up with the list of your requirements. Maybe it was a joint effort and you've forgotten – which, let's face it, would not be that surprising – or maybe Eric compiled it on the basis of what he thought you needed rather than what you said you wanted. I don't know. I don't even care. But I have the original in my office, with his signature on it, and I can tell you right now there is no mention of a swimming pool. He got what he asked for. As for you – I don't know *what* you want any more.'

'No?' Fry fired back. 'Well, it so happens I can help you with that. I can tell you exactly what I asked for, because I wrote it down.' He yanked out the table drawer viciously enough for the contents to spill across the floorboards. Among them was a small hardbacked ledger. He snatched it up and threw it into her lap so roughly that she covered her face with her hands. 'See for yourself.'

She was minded to throw it right back at him. But when she realised what it was, curiosity stopped her. She was holding something that many people considered priceless – the songbook of a rockstar, the place where music worth millions had its genesis. If her daughter ever asked how it felt to hold Jared Fry's songbook, she didn't want to have to confess that she didn't really know, she only had it for a second before throwing it at his head.

And then, she wanted to be able to call him a liar. She opened the book, looking for what he said was there.

'Daniel,' she said quietly after a moment. 'Look at this.' He got up and came to read it over her shoulder.

Fry hadn't invented it: it was a house-hunter's wish-list. Two people had worked on it: two hands and two pens had contributed their suggestions. A lot of it was scrawled in a thick black nylon-tip. Brodie flicked through the ledger and found most of the contents were set down in the same way. That was Jared Fry. Adding to the list, and in places amending it, was a ballpoint wielded by a more precise hand.

'Chandos?' asked Daniel.

Fry shrugged and nodded. Then he pointed. 'See?'

The first item on the list, in large black letters, was *Swimming pool*.

'I don't understand,' said Brodie blankly. 'This bears no resemblance to the list I was given. If I'd seen this list I'd never have suggested The Diligence.'

She looked to Fry, but there was no answer in his expression. He didn't believe in her list. She looked at Daniel.

Daniel knew she had neither imagined it nor remembered wrong. 'There were two lists,' he said simply.

Brodie was looking at him as if he was mad. 'Why?'

But Daniel didn't know either. 'Because this was the sort of place Chandos wanted, but he didn't think he could persuade Jared to buy it?'

Brodie was nodding slowly. 'I suppose. God knows, Devious is his middle name. He *could* have compiled two lists: the one in the book, so Jared believed his requirements were being taken into account, and the one that he gave to me. The amount of interest Jared was taking in the purchase, he was never going to realise he'd been conned until it was too late. And then' – she glared at him – 'he was going to blame me.'

Daniel was still troubled. 'Chandos doesn't strike me as a man who'd care so much about where he was going to live that he'd think it worth lying about.'

'He isn't.' Fry's gaze was autocratic. 'But then, I don't think he's the one who's lying.'

Brodie gritted her teeth and tried to remember the nice big cheque he'd signed for her.

Daniel paid them no heed. He was trying to work this out. 'So Chandos wrote up a list of features distinct from the one he and Jared worked on, and he gave it to you and sent you off house-hunting with it.'

'Because he wanted a house like The Diligence,' said Brodie.

'No,' said Daniel, and his voice was thin as if he was surprising himself. 'Because he wanted The Diligence.'

Brodie frowned, deeply sceptical. 'The place wasn't even for sale then.'

'No, it wasn't. But it was in the news. The planning application, remember? Chandos had seen it, he thought there was every chance you would have too.'

If anything, Brodie's puzzlement was deepening. 'What are you saying? That Eric decided Jared was going to buy this place, then gave me a wish-list that could only be met here?'

'I think so, yes. You said yourself, the requirements you were given it was a miracle you found anywhere to match them. Well no, it wasn't a miracle: the list was carefully tailored to minimise the competition.'

'And if I hadn't seen the story about The Diligence?'

'Knowing what's going on is part of your job,' said Daniel. 'But if you had missed it he'd have found some way to casually draw your attention to it.'

'But *why*?' demanded Brodie.

'Because he didn't want his fingerprints on it. He wanted it to be someone else's suggestion.'

Fry didn't even believe in a second list, but if there was one he didn't understand the reason for it any more than Brodie did. 'You're saying Eric wanted this place so much he was prepared to lie to me to get it.' Daniel nodded. 'I'm with her. Why?'

Daniel watched him for some indication that actually he knew, but there was none. 'Brodie, would you nip downstairs and get Jack?'

The words were casual enough. But when Brodie went to ask why his eyes stopped her dead. 'All right,' she said demurely, heading for the door.

When she was gone Fry relaxed a little. He sat down wearily on the sofa. All the fury, and the energy it had fuelled, had dissipated, leaving him tired and uncertain. 'You're wrong about this. Why would Eric want to come here? And if he did, why wouldn't he just tell me? I always end up doing what he wants. He knows that.'

Daniel's voice was quiet, apologetic. 'He wanted you to buy The Diligence because he knew what was in the garden. And...' He left the sentence unfinished.

They'd come too far for that. '*And?*' prompted Fry.

'And he didn't want you to know who turned you in.'

It was a long time since Jared Fry had had any colour to speak of. The living-dead make-up that was part of his stage persona was a flattery: when it came off he looked more corpse-like than ever.

Even so, whatever blood the heroin had spared him left his cheeks now. 'You think I killed her. That I killed her, and Eric knew. That eight years of protecting me were enough, and when he saw a chance to get the truth told he took it.' His voice was ghostly with shock.

Daniel nodded. 'Yes.'

'You're wrong. I didn't know Sasha Wade, and I didn't kill her.'

'But Jared – would you even know?'

'That I'd *killed* someone? Murdered a nineteen-year-old girl? Of *course* I'd know!'

'Do you remember threatening Brodie?' No answer came. None was needed: the look in the other man's eyes was enough. Daniel explained. 'When you went to her office you were as high as a kite and you told her to leave Chandos alone. You said if she didn't you'd burn her house down.'

No one's that good an actor: plainly Fry had no recollection of making the threat. He gasped for breath like a flying fish on the deck of a Whitbread racer. 'I said that? Why am I not behind bars?'

Daniel sighed. 'Because she didn't think you meant it, she didn't think you'd remember saying it, and she didn't think you'd be capable of doing anything about it even if you did.

'Maybe she should have told the police anyway. Maybe I should. We didn't know, then, that there was any connection between you and the dead girl. Even so, maybe we shouldn't have let it pass. Not everyone who makes threats will become violent, but most people who become violent first made threats.'

Fry was shaking his head in slow disbelief. 'I don't remember. I really don't remember.'

'I know,' said Daniel. 'Look, you didn't hurt Brodie, you didn't try to hurt her, maybe it was – literally – poppycock. But if you can forget that, that happened four days ago, why do you think your memory of eight years back can be trusted?'

'There's a difference,' struggled Fry. 'Between saying something stupid and picking up a rock and beating someone's head in! If I'd done that, I'd remember.'

'Is that how she died?' asked Daniel softly.

'I don't know!' shouted Fry. 'It was – an example. Words. Words I can do – at least, I could once. But killing somebody? I wouldn't know where to start.'

'By picking up a rock in the heat of the moment.'

'I don't know she was killed with a rock!' yelled Fry.

Footsteps on the stair and Brodie was back, alone. She sidled diffidently over to Daniel and whispered in his ear.

He turned to look at her. His face was blank. 'What?'

'I said,' she repeated with a kind of embarrassed restraint, 'he was out of the country when the girl went into the ground. And he had been for a week.'

It was as if he'd reported spotting a new comet only to have it come off when he polished his objective lens. On the heels of disbelief came mortification. He didn't know where to look, what to say. *Sorry* didn't really cover it.

All the same... 'Jared, I'm sorry. I thought – I was afraid... I didn't want to believe it but the facts seemed to point that way. I'm glad I was wrong.' He turned to leave, anticipating at every moment a furious hail of small objects, or possibly blows.

'Wait.' Fry's voice was hard, the quiver of panic replaced by an edge of steel. 'You aren't going anywhere.'

Daniel did as he was told. If Fry wanted to black his eye he thought it was the least he was owed. He'd called the man a murderer. He'd accused him of killing a teenage girl and not even remembering. If Fry wanted to beat him bloody he wouldn't raise a hand in his own defence.

'Not till we make some sense of this,' gritted Fry. 'You said Eric knew she was there.'

'It seemed the only explanation.'

'You thought that meant I'd put her there. But it didn't. So what does it mean instead?'

'I don't know,' admitted Daniel. 'I thought I did but I was wrong.'

'Damn sure you were wrong,' snarled Fry, 'but not about all of it.' He scowled at Brodie. 'You're sure the list Eric gave you is different to mine?'

'Yes,' she said. 'I'll print you a copy if you want.'

He shook his head, the rats' tails in his eyes. He didn't want to but he believed her. 'So why was Eric so determined to come here?'

'Maybe the items on the list were things he wanted,' suggested Brodie, 'but wanted you to pay for.'

Fry's face was dark and perplexed. 'He doesn't use the cellar or walk in the woods, and I haven't seen him looking at the view yet. No, Daniel's right – he gave you that list because this was where he wanted to come. He made it impossible for you to find us anywhere else. He wanted The Diligence, only he didn't want either of us to know that. For pity's sake, somebody, tell me why!'

Against his better judgement, still appalled at the magnitude of his error, Daniel was trying to find him an answer. His face wrinkled with the effort. Then it cleared.

Brodie saw it happen. She waited for him to speak. But this time he had to be sure: he went through it in his mind time and again, looking for traps. He wasn't accusing anyone of anything until he'd ruled out everything else.

Finally he said, 'There are two reasons for locking a door. To keep people in, and to keep people out.'

Jared Fry stared uncomprehending into his face. 'What the hell are you talking about?'

Daniel tried again. 'Hidden things have a habit of getting found. If you desperately need something to stay hidden you have two options. You can put it somewhere so remote that hopefully no one will ever look there. Or you can keep it close by, watch over it and make sure no one will ever look there.'

Brodie at least was beginning to see where he was going with this. 'Or you could do one, and afterwards realise it was a mistake. In which case, if you got the chance to put it right, you'd take it.'

Daniel nodded. 'He got away with it for eight years. Then he read about the plan to build more flats here. That would mean construction machinery and digging. New service pipes, more car parking, more of everything. A massive risk that she'd be found. But also an opportunity he'd never have again. Once he moved Jared in here he could make sure no one dug in the garden. At least, he thought he could.'

'But he didn't want anyone to know that buying The Diligence was his idea,' Brodie continued slowly, working it out, 'because one day the worst could happen. If she was found, he wanted it on record that it wasn't his idea to come here. So he hired me and provided me with a list of requirements that could hardly be satisfied anywhere else.'

Now even Fry was catching up. 'You're saying... *Eric* killed this girl? *Why?*'

'I have no idea,' admitted Daniel. 'Except I think it has something to do with that song. *Crucifiction.*'

'*My* song,' Fry said stubbornly.

'Your song, her song – if we knew for sure I think we'd know why she died.' Daniel's gaze dropped to the sofa. 'That's your song-book?' Fry nodded. 'How far back does it go?'

Fry gave a throaty laugh. 'All the way. How many songs do you think I've written?'

'So *Crucifiction* is in there? Can I see?'

Fry shrugged and opened the ledger. But for a moment he seemed reluctant to pass it over. As if it was a baby and he wasn't sure he was putting it in safe hands.

'Please,' said Daniel softly.

Fry gave it to him. 'Anyway,' he said roughly, 'if he'd gone to that much trouble Eric would hardly have let the builder dig her up after all!'

'I don't think he did,' said Daniel absently, poring over the pages. 'I think you did.'

Fry shook his head. 'I'd remember.'

'No,' said Daniel, 'you wouldn't.'

She was reluctant to contradict but Brodie knew Daniel was wrong again. 'Charlie asked Mr Wilmslow who OK'd him to dig there. He said it was Eric.'

Daniel thought for a moment. 'It can't have been. Not if we're right about any of this. Have you got your phone?'

Daniel had called Wilmslow three times a week for months during the work on his house: the number was branded on his brain. Brodie punched it in.

Wilmslow was working in his garden. Brodie could hear a strimmer in the background. 'Hello? Yes?'

She told him what she wanted so matter-of-factly that he answered without wondering if she had any right to ask. 'I told the police. I asked the big man and he said to go ahead.'

Brodie shook her head at Daniel. 'He says you're wrong.'

'May I?' He took the phone. 'Mr Wilmslow – Daniel Hood. Do you mean the big man with the beard – Eric Chandos?'

'What? No, the chap who's paying the bill. The owner. The big man.'

Daniel wanted it in words of one syllable. 'Who are you talking about? Who did you speak to about the test-pit?'

'Fry,' said Norman Wilmslow. 'He was a bit dozy on it, but I couldn't find Mr Chandos and it is Fry's house. I thought, if he don't mind a hole in his lawn why should anyone else?'

Daniel gave Brodie her phone back and for a moment they just looked at one another. Then Brodie nodded slowly. 'When the digger hit pipes behind the stables Mr Wilmslow needed new instructions. Jared was there and Eric wasn't. Wilmslow asked if he should sink a test-pit down the garden and Jared said yes. He didn't know there was any reason not to.'

Criminal detection is an intellectual exercise right up to the point where you remember that someone got hurt. That moment arrived for Brodie just then. It wasn't a puzzle: it concerned a girl's death, and the fact that she was nineteen and never got to be twenty, and if they were right someone they knew was responsible for that. For killing her. For shovelling her out of sight under the leafy ground and letting her family mourn in ignorance for eight years.

And this – Brodie swallowed – was a man she knew. In the Biblical sense if not, it now appeared, any other way. Her skin had thrilled to the touch of hands which had killed. For a moment there was a real danger she would throw up.

Not Daniel, who was preoccupied with the songbook, but Fry saw the nausea swamp her face and reached out to steady her. 'You OK?'

'Yes,' she answered quickly. Then, more honestly, 'No, not really, but thanks for asking. It's just, suddenly this is real. The skeleton in the garden was a real girl and we probably know her name and we probably know who killed her. All we don't know is why.'

Wordlessly, Daniel pushed the tray to the end of the table and put the songbook down, open, the pages scrawled in thick black ink. Brodie could make out the title at the top and not much else.

'See?' said Fry, suppressing the satisfaction in his voice because it might seem crass in the circumstances. 'I told you it was my song.'

But if what he'd seen had made Daniel revise his opinion he'd have said so. Brodie picked up the book.

It was heavier than she'd expected and three-quarters full. It was open about half way through. By knitting her brows and peering at the scrawl slightly sideways she was able to read what was written there – helped by the fact that the words were now quite familiar.

When she'd finished she looked at Daniel interrogatively. He looked away. Using her finger as a bookmark, she flicked back and forth through the pages. Then she saw what he had seen.

'Jared,' she asked carefully, 'how long does it take you to write a song?'

He shrugged. 'Depends.'

'I'm sure it does. But in general, are we talking hours or months?'

'A few hours for the first draft. I'll rework it over the next few days, then come back to it several times before we record it. That might take a couple of months. It might take longer.'

'And some come easier than others?'

He gave a mirthless grin. 'It's like giving birth. Sometimes it's a yell, a rush of blood and there's a baby in your arms, and sometimes it's out with the forceps.'

Brodie leafed through the book again, noting the dates by each title. 'You wrote more at the start of your career than you have recently.'

Fry was defensive. 'There's more to do now. We're on tour a lot of the year.'

'I'm sure,' nodded Brodie. 'And then – forgive me – by the time you wrote *Crucifiction* you were already on heroin?'

'Way before that. So?'

She sighed. 'Being stoned makes people feel creative but it's an illusion. I bet it was getting harder to put together songs that still looked good in the cold light of day six or seven years ago.'

'It was never easy,' gritted Fry.

'But the results used to be better,' Daniel said gently. 'You told me that.'

Jared Fry only bristled. '*Crucifiction's* a damn good song. Ask anyone.'

'Of course it is,' agreed Brodie. 'It's a classic of the genre. It defines you as an artist. I'm not knocking the song, I'm trying to understand how it came to be written. And why this song, and a lot of the songs that came after it, were written in a different way to the ones that went before.'

He didn't know what she meant. Frowning, he leaned over to look.

Brodie flicked the book back several pages. 'I know nothing about songwriting, all right? But this is what I'd expect – a lot of writing down, scribbling out, writing over, writing in the margin, starting again. This song, from 1995, was worked and reworked until it satisfied you. To judge from the different pens, you had several sessions with it. And then you were happy that you'd got it right. Yes?'

Fry nodded and then shrugged. He still didn't see what she was getting at, what she and Daniel had both seen.

'So why is *Crucifiction* different? Did it really spring from your brain word-perfect? Did you really not want to change anything from when it came into your head?'

There wasn't an alteration on the page. It seemed to have flowed from his brain, down his fingers and off the end of his pen in its finished state, exactly as he would sing it. Perfect.

Fry said off-handedly, 'I must have worked it out in my head, only written it down when it was right.'

'Perhaps,' said Daniel. He indicated the bottom of the page where a spider appeared to have got drunk and fallen into an inkwell. 'What's this?'

'That's the music,' said Fry through clenched teeth.

It wasn't formal notation such as classical musicians would be familiar with. Perhaps it would have made sense to another rockstar, or perhaps these dashes and squiggles were a language unique to Jared Fry. What was clear was that he'd written the music exactly as he'd written the words: in one great out-pouring of creativity, without a note being subsequently changed.

Brodie was nodding slowly, but not because she was convinced. 'Well, for whatever reason, you wrote *Crucifiction* in a different way to how you wrote all the earlier songs. But afterwards there are others written the same way. Not all of them. Half, maybe more, are scribbled and rubbed out and rewritten like the earlier ones. But among them are' – she flicked through the pages, counting – 'maybe twenty that look the way *Crucifiction* looks. As if you knew exactly what you wanted to say and how to say it before you ever opened this book.'

Daniel didn't take the book back. He knew what was in it. 'And after those twenty songs were written the muse departed. Everything you've produced since has been written the same way as your early songs: with a lot of effort, a lot of input, a lot of corrections and improvements. Just…'

He managed to stop the words but not the thought. 'Just not the same results?' said Fry bitterly. He didn't need anyone to point out that his talent was gone.

'I'm sorry,' murmured Daniel. 'I don't mean to hurt you. I'm trying to get at the truth.'

'Which is what? That I used to be a better songwriter than I am now? Hell, Daniel, I'd figured that out myself. What other revelations have you got lined up?'

Daniel's eyes were full of regrets. He knew exactly what he was about to do: destroy another human being. 'Jared, you didn't write those twenty songs. Sasha Wade wrote them. You just copied them down when you were too doped-up to remember.'

Deacon waited until Voss had returned from speaking to Brodie. 'What did she want?'

Voss explained discreetly into his ear.

Deacon didn't do discreet. 'Speak up, Charlie Voss.'

Voss sighed. 'She wanted to tell us that Daniel has worked out who killed Sasha Wade.'

'Oh? Who?'

'Jared Fry.'

That quiver like a small earthquake behind his craggy features was Deacon trying not to laugh. 'What did you tell her?'

'That Fry was several hundred miles and a body of water away, performing in front of several thousand people, when Sasha died.'

'That's our Daniel for you,' Deacon remarked tolerantly to Eric Chandos. 'Great thinker. Terrific thinker. You wouldn't believe the times he's been nearly right about things.'

'Which makes two of you,' smiled Chandos. It wasn't just confidence: it was an arrogance that would have cut patterns on glass.

'That's about par for the course,' nodded Deacon, refusing to rise. 'You come up with a theory, it isn't right; you try something else, that isn't right either. But you're getting closer all the time, and when you get it right you find the proof. Which is actually all that counts. Courts aren't interested in what I think. They're not even interested in what I know. They're interested in what I can prove.'

'And exactly what can you prove, Superintendent?' Chandos's bearded jaw jutted combatively.

So Deacon told him. 'I can prove that you were in possession of a black van the night one was seen down the garden here, at about the time and place that girl was buried. I can prove that you cleaned it thoroughly before passing it on to a dealer for resale. I can prove a connection between Fry and Sasha Wade – either they wrote that song together or one copied it from the other. And that's just now, Mr Chandos. Imagine what I'll be able to prove when I've had more than an hour to absorb the fact that you murdered a nineteen-year-old girl.'

Chandos remained unshaken. 'You can't prove that. You don't know that, and I doubt you even think it. You and I both know why we're having this conversation, and it's nothing to do with the girl in the garden.'

Deacon gave a shark's-tooth grin. 'You're good, I'll give you that. Most people in your position would be getting anxious around now. A bit breathless and dewy. And that includes the innocent ones. It takes nerve to just sit there saying, *Prove it*.'

'That's not what I said,' said Chandos calmly.

'Of course not,' agreed Deacon. 'Because that's something else innocent people don't do. They don't ask me to prove their guilt, they try to prove their innocence. They get quite upset when they can't.'

'It takes a lot to upset me. More than an honest mistake that's bound to get sorted at some point.'

'Well, that's a downright generous attitude,' said Deacon appreciatively. 'I've certainly made mistakes in my time, honest and otherwise. I've accused innocent men of crimes and let guilty men go free. The former is embarrassing, but only the latter costs me sleep. Because people who've killed once are always likely to do it again. Or something else vicious and damaging. Most people have basic inbuilt inhibitions to stop them really hurting someone, whatever the provocation. They recognise that even their worst enemy is another human being and you don't end someone's life just because you're angry.

'People who kill lack that mechanism. They don't get angrier than other people, they just find it easier to ignore the warning lights. Everyone *feels* they're more important than anyone else: those who kill really believe it. They put their own interests, desires, needs, whims even, ahead of other people's basic rights. And not just once but again and again. Sometimes we get them not because they've killed again but because they've done something else no reasonable person would do.'

'I understand what you're saying,' nodded Chandos, 'but you're wrong. I behaved badly towards Mrs Farrell – though of course it was she who behaved badly towards you – and for what it's worth I regret that. Our... involvement... was one of those things that comes out of nowhere, that don't even mean very much except for a few days when they mean everything.

'But that sort of thing happens to everyone. Sometimes you're the bandit, sometimes you're the coach. You have to be philosophical about it. In particular, you don't have to let it affect how you do your job. Accusing me of murder to pay back a personal grudge is unprofessional.'

Deacon's eyes were wide with admiration. 'Mr Chandos, it's a real treat for me to be dealing with an educated man for once. Sometimes you're the bandit and sometimes... I must remember that. Never got past O-levels myself so I wouldn't have thought to put it that way. With me, everything's black and white. Right or wrong.' His voice hardened so fractionally Chandos might have imagined it. 'True or false. No wonder Mrs Farrell was drawn to an erudite gentleman like yourself.

'But you're right, we should put that behind us. It has no bearing on what happened here eight years ago. The fact that I've seen you behaving like trash in recent days doesn't prove that you behaved the same way towards Sasha Wade.' Again the fractional change of tone, the distant rumble of shifting goalposts. 'But it does suggest you might have done. It's what I was saying about people who kill – they treat other people as if they have no value. As if using them is all right.'

Chandos kept a sofa in his office for the same reason Brodie had one in hers. His was bigger. Even so, Deacon just about filled it. He spread one broad hand on each arm.

'I've thought and thought about it, Mr Chandos, and I can only come up with three explanations for your behaviour. The kindest is that you were skittled by Mrs Farrell and didn't know what you were doing. Well, that I can understand. The second is that you knew what you were doing but you didn't care. Didn't care if you hurt her, certainly didn't care what effect it might have on me because you'd no reason to court my goodwill.'

Deacon regarded Chandos speculatively. 'And the third possibility is that you knew exactly what you were doing, and deliberately set out to anger me, and if it meant hurting Brodie, never mind. Which would make you one of those people we were talking about – the ones who ignore warning lights. I could believe that about you, Mr Chandos. I could believe you put so much more value on your own importance than anyone else's that you'd have no qualms about going through someone to get what you want. In this case, me hating your guts. The question then is, why?'

Chandos's gaze challenged him to find an answer. 'It'd be a pretty silly thing to do if I'd carried out the murder you were investigating.'

'That's what I thought too,' agreed Deacon. 'At first. Then I wondered if it wouldn't be a pretty smart thing to do.'

Eric Chandos leaned back in his expensive black leather chair, apparently seeking patience among the oak beams of the ceiling. 'All right, superintendent,' he said finally, 'have it your way. However often I tell you you're wrong, that I didn't know this girl and I certainly didn't kill her, I can't make you believe me. I think you're going to have to arrest me and charge me with something. Should I have my solicitor meet us at the police station?'

Nice normal people who don't commit terrible crimes but occasionally wonder what it would be like to be accused of one think that beating the rap depends on giving the right answers. On having a watertight alibi, and a few corruptible friends to vouch for it.

Here's a tip, only you didn't hear it from me. No alibi is as difficult to break as no alibi at all. The suspect detectives dread above all others is the one who denies, and continues to deny, all knowledge of the crime without providing any supporting evidence that can be checked and found wanting. 'I didn't do it; I had a headache and went to bed early; I didn't go out and no one saw me,' is a story that will stand up to anything short of, and sometimes even including, eyewitness testimony.

Of course, traces of the victim's blood on your boots will always be a problem.

Chandos may have known this, or he may simply have run out of different ways of saying, 'It wasn't me.' Either way, it was a good move. Charging someone starts a clock that runs as inexorably as anything in Poe. There's time to iron out some of the wrinkles, there isn't time to build a case. The material elements need to be in place first. Nine times out of ten, an officer given the choice Chandos was giving Deacon will show his suspect the door.

That isn't, of course, the end of the matter. It may be a reflection of how close he is to tying up the loose ends, that the detective will opt to release his suspect – knowing he'll be seeing more of him sooner rather than later – rather than risk compromising his case.

But the clock doesn't start ticking while the parties are merely chatting in the suspect's study, even after the tea and biscuits are gone and the questions have turned pointed. Deacon wasn't ready either to move up a gear or to finish. He dealt with the ultimatum the way he dealt with so many, by ignoring it.

'So it took Fry a couple of years to write that song of his? Seems a lot of effort for a page of scrawl. A few hundred words. Shakespeare wrote a couple of Henries, a Richard, that thing with the donkey and half a dozen sonnets in the same sort of time.'

'Perhaps he wasn't performing them as well,' smiled Chandos.

'Actually,' said Deacon, meeting his gaze in a way that was the human equivalent of bighorn sheep clashing heads in the mountains, 'I think he was.'

Chandos shrugged. 'He must have been better at it, then.'

'You can't say that,' said Jared Fry. Shock was a breathy pant in his voice. 'It isn't true.'

'I'm not suggesting,' said Daniel gently, 'you knew that's what you were doing. You use heroin because you think it takes you where the ideas are, and you come back with a new song in your head. But what if it's only there because someone put it there?'

Fry was as dismissive as only a scared man can be. 'You don't know what you're talking about. Creative artists have always taken drugs. Because it works. It filters out the garbage, opens the mind. It…'

'It left you vulnerable to a kind of post-hypnotic suggestion,' said Brodie plainly. 'You scored, you wandered off to Planet Zog and you came back with a brand new song buzzing round your head. And yes, some of them were yours, but some of them were Sasha's. They're so polished Eric must have dictated them to you word by word, and hummed you the tune, as you were surfacing. And you weren't even aware of it. The first you knew, you had a new song in your book, in your handwriting, and no memory of how it got there. But they weren't your songs.'

'But – how would he even know her… ?'

'I imagine she asked him to handle her career the way he'd handled yours,' said Brodie. 'She sang her songs for him and he realised what they were worth.'

'And he killed her for them?' Fry's deep voice soared.

'I think so. They got together while you were in Ireland. She ended up dead, he ended up with a book full of top-class songs. A God-send for a man whose milch-cow was drying up.'

'You don't remember writing them,' murmured Daniel. 'You told me that. You take psychotropic drugs, all you know is that when you come round you've done it again – written another great song. Only you haven't. You've just written it down.'

'You're crazy,' spat Fry, almost as if he believed it. 'You couldn't do that if you tried.'

Daniel shook his head. 'It's amazing what you can do when you try, if scruples don't get in the way. That's how brainwashing works.

You drug someone, tell him something while his conscious discrimination is off-line, and he wakes up believing it. It's how subliminal advertising was meant to work – and maybe does work, how would we know? We can't – any more than you could know that what was coming out of your head was someone else's thoughts.'

Fry hardly knew how to react. Men who have lost limbs report a space in which there's no pain because the nerves are traumatised. It was like that. Something vital to him, something precious and irreplaceable, had been taken from him, and the fact that it wasn't hurting yet was scant comfort. Grazed knees and paper-cuts hurt then heal. This was too big to hurt.

He said again, 'You're crazy.' But he knew it was the truth. Perhaps part of him had known all along, a detached part of his psyche that remained aware when the rest of him was cocooned in feather-bed layers of heroin, that was there when his manager took out the book from which he read, at intervals calculated to provide a undiminished reputation and the income that went with it, the regular bedtime story. Perhaps Daniel wasn't telling him what had happened so much as reminding him.

But didn't Fry want to hear it. If part of him already knew, the rest of him had walled it up out of his ken. Perhaps his addiction was less about self-indulgence than self-defence. He had come to terms – there had been no choice – with being an ex-songwriter, a flame that had burnt brightly and then died. He could live with that because his legacy to himself was some of the best songs he'd ever heard. Now he faced a more brutal reality: that those songs were in fact written by someone else. By a girl who, as his was fading, produced a talent so extraordinary she died of it.

His voice fell to a whisper. 'None of these songs was mine?'

Daniel Hood was a kind man. He knew that Fry had taken a pride in his work long after there was any reason to take pride in himself. He took no pleasure in wresting that from him. 'Of course they were,' he said quickly. 'All the early ones. Everything up to *Crucifiction,* and a lot of the later ones. You can tell which from the book, from the way they were written. That's still an impressive body of work, Jared.'

'I thought – I *believed* – I wrote them.'

'I know. And maybe without you they'd never have been written. Sasha Wade approached Chandos instead of some other manager because she was touched by your music. And it was you who made the songs – even her songs – famous. With Sasha performing it, maybe with anyone else performing it, *Crucifiction* might never have been more than a curiosity. I know this has come as a shock. But it doesn't mean there's nothing of you in those twenty-odd songs. If you'd known you were collaborating with Sasha Wade, you'd still be pretty damn pleased with them.'

Finally Fry sat down beside Brodie. Not from choice: his knees folded and the sofa caught him. The open book was in front of him on the table. The blocky scrawl gripped his eye. Reluctantly he flicked through the pages. But there was no missing, now it had been pointed out to him, the difference between those songs and the others. Between hers and his. He sat back, his head swimming. 'What do we do now?'

The explosion Brodie had been waiting for seemed to have fizzled out. The demon rocker slumped beside her like an orphaned child, waiting to be told what his future held. She slid her hand over his. 'We'll have to tell Superintendent Deacon. I imagine he'll want to move the interview down to Battle Alley.'

'What do you want me to do?'

'I don't think there's a lot *for* you to do,' said Daniel. 'You don't remember any of this, do you? Mr Deacon will want a statement from you, but there won't be much in it. The real evidence is the book. It'll come down to whether a jury puts the same interpretation on it that we have.'

Fry's head came up with that odd admixture of arrogance and fear. He was ashamed to ask but he needed an answer. 'What about *me*?'

Brodie squeezed his hand. 'I don't think any of this was your fault. You behaved stupidly – God, you behaved stupidly, you spent so much time on mind-altering drugs that you were never going to know you were being used – but you had no part in Sasha's death and no conscious involvement in the theft of her work. I don't think you're going to prison over this.'

'But Eric is.'

Daniel nodded. 'If we're right. And if Mr Deacon can prove it.' He was looking at the book. 'We ought to give this to him and explain what it means. Will you do that or should I?'

He might as well have asked Fry which kidney he wanted to donate. The book was his child, he hadn't ventured further than a few miles from it for ten years, and though he'd now discovered he wasn't after all its biological father he still didn't want strangers taking it away.

Brodie decided for him. 'I'll take it down. I need a word with Jack anyway.' She picked it up and Fry made no attempt to stop her.

In truth, Deacon was glad of the interruption. Interrogating Chandos was as much fun as kissing a porcupine: he'd be glad when he'd had enough. But it wasn't in him to be gracious. 'What does she want this time? Has Daniel decided it was all done with mirrors and a bit of Blue Tac?'

'She wants a word outside,' said Voss.

Deacon scowled but got up, unfolding stiffly. 'Maybe she's trying to keep you out of prison,' he grunted at Chandos.

'Maybe she's trying to save you from making a fool of yourself,' countered the manager.

As soon as Deacon closed the study door behind him, Brodie took him by the arm and steered him into the sitting-room. She pushed him into a chair, pulled up one for herself and fixed him in place with the story she had to tell.

Deacon listened in silence. It was impossible to judge if he believed it or was waiting for her to draw breath so he could tell her it was nonsense. But when she showed him the book he flicked back and forth between the two types of songs and understood the point she was making.

When she'd finished, still for a few moments he said nothing. Then: 'What does Fry think of this? Does he remember Chandos dictating the songs to him?'

Brodie shook her head. 'Not even when we drew him a picture. In spite of that, he knows it's the truth. It explains things he'd never understood. Why he can't write any more. Why, when he was still writing, he could only do it when he was stoned. Why Chandos never got him off the stuff. And of course, why he was so determined to have this house that he lied to Jared and me both.'

'That was a mistake,' reflected Deacon. 'He thought it was the only house in England where he would be safe from his past. In fact, it was only by returning here that he linked himself to Sasha Wade.' He looked again at the book. 'I like this. I like it a lot. It's good enough for me, but I'm not sure it'll be good enough for the Crown Prosecution Service.'

Brodie was thinking. 'What were you going to do? If I hadn't brought you this?'

'I was about to thank the man for his time, ask him to let me know before he went off on any foreign holidays, and leave,' Deacon said honestly.

'That's exactly what you should do.' There was an unholy gleam in Brodie's eye. 'Just don't go too far away.'

Chapter Twenty-Seven

'They've gone,' said Brodie.

Daniel nodded sombrely. 'Jack saw it too, then. The book was all he needed.'

'No, I don't mean they've arrested Eric,' said Brodie. 'They've just gone. Jack and Charlie Voss. I caught them just before they left.' This was true if misleading.

Daniel frowned. 'Didn't he look at the songbook?'

'Yes. And then he left.'

It was a complicated relationship between Daniel and Deacon. It wasn't made any simpler by Brodie's feelings for each of them, but even without her there would always have been friction. Deacon thought Daniel was put on earth to annoy him while Daniel thought Deacon's mission was to misunderstand him; wantonly and deliberately if it didn't happen naturally. He thought that was what had happened now. That if anyone else had noticed the discrepancy in how the songs were written – particularly if Deacon himself had noticed – he'd have been talking to the Director of Public Prosecutions right now. Piqued, and uncertain what to do next, Daniel subsided onto the sofa.

Fry said, 'Eric's downstairs?'

'Mm,' nodded Brodie absently. 'Well, there's no point us staying out of the way any longer, I suppose…'

Fry reached the stairs first.

Half way down Daniel realised the danger and tried to catch up with him. Brodie blocked his passage. 'Who are you trying to protect?' she hissed.

'Jared.'

'I don't think you need to.'

Chandos came out of the study as Fry reached the hall. 'You can show your face now, no one's going to stick a Litmus paper up your nose.'

Whatever he was expecting, it wasn't bodily assault. He was older than Fry but also bigger and stronger. Only a soul-deep rage he was incapable of containing blinded Fry to the inevitable outcome of a physical confrontation. Or perhaps he knew he was going to get beaten senseless but thought it was worth it. Welcomed the chance to swap internal wounds that killed without showing for external ones that only bled.

They rolled across the ancient floorboards like a novelty bowling-ball, arms, legs and profanities coming out at all angles. When it fetched up against the kitchen door it separated into two men again, one throwing blows like confetti, more concerned with the quantity than the aim, the other returning about one in five but actually doing some damage.

Finally Daniel managed to get past Brodie, got a hand in Fry's collar and yanked. The combatants fell apart. There was blood on Fry's face, uncomprehending fury in Chandos's. Fry wasn't even forming words any more, just howling like a trapped animal.

'Jared! Calm down. This isn't achieving anything.'

For a calculating man, Chandos was beside himself with rage. 'What the *** do you think you're *** doing, you *** *** little troll?' Brodie listened with interest. There were obscenities in there she hadn't heard before.

Between his bloody nose and his bruised ribs, and the pain in his heart, Fry could hardly speak. He fought weakly but failed to break Daniel's grip. 'I know what you did,' he gasped. 'You bastard. I know what you did *and* how you did it.'

Chandos didn't know what he knew. Plainly something had happened, and if he didn't know what at least he knew who to blame. He swatted Fry aside like a mosquito, which left him face to face with Daniel. 'You again! *Now* what have you been telling him? You're not going to be satisfied, are you, until you drive him completely off his head!'

Daniel had no chance to answer. Fry was back, his body bent like a bow with the bone-cracking power of his anger. But it wasn't just anger: there was grief and humiliation mixed in there, and together they flayed him and bared his workings to the world. Chandos wasn't exaggerating: Daniel too feared for his sanity.

Brodie was waiting for him to construct a sentence. Because she didn't think it was going to be what it should have been. She didn't think he was this overwrought for a nineteen-year-old girl he'd never met. She was right; and yet disappointed.

'You let me think *I* wrote those songs!' yelled Fry, his voice fragmenting. 'You *made* me think that! I believed they were mine.'

Chandos tried to brush the accusation aside. 'I don't know what you're talking about.'

Fry had been silenced for the last time. He seemed past caring what happened to him now. If Chandos wasn't who he thought he was, and even *he* wasn't who he thought he was, maybe it didn't matter what happened next. He had nothing left to lose.

'*Chimera. Hell Won't Wait. Crucifiction*, for God's sake! All the songs that people who don't even listen to demon rock know are mine. Only they're not. They were written by a girl who came to you for careers advice and never went home. You killed her, and you kept her songs and fed them to me one at a time, when I was so blitzed I wouldn't even notice.' He barked a desperate little laugh. 'I thought that was when I was at my most creative. I knew it would kill me, I came to realise it wasn't even good for my work long-term, but I thought if the heroin was helping me write songs like that it was a price worth paying. But I wasn't writing anything, was I? I was just taking them down.'

People who live through volcanic eruptions talk about an unnatural stillness falling immediately beforehand. It was like that with Chandos. Trying to fix it in her mind afterwards Brodie dismissed the obvious explanation, that he was frozen by shock. Nor was it the silence of defeat, of a man giving up. It was more as if time itself was stunned into pausing while he considered his next move. The look of furious exasperation had faded from his face but nothing came to replace it. Close enough to both Daniel and Fry to bang their heads together, he made no move of any kind. Stillness radiated from him in an expanding shell like fall-out, filling the room, filling the house around them, a stillness so profound it was not merely the absence of movement but the death of it. Unmoving himself, he was also the cause of immobility in others.

If his body was fixed, perhaps it was to free his mind. Behind the silence Brodie sensed the deep generator hum of high-speed calculation. The sound of a volcano thinking.

At length – and not one of them could have said how long the silence lasted – he said, so softly she had to strain to hear, 'When I first saw you on stage I thought you were going to take the world by storm. You were eighteen years old, you were hammering hell out of an old Yamaha guitar, and you looked like you'd crawled on your hands and knees over broken glass to get to where the music was. I didn't know if the raw power of your voice or the desolation of your vision was the more startling, but I thought you were the most exciting thing I'd ever listened to.'

He looked at Brodie then, and the sad ghost of a smile twitched the dark beard. 'You should have seen him then. The energy. The fierce determination to get his songs heard. You felt, if he had to, he'd kill for them. I thought, How can a boy who wants to be heard that much *not* go all the way? And I asked myself, How can you know that and not go with him?

'I had other commitments. I got rid of them. People – people in the business, people who knew what they were talking about – said I was crazy, that only amateurs put everything on one throw of the dice. But they hadn't seen what I'd seen, heard what I'd heard, and though I agreed with every word they said I still knew it was the right thing to do.'

Eric Chandos sighed, and lifted the broad shoulders in a world-weary shrug. 'I still think it was. Things didn't work out how I'd hoped but there were factors outside my control. By the time I realised the drug use had gone beyond recreational to full-blown dependence he was already a lost cause. I knew then I'd have to rethink the game plan, because commercial success was still a possibility but rewriting the standard for rock music no longer was. The hunger to be heard had gone. He'd found another way to dull the pain.'

Fry's gaze was hot, ashamed and accusatory. 'You could have helped. You could have got me clean. I don't remember you even trying.'

'That's kind of the point, Jared,' said Chandos drily. 'You don't remember. I did try. I tried very hard to talk some sense into you in those early years. I knew what you were risking, not just personally but professionally. There are rockstars who can manage an addiction and still be great. There are an awful lot more ex-rockstars, and people who never quite became rockstars, and people who had a great future behind them the first time they stuck a needle in their arm.'

Brodie waited but there seemed to be nothing more coming. 'So?' she prompted eventually.

'So?'

She breathed heavily at him. 'You'd taken risks to make a star of Jared and he was pickling his brain with jolly-juice. What did you do then? Find someone who could still write demon rock – and write it well enough for Souls to play it – and kill her for it?'

Chandos stared at her as if she was something he'd stepped in. 'Don't be absurd.'

'Don't lie to me!' snarled Fry. 'I want the truth. Those aren't my songs. I thought they were but they're not. She wrote them. Sasha…

Sasha...'

'Wade,' Daniel supplied softly.

'She wrote them, and then she died, and somehow I ended up writing them in my book.' Despite the tremor in his voice, Fry had a grip on his emotions for now. 'I know *I* didn't kill her, I was in Ireland when she died. But you were on your way home by then. You met her, didn't you? What happened?'

Chandos gave an irritable shrug. 'This is all a fiction. You do know that, don't you? A fairy story. Detective Superintendent Deacon has been asking me the same question for the last two hours: he went away because even he finally realised he was barking up the wrong tree. Doesn't that tell you something, Jared? Someone who really wanted to pin something really bad on me has just gone home. I know your mental powers aren't what they once were, but that should tell even you *something*.'

Brodie considered for a moment. 'If you want to believe you've convinced him of your innocence, don't let me spoil your day. But if the three of us are satisfied of your guilt you shouldn't count on Jack missing the point. Jack Deacon is many things, not all of them admirable, but one thing he isn't is gullible.

'You're not walking away from this, Eric. Not because of what we know: because of what Jack knows. You went to some trouble to distract him, but time was never going to be on your side. You made him angry. I dare say he's still angry, but now he's thinking as well and he'll be on your case until either you tell him what happened or he works it out for himself. Telling him might be easier.'

The way Chandos looked at her, for a moment she felt the quiver in her belly as her body responded to the proximity of his. As if he hadn't used her as a shield to hide behind and cast her off when her function was performed. As if he hadn't traded her happiness for his own safety, and not even carelessly but in full knowledge of what he was doing. She had every reason to hate this man. But the danger was, if he went on looking at her like that, she'd forgive him.

At least she recognised the danger. Daniel once said, when someone accused him of doing something courageous, that it wasn't necessary to be brave, only to play the part. Try as she might, she couldn't feel nothing for this man. But she could pretend to. She curled her lip and looked away.

Behind her back she heard Chandos sigh. 'Look. I didn't kill that girl. You can believe it or not, but it happens to be true. Yes, I met her. I found myself in possession of her songbook, and I used it to kick-start Jared when he lost his way. But I didn't kill her.'

Daniel's voice was low. 'Should I get Superintendent Deacon back here?'

Chandos shook his head. 'If anyone deserves to hear it first it's Jared, and it might be difficult for us to talk properly later. I'll tell you what happened – everything that happened. Then, if you want, you can call Deacon back and I'll tell him. But you'd better understand what the result of that will be. I'll be in trouble certainly, though perhaps not as much as you'd like. But I'll get through it. Jared won't. If you make this public, you won't just be destroying his future, you'll erase his past. You might as well slit his throat here and now.'

Fry was standing at the foot of the stairs, his hands stuffed in his pockets. Blood was smeared on his face and his shirt was torn. His eyes were angry and afraid and his body was tensed in a bitter resentful hunch. 'Keep talking.'

Chapter Twenty-Eight

The King's Hall in Belfast was used to staging big events: everything was ready, everyone knew what they were doing. Chandos spent a couple of hours there – no more, there was no need. He took the SeaCat to Stranraer and drove half the day and into the night, getting home red-eyed and exhausted in the early hours of Monday morning, June 16th.

There was no one else in the London house. Fry and Tommy were in Ireland with the band and Miriam the housekeeper had taken a fortnight's holiday while they were away. Chandos didn't have a PA at that time but he'd given the girl who did his secretarial work some time off as well. He got in at two in the morning, a time when even London is mostly asleep, and surprised a burglar.

At least, that was what he thought when he hauled himself upstairs, discarding clothes as he went, only to hear a soft sound from behind Fry's bedroom door. He stopped dead and looked for something heavy with which to arm himself.

As a household they didn't go in for bronze statuary, walking-sticks or golfclubs. The best he could do was a pseudo-Gothic mace Fry had used in the act until one day it rolled off the stage and broke someone's foot. Now they used it as a doorstop.

'You hit a nineteen-year-old girl with a *mace*?' breathed Brodie, horrified

'Of course I didn't,' snapped Chandos.

Thus armed, he crept to Fry's door, threw it open, threw the light-switch and had his weapon at the ready in less time than it takes to say it.

There was a little shriek of terror and Chandos found himself eye-balling a girl – his first thought was she was about twelve years old – wearing a t-shirt and underwear and nothing else, kneeling on Fry's bed where she had obviously been sleeping not long before.

'Who the hell are you?' he yelled, the backwash of fear coming out as fury. 'What the hell are you doing here? How the hell did you get in?'

She was white, shrinking from him. Her voice was tiny. 'I climbed in.'

'Climbed in? What do you mean you climbed in?'

She gestured at the bedroom window, then drew her hand back hard against her body before he got a chance to snap it off.

Chandos looked at the window, looked at the girl, looked at the window again. 'We're two storeys up!'

'Drainpipe...' she mumbled.

This was Sasha Wade, scion of an unknown house, so full of the music that nothing seemed too difficult, no risk too great, in the cause of liberating it. She reminded him of Fry. Of Fry when first Chandos saw him, three years before, a ragged eighteen-year-old with fallen angel eyes and the voice of a storm. The anger leached from him. 'What are you doing here?' he asked again. 'What do you want?'

'I wanted to see you.'

'Me?' Managers aren't used to that. 'Jared's away on tour.'

She knew. 'Ireland.'

Chandos nodded. 'So what do you want with me? And how long have you been here?'

'Since Saturday night,' she whispered, her eyes downcast. 'I was going to leave in the morning if you hadn't got back. I haven't taken anything,' she assured him anxiously. 'Except I made some coffee, but I'll pay for that. And soup. And there was some...'

'Never mind the food,' he snapped. 'You've been here two days? You climbed up a drainpipe and in through a window carelessly left open by a certain demon rocker who will be hearing all about it, then you set up camp in Jared's room. And you say you wanted to see me but I still don't know why. Do your parents know you're here? Maybe I should call the police.'

'No!' Her eyes flashed dramatically wide. 'My parents don't know I came. Nobody knows. I haven't done any harm. Five minutes of your time, that's all I want. I can tell you everything you need to hear in five minutes. Then you can throw me out if you want to. You can call the police if you want to.'

'Damn right I can call the police.' But the urgency had gone. It was impossible to feel threatened by a teenage waif in her underwear. 'Five minutes. And for heaven's sakes, put some clothes on.'

Unsure if dressing time was included in the five minutes, she talked as she scrambled into her jeans – fast, because five minutes isn't long to make a pitch the rest of your life is going to depend on.

'I write songs,' she gabbled. 'And sing. You think Jared's good? – I'm better. When you hear me sing you'll want to hear more. So will everyone. I'll sing with Souls or on my own, whatever you want. You want Jared to sing some of my songs, you can have that too. You don't know it now but you need me as much as I need you. I can give you songs to stop the world.'

It wasn't the first time Chandos had been ambushed by wannabes. At the start of his career he was afraid to send them away in case one of them really did have the Midas touch. Later he realised how very rare it was, how vanishingly small the risk of missing a genuine talent. Now he got rid of them as quickly as he could without resorting to actual bodily harm.

This girl was different. It was the way she used words. They danced for her. If she talked like that when she was trembling with fear and trying to find the left leg in her jeans in the middle of the night with no one here but him, what could she do with an audience? What might her songs be made of?

Warily, conscious that it might be a mistake, he said, 'Shall I find you a guitar?'

'Brought my own.' She produced it from beside the bed, a cheap acoustic guitar with a gaudy woven strap. She'd climbed a drainpipe with it on her back.

She sang the song the world would come to know as *Crucifiction*.

When she'd finished, her eyes shining with the effect she'd obviously had on him, Chandos just kept sitting on the edge of the bed, trying to breathe steadily. 'You wrote that?'

'Yes.'

'Words and music?'

'Yes.'

'Are there any more?'

There were many more. She sang eight or nine of them; which was the first he saw of her songbook. Or rather, as it turned out, her new songbook. 'I left the old one at home. Some of the stuff in it isn't that good. I copied the best ones into this.'

'How long have you been writing songs?'

'Since I was a kid. But mostly the last couple of years. Since I heard Jared. I knew what I wanted to say but till then I didn't know how to say it. But I do now. Don't I?'

He had to admit that she did. 'Listen, Sasha, I think you're right – you have a talent and it ought to be nurtured. Maybe I'm the one to do it, maybe not, but somebody should. We have to talk about this again, seriously, with your parents and maybe with a lawyer. But not in an empty house in the middle of the night. I at least have a reputation to lose.'

She laughed at that, a high bell-like chime that reminded him what her voice was capable of. Her pale skin glowed with excitement. She knew she was on the shore of the new world she'd been seeking. She knew he wasn't lying to her: she knew she'd got her break. She let him show her down through the house to the front door.

At which point a thought struck him. 'Have you anywhere you can go tonight?'

She gave an elfin shrug, genuinely uncaring. 'I'll wait on the station. There'll be a train in a couple of hours.'

She was nineteen and looked younger, a fey child alone in an unfamiliar city, a girl so set on her destiny she would break into the house of someone she thought could help her. He couldn't turn her out on the street at four in the morning. 'Go back to bed, I'll take you to the station after breakfast.'

'But you didn't,' hazarded Brodie softly.

'By breakfast she was dead.'

He'd gone to his own room then, and though he was exhausted by the long day his head was too full of possibilities to sleep. An hour ago he was a successful man, respected in the music industry, the man who'd produced the remarkable talent that was Jared Fry. Now he was going to do it again, with an unknown who sang like a harp and wrote like Dante. Once could be luck, but twice was a reputation that would sustain him for the rest of his career.

Eventually exhaustion won and he slept, dreaming of platinum records and white limousines.

He woke to a shock like melt-water pouring down his spine and the awareness of small, cool hands on his body.

He shot out the other side of the bed as if fired from a gun. He scrabbled for the bedside lamp, but he'd been away from home too long for it to come naturally to hand, he succeeded only in knocking it to the floor where it smashed. He kept going, groping for the light-switch beside the door.

When the light came on it found both of them naked, her kneeling on the bed, him spread-eagled against the wall, the bedclothes spilled in a line between them. He yelled, 'What are you *doing*?' in a voice that soared till it cracked.

There's a difference between elfin and elvish. She gave him an imp's smile. 'Casting couch.'

'You're nineteen years old!'

'Old enough. Even the law says so.'

Whatever the law said, whatever *she* said, she wasn't a woman. She hadn't a woman's body. It was small and spare, long thin bones under downy skin, small high breasts that would have gone unnoticed altogether if there'd been any flesh anywhere on her. With her cap of fair hair and her huge eyes she looked like a poster-child for a famine in Stockholm. Sleeping with her would be like sleeping with his niece.

'Will you for God's sake go and put some clothes on!'

'You haven't got any on.'

'This is my room!'

'It's big enough for two.'

Some of the shock was passing. One thing was certain: she wasn't big enough to rape him. 'Sasha, I don't know what you think you know about the music business but this isn't how it's done. Leastways, it isn't how I do it. You have talent and I want to promote it. If I'm right you'll make me a lot of money. I don't need any other kind of reward, and I'm not looking for a girlfriend young enough to be my daughter.'

'That's all right,' she said reassuringly, 'no one has to know. I won't make sheep's eyes at you at showbiz parties.'

'Damn right you won't, you'll be tucked up in bed saving your voice. Sasha, I'm not kidding – this is no part of the deal. It isn't necessary and I don't want it.'

'Why not?' She looked down at herself in surprise. 'What's wrong with it?'

'It's ten years too young, that's what!'

'I'm good,' she promised, as if that might be what was worrying him. 'I lived with a premier division footballer for two months.'

He found his mouth open and shut it. That might have been a non sequitur; on the other hand, sexual technique could have been part of the coaching programme, sandwiched between dribbling and tax avoidance. He opened the door and pointed. 'Bed.'

She patted the mattress. 'Got one here.'

He hardly knew what to make of her. He couldn't have made himself any clearer; she couldn't still think this was the price of his help; still she wanted to jump his bones and wouldn't take no for an answer. Leaving the door open he moved slowly back towards the bed. 'I don't want this,' he said again.

Naked as he was, her eyes seemed to strip him, flay him, get under his very skin. There was a directness in her gaze that was both unflinching and uncompromising. 'What do you think I am?' she demanded. 'A child? I'm not. I'm not sure I was a child when I was ten years old, I'm sure as hell not one now. I'm not jail-bait, if that's what scares you. My body is mine to give. I'd like to share it with you, at least for tonight, and not as a bribe and not because I think I'll get a hold over you but because it's late and it's cold, and I'm a long way from home, and we're both alone, and I think it would make us feel good. But I'm not going to beg. If you really want to sleep alone you can.'

He dared to let his eyes trace her outline, to linger on the long muscles of her thigh, the dip of her belly. He'd been on the road for a fortnight, and he was tired and in need of comfort. He'd have settled for hot chocolate but...

If he told her once more to go he thought she would. He said, uncertainly, 'What are your parents going to think?'

She shrugged, amused. 'I can't imagine telling them.'

She wasn't lying: she was good. She wore him out. Of course, after the day he'd had that wasn't difficult. When he had nothing left to give she pushed him onto his back and rolled off the edge of the bed, stretching as she rose, the early morning light gilding the contours of her body. Hovering on the cusp of sleep he watched with hooded eyes as she straightened and walked away, a slight pale figure at once frail and adamantine, strange and familiar. He heard the shower, then he slept.

Over a period of time, still sleeping, he became aware of something wrong. But not until he was awake did he realise what it was. The shower was still running.

His first fully conscious thought was that, having made all the running, now she regretted it and was trying to scrub every trace of him from her skin. He chewed his lip, wondering what he should do. He called her name; there was no answer. He got up, wrapping a sheet around him, and opened the bathroom door. 'Sasha, it's all right. Don't be upset. We'll forget it happened...'

She was sprawled in the cast iron bath, limbs splayed awkwardly, the water – cold now, there hadn't been time since his return to heat a full cylinder – beating down on her young body. She was the wrong way round, with her head on the taps, and he thought she'd fallen asleep with her chin on her shoulder. And then he saw she wasn't asleep.

'She'd slipped on the soap,' he said. His voice was wondrous with the banality of it. 'She was showering, she slipped on the soap and she banged her head on the taps. There was a graze on her temple, the sort of thing you get from walking into a cupboard door, the sort of thing that hurts for a couple of minutes but by the time you've found the Elastoplast you can't see where it was. But she was dead.'

Chandos saw their expressions and marshalled a wan smile. 'You don't believe me. I don't blame you – I didn't believe it either. You see what people manage to survive, you don't imagine people can die that easily.'

'They can,' murmured Daniel. 'They don't very often, but they can. The right injury to the right spot, and just occasionally some-one dies for almost no reason at all.'

The look Chandos gave him bordered on grateful. 'I kept having another look. I kept thinking, Don't panic, she'll wake up in a minute. But I knew she wouldn't.

'And I found myself thinking about all the other things I knew. That she wasn't a local girl. That she'd come to London without telling anyone what she was doing. That she'd broken into the house – which meant no one had seen her because they'd have called the police if they had.

'That she was nineteen years old and looked less than that, and that she died in my bathroom after we had sex. That was the one I couldn't get past. When the police came the press wouldn't be far behind. They'd get hold of a picture of her looking like a child and they'd crucify me. Even if I could convince the police I was telling the truth, the tabloids wouldn't care. I was a successful man in a glamorous industry, and there's nothing the tabloids like better than fêting you one week and stoning you the next.'

Somewhere in the telling he'd aged ten years. His skin was grey. His eyes were tired. His whole body had slumped now the secret he'd put everything into protecting was out.

'Anyway, why should the police believe me? They'd look at her and look at me, and wonder if I'd raped her and hit her to stop her screaming. They'd find out I was supposed to be in Belfast, that there was no one else in the house because I'd said I'd be gone for days yet, but I'd come back early and had sex with a young girl who then died in my bathroom. I could be charged; conceivably I could be convicted. Even if I wasn't the doubts would remain. People who'd begged to do business with me would stop returning my calls. Venues would be unavailable when I needed them, and as for supp-orting acts, forget it. Who wants to appear with a band managed by a paedophile? She wasn't under-age. But I'd pay for it as if she was.

'And it was too late to do anything for her. I asked myself if it was reasonable to have to pay with my career for her mistakes.'

And once the question was asked the answer was obvious. She was tiny: she fitted into a bin-liner. He brought his car to the back of the house.

Just in time he thought better of it. He meant to take her somewhere she would not be found; but if he was unlucky it made sense to ensure that no sign of her presence could be left in his car. He thought then of the old van. It was going to the dealer in the next few days, it could make one last run for him first.

But the sun was up and it was already too late to do anything more tonight. The long day passed minute by grudging minute. He was terrified that Miriam would return early, but his luck held and no one came to the house all day. He spent the morning agonising over where to take Sasha Wade, and in the afternoon he fetched the van and got together the tools he'd need. When darkness returned he carried the dead girl out to the vehicle, parked behind the house with the lights off, and left for Cheyne Warren. Passing through Horsham he dropped her clothes into a rubbish skip.

People with a body to dispose of always go somewhere they know, and nobody travels further than about a hundred miles. The Diligence Hotel suited Chandos on both counts. He hadn't been with the band when they stayed there but he had seen it, in fact more recently than they. As late as February 1997, looking for somewhere to spend a night on one of his pre-tour trips, he'd seen the sign for Cheyne Warren and remembered booking rooms there the previous autumn. But he'd found The Diligence closed, derelict amid its overgrown grounds. He'd driven on and passed the night somewhere else. But five months later he returned to The Diligence expecting to find it still empty.

It was a shock to find the place a building site. His first appalled thought was that he'd have to keep driving, find somewhere else, the black plastic bundle behind him becoming more threatening with every mile. Then he wondered if there was in fact any need. The gate was open: builders' carelessness, he assumed, not knowing one of the flats was already occupied. There was nothing to stop him driving through the yard and down the garden to where it stopped being overgrown and started being a wood. It was dark, no one would see him from the road. And if no one saw him no one would investigate what he was doing there.

It was a gamble. But so was turning round and starting to look, in an unfamiliar area in the middle of the night, for a safe place to dispose of a body. Every minute he was in this girl's company she was a danger to him. A minor accident on these narrow unlit roads could result in policemen taking his name and looking in his van. Whether or not it was sensible, he couldn't face prolonging this any further. He took a deep breath and drove through the courtyard and down to the wood.

In fact, no one disturbed him. Once he heard a car but supposed it was on the road. He paused, heart in his mouth, but the sound died and he thought it had passed. He kept digging.

It took longer than he'd expected. The sweat stung his eyes and bathed his body under his clothes but finally the job was done. It wasn't a very perfect grave, he had to bend her to fit where the trench snaked among the tree-roots and she'd stiffened enough to make that difficult. Somehow he managed, and he spread the earth over her like a quilt and hoped she'd sleep forever.

Only when he was leaving, still without headlights, did he see a car parked beside The Diligence that had not been there when he arrived. His heart lurched into his throat and he didn't know if he should stop or go on or leave the van and run. The last was the stupidest: the abandoned vehicle would be traced to him in hours. He decided to keep moving. If someone tried to stop him he'd know that he'd been observed.

But no lights sprang up, no voices rang out in challenge, and he reached the road daring to hope he was safe.

He drove by random ways for an hour, partly to break his trail, partly because he was still too shocked to plan. At first he told himself, *If there are no roadblocks in the next five miles I'm in the clear*; then, *If there's no hue-and-cry in the next half hour*; then, *If the police were out looking for me I'd have seen them by now.* As the short night began to lift, with no sign of pursuit he turned for home.

Chandos looked at Brodie and smiled tiredly. 'You'll have figured out the rest. When the papers reported plans for more development here it was as if someone hit me with a sock full of wet sand. I knew what they'd find. I'd been careful, I didn't think she could be traced to me, but I couldn't be sure. I had to prevent that work starting. I convinced Jared we should move out of town, and I gave you a list of requirements you could hardly satisfy anywhere but here. As it happened you'd read about the plans too. If you hadn't I'd have had to draw your attention to them. Discreetly.

'Somehow it all worked. Like everything else I'd done, the hard bits came together and some crazy little detail scuppered me. Like God was teasing me. Even the girl, who climbed up to an open window with a guitar on her back then died slipping on a bar of soap. How can you not believe in God,' he asked Daniel, 'when somebody up there is so obviously playing silly buggers?'

'How can you believe in God,' responded Daniel, 'and treat people like they're of no consequence?'

'I told you,' said Chandos tersely, 'it was too late to help her. She was already dead. She'd been dead for half an hour.'

'It wasn't Sasha I was thinking of.'

Chapter Twenty-Nine

All through the long telling Jared Fry had said nothing. Brodie looked at him now. He was ashen and hollow-cheeked, and he'd sunk onto the lower steps of the staircase as if his knees would no longer support him. Now he looked up. 'Finish it,' he grated.

Chandos thought he had. 'What do you mean?'

With a hand on the rail Fry jerked himself to his feet. His knuckles were clenched bloodless and his whole body shook. 'I mean, the part where you turn me into a mouthpiece for someone else's songs! The part where you decide I can't write any more, I'll never write anything worth listening to again, if you want to go on making money out of me you'll have to find some other way. The part where you wait till I'm stoned then feed me the songs of a dead nineteen-year-old girl and let me think they're mine.'

'Ah,' said Chandos. 'That.'

'Why do you think I've been shooting myself stupid for the last six years?' Fry shouted in a fury of grief. 'For fun? Because it made my life easier, or more rewarding? Because I liked waking up in my own vomit, and seeing from people's faces that I owed them apologies for things I didn't remember doing? Because it was fun knowing the band were carrying me, and all I brought them now was my name and the few good songs it was made on?

'Eric, the reason I take heroin in quantities that are not so much recreational as veterinary is that I thought that was how I wrote those songs! I thought that was how I got to where they were. I've thought that for six years, ever since the songs went where I couldn't follow. Now you're telling me they weren't even my songs. All the heroin did was knock me out long enough and bring me round stupid enough to believe that what I'd written down was my work. And it wasn't. It was hers.' He was almost crying.

'Yes, it was,' agreed Chandos. 'But don't kid yourself, that isn't why you're a junkie. I only started feeding you Sasha's songs when you stopped producing your own. You know this business, you've been in it long enough. One way or another you stay on top of the game, because if you don't there's always someone younger and hotter waiting to take over. You were taking heroin by the time you were twenty. By the time you were twenty-two it was taking you – consuming you, feeding on your body, your energy, your talent.'

He saw how Fry devoured the little compliment, the raw hunger in his eyes. 'Oh yes,' he said softly, 'you had talent. Those songs *could* have been yours: there was a time when you were that good. If you'd stayed clean; if you'd even stayed in control. That's what I expected when I took you on. Even when you started doing drugs I thought it was something we could manage – either sort out or work round. I had no idea how comprehensively it would destroy you as an artist.'

'You could have helped me – !'

'I *did* help you,' snapped Chandos. 'A lot of people tried to help you. You didn't want help. You were the great Jared Fry, the prince of demon rock, the poet of pain, and you liked it too much to want to change. Maybe I should have walked away at that point. You'd be dead by now if I had.

'Instead I looked for a way to keep you working. To keep you in the band. The songs were the only reason Souls For Satan didn't look for another front man, one they could count on. You'd used up everyone's goodwill, Jared. At first people make allowances; then they make excuses; then they make other arrangements. You had no friends left, except me.'

He paused, as if expecting one of them to mock that. He seemed surprised when no one did, took a moment to pick up the narrative again.

'And I had Sasha Wade's songbook. I'd buried her, I'd dumped her clothes, I'd smashed her guitar and burned the pieces, but I couldn't bring myself to burn her songs. I should have – they were the only link between her and me. But they'd mattered so much to her she'd died trying to get them heard, and it seemed callous. So I kept them.

'That year was a turning-point in more ways than one. It was when you made the jump from cult hero to international rockstar. It was when your drug habit started getting the upper hand. And it was when every song you wrote went from being better than the one before to being a little bit worse. I didn't even notice at first. But when I did and looked back, that was when it happened.'

Brodie risked a glance at Jared Fry. He looked frozen, his whole body locked with pain. He might have been stupid but he wasn't a fool: he knew what Chandos was telling him was essentially the truth. If he had been betrayed it was because his own frailty had made lies both possible and necessary.

'You went downhill from there,' Chandos continued remorseless-ly. 'Healthwise, as an artist, as a man. Six years ago I realised that the only way your career was going to survive – that *you* were going to survive – was if I gave you a talent transfusion. You'd passed out on the floor – and yes, you'd thrown up – and I looked at you and thought, Either I do this or I walk away now and read in tomorrow's papers that he died of an overdose.

'Well, I didn't walk away. I got you pumped out, I got you cleaned up, and while you were sleeping it off I took out Sasha's book. I picked a song and read the words to you, and whistled the tune. Over and over again, all the time you were coming round. When you opened your eyes I put a pen in your hand and your own book on your lap, and I read it again, word by word. And you wrote it down. An hour later you came lurching downstairs, babbling excitedly about how this great song had come to you while you were tripped out. And I had to pretend to be impressed.'

'*Crucifiction?*' whispered Fry.

'*Crucifiction*,' agreed Chandos. 'Which was of course a mistake. I'd been so stunned by what followed that I'd forgotten what she told me – that she'd copied it from an older collection that she left at home. I only remembered after it was too late: the song was recorded and selling faster than they could distribute it. And I thought I was dead.

'But nothing happened. No one came to accuse us of theft and murder. There was only adulation. From the fans, from the critics, from the industry. I wish I'd enjoyed it more. I was waiting for the second shoe to drop, but it never did. Finally I realised that the other book with the song in it must have been carefully packed up with all Sasha's possessions in cardboard boxes in her parents' loft, and even if they'd read it the chances of them listening to Jared Fry sing demon rock were vanishingly small. I'd got away with it. So a few months later I did it again.'

'All those songs,' moaned Fry. 'None of them mine?'

'None,' said Chandos; so far as Brodie could tell there wasn't an ounce of feeling in how he said it. 'What you were writing by then wasn't just crap, it was trite crap. This was the only way I could get a song worth recording out of you. I tried not to be greedy. We could keep going on a couple of hits and a few make-weights each year. Even so, eventually the well ran dry. By last year all Sasha's songs had been used. All that was left was you. And I don't have to ask, do I, how much useful work you've done this last year.'

He didn't. Neither did Brodie. The answer was writ clear on Fry's face. 'You let me think I wrote her songs.' It was more than grief in his voice, it was bereavement.

'And now you know you didn't,' said Chandos coldly. 'You've had six years of success that you didn't earn. If you're looking for an apology, Jared, I don't think I owe you one. I didn't ruin your career, I prolonged it way beyond the point where it would have imploded. You want to talk about debts, let's talk about what you owe me. I didn't kill that girl for you – I didn't kill her at all – but I took risks for you that I didn't need to. I kept you at the top when it would have been easier to let you fall. What you are today you owe to me.'

Scorn twisted his lip. 'What you'll be next month, of course, will be all your own doing. Anybody want to start a book on it? A gibbering wreck in the back ward of a psychiatric hospital? Another showbiz suicide? Or just a bore leaning on a club bar, bumming the price of a fix off people in return for telling them how he used to be Jared Fry?'

What escaped Fry then was something between a sob and a howl, a tortured sound racked from a tormented soul, and he turned and scrambled up the stairs. They could hear his steps stumbling upwards long after he was gone from sight.

'You really are a shit, aren't you?' Brodie said quietly. She had her phone in her hand, her thumb on speed-dial. 'If you want to run neither of us is going to waste much effort chasing you. But I imagine Jack will.'

Chandos eyed her loftily. 'Why should I run? I want to sort this out. Maybe I'll go to prison but it won't be for long. It wasn't murder, it wasn't manslaughter, it wasn't rape. I failed to report a death. I carried out an unauthorised interment. I breached the copyright on some songs. Like I say, it can be fixed. I can do a couple of years if I have to. Compared with keeping Jared on track it'll be a holiday. And I'll come back ready to do some real work for a real star.'

'And Jared?' asked Daniel, tight-lipped. 'You've destroyed him – you do know that? He'll never recover from this. He hasn't the strength to do it alone and there's no one to help him. His friends are gone, his career is gone, you've even managed to ruin his legacy. You brought him to this, and not for his benefit but for yours. Now you've had everything he had to give, will you really let him rot?'

Because Daniel was shorter, Chandos could look down his nose at him without tilting his head back. He said simply, 'Yes.'

Leaving The Diligence, Deacon had driven into Cheyne Warren and parked outside the grocer's. The minutes passed and his phone remained silent. Half a dozen times he checked that he hadn't inadvertently switched it off.

When Voss saw steam starting to come from his ears he went into the shop and came back with ice-creams. 'She'll call when there's something to say.'

'You reckon?' Deacon took a fierce bite out of his flake. 'Maybe she's giving him a head-start.'

'You don't believe that.'

He considered for a moment. 'Damned if I know what to believe, Charlie Voss. To be honest, I don't know what she's doing there at all.'

'I do.'

Deacon sniffed glumly. 'Me too. After everything he's done to her, after everything she's said, she couldn't resist the opportunity to help him out one last time.'

Voss reflected for a moment. 'Permission to speak freely, sir?'

Deacon peered at him. 'Go on.'

'Stop talking like a bloody fool. Sir. She isn't there to help Eric Chandos. She's there to help you.'

He thought about that. He still didn't believe it. He didn't dare believe it. And the phone still didn't ring.

And then it did.

They went back into Chandos's study. Brodie and Daniel waited in the hall. But they weren't there long. Deacon didn't need the full-and-frank version, just the bones of what had happened and to know Chandos was ready to make a statement. That would be done at Battle Alley, with all appropriate formalities. Deacon cautioned him and let him gather a few belongings, then they headed out to the cars.

Jared Fry met them in the courtyard. He'd composed himself a little since fleeing upstairs. Deacon guessed that if he looked he'd see a fresh needle-track under his sleeve. He said carefully, 'As I understand it you had no part in the death or disposal of Sasha Wade. Unless new evidence emerges during interview I don't expect to charge you. But I will need a statement, and you'll need to contact your solicitor to deal with the civil complications.'

'Complications.' Fry seemed to be trying the word for size. Then he jerked a nod at Chandos. 'Can I – I don't know – say goodbye? We were friends for a long time.'

Deacon shrugged. 'Make it quick.'

Fry moved close enough to Chandos to shake his hand but then didn't. His fists were in his back pockets. His voice was low. 'I don't suppose I'll see you again.'

'Don't be too sure,' Chandos drawled lazily. 'You might come through this.'

Fry smiled. It was an odd smile: those watching saw different things in it. Deacon saw bitterness, Voss saw regret. Brodie, rather further away, thought that despite all that had happened she saw a kind of affection. Daniel saw resolve.

Then Fry took his hands from his pockets and raised them awkwardly, as if to clasp the taller man's shoulders. Instead, at the last moment, his expression mutating to what everyone saw as implacable, he punched him under the ear.

It wasn't that savage a blow. For a moment no one understood the look of sheer God-forsaken shock that swamped Chandos's expression or the way his body went weak and tottered before he fell to his knees. Fry opened his hand and something fell light on the cobbles.

Daniel, too far away to see what it was, nevertheless knew. 'Oh no.' And Brodie, absorbing the knowledge directly from his mind in that near-telepathic way they had that drove Deacon crazy, put her hand over her mouth.

'What the *hell*?' Deacon had hold of Fry before he even knew what had happened, because experience told him it wasn't a surfeit of emotion at a comradely punch that had downed Eric Chandos. Voss moved to support the stricken man.

Daniel said tightly, 'Ambulance.' And when Brodie went on staring in unmoving horror he reached out and shook her fiercely. 'Ambulance! Quickly.'

With his free hand Deacon reached down and picked up the plastic syringe which had fallen from Fry's grasp onto the cobbles. It was a large syringe, and it was empty.

Chapter Thirty

It was late evening before Deacon called it a day.

There had been a lot to do. He'd booked Jared Fry into the custody suite on a charge – for the moment: this could change – of attempted murder, but it was soon evident he couldn't stay there. The police surgeon wanted him on suicide watch in a secure psychiatric unit as soon as it could be arranged.

'You're serious? You think he could top himself?'

Dr Galbraith pulled down his lower lid with a fingertip. 'Look closely. Am I laughing?'

Deacon had no reason to debate the point. 'It's your call. But I'd have thought he'd had enough excitement for one day.'

Galbraith was a big man, a little shorter than Deacon but fatter, substantial in every way. He nodded. 'Enough for a lifetime even. That's the problem. He's burned all his boats, razed his bridges, cut the only lifeline he's known for ten years. When the reality of that strikes him he'll wish he'd emptied that syringe into himself.'

'Any word from the hospital?'

'Chandos is alive – well, no one's pronounced him dead. He's on a ventilator while they try to clean up his blood. No one will speculate on how successful that'll be. The needle grazed his carotid artery. If his brain had taken the full load he'd be dead now but it got some of it. Best guess? – he won't wake up. He might remain in a persistent vegetative state or he might die when they pull the plug on him. I don't think there's much chance of a significant recovery.'

'So Fry's going down for murder.'

Galbraith shrugged. 'Unless Chandos keeps on ticking over. But every way that counts it was murder.'

Deacon shook his head, half bitterly, half in wonder. 'This bloody job. You start off with a body and a guy who deserves to be done for murder, only it turns out he probably didn't kill anyone; and you end up with another guy who probably will be charged with murder and maybe doesn't deserve it.'

'Unless it was a bizarre accident where Mr Chandos tripped and fell on a loaded syringe,' said Dr Galbraith severely, 'whoever shot heroin into his neck is responsible for his condition. Murder is, of course, a legal concept.'

It had been a pretty half-hearted attempt to defend the demon rocker and Deacon gave it up without further argument. 'Oh, it was murder all right. It was deliberate and premeditated, and it wasn't self-defence, and whether or not Chandos is still breathing a year from now, Fry ended his life. The only' – he managed just in time to avoid saying *good* – 'thing about it is, it was Chandos's actions which reduced Fry to the state in which he committed that crime. A good brief will make a touching plea in mitigation. He won't get Fry off but he'll halve the time he has to serve.'

Galbraith was watching him. 'You seem to have a degree of sympathy for this young man. You'd be glad to see him out sooner rather than later?'

Deacon knuckled his eyes wearily. 'He isn't coming out at all and we both know it. There's no way Fry will serve five years in prison. It'll be a major achievement keeping him alive long enough to stand trial. And yes, since you ask, I'm sorry for that. It may not be saying much but he was a better man than the man he stabbed. But I'm only the detective, thank God, not the judge or the jury. My role in all this is almost done.'

He walked home. He threw his coat at the rack in the hall and missed. He fed the cat. He stood in the kitchen watching it eat for a minute, head bowed, chin on his chest. Then he picked up his coat and went out again.

He wasn't sure where he'd find them except that they'd be together. He swung by the netting-shed but Brodie's car was nowhere to be seen so he walked on, up through the town to Chiffney Road. At the end of the drive he hesitated. It was too late to be calling on anyone he wasn't planning to arrest. He should go home and see her tomorrow.

A light burned over the front door. Now another came on in the hall, spilling onto the gravel as the door opened. 'Jack. Come inside.'

It was Daniel. Deacon hesitated a moment longer, then trudged up the steps. 'Where's Brodie?'

'She went to bed an hour ago. She took a sleeping pill.'

'You're staying here tonight?'

'I said I would.'

Deacon didn't enquire any deeper; didn't need to.

'Any news?'

'No,' said Deacon. 'Nor likely to be until they need the plug for the vacuum.'

Daniel often found it hard to know when Deacon was pretending to be a callous sod and when he was actually being one. 'And Jared?'

'Being watched. I suppose, being treated.'

'You suppose.'

The big man shrugged. 'I catch them, somebody else deals with them. Galbraith says he's in the right place. That's good enough for me.'

'Prison, even a prison hospital, will be hard on him.'

'What's the alternative? He may have been provoked, he may have done the world a favour, but he still stabbed a hypodermic needle into somebody's neck and pumped his brain full of heroin. *I'd* give the guy a medal but I doubt a court'll feel the same way.'

'Did you get the story out of Chandos first?'

'Pretty much. I'll want to talk to you and Brodie in the morning, you can fill in anything I missed, but I think I got most of it. He said it was an accident. Sasha Wade's death. That it was an accident and he wasn't even in the room.'

'He told us the same thing,' said Daniel.

'Did you believe him?'

'I had no reason not to. He seemed to be telling the truth. He did-n't think he was in too much trouble.'

The irony of that was too keen to need comment. Deacon sighed. 'I'll go see the Wades tomorrow. It isn't the news they want but maybe this long after it's better than none.'

Daniel only nodded.

They were in Brodie's sitting-room. Deacon made no move to go. 'How did she seem?'

Daniel gave a helpless little shrug. 'You know Brodie – it can be hard to tell. She was shocked – of course she was, we all were. I never saw it coming. I knew how distressed Jared was but it never occurred to me he'd do something like that. Maybe it should have done. An hour before they'd been punching one another round the hall floor. And I knew there was heroin upstairs. I just never *thought*...'

'Of course you didn't,' said Deacon. 'I knew all that too, but I didn't realise what was happening until Chandos hit the deck. None of us has any reason to beat ourselves up over this.'

Daniel said quietly, 'Brodie thinks she has.'

Deacon considered. 'Well, maybe Brodie has.'

Daniel bit his lip. His opinion wasn't being asked and he'd no right to offer it. But Brodie's happiness mattered to him, too much to jeopardise it for the sake of politeness, so he gave it anyway. 'Jack, you have two options. You can forgive and forget – and I do mean both – and get on with your lives as if this never happened. Or you can nurse the grudge and lose her. I don't think there's a third way.'

'What does she want?'

'Ask her.'

'You know.'

'So do you.'

Deacon straightened up against the back of the sofa. It was a big room in a big Victorian house: even so he seemed to fill it. He fixed the younger man with an eye like a spear. 'And what about you, Daniel? What do you want?'

Daniel was surprised. 'What do you mean? I don't come into this.'

Deacon barked a bitter little laugh. 'Can I have that in writing?'

'Yes, if you want,' said Daniel. 'This isn't about me. None of this is about me. Something happened between you and Brodie, and it's you and her that have to resolve it. Talk to *her* about it, not to me.'

'Hm.'

There is a thing in seismology called a Long Period Event. It's the deep subterranean sound a volcano makes when it's getting ready to blow. If you could put your ear to the ground at just the right moment it would sound pretty much like *Hm*.

'I will,' said Deacon. 'Tomorrow. As soon as she gets the Mickey Finn out of her system. We'll talk and we'll sort it out, and maybe I can't promise it'll be like it never happened but I will bury the hatchet and I won't mark the spot. Will that do?'

It was more than Daniel had hoped for. 'Yes.'

Still Deacon kept sitting.

'What?'

Deacon sighed. At least, you'd have to call it a sigh because there aren't any other words, but there was nothing wistful about it, nothing gentle or piquant. A sense of foreboding surrounded the sofa. 'You want the God-honest truth, Daniel? I'm a little afraid of you. Of what you're going to cost me.'

For a split second Daniel tried not to understand. To react with astonishment, his pale brows climbing, his pale eyes wide. But even before the new expression had settled on his face he'd rejected it as disingenuous. He might wish he didn't know what Deacon meant but in fact he did and to pretend otherwise – even by the flicker of an expression – was tantamount to lying. He swallowed and his gaze dropped. His voice was low. 'I've told you. You have nothing to fear from me.'

'Yes, you have told me that, haven't you, Daniel?' said Deacon. 'And I know it's the truth because you wouldn't lie to me. Not to me, not to anyone. Not *for* anyone. But then, it's not entirely up to you, is it? Maybe you can control your own feelings, but you can't control Brodie's.'

'I know exactly how Brodie feels about me,' Daniel said softly. 'And it's no threat to you.'

'And when she realises how you feel about her?'

'She's not going to hear it from me. And you can't – you simply cannot – be stupid enough to let her hear it from you.'

Big, strong men in powerful positions don't often get called stupid. Perhaps, not often enough. Deacon felt his muscles contract as if violence was an option. He made a determined effort to relax them. 'I'm not sure it would be stupid. I think it might be the only responsible – the only decent – thing to do.

'But you're right, I'm not going to do it. I'm not going to gamble when the stakes are this high. It does nothing for a man's pride, but if the only way I can keep her is by keeping from her the fact that she could have you instead, that's what I'll do.

'But Brodie is nobody's fool. You and me deciding to keep her in the dark is no guarantee she won't find the light-switch. If she does, the shit's going to hit the fan big-time. She's bound to feel used. Again. I can't see her forgiving either of us.'

'Then I'll tell you what I told her,' Daniel said, and his eyes as they came up were hard. 'If she asks you'll have to tell her the truth. Make sure you never give her reason to ask.'

Deacon went on staring at him, taking that in. A flurry of tiny urges hit him like hail. For a second he wanted nothing so much as to walk away from this and not be beholden to anyone for his happiness. For a second he wanted to wake Brodie, put the facts before her and make her choose. For slightly longer, and not for the first time, he wanted to knock Daniel Hood into the middle of next week. He resisted them all, aware that whatever satisfaction they might afford him would be transient and every one would leave him – leave them all – in a more difficult position than where they were right now.

Yet doing nothing seemed only a temporary solution too. Deacon's voice was the growl of a distant avalanche. 'You're in my way, Daniel. Everywhere I look I see your shadow over my future. You may not mean to come between me and Brodie: you say that isn't what you want and I believe you. But I'm afraid you're going to do it anyway. I'm afraid that one day it's going to be you and me rolling round the hall floor, punching one another bloody.

'And while I know I can beat the crap out of you, I'm not sure I can win.'